## JUPITER'S GREAT RED SPOT WAS
*BLEEDING* . . .

The giant planet's most impressive feature,
twice the diameter of Earth itself,
was sending out reddish streamers tens of
thousands of miles long, drawn by an
unimaginably huge vortex of clouds that
swept around the planet at a million miles
an hour.

Jameson tried to grasp the sc█████████
colossal events he w██ ███████████
whipping shapes w████████████████
that spinning vortex██████████████
moving with a speed████████████████
have shorn Earth in t██████████████
left it a polished ball, g████ ███ the heat
of friction.

The raging vortex had marched from
horizon to horizon, and he could see it
against the engulfing darkness, a tenuous
pillar of cloud extending thousands of miles
into space in a coiled loop that narrowed to
end in a gossamer thread somewhere inside
the orbit of Jupiter V . . .

*A thread whose tip was a glowing blue spark* . . .

# The Jupiter Theft

**DONALD MOFFITT**

SPHERE BOOKS LIMITED
30/32 Gray's Inn Road, London WC1X 8JL

First published in Great Britain by Sphere Books
Ltd 1979
Copyright © 1977, 1979 by Donald Moffitt
Published by arrangement with the author and
his agents

*For Ann, whose energy is greater than her
mass*

Set in Monotype Plantin

Printed in Great Britain by
C. Nicholls & Company Ltd
The Philips Park Press, Manchester

# CHAPTER ONE

The Swan was rising.

Deneb popped up on schedule, a bright spark above the crater rim. The giant X-ray telescope anchored in the dust of the Korolev Basin revolved in its heavy turret to take an optical bearing on it. The telescope's rudimentary brain made a minor adjustment in alignment, plugged itself into the Farside computer's cesium clock, and waited patiently for the object it had been told to track.

A sizzle of X-rays bounced off the nest of paraboloid reflectors and hit the scanning focus. The telescope became mildly attentive. It was several seconds too early for the appearance of Cygnus X-1.

Then Cygnus X-1 itself rose above the bleak lunar horizon, right where it was supposed to be. Something was very wrong.

The telescope called for help. It took the Farside computer about twelve nanoseconds to check all the possibilities against the star charts stored in its memory. None of them fit. It took another fraction of a second to rule out instrumentation errors. Then the computer followed its standing instructions and alerted the people.

The alarm went off with a ping, and the new duty tech, startled, dropped her stylus and lightpad. Anyone could tell she hadn't been on the Moon long. She bent to catch them much too quickly, and the abrupt motion lifted her bare feet right off the floor. Then she lost track of her centre of mass, toppled over all the way, and went sprawling face downward in slow motion.

The junior astronomy resident grabbed a handful of her smock and set her on her feet again before her eighteen pounds could hit bottom. 'Relax,' he said with an irritating grin. 'You'll get used to it.'

He was a six-month veteran of Farside Station himself, a brash, freckled young man who affected faded reg shorts and a shaved chest with his ident disc pasted on it. His name was Kerry, and he fancied himself irresistible. He handed the lightpad back to her with an unnecessary flourish.

5

Flustered, the duty tech turned to the monitor wall and located the flashing amber light among the banks of glowing buttons and display screens. She began logging the data flickering on the LED panel below it. Suddenly, her eyes widened.

'A new X-ray source in Cygnus,' she said. 'A strong one.'

He leaned over to see. 'It must be Cyg X-1.'

'No. There's a definite separation. Besides, this one isn't pulsing.'

'It's Cyg X-3 then.'

'It isn't, I tell you. The computer's already checked for position and emission characteristics.'

She wiped the lightpad, thumbing her notes into the computer's temporary memory register, and turned to face him. She was a small, sturdy young woman with a tight, pretty face and a cap of dark hair. Her ident disc said MAYBURY.

'We're famous then.' He grinned, 'It happened during our shift. How about celebrating with me when we go off duty? I've got a ten-pack in my coop. Genuine bonded joints – gold label, no synthetics.'

He leered. Like most of the station's female staffers, she'd elected to go braless in the Moon's less-demanding gravity, and there was an exaggerated tidal motion under her smock.

Before she could squelch him, another ping came from the board.

'The computer wants to divert Polyphemus,' she said, frowning.

'Why is it bothering to ask?'

'Dr. Shevchenko's using Polyphemus this month. He's touchy.'

'It's your decision.'

The duty tech bit her lip and after a moment's hesitation punched in the authorization. The computer thanked her, and pinpricks of coloured light began to ripple across the huge circular grid mounted overhead. Dotted lines streamed from the pinpricks, forming a holo image that seemed to converge in infinity. The tech and the resident turned instinctively towards the south observation window. There was a rustle of movement across the floor of the dome as more people turned to stare. Polyphemus in action was an impressive sight.

Out there on the pockmarked landscape a field of enormous metal flowers stretched as far as the eye could see, disappearing

6

over the sharp curve of the lunar horizon, only a couple of miles distant, without diminishing in scale the way Earth-bred eyes said they ought to. Each of those tremendous bowls was as big across as a football field, and there were more than two thousand of them, covering thirty square miles of the Korolev Basin. Now, as the observatory staff fell silent, the whole vast array swivelled in unison until all of them faced the same patch of sky.

They were aimed at the constellation of the Swan, still low on the horizon. The duty tech turned her face in the same direction and located Cygnus: a glittering cross with Deneb blazing at its tip. No one could see Cygnus X-1, of course, but Maybury knew it was there, near the place where the arms of the cross intersected. She was very glad it was ten thousand light-years away.

She shuddered, trying to imagine it. The thing called Cyg X-1 was an X-ray inferno, shedding an invisible glare equal to the total energy output of ten thousand suns. If it had any planets, it had fried them long ago.

Vampire stars – that was what X-ray sources like Cyg X-1 generally turned out to be: black holes or neutron stars that circled a blue supergiant companion, relentlessly sucking away its gases. As the gas fell into that terrible gravitational field, it was squeezed, bruised, heated to temperatures of up to 100 million degrees Kelvin. In the process it gave off that raging hellfire of X-rays.

The odds were that the new source in Cygnus would turn out to be something similar. The evolution of such X-ray binaries had been well understood since the late twentieth century. A massive star swelled as it burned up its hydrogen fuel, overflowing its Roche lobe and contributing mass to its companion. A supernova explosion in the burnt-out star left a black hole behind. And then, for a brief period of thirty or forty thousand years, a reversal of the mass exchange as the companion star in turn burned up its hydrogen and bloated to a blue supergiant, while the relentless hole devoured its substance. The Farside computer would be comparing its X-ray and radio images now, trying to fit its accumulating data into such a picture.

Another ping brought her attention back to the board. The junior resident peered over her shoulder.

'The computer's found something it can't handle,' he mur-

7

mured. 'It's just plugged itself in to the data centre at Mare Imbrium.'

The two computers, on opposite sides of the Moon, began exchanging data. After a couple of seconds the console buzzed to catch the human's attention, and a new request flowed across the screen.

'Now it wants the use of the five-hundred-inch reflector,' the resident said.

The tech bit her lip again, 'I'd better get Dr. Ruiz,' she said. 'He won't like it. He was up all night.'

But the duty tech already had spoken into her lapel communicator and asked the desk to wake up Farside's director.

By the time Dr. Ruiz arrived, green-smocked technicians and off-duty personnel were milling around the area. Word had spread quickly that something was going on, and curious faces peered into the glass-walled monitor booth.

Ruiz pushed through the crowd and closed the door of the booth behind him. He was a tall, gaunt man, slightly stooped, with hollow cheeks and a leathery complexion. His knobbly legs showed the effects of childhood malnourishment. His eyes were bleary with lack of sleep, and he was still tucking his singlet into his baggy shorts.

'I'm sorry, Dr. Ruiz, but—'

He waved her apology aside, 'What's this about the computer asking to divert the Sagan reflector?'

'It's true, Doctor. It's already diverted the Polyphemus array. Now it apparently wants to try for a counterpart image at the visible wavelengths. But with optical-viewing time booked three months in advance, I thought I'd better—'

'Yes, yes. You did the right thing to call me.' The director's eyes already were roving restlessly over the winking lights and flickering data screens of the big board. 'What have you got so far?'

The tech turned on her lightpad. Her handwriting and underlinings, in scratches of blue lightning on the pad's polycrystalline surface, crowded the computer-generated script she had dialled in from the board.

'Well, for one thing it doesn't pulse. It just gives off a steady X-ray emission consistent with a point source.'

'Hmmm. How about the possibility of sinusoidal variation with a period of several hours, like Cyg X-3?'

She shook her head firmly. 'The computer's been tracking it

long enough to have detected a curve. It's a radio source, too. We have a fix on it with Polyphemus.'

Ruiz raised a shaggy eyebrow. 'You diverted Polyphemus?'

She stood her ground, 'Yes, Doctor. I'm authorized to—'

'Don't worry about it.' He laughed. 'I'll deal with Dr. Shevchenko. You're doing fine so far. Go on.'

The junior resident butted in, trying to get himself noticed. 'Excuse me, Dr. Ruiz, but the X-ray source is only a couple of seconds of arc from Cyg X-1. It confuses the telescope at first. Doesn't that suggest that it's been occulted by X-1 until now?'

'And what do *you* say' – Ruiz squinted at the duty tech's ident disc – 'Mizz Maybury?'

The tech blushed. 'It's only twenty-eight days since the last sighting. Cyg X-1 is over ten thousand light-years away. The new source *couldn't* have been hiding behind it. For the apparent separation to increase that much, it would have to be moving laterally at several hundred times the speed of light.'

'And what does *that* suggest?'

Maybury gave the junior resident an apologetic glance. 'That it's the other way around. The new source may have been masked by Cyg X-1, but it's closer to the solar system.'

'My thoughts exactly.'

Ruiz walked over to the observation window, an imposing and dignified figure despite his baggy shorts, his knobby joints, the legs twisted by rickets that were his legacy from his childhood in New Manhattan. He looked out at the starry sky and located the Swan. He stared at it a long time, as if he were making up his mind about something.

With a casualness that made the other two gasp, Ruiz turned back to the board and punched in an authorization for the immediate use of the 500-inch Sagan mirror in the Tsiolkovsky crater. Diverting the giant telescope from high-priority projects wasn't something you did lightly, even if you were the director of Farside Station.

Instantly, a stunning image sprang into life on the photoplastic viewplate. It was truer and richer than the images that had been possible on the obsolete photographic emulsions of the twentieth century. There was no graininess with enlargement. They were seeing, in real time, exactly what the big eye was seeing halfway across the Moon.

There was an illusion of stars swimming across the plate, as electrical potentials changed on the plastic's surface. The stars halted as the Farside computer locked the telescope into the Polyphemus radio array.

The blue supergiant known as HDE 226868 was plainly visible as a bloated disc, thanks to computer enhancement of thousands of separate millisecond-long exposures. You could even see the pronounced bulge at one side, where its substance was being sucked away by its invisible companion.

You couldn't see Cyg X-1 itself, of course. Black holes swallow their own light, the way they swallow everything else.

Ruiz made the computer generate a phantom image derived from radio waves and X-ray scatter. A fuzzy speck of cotton appeared opposite the tip of the bulge. He shifted focus and found another cotton ball halfway between Cyg X-1 and Deneb. Whatever the new source was, it wasn't part of a binary. He frowned.

Maybury had been busy comparing her first entries on the lightpad with the updated figures on the board. 'Dr. Ruiz,' she said in a puzzled tone, 'there's no proper motion that the computer can detect. I know the observational sample is still very small, but the new object seems to have stopped its lateral movement.' She hesitated. 'That would mean that it's changed direction twice in the last twenty-eight days.'

The junior astronomy resident snorted. 'That's impossible!'

Nobody paid any attention. Ruiz looked thoughtful. 'Mizz Maybury...'

She was way ahead of him. She scribbled a question on her lightpad and read off the answer that appeared a moment later.

'The computer says that both the radio waves and X-ray emissions are blue-shifted,' she said. 'It's been compensating for our benefit.'

'That means the object is moving toward us,' the resident said brightly.

Ruiz switched off the ghost image and stared intently at the place where it had been. There was nothing visible.

But Deneb jiggled.

The others saw it too. All of a sudden the room was very quiet.

'Mizz Maybury,' Ruiz said, 'will you ask the computer to generate a star chart on this screen? Just the main reference points will do.'

'I'll do it,' the junior resident offered.

A scattering of white crosses appeared on the screen, canceling out the stars. But Deneb was still there, displaced inward toward the cotton ball.

'It's bending light, whatever it is,' Ruiz said. 'And it's between us and—'

Angry squawking from the wall communicator interrupted him. He looked up and saw the apoplectic face of Dr. Mackie, the chief astronomer at the Sagan dome.

'Dr. Ruiz!' Mackie sputtered. 'I must protest at the high-handed manner in which you preempted the schedule of the five-hundred-inch mirror. There are such things as review boards, and I can assure you that—'

'Calm down, Horace,' Ruiz said. 'I think you'd better get over here right away.'

Mackie's truculence faded suddenly. 'What have you got?' he said carefully.

'I'm not sure, but I want you in on it. Requisition the courier rocket. If you leave right away, you can be here in an hour.'

As soon as Mackie switched off, Ruiz called Central Communications. 'Put me through to the Mars station. Personal, direct to Dr. Larrabee at the Syrtis Major radio observatory. Wake him up if he's asleep.'

'You're on, Doctor.' Communications said.

Ruiz spoke rapidly and precisely into the communicator, giving coordinates, explaining the situation in as few words as possible. '. . . And, Larry,' he finished, 'don't waste time calling me back for a confirmation. Just do it.'

He switched off and settled back in one of the swivel chairs. 'How about some coffee while we're waiting?' he said.

The wait was over an hour. There could be no such thing as a conversation with Mars, particularly when Mars was on the other side of the Sun, as it was now. As the crow flies, it would take radio waves a bit more than twenty minutes to travel one way. But the crow wouldn't fly through the Sun. The message had to be bounced off the relay satellite orbiting Venus, currently a quarter orbit ahead of Earth, and in line of sight with both Earth and Mars. The round trip for an exchange of messages, with the detour, would take about an hour even if Larrabee answered immediately.

He answered almost immediately. Ruiz was into his third cup of lukewarm coffee when Larrabee's voice came out of the wall, clear as a bell, with all the interplanetary static edited out by the computer. Voice transmissions from Mars were sent in pulse-code modulation with triple redundancy, and in the un-likely event that any particular pulse was wiped out all three times, the gap was too infinitesimal for the human ear to detect.

'I don't know what this is all about, Hernando,' a cheerful baritone said, 'but I'll take your word for it that it's important. We're zeroing in on your Cygnus Source now. Just sit tight a couple more minutes. I'll keep the beam open. You owe me a drink when I get back.'

Ruiz sipped another cup while the resident, Kerry, hovered around him and Maybury punched setups into the board. The new shift had arrived, and they were tiptoeing around, trying not to look curious. Ten minutes later, lights started blinking all over the board as the Mars computer fed data via radio into the Farside computer's memory buffer register. The computer, consulting its hydrogen maser clock, corrected for transmission delay.

Before mankind had set up shop on Mars, astronomers had had to wait six months to measure parallax. You took a picture of your target star, and when the Earth had travelled halfway around the sun you took another picture on the same plate and measured the apparent shift. Now you could triangulate by taking sightings from the Moon and Mars simultaneously.

Ruiz watched the figures unreeling on the LED displays, his coffee forgotten. In his mind he translated them into a triangle with a base line that was 234 million miles wide. If the X-ray source was anywhere within a hundred light-years, he'd get reliable results.

Two glowing dots appeared on the viewplate against a back-ground of stars; the computer had enough data now to attempt a preliminary visualization. Who had asked it to do that? He looked up – that girl Maybury. She was efficient. That fool with the shaved chest was doing nothing except stand around looking important.

Ruiz looked back at the screen and blinked. The dots had stopped jiggling. They were impossibly far apart. The paral-lactic shift was . . . huge!

The dammed thing was less than a light-year away!

He snatched the lightpad from a startled Mizz Maybury and made his own rough calculation. His answer approximated the computer's average figure: a distance of about half a light-year. The Cygnus source was *close* – closer than any stellar object

12

had a right to be. And it was blue-shifting. And there was no proper motion. All the motion was head-on.

Something soft nudged his arm: Mizz Maybury's breast. She was leaning across him, thrusting a piece of paper in front of him, trying to get his attention.

'Dr. Ruiz!' she said urgently. 'I thought you might want – that is – I asked the computer to pull out the most recent planetary data. The positions of the outer planets – I mean, there's a discrepancy of several seconds in the longitude and declination of both Neptune and Pluto. It might turn out to be simple observational error, but—'

He waved her aside. 'In a moment, Mizz Maybury.' He was staring intently at the screen that showed the values for the base angles. The computer was constantly updating them as it refined and reaveraged its data. They held steady up to the eighth decimal point, then jumped back and forth a good deal, but the trend of the figures was definitely higher.

The thing had to be moving *fast* to show any noticeable change in that short a time. Ruiz was almost afraid to ask how fast. But he wiped the lightpad and scribbled an order for the computer to pin a tentative value on the blue shift and try to correlate it with the changing parallax. There was a pause of several seconds while the computer searched its peripheral memories for an appropriate programme; then figures began to flow across the lightpad, while a duplicate column of numbers marched across one of the display screens.

He heard a gasp behind him, Maybury was looking over his shoulder.

'That's right.' he said. 'It appears to be moving towards us at something more than ninety-eight per cent of the speed of light.'

Over at the data screen the junior resident cleared his throat. He was perspiring, and the green ident disc on his chest was coming unstuck. 'That means it'll be in the vicinity of the solar system in about six months,' he said.

'At its present speed, yes,' Ruiz said.

He drummed his fingers on the arm of the chair. Finally he said, 'I don't suppose we'll really have enough data till we've observed it for a few more days, but why don't you have the computer generate a projection of the path of the Cygnus Source through the solar system.'

Maybury and the young man got busy over at one of the

consoles. Ruiz could hear them whispering together, having some kind of dispute, but he wasn't paying attention. He was thinking about the trip to Earth he'd probably be making some time in the next twelve hours, dreading it. He glanced up and saw the junior resident, an angry flush on his face and chest, step away from the console and stare sulkily out the observation window. Maybury was hunched over, shoulders tense, her fingers flying over the lightboard, her bare toes twiddling in unconscious rhythm. At last she straightened up and turned in her chair.

A flat disc grew in the square darkness of the holo well. It looked something like a target, with the sun and the orbits of the inner planets crowded together to make a bull's-eye. In the computer's stylized representation Pluto's orbit was a tilted hoop intersecting the orbit of Neptune, which had briefly replaced it as the outermost planet beginning in 1987.

A yellow dotted line with an arrowhead represented the probable course of the Cygnus Source. It wiggled back and forth a bit as the computer changed its mind, but it always intersected the plane of the ecliptic somewhere near the edge of the bull's-eye.

Ruiz canted the image for better perspective and zoomed in so that Jupiter's orbit was outermost. Now he could see the positions of the inner planets – coloured beads strung on those glowing tracks, and necessarily out of scale. Six months hence, Mars would just have overtaken Jupiter and Earth would be rounding the Sun to catch up.

That X-ray holocaust from Cygnus was going to penetrate the plane of the solar system somewhere between the orbits of Jupiter and Mars. It would pass within 4 A.U.s of Earth.

Ruiz rose out of his chair very carefully, like an old man, and walked over to the observation window. He took another long look at Cygnus, knowing it was futile. If the 500-inch telescope couldn't see anything, he certainly wasn't going to see anything with the naked eye. The duty tech made no attempt to follow him with her piece of paper. Even the junior resident had sense enough not to say anything.

Dr. Mackie arrived a few minutes later, still wearing his pressure suit, his helmet tucked under his arm and his turkey neck sticking out of the collar ring. He saw the look on Ruiz's face. 'What's wrong?' he said.

Ruiz was a tough old bird. He had grown up in the squalor

14

of a refugee camp on Long Island in the years after most of Manhattan had been rendered uninhabitable by the bomb, made of stolen reactor wastes, set off by the New England Separatists in 1998. He had clawed his way to the top on his own merits, despite the twin handicaps of poverty and a provisional ident. There wasn't much that could unnerve him.

But now his face was grey as he turned to Mackie.

'I'm putting you in charge, Horace,' he said. 'I'm going down to Earth to tell them that the human race has just been sentenced to death.'


## CHAPTER TWO

Tod Jameson flung up a gauntleted hand to protect his faceplate and yelled '*Wei hsien!*'

He grabbed a startled Li Chen-yung by an air hose and spun him around. There was just enough time to plant both boots against Li's quilted blue spacesuit and give him a mighty shove; then the flat, perforated pad of the landing leg went sailing past his head like a gigantic flyswatter. Its stately slow motion was deceptive. There was enough mass behind the pad to grind him into the hull like a bug. His spine crawling, Jameson saw it crunch its way through several honeycomb layers of the Callisto lander's skin and embed itself there, trailing springs and broken struts.

He was drifting outward in a direction opposite to the shove he'd given Li. Earth filled the sky, a colossal backdrop of sparkling blue-and-white whorls. Against it was silhouetted the unfinished framework of the Jupiter ship, just a couple of miles off, a spidery wheel with a spear through the hub.

Li's voice crackled in his helmet. 'Thanks, buddy,' he said.

'*Hwan-ying,*' Jameson replied. He wondered if his Chinese sounded as stilted as Li's English.

He located Li, a starfish shape floating in emptiness, pinwheeling crazily. As he watched, Li brought the spin under control and fired a short, economical burst from his suit jets that sent him back toward the squat bulk of the landing vehicle.

Jameson aimed himself carefully and fired his own thruster. He braked expertly within reach of a strut and hooked one foot under it. Li was already there, inspecting the mangled locking mechanism of the landing foot that had almost killed them both.

'Missing bolt,' Li said, pointing a sausagelike finger. 'Big spring in leg tear loose.'

'*K'an-yi-k'an*,' Jameson said.

They both looked up at the place where the lander had kicked a hole in its own side. The skeleton leg was sticking out ignominiously, its foot buried in the lander's aluminium hide. The image was so anthropomorphic that they both laughed.

'What if that happen while we orbit Callisto?' Li said, his broad peasant features suddenly serious inside his fishbowl.

'*Bu-hau*,' Jameson began. '*Bu-dau shem . . .*' He floundered, trying to think of the word for 'abort', and gave up. 'We'd have to scrub the mission,' he finished lamely in English.

His suit radio buzzed, and Jameson tongued the switch that put him on closed circuit. 'We're sending a repair crew right away,' Sue Jarowski's husky voice said. 'Are you and your Chinese friend all right?'

'We're fine,' Jameson said. 'No injuries. But it looks as if the lander's been holed. We're doing a damage inventory now.'

Li had turned away discreetly so that Jameson wouldn't see his lips move while he reported on his own scrambled circuit. It was a meaningless courtesy. Both of them knew perfectly well that Li's people, in the sequestered pod they had attached to the rim of the international space station a few miles away, were busily processing all American message traffic, just as the Americans routinely unscrambled all Chinese transmissions.

The ritual spying had become a way of life during the year-long preparations for the joint Chinese–American Jupiter mission – like the elaborate charade of speaking the other side's language during mission exercises.

The big prize in the game was the new boron fusion/fission engine that was going to power the Jupiter ship, courtesy of the United States. The Chinese didn't have one yet, though they were said to be working on it furiously.

Jameson was familiar with the basic principle You inject a proton into boron 11, with its six neutrons and five protons, and you get an unstable nucleus that explodes into three helium nuclei, with two protons and two neutrons apiece. But it took temperatures in the billions of degrees to start boron fission.

So to get the hot protons needed to trigger the boron reaction, you had to have a fusion reaction first. That was being

16

supplied, courtesy of the Chinese, via a more conventional deuterium-tritium fusion, triggered by carbon dioxide lasers.

The security problems at the interface of the two systems were nightmarish.

The daily American security sweeps constantly uncovered one ingenious Chinese spy device after another hidden in and around the still-empty engine modules. They were deactivated without comment. Both sides pretended they weren't there.

It was a hell of a basis for travelling to another planet, but it was the only way it was going to get done. America and the China Coalition were the only two political entities that had the resources and the motivation. The European Space Agency was too fragmented by intramural squabbles. Greater Japan stuck pretty close to Earth orbit and applications satellites of a practical nature. And Russia – what was left of it after the Chinese police action of 2003–2008 – was no longer a spacefaring nation.

Jameson looked at Li and grinned. It was a good thing that both sides had a healthy share of get-the-job-done types like Li and himself. Best to leave the rest of it to the politicians and the security men.

Li grinned back. 'You look more Chinese than I do, old buddy,' he said. 'Are you sure we're not getting to you?'

Jameson knew what he meant. In zero-g conditions, some of the body fluid tends to migrate upward to the face. Jameson's normally lean face was temporarily puffy, cheeks risen and his grey eyes slitted. He was also an inch taller, thanks to a stretched spine.

'*Wo ma?*' Jameson said innocently. '*Wo pu-shih Chung-gwa-jen.*'

Li laughed, a little constrained by all of the listening ears. The two of them pulled themselves from handhold to handhold across the curving surface of the Callisto lander, towards the embedded footpad. There was a lot of debris floating around: pieces of the locking mechanism, fragments of hardened foam insulation. Something the size and shape of a pot lid drifted past lazily. Li made a grab at it, but Jameson netted it first.

He turned it over in his gloved hands, anchoring himself with the toe of a boot. It was a bolt head – the one missing from the locking mechanism.

He saw why it had broken loose: someone had sawed the head off the bolt and substituted this hollowed-out fake. Inside was something that he guessed was part of an X-ray camera. It seemed to be a lensless system depending on folded optics and a paper-thin electronics sandwich of an image plane that transmitted the pictures on its face through a pea-size FM device. The capsule of radioactives seemed to be missing, fortunately.

He looked reprovingly at Li. Li looked back blandly through his visor, without even the grace to blush. He probably hadn't known the thing was there. After all, it had almost killed him too.

Why? Jameson wrinkled his forehead and had the answer immediately. The Callisto lander would normally be tucked up in an external module next to an engine pod. The Chinese hoped to get a few pictures that would give an insignificant clue or two to the size and configuration of some component of the boron drive, so they could add the information to all their other pieces. They were capable of going to ridiculous lengths. The other day someone had caught a Chinese engineer with millimeter markings painted on his thumbnail, sneaking a measurement of one of the unconnected fuel pellet delivery pipes.

He stowed the bogus bolt head in a leg pocket of his spacesuit. He'd turn it over to one of the security boys later. No official complaint would ever be lodged. The polite fictions that made the joint mission possible had to be maintained at all costs.

Li had looked away nonchalantly while Jameson pocketed the spy device. He'd be talking to his own security representatives later. Now he said, as if nothing had happened, 'Here they come now.'

Jameson craned his neck and saw reflected earthlight glinting off an open tetrahedral framework festooned with clinging objects. It was about a half mile away. Whoever was jockeying the repair rig was good; he'd coasted all the way without correction. Suddenly there were a couple of brief flares of hydrazine jets, and the thing was hanging motionless in reference to the Callisto lander.

Two bulky dolls floated from the cage: the co-foremen. Jameson could make out the American-flag shoulder patch on one and the red-star patch on the other. They conferred briefly, helmets together, and then two repair lobsters detached themselves from the frame, accompanied by a swarm of spacesuited attendants.

Sue Jarowski's voice sounded in his helmet again. 'Mission Control says you and Li can call it a day, Tod. They're scratching the training exercise until Thursday.'

Jameson conjured up an image of Sue's face while she talked: dark hair, strong almost-pretty features with wide cheekbones, snub nose, generous mouth. She was crisp and alert, and a damn fine communications officer.

'I think I'll stick around here, Sue, until they finish the repair. I can borrow a bottle of air from the repair crew.'

Sue hesitated, then said 'Ray Caffrey wants to see you.'

'I'll bet he does. Tell him I'll check in with him later.'

Caffrey was the security rep. On the official mission roster he was listed as 'Safety Engineer'.

'I understand. I'll tell Ray.'

Jameson turned back toward the repair rig. The two lobsters, bright orange against blackness, were manoeuvring themselves into position, getting a helpful nudge or two from the men swarming around them. A repair lobster was nothing more than a simple cylinder with a plastic bubble for the head of its operator at one end. It got its name from the two big clawlike waldos at the forward end and the twin rows of smaller specialized limbs down its ventral surface.

One of the lobsters anchored itself on the Callisto lander's hull and grasped the embedded landing foot. It tugged gently, trying to do as little further damage as possible. The leg came free. There was a little frosty explosion of particles of trapped air. A couple of space-suited men took charge of the damaged leg and ferried it back to the repair frame. One was Chinese, one American. Jameson grinned without humour. Even the garbage detail had to be binational.

There was a frying sound in his helmet, and Li's voice said: 'I be going back to Eurostation now. See you Thursday.'

Li's stocky figure was already mounting his scooter. He gave it a couple of squirts, aiming it toward the big wheel in the distance.

'You're not going to watch the repair?' Jameson said in careful Standard Mandarin.

'No. What for?'

Li hunched over the steering bar, and the scooter dwindled against the stars. Jameson watched it until it was too small to see. Li obviously had been recalled to explain why he hadn't managed to retrieve the spy camera first. Perhaps if those security clowns had had the sense to confide in Li, he would have.

Jameson sighed. It was a sticky business. As co-commanders of the Callisto lander, he and Li would depend on each other utterly when they set down on the frozen surface of the Jovian moon. They had to trust each other without reservation. But Li had his loyalties, just as Jameson did. Jameson shrugged mentally. You had to work within the system.

He gave a start as a pair of mittened paws grasped his upper arms and a helmet clinked against his. He found himself staring into the raw red features of the U.S. repair-crew foreman, a likable, plain-spoken man named Grogan. Grogan was being smart enough not to use his suit radio.

'Beg pardon, sir,' Grogan said, 'but what's going on? We saw the landing leg spring loose through the telescope, but that's all.'

Jameson pressed his helmet against the other man's. 'Tell you all about it later. For now, just make sure that everything you replace in the locking mechanism is all right. Particularly the bolts.'

Grogan's corned-beef face split in a grin. 'Got you, sir. I'll check out the replacement parts myself.'

He gave a push and launched himself towards the sleeve of the landing gear. The Chinese foreman was fishing around in the tangled mess and passing broken pieces to a crewman with a sack. Grogan stationed himself there, the lines of his body looking belligerent even through the bloat of the spacesuit. Jameson relaxed.

The other lobster brought over a replacement leg, an articulated metal lattice five metres long, with the flat mesh pad of the landing foot at one end. Swimming behind it was a four-man crew with laser cutting torches.

Jameson waited until they were finished, then hitched a ride back on the repair frame. Clinging to a crossbar, he watched Eurostation grow in his vision. The great wheel was surrounded by a random collection of orbital constructions and the parked shuttles of half a dozen nations hanging like gnats above its hub. That glittering spider web suspended a couple of kilometres beyond the rim was their radiotelescope, leased to all comers, and the pool of quicksilver trapped in a cage was one of the solar collectors. The spinning cross with the tin cans at the ends of the arms was one of the earlier stations, still in use as an isolation lab.

But it was Eurostation itself, rotating ponderously against the stars, that dominated that floating junkyard. It had been growing for fifty years. The inner rim, only six hundred feet in diameter, had been the original station back in the early decades of the century. Now it was a low-g hospital, among other things. It was connected by six vast spokes to the outer rim, more than a half mile across. Future expansion would have to be done laterally, turning the wheel gradually into a cylinder, unless they wanted to slow the rotation. An exception was the blister the Chinese had attached to the rim – a spartan environment where they could practise their state religion uncontaminated by Eurostation's amenities.

The hub of the station reared in front of him like a metal cliff. Jameson detached himself from the repair rig and kicked himself towards it. The rig continued on towards the floating corral where the construction equipment was parked.

Jameson's boots hit the metal and stuck. He found a convenient handhold and looked around for a single-lock. They weren't going to open one of the yawning docking adapters for one man.

The surface he was clinging to – a flat disc a hundred metres in diameter, painted with bright targets – didn't share the station's rotation. Otherwise he'd have found himself sliding inexorably toward the edge and out into space. Actually it was the base of a shallow, truncated cone that floated free within the station's hub – a little space station in its own right. The station personnel – depending on their origin – called it the *Kupplung* or the *Embrayage* or the Clutch.

He crawled towards one of the open manholes, electrostatically sticky, and levered himself inside. He closed the cover behind him and pressed the big red button next to the inner door. Air hissed into the lock. After an interval, the inner door spun open, and a bored attendant with a German-Swiss accent helped him off with his suit. Jameson headed immediately for the men's showers and peeled off his wilted liner in a cubicle smelling of sweat, steel, and rubber. After six hours in a spacesuit, it was a relief to zip himself into a showerbag set for needle spray. He emerged, refreshed, in a clean singlet and shorts, and joined the crowd of off-shift construction workers waiting in the outer corridor.

If they had been standing instead of drifting in random orientations along the walls, Jameson would have stood half a head above most of them. He was tall for a spaceman, but he made up for it by being greyhound-lean. Actually, he was well within the mass limits. Jameson had the frank eyes and square-jawed good looks that delighted the Space Resources Agency's pressecs and accredited newsies. He looked the part, hanging casually from a holdbar with one big-knuckled, competent-looking hand and keeping a firm grip on an SRA blue nylon zip bag with the other.

A chime sounded. The drifting men began to settle towards the curving wall as imperceptibily it became a floor. The clutch was matching its spin to that of the station. There was a gentle lurch, and clutch and station mated with a resounding clang that shuddered through the chamber. The row of doors underfoot slid open and the waiting men dropped through. Jameson hurried through with the crowd. He repressed a shiver as he floated past the rubber-gasketed doorframe. The shearing action from a mismatched spin could slice a man neatly in half – but of course it couldn't happen; the doors wouldn't open unless the safety locks were firmly engaged.

He sank, feather-light, to the deck, and got a surprise: Caffrey was waiting for him in the reception area.

Jameson tossed the fake bolt head at him. 'Here you go, Ray. The latest Chinese contribution to space cooperation.'

Caffrey looked uncomfortable. 'I'll need a report from you,' he said. 'Let's go to my office for a debriefing.'

'Can't it wait? I'm bushed.'

'Sorry, Commander. You know how it is.'

Jameson grimaced. 'Okay. But I can't add much to what you already saw through my helmet camera.'

He followed Caffrey to a dropcage, bracing his hands against the ceiling as it plunged down its shaft towards the outer rim of the station. Free fall was too slow for the first stage of the trip and too dangerous for the last stages – especially for newcomers. There was one in the cage now, a mousy man in a drab Earth-style business blouse, who yelped in surprise as he bobbed to the top of the cage and bumped his head. One of the construction men, laughing, pulled him down and warned him about the gradient. Caffrey maintained a tight-lipped silence, his expression discouraging conversation from Jameson. He had the spy camera tucked under his tunic.

They got out at the rim, in the main corridor that circled the station. There was an electric trolley and a carpeted walkway. The carpeting felt luxurious under Jameson's bare toes. The lighting was soft, and a hidden speaker played an unobtrusive slipbeat, nines against sevens. The European Space Agency did everything up brown for its clients. They kept their big wheel spinning at a comfortable half-g at the rim, which made it easier for people stopping over on their way back from the Moon or Mars to readjust to Earth gravity. The five restaurants were excellent, and the Swiss ran a four-star hotel.

They passed through the American lounge on their way to Caffrey's office. A clutter of chairs and little tables were arranged around a central well, circled by a low railing, that looked down on the stars. The far wall was a spectacular row of tall, narrow windows that showed the stars streaming slowly by, their flight showing no detectable arc here in this fractional slice of the station's vast circumference. A couple of dozen off-duty members of the Jupiter crew were there, socializing with construction workers and transients. There were no Europeans there, except for the bartender and a couple of stewards. This part of the wheel was U.S. diplomatic territory for the present.

Mike Berry waved at him from the other side of the room. He was playing a game of low-gravity darts with a rumpled, bearlike man who looked like a construction worker, but actually was the mission geologist, Omar Tuttle. Berry was a physicist, one of the two fusion specialists in charge of the boron drive. He was thin and thirtyish, with unkempt brown hair and a long, homely face animated by boyish enthusiasm. It was his first trip into space, and Jameson had been assigned to him as big brother during his astronaut training.

The moment of inattention cost Berry his point. His dart strayed sideways under the influence of the Coriolis force and missed the target entirely. One of the construction workers heckled him good-naturedly, and Tuttle, sipping his reconstituted beer, smiled in satisfaction.

'Tod...'

It was Sue Jarowski. He'd almost collided with her. She smiled up at him, appealingly gaminelike with her dark, cropped hair and a man's faded workshirt with pushed-up sleeves she'd borrowed somewhere. Jameson wondered if the shirt were his. He and Sue had spent a couple of sleep periods together, back when the mission personnel were still sorting

23

themselves out, but for some reason they hadn't seen much of each other since.

'Sue! How goes it?'

She put a hand on his arm. 'Are you just going off duty? Why don't you join Dmitri and me for a drink?'

He looked past her to where Dmitri Galkin, the junior biologist-cum-life-support tech, was sitting on an airpuff, contemplating a lipped cup with some greenish liquid in it. Dmitri met his eye and glanced away, looking miffed.

'I can't right now, Sue. I'm on my way to Security.'

He shrugged helplessly, and she followed his gaze to where Caffrey was waiting impatiently by the exit.

'Will I see you later?' Sue said. 'Why don't you stop by the lounge when Caffrey's through with you?'

She gave his arm a squeeze. He smiled back at her.

'I'll do that.'

When they reached the security rep's quarters, Caffrey carefully locked the X-ray spy camera away in a cabinet. He indicated a chair. 'Sit down, Commander,' he said.

Jameson sat down. Caffrey's manner was strangely formal. He was usually a fairly regular guy for a security rep. And this wasn't the comfortable armchair he usually sat in during debriefings. It was a fully equipped interrogation seat, with accessory plugs, ankle and wrist straps, and a head clamp. It tilted and swivelled to give its occupant a sense of psychological helplessness.

'What do you want to know, Ray?' Jameson said.

The security man didn't answer. He pressed a buzzer on his desk.

'It's up to the top brass, of course.' Jameson went on, trying to keep his voice conversational, 'but maybe this time we ought to lodge a formal protest. Bugging the lander is one thing, but this time it endangered the mission. If that landing leg had given way when we touched down on Callisto, Li and I could have been killed.'

'Don't say anything yet, Commander,' Caffrey said.

The door opened and a tall, unsmiling man in grey coveralls came through. Jameson didn't recognize him, but he knew the type. It was some functionary from the Reliability Board.

'This is Commander Jameson. Doctor,' Caffrey said.

Jameson looked up at the RB psychologist and said, in a feeble attempt at a joke, 'You going to strap me in, Doc?'

'That won't be necessary,' the RB man said. There wasn't a trace of humour in his words. 'Just grasp those armrests. That's right. Now put your head back against the backrest while I adjust it. That's the way.'

He had Jameson hooked up in a few minutes: skin electrodes, blood-pressure cuff, EEG cap, electromyograph, voice analyzer, and the rest of them. They were all plugged into a little averaging computer marked RESTRICTED USE. He positioned a little device on a rolling stand in front of Jameson's face to record changes in retinal colour and pupil size, and sat back waiting for Jameson to utter the first word. It was a familiar RB gambit.

Jameson fought back his anger. 'You know, I was checked out thoroughly at the start of the project,' he said. 'Everybody was.'

'Nothing to get concerned about, Commander Jameson,' the psychologist said soothingly. 'You've been working closely with your Chinese counterpart for some time now. This is just a routine test. Everybody's going to have one.'

It was easy for Jameson. He'd grown up as a Guvie brat. He'd been taking tests since his kidcare days: tests to get into the right schools, tests to qualify for government employment and housing and food chits, tests to get into the Space Resources Academy. It got to be second nature. You learned to give them what they wanted.

'You speak Chinese rather well, Commander. Not just the vocabulary – the four tones seem to come naturally to you. Most Westerners have trouble with them.'

'I just have a good ear, I guess.'

'Do you feel any special affinity for the Chinese?'

He kept his voice carefully neutral. 'They're okay.'

'Li Chen-yung in particular?'

'Li's all right.'

'You're not being very responsive, Commander.'

'Li's my partner in this exercise. We have to mesh as a team. Our staying alive depends on our trusting each other. Up to a point.'

'Up to a point?'

'Yes'.

'Hmm.' It was possible for Jameson to read those steely eyes. 'Do you feel anger toward Li over the incident with the spy camera?'

25

'No. Li probably didn't know it was there.'

The RB interrogator studied the little hooded screen on his computer. He punched for various readings. Jameson knew it was showing his anger and resentment. That didn't matter; his feelings would be interpreted as anger toward Li and the Chinese. A little anxiety and resentment about being grilled was normal anyway, no matter how reliable you were.

The questioning took about an hour. It was a fairly standard RB mix, with a new version of the authority-acceptance index and the same tired questions on alcohol and drug dependence he'd been answering for twenty years. It ended with a sexual orientation series, complete with flash holos, a needle sampling his blood, and a very uncomfortable metal codpiece with leads hooked to the computer. So far as he could tell, no drugs were being fed into his bloodstream via the needle, so the test was routine. There was no particular reason for it, which made it all the more insulting.

The RB man folded up his instruments and left. Jameson swabbed electrode paste off his forearm with an alcohol-soaked gauze pad. 'Finished with me?' he asked Caffrey in a level voice. 'Or did you want to do that debriefing?'

Caffrey flushed. 'No, you can go now.'

The lounge had emptied out somewhat by the time Jameson returned. Sue was sitting alone at one of the little plastic tables surrounding the central floor well. There was no sign of Dmitri. Jameson drew himself a beer and joined her.

'What was that all about?' she said.

'Reliability test.' He grimaced. 'Some arbee I never saw before. I guess they're worried about my getting contaminated, working with Li.' He drained half his beer and slammed the mug down too hard. The pinkish brew sloshed over the lip of the mug and splashed on the table.

'They've got to be careful,' she said reasonably.

'They can be so careful that they'll endanger the mission. The way Li's people almost did.'

She looked around uneasily. 'You shouldn't talk like that, Tod. Someone might misinterpret what you said about endangering the mission.'

'Dammit!' he flared. 'I'm no Rad! They ought to know that by now. I had my first arbee screening when I was only six years old, when GovCorp transferred my father to another city. I went to Federal schools from kindergarten on. It's fragging humiliating to be treated like some Privie slob who might have a nuke hidden up his sleeve!'

'My father came from the Private Sector,' she said quietly.

He covered her hand with his. 'I'm sorry.' he said contritely. 'I didn't mean that. I've got PriSec blood in my own veins, a couple of generations back. Everybody does.'

'I know,' she said wryly. 'We're the salt of the Earth. At least that's what the government keeps telling us.'

She gave him a warm smile. He held on to her hand. He'd forgotten how pretty she was. The two of them had meshed well during their brief experiment together during the early days of mission training. It had been the policy of the Space Resources Agency to balance the sexes ever since the scandal of the second Mars mission, early in the century. It was the only sensible way to deal with the inevitable tensions. Even the Chinese paired their crew members, though for public consumption they made much of 'comradeship' and 'Socialist chastity'.

Neither he nor Sue was attached at the moment, if you didn't count Dmitri. He leaned across the table, her hand warm in his. Her dark eyes looked expectantly at him. 'Sue . . .' he began.

'Hey, we're not interrupting anything, are we?'

He turned his head and saw Mike Berry standing there, a broken-nailed clump of fingers around a pink beer, the other hand resting on Maggie MacInnes's shoulder.

Maggie was a computer tech, a lean, freckly woman with an impertinent nose and carroty hair worn a little too long for space. She wasn't wearing anybody's shirt, just issued shorts and an improvised crisscrossed halter that tied behind her neck, baring skinny shoulder blades. Her rangy figure made Sue look a little chunky. Jameson didn't know Maggie very well, but after he and Li finished their current schedule of EVA exercises they would be working with Maggie and her counterpart, Jen Mei-mei, plotting orbits and landing approaches.

'No,' he said reluctantly. 'Have a seat.'

Sue unobtrusively pulled her hand away from Jameson's. She smiled a greeting and pushed over to make room.

Berry kicked a couple of airpuffs over, and he and Maggie plumped down on them. 'I hear you've got the security types buzzing, old chum.' he said.

Jameson looked up, surprised. 'How'd you hear that?'

'Oh, word gets around.' Berry hunched over, looking conspiratorial. He brushed his hair forward and narrowed his eyes, in an uncanny imitation of the RB interrogator Jameson had just left. 'What's that?' he said. 'You say this Commander Jameson wants us to lodge a protest with the Chinese over their spy camera? Impossible.'

Jameson laughed. 'Mike, you ought to be on holovision.'

Berry held up a hand. He changed his body language and became Caffrey, frozen-faced and wary. 'Why impossible?' Instantly he was the RB man again. 'Because then the Chinese would lodge a protest with *us*, over the holo scanner we planted in their dormitory. It's a fair exchange. *They* don't find out about our boron engine, and *we* don't find out about their sex lives.'

Maggie was laughing too, but Sue looked uncomfortable.

'But when did you meet—' Jameson began.

'You weren't alone, old chum. They're doing everybody. Doctor Von Hotseat just arrived this morning on the Earth shuttle. Tuttle's in there with him now. If you want to know, they started with me, while you were still floating around outside. Wanted to know if I believed in the free exchange of scientific information and all that.'

'See,' Sue said to Jameson. 'I told you not to take it personally.'

Berry raised a bushy eyebrow. 'What's this?'

'Oh, I was just sounding off about Security,' Jameson said. He took a swallow of beer and wiped his mouth with the back of his hand.

Maggie spoke up. 'I know what you mean. I never thought I'd get approved for this mission at all. They rescreened me twice. I even had to sign a braindip release.'

Jameson wasn't surprised. Maggie spoke with an unmistakable Yankee twang. People were more tolerant these days, but when Jameson had been growing up there still had been a lingering bitterness over all the ugliness of the New England Secession, and the loss of so many occupation troops during the pacification. Of course, it had been tough on the New Englanders and eastern Canadians too; particularly the use of nukes.

It couldn't have been easy for Maggie, getting this far in the space programme. Since reunification, New Englanders and Canadian annexees were theoretically entitled to full citizenship

28

with all its rights, but there was always that coded notation in their passbooks. There were far fewer restrictions on the children and grandchildren of the Russian refugees of the 2010's.

Sue changed the subject diplomatically. 'Look,' she said. 'I've never seen Jupiter so bright!'

Jameson looked down into the stars. The splendid gem that was Jupiter had just come into view in the glassed, rail-encircled well set into the carpeted floor of the space lounge. It drifted slowly past as the great wheel of the space station turned majestically on its axis. Of all the points of light visible, it was the most brilliant.

The four of them watched it in silence until it disappeared almost beneath their feet. A minute later, the window was full of Earth, blue and dazzling against the threadbare fabric of the night. Beneath the swirling clouds he could make out the brownish outlines of the continents, the elephant wrinkles of mountain chains, the patches of lucent green at the poles, where the Arctic wastes had been planted in snow rice. It all seemed familiar and comforting and close.

'What do you suppose we'll find when we get there?' Maggie said in a voice that was almost a whisper.

Jameson knew what she was feeling. It got to you every once in a while, that moment of strangeness when you caught a glimpse of that distant spark and realized it was a *place*. That you were actually going to go there across the enormous dark gulf, with a hundred members of your species, in a fragile hollow ring of drawn metal and spun plastic foam.

Maggie was looking directly at him. He saw her shiver.

'On Io,' Berry said, 'sulphur and sodium. On Callisto, lots of pebbles. What else?'

'Why not life?' Sue said. 'No, wait a minute, listen. After all, Callisto's got an atmosphere of sorts, and it's far enough from Jupiter so that it doesn't get the same dose of radiation as the other three Galilean satellites. Dmitri says that, given ammonia frost and evaporate salts, and the existence of molecular hydrogen . . .'

In a few moments the four of them were having the usual animated arguments about life on the Jovian moons – life on Jupiter itself. It was the major after-hours pastime of the entire Jupiter crew, Americans and Chinese alike. Soon it would be settled once and for all.

'. . . I see a giant lipid, floating in a pool of methane,' Berry

29

was saying, stroking his scraggy beard and peering into his beer as if it were a crystal ball. He had an exaggerated gypsy accent. 'A very complex molecule, like chicken fat. No, no, it's not a lipid after all. It's a lipoprotein, in a cloud of sulphur! It's saying "Earthman beware..."'

Jameson stopped listening. He was staring into the bowl of stars at his feet. Earth was gone. Jupiter swung into view again among the wheeling stars. It was clear and steady-bright, and it was half a billion miles away.

Maggie said it for him. She caught his eye across the table and said, 'It's a long way down, isn't it?'

## CHAPTER THREE

'Can't you scientist fellows do something to stop it?' demanded the Undersecretary for the Department of Urban Safety. He was a large beefy man in a conservative lace suit over a crimson body stocking.

'No.' Ruiz said bluntly.

*Ass*, he was thinking. But he kept his expression neutral as he looked around the horseshoe table at the assorted bureaucrats sitting there. There wasn't a flicker of comprehension on any of those well-fed faces, except perhaps for Fred Van Eyck, deputy administrator for the Space Resources Agency.

The conference room was deep underground, buried beneath the National Intelligence Bureau's reinforced-concrete antheap somewhere north of Washington. They had hustled him here as soon as he arrived on Earth. They had told him it was because the huge parabolic antennae on the roof of NIB headquarters offered a convenient – and secure — channel of communication with the Moon. But they hadn't allowed him near a communications terminal since his arrival.

Ruiz was tired, and his legs ached from the unaccustomed gravity. His body clock hadn't had time to adjust to terrestrial rhythms. His head was muzzy, and there was a bad taste in his mouth, and he felt seedy in the vending-machine disposasuit he'd been wearing for the last two days. They had promised him an audience with the President, but so far he'd spent most of his time talking to a parade of obvious gumshoes from the NIB and the Reliability Board.

They seemed to think that the Cygnus source was a political problem. Make the right policy decision and it would go away. Now they'd assembled this ad hoc committee and allowed him to drop his bombshell.

Over in the corner, a government newsie from the Federal Broadcasting Agency was taping the proceedings with a holo-scan. An NIB agent was supervising him, carefully collecting each spool as it was finished and locking it away under seal.

'Why not?' the undersecretary insisted. 'We give you fellows a big enough budget to fritter away out there in space. Can't you fire a rocket at it or something? Blow it up with a nuclear bomb?'

Ruiz looked helplessly at Fred Van Eyck for support. Fred was the only person present who knew an asteroid from a black hole, but he refused to meet Ruiz's eye.

Ruiz took a deep breath. 'Mr. Undersecretary,' he said, choosing his words carefully. 'We're talking about a stellar object approaching the solar system at very nearly the speed of light. Try to imagine a body many times larger than Earth giving off energy equal to an explosion of ten to the fourteen power megatons every *second*. That's on the order of a trillion times our most powerful fusion device. It would be like trying to stop a forest fire by throwing a firecracker at it.'

The undersecretary thrust his jaw out stubbornly. 'But couldn't you—'

'Let me put it another way,' Ruiz said. 'If you launched a nuclear bomb every hour on the hour for the next hundred million years, and timed them all to arrive at once, you *might* make an impression on an X-ray source like the Cygnus object. That's assuming, of course, that you could deliver them within a million miles of the thing without having them melt. And that you could intercept a target that's travelling at close to the speed of light.'

Out of the corner of his eye Ruiz saw Fred Van Eyck wince.

'Dammed scientists bring us nothing but trouble,' the Undersecretary grumbled. 'They ought to cut off your appropriation.'

Someone cleared his throat. It was Hoskins of the Civil Liberties Control Board. 'Dr. Ruiz, do I understand you say that there's no way we can ... *evade* this thing?' He coughed delicately. 'That is to say, couldn't a select group of persons – government officials and so forth, and their families – wait it out on the Moon, or on Mars?'

'No, Mr. Hoskins. Mars will be baked to a cinder too. There's no place to hide.'

At the far end of the curving table, just out of range of the holoscan, General Harris, NIB's owlish director, drummed his fingers on the transparent plastic surface. 'How about digging in?' he said. 'Caves, underground shelters?'

Ruiz stared unflinchingly into the hooded eyes. 'The Earth's crust will be sterilized,' he said. 'Down to the bacteria at the bottom of the deepest mine shaft.'

There was a stirring around the table. The magnitude of the situation was finally beginning to sink in.

'But this is serious.' The speaker was Norman Slade of the Public Opinion Monitoring Board. He was a waxy, narrow-faced man in one of the iridescent kaleidosuits that were popular this season among middle-aged swingers. He made a gesture with one hand, and the lenticule-impressed patterns on his sleeve rippled across the spectrum with a three-dimensional effect. 'If this gets out to the public, there'll be no controlling the population in the large urban centres. We'll have panic, rioting, civil breakdown. And every half-baked terrorist group will—'

'How long can we keep it under wraps?' interrupted the Public Safety Commission's Rumford. He turned a large shaggy head toward the NIB director. 'Who knows about this so far?'

'We moved in while Dr. Ruiz was still en route to Earth. A junior astronomy resident at Farside alerted us in time. We were able to place the duty tech under arrest and seal off the observatory. Dr. Mackie is co-operating, of course. We don't think anybody on the Farside staff talked to anybody outside, but we've cancelled all leaves from the Moon anyway. We're censoring all transmissions from there.'

'How about the Chinese?' Rumford said.

'That's classified,' General Harris said blandly.

*The Hell with them,* Ruiz thought. Maliciously, he said: 'You can assume the Chinese know everything we do. They monitor our transmissions with their synchronous lunar satellite, including what goes in and out of the Farside computer. And they've got a pretty good observatory of their own in the Jules Verne crater.'

'The Chinese will keep it under wraps too,' Slade said confidently. 'They won't want to panic their own population.'

Rumford shook his great mane. 'The danger is that the Chinese might decide to leak the information *here*. Stir up our Rads. Exploit the unrest.'

That was too much for Ruiz. He exploded. 'For heaven's sake, don't any of you people have any conception of what this is all about? We're talking about the end of all life on Earth – about six months from now. How is anybody going to exploit *that*?'

The NIB director looked at him coldly. 'We appreciate your feelings, Doctor. We understand that as a scientist your perspectives are different. But we'll expect your full cooperation. I remind you that the penalties for violating provisions of the National Information Act are quite severe.'

Ruiz stared back just as coldly. 'I understand completely. Don't worry, I'll keep my mouth shut.'

'Fine. I'll also remind you that the penalties extend to the withholding of information, intentional or otherwise.'

'What information?' Ruiz asked angrily. 'I've been kept in isolation since I left the Moon five days ago. I haven't the faintest idea of what data the observatory may have developed since then.'

'All transmissions from the Moon have been classified until further notice.'

'And you want a pliant *cofrade* like Mackie at that end of the cover-up, do you? That's it, eh? I'm not a member of the club. Let me tell you something, General, You know it already. You need my help, whether you like it or not.'

Ruiz was shaking when he finished, his skin covered with cold sweat, and he cursed himself for it.

The NIB director looked at him shrewdly. 'What is it that you want, Doctor?'

Ruiz took a breath. 'Send me back to the Moon.'

'That's impossible . . . for the time being.'

'Then let me talk to Mackie. And I'll need a computer terminal.'

Ruiz waited. The terminal was what he really wanted. He knew, realistically, that they weren't going to let him return to Farside.

The NIB director pursed his lips. 'All right,' he said finally. He pressed a buzzer, and an aide came in. 'Take Dr. Ruiz back to his quarters,' he said.

Ruiz limped out, following the aide past the armed guards.

No one spoke to him. Before the door swung shut behind him, he could hear them starting to argue. Fred Van Eyck's voice cut in, soothing and reasonable: '. . . no harm in letting him . . .'

His quarters were comfortable, impersonal, and windowless. There was a fold-out kitchen, well stocked with food and liquor, and a small bath. There was no phone or holoset, but a previous occupant had left a collection of battered and fading erasabooks and some spare spools in a drawer. Ruiz took a shower, put on a paper robe he found in the closet, and sat down to wait.

An hour later the door opened and two grim-faced agents came through, wheeling a portable computer terminal with a standard communicator plugged in to it. They nodded at Ruiz and hooked it into a thick socket in the baseboard. They left, and General Harris entered, followed by a silent man in a non-descript polka-dot suit. The man did things to the terminal and it came to life. He stepped back, lounging against the wall, not bothering to conceal the holocorder in his hand.

'All the signals go through a scrambler circuit,' the NIB director said, tight-lipped, 'but watch what you say anyway.'

The screen flickered, and Ruiz was looking at Horace Mackie's long, mournful face. In the background was the banked instrument panel of the monitor booth at Farside. An armed guard in NIB green hovered just behind Mackie.

Mackie squinted at him. 'Dr. Ruiz, is that you? Listen, I had nothing to do with my being named acting director—'

The NIB chief leaned past Ruiz and shut off the sound. Mackie's lips continued to move for the next second and a half, until the image from Earth reached the Moon. The armed guard said something to him, and he flushed. The sound went on again.

'Never mind all that, Horace,' Ruiz said gently. 'Just give me what you've got.'

Another second-and-a-half delay, and Mackie nodded, 'We still haven't picked up the thing optically. It seems to be a dark body, of about two-thirds Jovian mass.'

'Is that all?' Ruiz said, surprised.

'Yes, we've had a fix on it for the last four days with the big gravitational wave detector at L-5, and we've been taking more or less continuous readings of perturbations of the outer planets, and the computer estimates that the current mass—'

'Horace. Wait a minute. What do you mean by *current mass*?'

34

It was another second and a half before Mackie knew he'd been interrupted. He blinked and said 'That was the next thing I was going to tell you about. The mass of the Cygnus object seems to be decreasing.'

'Decreasing? By what factor?'

'It's lost about two per cent of its mass in the last four days.'

'What about X-ray and gamma emission?'

'That's decreasing too.'

'You mean *increasing*! That mass is turning into *something*!'

'No, no, we're quite sure. X-ray luminosity is definitely decreasing on what seems to be the beginning of a hyperbolic curve.'

The NIB director growled in his throat. 'What's going on? What's this all about?'

'Shut up,' Ruiz said. He leaned forward into the screen. 'Horace, listen to me. Have you checked for parallactic shift since I left?'

Mackie looked uncomfortable. 'Uh, no. They won't let me communicate with Dr. Larrabee. I'm assuming the previous estimate holds – minus, of course, the distance it would have travelled in five days at approximately light-speed.'

Ruiz turned to the NIB director. 'I want to talk to Mars,' he said.

Harris hesitated a bare fraction of a second. His craggy face and bald dome looked like something carved out of granite. *His Nibs*, the press liked to call him. He turned steely eyes on Ruiz. 'Write down what you want to ask Dr. Larrabee,' he said.

Ruiz tore off a corner of his robe and scribbled on it. The man in the polka-dot suit left his position by the wall and took the scrap of paper from him. General Harris nodded imperceptibly, and the man left.

'It'll be at least an hour,' Ruiz said.

'I'll wait,' the general said. He walked over to the pull-out kitchen and poured two glasses of Brazilian scotch. He handed one to Ruiz. Ruiz switched off Mackie's face and took a sip.

An hour and a half later the console buzzed and the screen lit up with the words STAND BY FOR VOICE TRANSMISSION. Ruiz put down his drink and turned up the sound.

'What the hell is going on, Hernando?' Larrabee's voice blurted, sounding aggrieved. 'One of my chief assistant bottle washers for these past three years turns out to be an NIB goon, and he tells me—' There was a faint scuffling sound, and

Larrabee's muffled 'Get your hands off me, Grover . . .' and a fade-out. After a moment, Larrabee came back with 'Here are the numbers. I've fed them to the Farside computer, as you asked.' He read off the base angles, sounding curt, and then the transmission abruptly terminated.

Mackie came back on the screen, looking anxious. 'I assume I'm plugged in to the computer,' Ruiz said. Without waiting for an answer, he began typing his query. He could see Mackie turning to follow the proceedings on some screen out of camera range. The answer came back in the fraction of a second it took Ruiz to lift his fingers from the keys.

'Well?' the NIB director said.

'The Cygnus object is slowing down,' Ruiz said. 'That's what it's doing with all the mass it's throwing away. The energies involved would have to be . . . enormous . . . for it to decelerate like that.'

'Never mind all that!' Harris snapped. 'What does it mean?'

'Mean?' Ruiz passed a hand wearily over his eyes. 'It means we've got a reprieve. By the time the Cygnus object arrives, it'll be a good deal more tame. And considerably shrunken.'

'Time,' the general mused. 'If it's slowing down, we'll have more time to get ready . . .'

'Didn't you hear what I said? You can call off your dammed national emergency. If the trend of those curves continues, it won't be shedding any dangerous amount of X-rays and gamma radiation by the time it gets here. It won't be colliding with interstellar hydrogen at relativistic speeds any more! And it won't have as large a gravitational scoop. And its cross section will be smaller.'

The NIB director looked at the screen. 'Do you verify that, Dr. Mackie?' he said.

There was a three-second delay, and Mackie jerked into response. 'Er . . . we'll have to continue our observations for some time, of course, but—'

'Why don't you tell him the Cygnus object's rate of deceleration, Horace?' Ruiz said.

Mackie maundered on until Ruiz's words reached him, then said 'Uh . . . why, approximately nine hundred eighty centimetres per second per second.'

'Is that figure supposed to mean something to me?' Harris said.

'It's an interesting coincidence, that's all,' Ruiz said. 'The

Cygnus object happens to be braking at just about one gravity.'

'I don't see . . .'

'Don't you understand yet, man?' In his impatience, Ruiz had reverted to his New Manhattan accent. 'It's not passing through any more. It's going to park here.'


## CHAPTER FOUR

The saloon smelled of fresh paint and new insulation. They were still putting the finishing touches on it. Tubular metal scaffolding was stacked haphazardly against the bulge of the far wall, where carpenters and foamwrights were installing a small stage to be used for concerts and amateur theatricals. Rows of mismatched folding and inflatable chairs had been hastily set up for the meeting. The curving chamber was one of the few places in the American sector of the ship that was roomy enough to seat this many crew members at once.

Jameson filed in with the rest, looking over the heads in front of him. There was a lot of joking and good-natured jostling. It felt good having weight on his feet again. They'd been spinning in the Jupiter ship at a full g for a couple of days now as part of the final shakedown – though during the actual voyage the 200-metre ring would be stressed at only two-thirds of a g.

A small, wiry man in a stained overshirt bumped into him; it was Kiernan, one of the hydroponicists. 'What's the Old Man want?' he said. 'I've got two hundred trays of wingbean seedlings to set out.'

'Your guess is as good as mine.' Jameson said.

Jameson found an empty seat near the back and sat down. The saloon was filling up fast. A couple of minutes later, Maggie MacInnes slid in next to him. A bony hip bumped his. She turned her head and blinked orange eyelashes. 'Hi,' she said. 'We haven't seen much of you these days.'

'Li and I pretty well wrapped up the landing exercises a month ago,' he said. 'I've been working for Captain Boyle. Got to earn my keep while we're getting there.'

She brushed a loose strand of red hair from her cheek. 'I'm glad you're going to be one of the execs in charge,' she said.

'I'm just third officer. By the way, that was a nice set of trajectory parameters you sent up yesterday. I recognized your touch.'

She shrugged freckled shoulders. 'I want to get to Jupiter in one piece too.'

The buzz of conversation around them died down as Captain Boyle came in and took his place on the little raised platform with the folding Moog and the music stands. He smiled and nodded at a couple of people in the front row, then stood in an easy posture, one thumb hooked into his harness, while he waited for everyone's full attention.

Boyle was a big imposing man with a red face and a thick, powerful neck. His cap of tight curls was thinning, and under the harness straps and the fresh uniform blouse donned for the occasion his wide shoulders and bull-like chest were tending toward bulk, but his waist was as trim as it had been when he commanded the expedition that had begun the work of seeding the Venusian clouds with life. Like many big men, he moved well, and in a way that inspired instant confidence.

'Ladies, gentlemen, and all you others,' he began; there was a dutiful laugh. 'I won't keep you long. I just want you all to know that, as of a couple of hours ago, our mission is officially go.' He drew a length of message strip out of the pocket of his shorts and waved it at them, 'I've just received confirmation from Earth of our original target date—' A ragged cheer went up, and in the second row Mike Berry stood up and raised clasped hands in a victory gesture. Captain Boyle motioned for silence and went on. 'I know that there have been times in the last year and a half when some of you thought we'd never make it' – groans from the audience – 'but I want to say that I'm proud of you and all your efforts.'

His manner became more serious. 'At this moment, over in the opposite side of the ship, Captain Hsieh is giving essentially the same message to his crew. A great new era in the exploration of space is about to begin. As representatives of the human race, we are going to' – he cleared his throat and looked a little embarrassed – 'to carry the banner of mankind farther from our home planet than we've ever gone before – ten times as far . . .'

Maggie nudged Jameson. 'Some pressec wrote that for him,' she whispered.

Jameson frowned her into subsiding. Boyle's awkward words had stirred him more than all the slick panegyrics he'd heard on the holoset in the last couple of years. He didn't think anybody had written them for him.

Boyle was going on more briskly. 'We'll be having a joint party with our Chinese crewmates tomorrow night' – there was a rustle of interest; the Chinese had remained correct but aloof during training, and get-togethers where you could socialize with them were rare – 'but tonight I'm inviting you all to a party of our own in the bubble lounge at Eurostation. Drinks and eats are on me.' Somebody whistled appreciatively; the bubble lounge was expensive.

He waved them into silence again. 'We'll be essentially finishing our training sessions in the next week, except for wrapups. During the six weeks before countdown, there'll only be routine maintenance while the Earth crews finish up outfitting. I'm happy to say that there'll be Earth furloughs for all of you on a staggered schedule.'

Maggie turned to Jameson, her face shining. 'Earth! I've been breathing canned air for six months now.'

Jameson drew a deep breath. It was real now. This was what all the hard work had been for. He realized that until this moment he hadn't really believed in it.

Around them, people had begun to chatter, to move restlessly in their seats. Captain Boyle held up his hand for silence again.

'Before we break this up, there are a couple of people I want you to meet. You'll be seeing a lot of them.'

There was a stir of interest. Maggie was leaning to her left to see, a skinny thigh pressed against his.

A sandy-haired fellow with boyish, snub-nosed features and well-muscled shoulders under a sleeveless jersey came in through the door behind Boyle, moving in a catlike crouch that showed he'd spent a lot of time in low gravity. He waved at someone in the audience and took his place beside the captain.

'Most of you know Jack Gifford,' Boyle said. 'Jack worked right alongside Roy Jenkins as an alternate during the initial training exercises, and SRA's been keeping him up to date right along. I'm sorry to have to tell you that Roy's been scrubbed for medical reasons. We'll all miss him. Jack will take his place as probe tech.'

Gifford smiled and nodded and took his place in the audience, squeezing in next to Sue Jarowski. He immediately struck up a conversation with her, something involving huge gestures. A couple of seats away, Dmitri looked unhappy.

Another man had slipped in through the door behind Boyle. He had a seal's head, sleek and shiny, and a triangular face with the kind of sallow complexion that always shows a subsurface smear of blue whiskers. The head seemed too small for the massive slope of shoulders and the bunched muscles that stretched the sleeves of his T-shirt. He was wearing a pair of heavy boots with thick gum soles. They struck Jameson as out of place in space, where the soles of your feet were among your most important sense organs.

This is Emmet Klein,' Boyle said. 'He'll be replacing Ham Bailey in charge of Stores.' He cleared his throat. 'Bailey will be returning Earthside for re-assignment. Our new stores exec is fully qualified – he's had three years at Mars Station and more recently has been working at the shuttle-launch complex at Salt Lake. I'm sure you'll all get along fine with him.'

Maggie poked Jameson. 'What do you think?'

Jameson frowned. 'I don't understand,' he said. 'If Bailey had to be reassigned, why didn't they replace him with Vitali or Michaels – somebody who's familiar with the mission? Mars and Salt Lake are impressive assignments, but they're ground-based.'

People were standing up. A small knot of men and women clustered around Klein and Gifford, all talking at once. Klein looked uncomfortable. Jameson felt sorry for him.

'Meeting's over,' Maggie said, getting up. 'Are you going to be at the party tonight?'

'Wouldn't miss it,' Jameson said. 'First I've got to go over to China country and talk to Li about closing down the lander and getting it podded.'

Captain Boyle was coming down the aisle, heading for the exit. Jameson stepped out and stopped him.

'What's all this about reassigning Ham, Skipper?' he inquired. 'He's the best stores exec we've ever had. He's been checked out for the mission for a year.'

Was Boyle avoiding his eyes? 'I don't know, Commander,' he said brusquely. 'I don't make policy. They do that down at Space Center.'

'Nothing medical, I hope?'

'Bailey's fine.'

'That's good to know. I'll look forward to helping give him a good send-off at the party.'

40

The captain's red face seemed to get a shade redder. 'He won't be at the party,' he said. 'He'll be leaving on the next shuttle.' He looked at his watch. 'About ten minutes from now.'

Captain Boyle's party was turning into a noisy success. Most of the crew had made some effort to dress up in Earthside clothes for the occasion, and there was a glitter of bright colours and iridescent fabrics. A couple of the younger dancers of both sexes wore little more than sparklepaint and stickumcups, but Beth Oliver, the beautiful and sought-after chemistry chief, was stunning in a full-length kaleidogown that shifted from endlessly flowering geometric patterns that spilled out of scores of focal points to an eye-boggling infinite-depth effect as she twisted in time to the thrumming slipbeat. The dancers took advantage of the low gravity in the bubble lounge to do complicated midair pirouettes, sometimes joined and sometimes in facing pairs.

The bubble lounge, halfway up one of Eurostation's main spokes, had a dreamlike quarter-gravity that went with the imaginative decor: space itself. The six enormous lobes of clear Lexan, bunched around the central shaft, brought the universe inside – an illusion that the designers had deliberately fostered by using the barest minimum of silvery, deceptively fragile-looking ribs to support the transparent plastic, and by hologenerated sparks of light that flickered on and off throughout the interior, like stars passing through. Directly above, you could see the diminishing spoke and the hub of the station, but everywhere else you saw only stars, drifting by like a million Christmas lights.

Jameson, a lidded drink in his hand, was part of the group gathered around the Moog. Mike Berry was at the keyboards, rapping out a creditable slipbeat. He'd dialled in a seventeen-bar ground that the Moog repeated over and over again, with random computer variations of timbre and ornamentation, and there was some kind of raga, also computer generated, weaving in and out of it. He'd punched in three basic beats that slid through one another with hypnotic insistence, and over the whole framework he was improvising a primitive but energetic mélange of chords and runs that contained fragments of some of the more popular recent hits.

'Want to spell me, old chum?' Berry asked Jameson.

'No thanks,' Jameson said. 'I'd rather enjoy my drink. I'll suffer along with you.'

Maggie leaning over the console, her hand on Berry's shoulder, looked up and said, 'Why don't you? Mike tells me you're good.'

Jameson laughed. 'I noodle around a little – old music mostly. I'm no good at party stuff. I'd kill the dancing.'

'He's right,' Berry said. 'No sense of rhythm – even with the Moog to help him. He's better off poking around with Bach and Mozart and Farnaby and all those ancient foot-tappers he likes.'

'I don't like committee music,' Jameson said good-naturedly. 'At least the Chinese leave out the aleatory computer input.'

'He has a hyper ear for tone, though, I'll give him that,' Berry went on imperturbably. 'Did you know that behind that standard face lurks a gift of absolute pitch?'

'Is that true?' Maggie said.

Berry answered for him. 'Of course, absolute pitch has nothing to do with musical talent. It's just a freak ability.'

'Mike, on the other hand, has talent but a tin ear,' Jameson said. 'Haven't you noticed that the Moog's out of tune? The last person who used it must have been fooling around with an enharmonic change between F sharp and G flat. I've been wincing for the last half-hour. You better clear the instructions and get it back to equal temperament.'

Unabashed, Berry went on playing.

'Can you really tell?' Maggie said.

Jameson's attention was distracted by the sight of Sue Jarowski drifting over, with the new man, Gifford, in tow like a magnetized particle. Sue was wearing an off-the-bosom chlamys with what seemed to be nothing more than a spray-on on the revealed side. 'Sure,' he said absently. 'Won a lot of bets with it when I was a cadet – earned my pocket money that way. Used to bet I could tell a fellow what note his boot was squeaking on, or whether somebody had just belched in B flat or B natural.'

'Maggie's an antiquarian too,' Berry said. 'Collects old things.'

'Old physicists, you mean?' Jameson said automatically.

Maggie laughed. 'Nothing too really hyper,' she said 'Twenteth-century plastic bottles, mostly.'

'Expensive hobby,' Jameson said.

Sue and Gifford pushed their way through the circle surrounding the Moog. Dmitri was hovering miserably nearby. Sue gave them all a big, earthy smile. Jameson wondered if he could pry Sue away from the party before Gifford did.

Berry lit up a joint and let the Moog do the work while his hands were busy. The dancers didn't seem to notice. With Berry no longer hammering away, the computer reached into its memory and filled in the gap with a standard contrapuntal theme that would go with the raga. It sounded fine.

'Have a gasp,' Berry said, passing the joint to Gifford. 'This is all organic – no synthetic THC added.'

'Thanks,' Gifford said, taking a drag and passing it to Sue. 'Too bad about Roy, but his hard luck's my ticket to Jupiter.'

'Glad to have you aboard,' Jameson said.

'Oh, here's our other new man,' Sue said. 'Hi.'

Jameson looked around and saw Klein standing on the fringes of the group, a plastic-lidded mug in his hand, his eyes roving over the dancers across the way. He turned around and nodded – reluctantly, it seemed to Jameson.

'Hey, you were on Mars,' Gifford said. 'Do you know Raul Peterson? Stocky guy. Seismologist assigned to Tharsis.'

'I was at Syrtis Major,' Klein explained. 'Excuse me.'

He threaded his way through the crowd and walked in his heavy boots over to the circular bar that skirted the centre of the lounge. The two barwomen were both busy, so Klein reached across to help himself. As Jameson watched, Klein thumbed his mug open and started to pour himself a cup of coffee. Just as Jameson was thinking that it was a little odd for Klein to be drinking coffee this early in the party, there was a scream and a little flurry of confusion up at the bar. Klein had managed to spill hot coffee over Beth Oliver, and himself too. The coffee had streamed right past the rim of the mug and splashed them both. Klein hadn't allowed for the sidewise curving effect of the Coriolis force when he poured. It seemed an odd lapse for someone who was supposed to be used to space.

Klein, his sallow face turning livid, was apologizing to Beth, and the United German barmaid was hurrying over with a damp cloth to mop up Beth's kaleidogown. Jameson craned his neck to see above the heads of the crowd, but then Sue, her voice raised against the din, was saying something to him, and he forgot about Klein.

By the time the intruder from Cygnus crossed the orbit of Neptune, its mass had shrunk to approximately that of the planet Earth. It could be picked up visually now by the 500-inch Sagan reflector on the Moon and the smaller mirror at L-5. With computer enhancement of the images, its surface features – if you could call them that – could be seen quite plainly.

The Cygnus Object, as the freepie media called it now that its existence no longer could be kept a secret, turned out indeed to be an Earth-size plant, its surface masked by clouds of boiling hydrogen. It even had a moon – a seared, rocky body a couple of thousand miles in diameter – and it also had an inexplicable wobble, as if it were rotating about a common centre of gravity with some massive object, one that the telescopes could not detect.

It was going to intersect the plane of the solar system at a shallow angle – about seventeen degrees from the ecliptic – and its speed was now low enough, at some fourteen miles per second, to assure that it would be captured by the Sun.

There was going to be a new planet in the solar system.

There was no hint in any of the stories that the Cygnus Object once had been a dangerous emitter of X-rays whose passage might have wiped Earth clean of life. There was no mention of the fact that it had shrunk from near-Jovian size in a matter of six months. Or, that against all natural law, it had unaccountably slowed to its present sedate speed from a velocity approaching that of light.

Fortunately for the authorities, the wandering planet had been obeying the laws of physics ever since it had come close enough to the solar system for Earthbound observatories and hundreds of amateur astronomers throughout the world to notice it, or its effects.

Independent observers were finding it remarkably difficult to get corroborating data from Farside or the Chinese observatory in the Jules Verne crater – though the Chinese claimed to have discovered the Cygnus Object first. Farside had issued a terse pressfax release just in time to prevent the Greater Japan observatory at Vladivostok from establishing a prior claim, and had said little since. Farside's new director, Dr. Horace Mackie, was nowhere near as communicative and co-operative as Dr. Ruiz had been, and the man who had succeeded Mackie at the Sagan dome, a young former resident

44

named Kerry, did nothing but spout officialese and academic doubletalk.

The newsies relied mostly on European and Japanese sources. There were enough compulsive talkers with Ph.D.s to give them all the copy and vids they needed about dead planets, torn from their suns, wandering through the void between the stars for millions of years. The story provided a brief circus for the public, and then it began to fade from the news.

Mizz Maybury was the first to notice anything.

She was on duty in the monitoring booth that shift. For company she had a silent, flat-faced assistant named Sorg, who she knew worked for the NIB. There had been a lot of them ever since Dr. Mackie had become director: extra people, new arrivals from Earth or Mare Imbrium who didn't seem to be doing anything much, or who, if they did, weren't very good at their jobs.

'Set up the board for a visual fix on the visitor,' she said, glancing at her worksheet instructions. 'I'm supposed to run some spectra tests this shift. You can use the small refractor.'

Sullenly, Sorg moved toward the panel. Maybury shuddered as he passed her. He was a pale young man, short and stocky. She didn't like the way he kept sneaking glances at her when he thought she wasn't looking.

Unconsciously her hand strayed to the dollar-sized shaved spot on her skull, where she'd been braindipped. The hair was starting to grow back, and it itched. They had told her that removing the tiny sample of cortical tissue for chemical monitoring during questioning – they took less than a cubic millimetre – couldn't possibly harm her. She'd hardly felt the prick of the dialytrode needle as it penetrated her scalp. But all the same, she hadn't felt the same since her arrest. It was more than a little scary to be locked up in a tiny room for a week while those dreadful men shouted at you and asked you questions and made all sorts of terrible accusations just to see how you'd react. They'd even told her that Dr. Ruiz had confessed that she had helped him sell information about the Cygnus Object to the Chinese She *knew* that couldn't be true. And then, when they couldn't shake her, all the questions about who she'd talked to since the sighting. All of them had been checked out, including her ailing grandmother on Earth. Finally, when they were grudgingly satisfied, all the warnings – threats, really – about not discussing her work with *anybody*

45

– not even her co-workers at Farside. She hadn't been allowed her sixth month Earth furlough, and even a pass to Mare Imbrium was hardly worth it any more, with the government hassle.

For once, Sorg had managed to talk to the Farside computer without being asked to repeat himself. The photoplastic plate in front of her came to life with the Cygnus Object's hazy disc. The speck of light off to the side was its moon.

Maybury applied herself to her job. While she was at it, she hooked in the bolometer and took the planet's temperature.

It was *hot*, despite its long sojourn in the chilly depths of interstellar space. No walking barefoot on its still-unseen surface unless you wanted to burn your feet! That terrifying blast of X-rays as it ploughed its way through the interstellar hydrogen must have warmed it up considerably – and warmed it all the way through. The surface temperature hadn't dropped by any noticeable fraction of a degree since the last bolometer reading.

She finished her measurements. Another moment and she would have told Sorg to switch off the image. But she just happened to be still looking at the plate when it happened.

A first-magnitude star suddenly bloomed between the planet and its moon.

Almost at the same moment, an enormous whirlpool of hydrogen clouds began to form on the side of the planet facing the star.

Maybury blinked, unable to believe her eyes. Meteorological phenomena thousands of miles across just didn't develop in the space of a few minutes.

She looked across at Sorg and hesitated. She really should call Dr. Mackie at this point. If anything interesting was developing, she'd probably be shooed out of the booth. That's the way things had been going at Farside since Dr. Ruiz had left. Her small jaw tightened stubbornly as professional pride took over. Sorg, lounging against a console, hadn't noticed anything. She punched her queries into her lightpad and thumbed them into the computer.

Data began to dance across the lightpad; she had told the computer not to duplicate the display on any of the data boards. She watched for several minutes, then set the computer to continuously monitor the planet's position against the solar orbit the observatory had plotted.

46

Sorg was sauntering over in her direction. She looked down into the photoplastic plate – hooded to keep out stray light — and gasped.

The new star was moving.

It was moving fast enough for the eye to see – about as fast as the second hand on an analog-style watch. From its initial position of about three planetary diameters from the Cygnus Object, it crossed in *front* of the planet.

It wasn't a star. It was something bright in orbit around the planet. A pinpoint of brilliant blue-white light.

She did a quick mental calculation, timing its passage across the face of the planet. It covered the 8,000 miles in twelve seconds.

The thing was whipping around the shrouded planet at something more than two million miles per hour. And it was picking up speed. It winked out as the planet eclipsed it. The eclipse lasted some nine seconds.

It was accelerating at – her forehead wrinkled with disbelief – at a rate equal to tens of thousands of gravities! And why wasn't it flying into a higher orbit? What tremendous force could be tying it down like that?

There was something else. The whirlpool of clouds was moving across the smudged face of the planet, following the moving star. She tried to imagine what a hurricane with winds of more than two million miles per hour would do to a landscape.

She reached for the communicator button. A hand slapped down over it before she could press it.

'What are you doing?' Sorg snapped.

'I'm calling Dr. Mackie,' she said. 'Now get your hand off that button.'

Mackie took twenty minutes to arrive. By that time, the orbiting spark was whizzing round and round too fast for the eye to follow. It looked like a hoop of glowing wire around the planet – a ring of etched light.

The hydrogen whirlpool was no longer distinguishable. In its place was a blurred white band girdling the planet. The rest of the cloudy surface seemed to be seething violently.

And if you looked closely, you could see a rim of ghostly spider webs connecting the planet's blurred belt with that strange shining halo. The effect was nothing at all like Saturn's rings. It was a totally unfamiliar phenomenon.

"What's this, what's this?" Mackie fussed. His tone seemed to accuse her of being responsible for something untoward.

She tried to tell him about the circling spark that was responsible for that ring of light, but he dismissed her impatiently. He pursed his lips disapprovingly when she attempted to explain about an acceleration of hundreds of thousands of feet per second per second. He wouldn't believe it until he'd resurrected the vids himself from the data banks.

But he didn't kick her out of the booth, and she was grateful for that. There was a lot of work to do, and the two of them got busy. Neither of them noticed when Sorg slipped from the room.

Maybury worked straight through the end of her shift, and stayed on with the extra people Mackie had called in to help. He kept them all very busy with visual observations, spectra and bolometer readings – becoming very excited at the rise in surface temperature detectable over the next few hours, caused, most probably, by the scouring friction of those million-mile winds.

But it never occurred to him to recheck the planet's solar orbit. Maybury finally was able to get his attention long enough to show him the numbers still unreeling on her lightpad.

'Good God!' he said, when he finally assimilated it. 'I wish Ruiz were here!'

There was no doubt about it. The planet from Cygnus was moving again.

It was a course correction. It was against all the rules of celestial mechanics. Not even the powerful gravitational tug of Jupiter could account for the planet's being torn from its solar orbit that way.

Mackie made everybody drop everything and apply themselves to this new phenomenon. So he was caught flat-footed ten hours later, when the wire hoop of light flickered and faded and became a spark again – a spark that slowed over the next twenty minutes and then abruptly extinguished itself.

The planet and its blistered moon had stopped changing direction. They were hurtling along a new path, but one that obeyed Newton's laws of motion.

Maybury stood on tiptoe and peered past Mackie's stooped shoulders to the viewplate. Mackie had plugged in the Sagan reflector, with Kerry's assent, and the view of the planet's disc was magnificent.

The face of the planet lay bare: a smooth rocky desert shorn of its hydrogen clouds except for a few wispy remnants.

It was dead now. That was the inescapable impression you got, looking at it. It had roused itself briefly and mysteriously, and now it was an inert ball of cooling rock.

But that last burst of effort had done its work.

Maybury tiptoed away and asked the computer for an entirely unauthorized projection of the planet's new trajectory. The answer made her gasp; she'd have to show it to Dr. Mackie as soon as she could tear him away from the viewplate.

There was no doubt about it.

The planet from Cygnus was going into orbit around Jupiter.

Ruiz fed a newdollar into the slot and fidgeted impatiently until a holofax dropped into the tray. The news machine in the beachfront refreshment pavilion was the only one he'd been able to find in the whole government rest camp, except for the one in the lobby, and he didn't feel like walking across a quarter mile of hot sand to get there. Workers who were lucky enough to rate a free vacation on the Nevada coast weren't much interested in news of the outside world.

For Ruiz it was different. He chafed at the long absence from his work. It was exasperating not to know what was going on with the Cygnus Object – except for the sanitized snippets of information released to the general public. It was exasperating – and humiliating – not to be able to get through to his former colleagues on the Moon; there was always some 'difficulty.' Oh, they were sugar-coating his enforced sabbatical, with make-work assignments and the lecture obligations that they'd discovered in the small print of his contract, and privileged holidays like this one. Until the government figured out what to do with him.

He was an embarrassment. The government didn't like to admit mistakes. Ruiz was a leftover mistake.

The mistake had begun when they put him under house arrest almost as soon as he stepped off the Moon shuttle. The end of the world was politically sensitive information, it seemed. They just didn't trust him not to blab.

Now that it appeared that the world wasn't going to end after all, they didn't trust him to cooperate with the cover-up which was in full swing now. It wouldn't do at all to let a powderkeg population of a billion know that their government had suppressed doomsday. Ruiz had too crusty a reputation. It was safer to have a poor frightened hack like Horace Mackie in charge of the crucial flow of information at Farside.

Ruiz squinted at the garish yellow ball of the Sun, shedding its fierce light on the herds of naked people facing seaward. It warmed his chill bones, baking out the old pains. He supposed he was lucky to be enjoying the luxury of Govpark instead of shivering in an isolation cell somewhere. Probably he could thank Harris for that; the man had brains enough to realize that Ruiz, despite his origins, couldn't possibly have gotten where he was in GovCorp unless he had *some* discretion.

Ruiz sighed. Why couldn't they understand that he had no desire at all to stir up problems? All he wanted was to get back to the Moon, where he could be useful.

A pair of young Govgirls strolled by, big and healthy and tanned, wearing only the briefest of fronties, white teeth flashing, repellesprayed hair still shaking out beads of salt water from their swim. They gave him a cursory glance, then walked on.

Ruiz didn't belong here, with his seamed face and knobby joints, his hollow chest and baggy jockstrap. He stood there in the hot, insistent sun, squinting at the fax sheet, looking for all the world like some undernourished Privie who'd gotten in by mistake.

He was blocking the entrance to an eats booth, but he didn't notice the annoyed glances he was getting from people who had to squeeze past him. He was studying the sheet in his hands with growing rage.

The holofax showed a scarred rocky globe with a headline in three-dimensional block letters hanging in front of it. The headline read:

NEW MOON FOR JUPITER?

He tilted the fax first to one side, then the other, to see the part of the planetary surface the letters were obscuring. There were no surprises: just scorched rock like the rest of it. He snorted in disgust and read the brief story floating in white type in the illusory space beneath the sphere. There were no surprises there, either. It was substantially what he'd overheard a few minutes earlier when some bather had walked by with portable holovid blaring:

*. . . according to Farside director Dr. Horace Mackie, scientists have now updated and corrected their original computations, and it appears that the wandering planet will take up an orbit around Jupiter instead of orbiting the Sun, as had originally been theorized . . .*

Ruiz crumpled the holofax angrily and dropped it on the boardwalk. So that was the pap they were going to feed the public! Updated computations!

It had taken some unimaginable force to tear that planetary mass from its solar orbit and aim it so that it would be captured by Jupiter. The universe was turning out to be a very queer place indeed, and here he was, stuck in this expensive sandbox for spoiled Guvie brats, while a stuffed gabacho like Mackie had all of Farside's facilities to play with.

Hot tears of frustration in his eyes, Ruiz stared out over the water. Swarms of boisterous pink bathers splashed in the near surf, and farther out bright little sailboats bobbed against the translucent sky. It was hard to believe that this sparkling bay once had been known as Death Valley, before the '09 earthquake had split the coast open and opened a channel to the sea.

He shook his head; best take advantage of it while he could. There'd been nothing like it for people like him while he was scrabbling for survival in the stinking tents of New Manhattan.

Ruiz hitched up his jockstrap and picked his way awkwardly through the sprawled sunbathers to the water's edge. After a dip, he felt better. He picked up his gear and started the long trudge across the desert sands towards his assigned hospice. He'd give it one more try. Maybe this time they'd let him talk to Mackie. He pretended elaborately not to notice the arbee in the striped robe and mirrorglasses who followed him back.


CHAPTER FIVE

'Sorry I'm late,' Li said. 'Struggle Group meeting.' He made a wry face. 'We had to elect a new leader, and the self-criticism dragged on longer than usual.'

'*Yuan yu,*' Jameson said, giving Li a crooked grin of sympathy. 'I thought Chu Lo was Struggle Group leader.'

'Didn't you hear? Chu Lo got rotated Earth. They send up new biologist this morning. Lady name Tu Jue-chen.'

'Who's the new leader?'

'Tu Jue-chen,' Li said blandly. 'Only democratic way.'

Jameson diplomatically said nothing. If Peking Center wanted to replace their political watchdog this close to countdown, it was their business. He was just thankful that it was a biologist and not somebody involved in the operational safety of the spaceship.

The two of them set off down the corridor towards Stores, helmets tucked under their arms. The great ship was eerily silent, sound smothered in foam. A quarter of the crew was on Earth leave, or at Eurostation awaiting transportation. There was ample room in the 600-foot doughnut of the spin section to dilute the rest of the crew – now grown to almost eighty people.

The sandalled feet of an approaching crewman came into view as they advanced along the upward-curving floor, and gradually the rest of him emerged from the ceiling's eclipse. It was Kiernan, the wiry little hydroponicist, muttering to himself. As he drew abreast, he said, 'If you're headed for Stores, that new bastard's going to give you a hard time.'

'What's the matter?' Jameson asked.

Kiernan jerked his head angrily toward the exit. 'I wanted to check out a couple of parts bins to use for seedlings. They're just the right size. Wang and I punch holes in them for drainage. This Klein makes a big deal out of it. Says they're not authorized for that use – tells me to make out a requisition and he'll have the *proper* equipment shipped over from Eurostation, and in the meantime I lose two days!'

'By the book,' Jameson said. 'One of those.'

Kiernan disappeared down the corridor, still muttering. Jameson and Li turned into the next crosstube and found themselves in the supply bay.

There was some kind of argument going on at the desk. As they drew closer, Jameson recognized Chief Grogan. Grogan's enormous competence had gotten him promoted from the original construction crew, and he would be coming along to Jupiter.

'Look,' Grogan was growling with forced patience, 'I got five men waiting at the airlock to go on outside detail. I gotta have fresh charges for their scooters.'

On the other side of the counter, Klein's narrow face was set woodenly. 'I can't issue you the new charges until you turn in the empties,' he said expressionlessly. 'Those are the rules.'

'Rules hell!' Grogan said. 'Those fragging scooters are tethered outside. I gotta go all the way back to the air lock, put a man in a spacesuit, wait till he vacs the lock, wait till he matches hub spin, goes out, gets the charges, matches spin again, waits for the air pumps, and hands me the tanks like a good little boy! Then I trot all the way down here and say, please, sir, can I have my charges now, sir? And in the meantime I waste an hour of the shift.' Grogan's brick-coloured face contorted with the effort of being polite. 'Look, why can't you just issue me the replacements and leave the paperwork for later. I'll bring the empties down at the end of the shift. Bailey always used to—'

'Bailey isn't here any more,' Klein said.

'But—'

'I'm responsible for everything that goes out of here,' Klein said. 'You don't get new charges until you account for the old ones. If you want to fill out a lost or damaged report . . .'

Grogan made a choking sound. He spat out a rude word and stormed out. Klein's eyes flickered over Jameson and Li. 'Yes Commander,' he said. 'What can I do for you?'

'*Tongzhi Li, ching*,' Jameson said to Li. 'Can we have that shopping list?'

Li extracted a crumpled sheet of paper from a leg pocket and held it out to Klein. Klein didn't take it.

'Just a minute,' Klein said. 'I'll get *Tongzhi* Chia in on this.'

'We're kind of in a hurry,' Jameson said. 'We've got to finish up outside before Communications closes down. Chia doesn't mind, and it's okay with Li and me—'

'It's not okay with *me*, Commander,' Klein said. 'Wait here.'

He came back with Chia Lan-ying. The Chinese stores exec was breathtakingly lovely, with a tiny flower face and great dark eyes. She moved with brisk efficiency. She was wearing a blue smock with sleeves pushed up. Her little delicate fingers were grimy and ink-stained, and there was a smudge on her cheek. Jameson had always known her to be cheerful and cooperative, but today she seemed unhappy.

'*Hau-a, Tongzhi Li*,' she said severely, and then to Jameson 'Hello, Commander.'

'All right,' Klein said, 'let's start checking these things off. Do you have your book?'

'I can start getting those latch seals,' Jameson said. 'I know where Bailey kept them.' He took a step past Klein and the girl.

53

'Just stay on your side of the counter, Commander,' Klein said in a flat tone. 'Nobody except authorized personnel takes anything out of those bins.'

Jameson's lips tightened, but he caught himself before saying anything. 'All right,' he said. 'But hurry it up, will you?'

Klein took his time. He fussed and nitpicked over everything. Jameson could see Chia Lan-ying developing more and more of a strained look; her response to Klein was a sort of tight courtesy. Jameson could understand it. It was no use trying to hurry Klein. If you got him off the track, it just had to be done over again. The pile of items on the counter grew as the harried clerks fetched them, one chit at a time. Finally Klein looked up.

'I guess that does it, Commander,' he said. 'Will you verify the list?'

'I don't have to. I've been keeping track as we went along. Just hand me that thing and Li and I will sign it.'

'We'll have to check it all off. I'll read off the items.'

Jameson restrained his impatience. They got through the list faster than he had expected. Klein actually smiled when they finished. Li, his face neutral, began to stuff things into a sack.

'Want to help me with this air tank, Lan-ying?' Jameson said. When Bailey had been stores exec, he'd often deferred to his Chinese co-worker, with her deft fingers.

'I'll do that,' Klein said harshly.

The girl stepped back. Startled, Jameson couldn't think of anything to say as he felt Klein fumbling at the valve connections behind his back.

'Don't you know any better than to let a chi-com fool with your life-support equipment?' Klein whispered in his ear, loudly enough to embarrass Chia Lan-ying, who moved off and began to busy herself with a binder. 'It's against regs – and for a damn good reason. Any accidents where there's the slightest chance the other side gets blamed – *either* side, Commander – and it could bollix up the whole mission. Think about it'

Klein unlatched Jameson's depleted tank, chalked it with an X, and added it to a pile of tanks in a canvas cart. He picked up a fresh tank from the pile of equipment on the counter and fastened it to Jameson's harness.

'Careful when you screw in the T-valve on the switchover,' Jameson said mildly. 'It's a little tricky on this suit.'

'I've done this before,' Klein said irritably. 'There you go, all set.'

'Did you check the safety on the pressure-relief valve?' Jameson asked.

'It's all right, I said,' Klein snapped. He flipped all the latches shut, then moved away.

'Let's go, Li,' Jameson said. They picked up their sacks and left.

Li waited until they were in the tubeway. 'Not a very likable man, this Klein.'

Jameson's accumulated irritation broke through and aimed itself at Li. A little bit of shamefaced loyalty to his own side was mixed in with it. 'He doesn't have to be likable,' he said shortly. 'Just so long as he does his job.'

They walked to the nearest lift shaft in silence. They had to wait about five minutes. The wraparound door revolved to open, and Grogan and an assistant staggered out, hugging bulky scooter reaction tanks. Grogan grimaced at Jameson as he stepped past him. 'Don't empty your pissbottle while you're out there, Commander,' he said. 'That Klein joker'll make you go back and count all the crystals.'

Jameson laughed and stepped inside. Li crowded in with him. The door slid shut with a hiss, and the circular platform began to rise. The lift shaft ran through one of the three equidistant spokes that connected the ship's main ring to the hub and the thousand-foot spear that ran through it. It was three hundred feet to the hub – too far to walk and impossible to leap when the ship was under spin. Jameson felt his weight dropping fast as they ascended. The Coriolis force pushed at him. jamming him against the mesh wall of the cage. Then the cage stopped, the invisible fist released him, and he was so close to weightlessness that it made no difference.

Four of Grogan's men were in the spinlock antechamber, playing a dispirited game of cards on a magnetic board that kept getting away from them. They were in skivvies and sticky-slippers, their spacesuits bobbing from hooks on the wall behind them. They didn't bother to look up as Jameson and Li unfastened the hatch to the spinlock and dove inside.

Jameson and Li helped each other with their helmets and gloves, then vacced the lock. The spinlock was an unpleasant place to be in for any length of time; though your weight was negligible this close to the centre of the ship, the gradient between head and feet was quite noticeable. It made people feel odd, disoriented, a little nauseated. Through the little safety window Jameson could see the metal skin of the ship's central shaft reeling past at two revolutions per minute. The wheel's hub slid around the axle on frictionless bearings – the perfect ball bearings that had been cast under weightless conditions in one of the space factories swarming around Eurostation. Of course, total frictionlessness was impossible to achieve, but this came close enough; the minute amount of spin that was imparted to the thousand-foot axis of the ship was easily corrected once or twice a day by a modest computer-regulated flywheel.

Li released the brake. The anti-spin jets fired automatically, as soon as the computer verified that neither of the other two spinlocks had open outer doors. The unpleasant feeling disappeared as body fluids redistributed themselves. Jameson's sinuses cleared. Through the little window he could see the motion of the inner hull slow down and stop. The spinlock fastened itself to the long shaft of the inner hull. Now the 600-foot wheel of the spin section was sliding around the spinlock's outer ring of frictionless bearings in their Teflon track.

The two spacesuited figures pulled themselves aft along the webbing and cordage that restrained cargo. No-g wasn't good for much of anything except stowage and the super-growth section of the hydroponics system. The boron fusion/fission engine was all the way aft, off limits behind thick bulkheads. Jameson could see the dull red glow of the warning lights in the murky distance – though this airless tunnel ought to be deterrent enough.

Jameson and Li emerged through a hatch roughly halfway down the tunnel. There was a dazzle of stars around them. Jameson pulled himself out on the hull and perched on a railing, enjoying the view. This was the only position where you could get some impression of the whole colossal work of engineering that was the ship. He was straddling a gigantic oar, with the bulbous knob of the command centre at its forward end and the flaring skirt of the drive section at the rear. A small forest of antennae sprouted from the mushroom bulge of the bridge, and there was a cluster of spherical fuel tanks aft for the hydrogen-fusion part of the boron cycle. Otherwise the huge shaft was unbroken, except for the protective housings that held the Callistro lander and the automated probes.

But ahead of him, no more than fifty feet from where he sat, was the rotating bushing that contained the spinlocks and to which the three main spokes of the wheel were attached. He looked up and saw the great revolving circle he would be living in for the next year, as it swept steadily past the stars twice every minute. Here and there on the facing rim he saw little squares of light: illuminated ports. The ship would be ablaze with them when it began its outward journey.

'Come on, buddy,' Li's voice said in his ear. 'We've got a lot to do.'

Reluctantly Jameson dragged his eyes away from the stupendous moving archway above him. The whirling steel face in front of him was grinding away like a titan's mill, its flailing arms as thick around as the first moon rocket had been. Jameson shuddered at the thought of the mass and momentum behind that motion. It made him feel like a fly clinging to a power turbine housing. He turned away from it and crawled along a guiderail toward the plastic blister covering the lander.

Mothballing the lander was slow work. You couldn't open the sack to look for the various small items you needed, because everything tended to float out at once; instead you had to feel around inside through an inverted sleeve, and with gloves on it was hard to trace the shapes of different objects. After an hour of it, Jameson and Li were getting impatient – and careless.

Li was inside the blister when it happened. Jameson was outside, floating about two feet above the surface. He had just let go of his handhold so he could use both hands to get a tube of epoxy out of the sack.

Just at that moment there was a fluttering hiss inside his helmet as his number one air tank ran out and the switchover cycle to number two began.

And then he got a kick in the back.

He grabbed wildly for his handhold as he started to tumble, but he was too late. The jet of escaping air had nudged him a foot out of reach. It might as well have been a mile.

He was cartwheeling out of control. He hadn't bothered with suit jets for this job. Neither had Li. The valve of his number two tank was wide open and shooting him through space like a rocket. Before he could reach around behind him to try to do something about it, he had a new problem.

He was being squirted in a looping path towards the churning maw of the ship's hub. An enormous metal arm swept past his vision. The entire mass of the wheel itself, a quarter of a million tons, was concentrated at the end of it.

There was no way he could stop himself. Helplessly he watched the next arm swoop down on him. With luck, it would barely miss him, and then, ten seconds later, the third spoke would bat him with the full momentum of the ship and slam him into the massive bushing that contained the spinlocks.

They'd have to scrape him off with butter knives.

Desperately he flicked out the sack he was holding. If he let go, was there enough mass inside it to push him in the opposite direction? Not a chance, with his inertia.

Instead he hung on. The sack curled itself around the descending spoke. There was a jolt that almost tore his arm off, and then he was sailing outward. The outer rim of the ship flashed by him. He saw a lighted port with a face behind it. The ship seemed to shrink. A minute later it was a child's top, spinning in the void, and he was soaring up into eternal night. The air was gone from his helmet. He closed his eyes to save them, there was a fire in his chest as he sucked on vacuum, and then all his consciousness gathered itself into a single bright dot that shrank the way the ship had done. There was time to think that Li, still inside the lander pod, probably didn't know yet what had happened, and if he did know there was nothing he could do about it, and then all the time was gone, along with the rest of that bright dot.

The light was too bright on his eyelids. He had the world's worst headache. He was naked between clean sheets. There was weight on him, about two-thirds Earthweight, and he could smell ship's air. He opened his eyes and sat up. He immediately regretted it. A heavy liquid seemed to be sloshing around inside his head.

'That's a beautiful pair of bloodshot eyes,' a voice said.

It was Doc Brough. He was leaning over the narrow cot, a plump, sandy-haired man in shorts and a shirt with the tail hanging out. This was a cubicle in the ship's infirmary. Over by the canvas wall, Li was standing next to Grogan. They both looked uncomfortable.

'You can thank those two,' Brough went on. 'Comrade Li saw you sailing out to never-never land. Another minute and you'd have been invisible. They might have located you with radar in a day or two. Chief Grogan was just coming out of the outside lock with a couple of fresh scooter charges. He saw Li waving and pointing over by the lander pod. He didn't even wait to put the charge in the scooter. He just jetted himself after you, riding the tank and steering by the seat of his pants. Damn lucky he didn't cook his thighs and wherewithal. He'll be walking gingerly a few days, I'll tell you. Shared his air with you on the way back and got you down here. Don't worry, you aren't a vegetable. You weren't breathing space for more than a minute or two.'

Grogan lumbered over to the bed and took a widelegged stance. 'Anybody ever teach you to check your valves?' he growled. 'One arm of your T-valve was shut off tight. You vented your whole number two tank through the pressure-relief valve. And the safety came loose – wasn't screwed in right.'

'Thanks, Chief,' Jameson said.

Grogan growled again and left with a curious gait. No one would comment on it unless they wanted a flattened nose. Li came over. 'Schedule's shot to hell,' he said. 'I'll go over the report with you when you feel up to it.'

'Thanks, Li,' Jameson said. 'Excuse me. *Hsieh-hsieh, Tongzhi.*'

'Don't overdo it, buddy,' Li said with a quick grin, and left.

Jameson swung his legs over the side of the cot and stood up. 'Where's my shorts, Doc?' he asked.

Brough said, 'Get the hell back on that bed. You're not leaving here till I run a couple of tests.'

'Can't wait, Doc,' Jameson said, padding over to the locker near the entrance flap. 'I've got to see the captain.'

Captain Boyle was unhelpful. 'File your complaint if you like,' he said stiffly. 'But I won't recommend Klein's transfer.'

'Captain,' Jameson said, just as stiffly, 'Klein almost killed me. And on top of that, he's a damn bad stores exec.'

'He'll learn.'

'Learn, hell! At whose expense? It's going to be a long trip, Captain. You know we can't afford baggage like Klein. What's he doing here? What strings did he pull?'

'I won't discuss it further, Commander,' Boyle said.

'All right Captain, if that's the way you want it. But I don't understand what's going on here.'

He turned to go. Boyle touched his arm. 'Tod . . .' he said. He seemed uncomfortable about something.

'Yes, sir?'

'I'd help you if I could. But I'll give you a piece of advice instead. Don't file that complaint. It won't do any good, and the people down below don't like static.'

'Thanks for the advice, Captain,' Jameson said. 'You'll find the complaint on your desk in the morning.' His eyes held Boyle's for a moment, and he walked out.

Sue was coming down the passageway, a sheaf of reports in her hand. She was wearing a duty tabard over her shirt and shorts, unbelted and flapping open at the sides. 'How are you feeling?' she said. 'I stopped down at sickbay when I got off, but you'd already left.'

'I'm fine,' he said. 'If my ears would stop ringing.'

'That Klein!' she said. For a moment her face flushed.

'Hey, don't take it personally!'

'I can't help it! I know that . . .' Her voice dropped, and she looked nervously around the corridor. 'Captain Boyle was on the beam to Earth, raising ten different kinds of hell. I put the calls through. But he didn't get anywhere with those stonewallahs at Mishcon! He was furious!'

He looked at her. Her chest under the tabard was rising and falling fast. 'You bunking with the Giff tonight?' he said evenly.

She laughed. 'No. He's still sampling. I think it's Beth Oliver at the moment.'

'Make room for a broken-down spacie? I've still got three days till Earth leave.'

'Any time, Tod,' she said. They squeezed hands, and she took her reports through to the captain's quarters.

The shirt-sleeved young flight controller sat at his console, his finger poised above the firing button. He hesitated, then lifted the finger to a position in front of his face and studied it with undisguised admiration.

'This little pinkie's worth a half billion newbucks, do you realize that?' he said with simulated awe. 'That's what it's gonna cost the government a couple of seconds from now. Do you think it knows? Can fingers think?'

'Come on, Bedford, quit clowning,' the controller next to him said. 'Push the damn button and get it over with. The course alteration's all plugged in. I don't wanna have to ask for a recomp.'

'Ah, brief moment of glory' Bedford said theatrically, and stabbed at the red button.

Nothing happened. Nothing was going to happen until the radio signal reached the vicinity of Jupiter, some forty-plus minutes from now. And they wouldn't know if it had worked for another forty-plus minutes, when the telemetry data struggled all the way back.

There wasn't much to do until then, so the dozen men on the team leaned back in their swivel chairs, sipped coffee, and traded desultory conversation.

The officials gathered in the glass booth at the rear of the room were more agitated. Shevchenko, the astronomer whose programme was being superseded, was staring at the screen, looking grim. Beside him, the administrator for the Space Resources Agency, Harrison Richards, was biting his aristocratic lip as he watched half a billion dollars of his budget go down the drain for a project that hadn't been in the year's estimates. The deputy administrator, Fred Van Eyck, bespectacled and neat in crisp grey business pyjamas, was nursemaiding a group of VIPs from Washington, keeping them occupied and harmless with babytalk about the technical details of the mission. But there was sweat glistening on his high-domed forehead.

'Two years,' Shevchenko said bitterly. 'Two years' planning down the drain.' He was a small, untidy man with crumbs of food showing in the tangled oval around his mouth that he called a beard. He was wearing academic denims, faded and rumple-treated, with simulated patches badly dyed at the knees and elbows. Shevchenko's parents had been part of the enormous wave of immigrants from a devastated Soviet Union in the 2010s, and, like so many second-generation Russians, he had an aggressive drive to succeed that sometimes irritated his more-secure colleagues.

Administrator Richards glanced nervously at the Washington bunch. Van Eyck was still keeping them busy. Shevchenko was definitely not playing the game, airing his gripes in their presence.

'We'll tack as many of your experiments as we can onto the manned mission next month, Alex,' he said soothingly. 'We ought to be able to salvage most of your programme.'

'Salvage?' Shevchenko complained, spraying saliva with the sibilant. 'And can you promise me that those cloudtop features

61

in the south tropical zone will still be there six months from now? Eh, eh, tell me that!'

'There she goes!' one of the flight-dynamics engineers called from the front row of consoles.

With relief, Richards turned away from Shevchenko and looked up at the big central screen along with the rest of them. Van Eyck's smooth, low-key spiel trailed off as the Washington people strained eagerly to see.

The vast orb of Jupiter was moving right and off screen, as the robot probe, half a billion miles away, swung on its axis. For a moment there was a stunning closeup view of Io in crescent phase, surrounded by the spooky yellow glow of sodium emission. Then the picture jumped and blurred as the probe's thrusters fired a long burst, kicking it into a higher orbit.

'That does it,' Shevchenko said, looking close to tears. 'No more fuel reserves now. There goes our cloudtop orbit.' There was garlic on his breath. Richards moved away from him.

'You can see the captured planet and its moon now,' Van Eyck was telling the VIP's. 'We think the moon will take up an independent orbit around Jupiter. The planet won't be able to hold on to it now.' He turned and spoke into a microphone. 'How does our probe look, fellows?' he said.

The answer crackled through a loudspeaker in the booth as one of the flight controllers answered. 'Right on target, Dr. Van Eyck.'

One of the VIP's frowned importantly. It was MacPhail, the senator from Newfoundland, a big, portly man in a polyester kilt. Though his constituency was small, he was a power on the budget committee. 'I couldn't help overhearing what Dr. Richards said to Dr. Shevchenko. I know you people are anxious to get a look at this planet from outside the solar system, but isn't it a fact that you're altering the course of your probe with no ... *definite* object? And in the meantime you've scratched a very expensive programme that *was* planned with a view towards the efficient expenditure of tax dollars.'

Richards interposed himself hastily. 'I appreciate your concern, Senator,' he said. 'But part of the original purpose of this unmanned mission was to insure the safety of the Jupiter crew.'

'I still think—'

'Come off it Angus,' said one of the other VIPs. It was Rumford of the Public Safety Commission, bearish and bleary-eyed after his Earth-Moon flight. 'You know perfectly well that this is still a security matter. Don't you remember the flap when we first discovered the thing and we came to your committee for funds to move troops and Reliability units into the major population centres? That thing may still have some surprises in it, and we're *not* about to risk any public unrest at this point.'

MacPhail flushed. Van Eyck stepped smoothly into the situation.

'Let's have some magnification, have a closer look,' he said.

He pressed a button, and the disc of the planet from Cygnus began to swell on the screen. The shadow of its moon had taken a small bite out of its edge.

'How did you do that?' someone asked. 'I thought you needed an hour and a half for the radio waves to make a round trip.'

'Oh, the picture information is already here in the computer's accumulator vat – it's just like blowing up a high-resolution photo.'

Three-quarters of an hour before, the camera must have been in the middle of one of its back-and-forth pans to the Cygnus Object's moon. Still zooming in, the camera was focusing on the space between the two planetary objects. Sunlight glinted off something in the void.

'Good Lord!' Richards said. 'What are those?'

The camera was still zooming in, allowing a tantalizing glimpse of something unnaturally angular.

Then there was a dazzle of ruby light, and the screen went blank.

'Bedford!' Van Eyck roared through his microphone. 'Get that picture back on!'

There was consternation among the ranked consoles down below. The flight controllers, some of them half out of their seats, were scrabbling over their buttons and dials. One of the systems-operation engineers had left his chair entirely and was leaning over the telemetry officer, yelling in his ear.

'It's dead, sir,' Bedford's voice came over the speaker. 'The probe's dead. The instruments say that everything heated up – fast! Then it died on us.'

# CHAPTER SIX

For a moment, as the ablative port shields shredded and whipped away into the wind, Jameson caught a fine view of Greater Houston spread out below him: a glittering sprawl of bright cuboid shapes stretching for a hundred miles along the Gulf Coast. Inland, at the centre of that vast multicoloured jumble, was the graceful mile-high stalk of the Federal Tower, its entire south face a shimmering parabolic cliff reflecting the sunlight of the hundred acres of solar collectors skirting its base towards a focus at the Houston Electrical Authority plant across the river. It was in use after forty years, despite the gradual conversion of fusion power that had begun in the early decades of the century.

Offshore, rising from the rich blue waters of the Gulf, he could see the moored ranks of thousands of wind machines bobbing on their submerged floats: delicate-looking lattices hundreds of feet high, with propeller blades spinning like bright dewdrops all across the spider-web surfaces.

As far as the eye could see, across the surrounding Texas countryside, were the shining spokes of the solar farms, alternating with green strips of cropland growing chimeric soycorn and peanuts and wingbeans – food and energy for the megalopolis and its satellite cities. More than a hundred million people, the largest urban population in North America, lived in the Houston-San Antonio-Dallasworth triangle.

The horizon tilted as the great shuttlecraft banked towards the Dallasworth spaceport. Jameson settled back and watched the landscape flash by beneath him. The solar farms gave way to a drab patchwork of farmland dotted with small skyscrapers. After another ten minutes the green became increasingly pebbled with dull grey, as Dallasworth's outskirts yearned toward merger with Houston. Then the shuttlecraft banked again and dropped like a stone as it entered its final glide path. There were audible gasps from the more inexperienced travellers. Jameson had a glimpse of looping freeways, a blurred impression of serried roofs, horizon to horizon, and then the huge mantawinged craft dipped and skidded to an abrupt stop.

The pilot was skilful; re-entry vehicles have all the responsiveness of a brick at their 200-mph landing speed. Only a mild jolt threw Jameson and the other passengers forward against the corsets that encased them from armpit to hip. He could see his seatmate, a pert little brunette from the Moon, wince as the stretchband briefly flattened her breasts, and then the automatic clamps snapped free, a chime sounded, and the passengers began peeling themselves out of their cocoons.

'Please stay in your seats, ladies and gentlemen,' the pilot's voice came over the com. 'The conveyor will hook up as soon as our outer skin cools off a bit.'

No one paid attention. The passengers were struggling to their feet, jolly and befuddled by the drinks and joints they'd been served before re-entry. More than a hundred of them were milling noisily in the narrow aisles: tourists returning from Mare Imbrium and Eurostation's vacation inn, lunies, scientific and support personnel. They clutched their little souvenir packs with the ounce of Moon rock and the bottle of vacuum, and called back and forth to one another.

'How does it feel to have Earthweight on you again?' Jameson said to the woman. She very sensibly had remained in her seat while they were waiting.

'Good,' she said, flashing him a smile. 'I haven't been back for almost a year.'

'Oh?' He raised his eyebrows. 'I thought you Farside people got terrestrial furlough every six months.'

'I . . . I couldn't get away,' she said. There was an awkward silence. She suddenly seemed preoccupied.

'Well . . .' Jameson said. 'Planning to spend your leave in this area? There's certainly a lot to do. You're just in time for the start of the Houston theatre season, and the San Antone Fiesta.'

'No,' she said. 'I'll be taking the tube to Nevada.' She stood up. 'It was nice meeting you, Commander Jameson. Have a good leave, and good luck on your mission.'

She shook hands with him and disappeared into the crowd that was flowing toward the exit. The conveyor had arrived with a thud against the hull, and the big oval port swung inward. Jameson watched her go with faint regret. He had been on the verge of asking her to dinner.

He joined the surge to the exit, a tall, lean figure with his black hair cut spaceman-short. He looked cool and neat in lightweight grey slacks and an open-necked white shirt. He carried nothing but a small zipbag.

A beefy tourist, loaded down with cameras, last-minute pur-chases, and a bulging shoulder bag that had doubtless seemed light on the Moon, bumped into him. Jameson helped him re-trieve a gift-wrapped bottle of champagne from Eurostation – one that had come from Earth in the first place. 'Thanks,' the man said. There was hash on his breath. 'What a trip, but there's no place like home, right?' Jameson agreed with him politely and helped him negotiate the moving belt to the ter-minal. Around him cameras were clicking as they were carried past the controversial memorial statue of John F. Kennedy, an heroic nude more than fifty metres high, moulded of gleaming polymers; the figure balanced a representation of the Moon in one hand and held a rocket aloft like a sword in the other.

His clearance through customs was fast. The inspector flip-ped to the holopic in Jameson's ident-book and said, 'Hey, you're not the Commander Jameson that's going to Jupiter?'

'I'm the one,' Jameson said.

The inspector snapped the book shut and shoved it briefly under the scanner linked to the federal computer. There was no warning light that would have indicated a citizen with re-stricted rights or someone travelling without authorization. The computer noted Jameson's position on the planet, along with the last known positions of a billion other Americans, and sent the appropriate signals to both the central locator files and Jameson's own biographical file. It also automatically deducted his port-entry fee from his bank account.

'Nothing to declare, right, Commander?' the inspector asked cheerfully.

'Not a thing.'

The inspector slid the zipbag over to him, unopened, and handed him back his book. 'Enjoy your stay, Commander,' he said. 'And give our regards to the beasties on Jupiter.'

'I'll do that.' Jameson laughed. He took his bag and headed for the slideway to the levi-car terminal.

He'd just missed a car. He was in time to see it rolling down the tube, retracting its landing wheels from the tunnel's side flanges as it picked up speed and began to levitate.

The next car slid in a minute later, a long sleek, windowless bullet, painted with graffiti. It was amazing how teenagers painted their slogans on the hulls during the few seconds a levi-car was at rest.

Curved sections of hull swung open and became ramps.

Jameson boarded with long strides, found a seat, and sat down. He kept his zipbag in his lap. The hull sealed itself shut, and the levi-car launched itself smoothly down the tube.

The car rocked slightly as the side wheels retracted and the vehicle began to hover above the guideway, riding on a cushion of magnetic flux. Shielding coils under the floor protected the passengers from the intense fields generated by the superconducting levitation magnets. There was a momentary feeling of lag as the car's bullet nose penetrated the elastic petals of the first tunnel seal, a second momentary resistance, and then the car was hurtling down the evacuated tubeway in full electromagnetic flight. Jameson raised his eyes to the display board at the front of the car. The reeling numbers told him that Greater Houston was 221 miles away, that they were building quickly toward their optimum 600-mph speed, and that E.T.A. was approximately 23 minutes.

His seat companion was a priest, a large jolly woman with close-cropped hair, wearing a grey cassock with a government badge and serial number pinned below one shoulder. 'Your first visit to Houston?' she asked.

'Yes, Parent,' Jameson said, remembering his manners. His own family had been nominal members of the Church of the Reborn – his father, he suspected, for career purposes, though all registered religions were theoretically equal in the eyes of the government. 'How could you tell?'

The priest laughed. 'You had that eager look. It always shows. I hope Houston won't disappoint you.'

'I'm sure it won't. I'm a small-town boy myself. I'm looking forward to my choice of theatres, concerts, the holo pageants ...'

'And some earthier amusements too, I don't doubt,' the priest said, a twinkle in her eye. 'You look like a healthy young man. I won't preach at you – the Good Lord knows that clergypersons have a stuffy enough reputation as it is – but take my advice and stay away from Privatetown. You'll have plenty of fun without slumming – and it could be dangerous.'

'Thanks for the advice, Parent,' Jameson said, grinning. 'I'll bear that in mind.'

'You young people.' The priest sighed. 'Well, remember to keep a tight grip on your bankchip.'

She went back to reading her breviary, an old-fashioned LED model with start-and-stop scanning, and Jameson amused himself by studying his fellow passengers. They were mostly civil-service bankers and brokers, wearing conservative candy-stripe or polka-dot suits, with a sprinkling of Partnership entrepreneurs, noses buried in the evening business faxes. Farther up, in an aisle seat, was a rich Privie in a gaudy ruffled suit with enormous puff sleeves, talking too loudly to his seatmate, a clerkish little man in olive drab who kept trying to shrink away from him. Jameson reminded himself that he wasn't prejudiced. Two Indian businessmen were seated across the way, probably on their way to the Federal Tower to sell India-Burma technology or buy American rice or soycorn.

At the Greater Houston terminal, Jameson said good-bye to the priest and let himself be swept along by the crowd to the bustling upper level. He followed a blinking floor pattern to the cab stand. Ignoring the swarms of scruffy-looking hustlers who clamoured at him, he chose a reliable-looking flywheel trike and rapped on the driver's compartment at the rear. The driver looked him over from inside his Lexiglass pod, nodded, and pressed the latch release. Jameson stepped quickly inside the front bubble and lowered the canopy over himself – but not before he had had to throw a scattering of bucks at the urchins who were pursuing him.

'The MacDonald Towers,' he said.

The driver engaged the superflywheel, and the three-wheeler pulled out into traffic. Through a gap on the far side of one of Houston's celebrated people plazas he caught a glimpse of the Federal Tower. Seen from ground level, it was a stupendous brown obelisk rising into the sky, its mirror side curving impossibly outward.

Then the streets became less fashionable. The driver speeded up and kept to the middle of the roadway as they passed dank alleys where sullen men in faded, once-gaudy clothing loitered and illegal lean-tos made of discarded sheets of plastic or cardboard sheltered whole families in a space large enough for only a couple of mattresses and a few cooking utensils. There were women here who would sell themselves for a bowl of snow rice, and men who would slit your throat for a newbuck. The sidewalks were swarming with them – hordes of noisy, shabby people who jostled one another, bargained at makeshift stalls that sold cast-off junk – all managing to exist somehow on little more than the Federal subsidy. Flics buzzed around a ramshackle butcher's stall festooned with the carcasses of what looked like – Jameson strained to see – skinned rats; he told himself they must be beef hamsters.

A potbellied child with broomstick arms and legs darted out in front of the cab. The driver cursed, braked, and managed to swerve around him.

'Bad place to get caught,' he told Jameson through the battered speaker. 'Driver I know ran over a kid near here. Accident – the kid ran outa nowhere. But the crowd dragged him outa his cab and beat him to death, while the fed on the beat looked the other way. Left the passenger alone, though. Somebody even got him another cab.'

'That's comforting,' Jameson said.

'Yeah, I dint wanna take the long way round. Wheel's running down. Gotta recharge it after this trip.'

'You must be having a good day, then,' Jameson said. The kind of vacuum-sealed fibre composite flywheels used in small taxicabs generally stored enough energy for two or three hundred miles of city driving.

'Not bad,' the driver said noncommittally.

Jameson knew he was in for it. When a fare got taken to a luxury complex like the MacDonald Towers, he got taken by the cabbie too. But Jameson had decided to splurge on his last vacation before leaving Earth for the next year and a half.

The Towers were built on a tooth of land projecting into Galveston Bay. The old Lyndon B. Johnson Space Center had once stood here, before it was dismantled at the turn of the century. Now it was a parklike preserve that occupied a half-mile strip along the shore. Farther inland was a smudge in the sky that indicated residential and industrial areas, but over the water the sky was clear and blue.

He could see the harlequin splendour of the Towers now – candied minarets that looked like something out of a fairytale. The late-afternoon sunlight sparkled on intricate balconies, hanging shrubs, and the soaring fantasy-arches that branched from each of the four bases to recurve and join in the centre of the glittering complex.

The three-wheeler pulled into a wide circular drive, between two pillboxes joined by an overhead portcullis. The driver flashed something, and a bored Marine guard nodded him through. Jameson caught sight of a few listless beggars loitering hopefully outside the gate, and then they were bumping along past green lawns and fountains and massed floral displays. The fare came to a hundred dollars even. Jameson thumbed an added twenty-per cent tip into his credit transfer chip and inserted it briefly in the slot. The driver had to manually transmit the transaction to the dispatching computer by radio, but after a moment there was a beep and the passenger canopy unlatched.

'You're welcome,' Jameson said, and climbed out of the pod. Instantly he was assailed by a dozen dirty ragged urchins competing for his attention and his zipbag. How they managed to sneak onto the grounds was a mystery. Before the hefty Marine doorman was able to shoo them away – using the butt of his submachine gun rather too freely, Jameson thought – his left shoe had been shined, a deft little hand had explored the inside of the wrong pocket for his bankchip, and an enterprising eight-year-old had offered his virgin sister.

'This way sir,' the doorman said, and Jameson followed him into the lobby.

The lobby was a four-acre parkland of winding mosaic paths, impossibly brilliant flower beds, gaudy pavilions where people sat and watched the passing scene. There was a lake in the centre with tiny barges, each holding a low mushroom table and four chairs. Waitresses in swimsuits pushed floating trays of drinks to the patrons. People in holiday clothes strolled along the geometric walks, past peppermint kiosks. Around the vast perimeter was an arched arcade with cafés and theatres and shops.

Jameson was too tired to make plans. All he wanted was a hot shower, a change of clothing chosen from his room vid, a few drinks, and an early dinner at one of the restaurants up top. Then a fresh start in the morning – maybe shark fishing in the bay, or some skiing at the hotel's indoor fluoroslope.

He threaded his way through the jostling, good-natured lobby crowds towards the spiral elevator platform. One of the bubble cars had just alighted. It opened like a flower, and a dozen people stepped out. One of them was a tall, skinny redhead in a green jumpsuit. Their eyes met in mutual surprise.

'Tod!' she said.

'Maggie! Maggie MacInnes! What are you doing here?'

The question seemed to startle her, Then she recovered, and freckles crowded one another around a wide grin. 'I live here,' she said.

70

It was Jameson's turn to be startled. He looked around the vast cylindrical chasm of the lobbyscape, his posture unconsciously conveying the outrage of the ruinous daily rates, and gulped 'You live *here*?'

Maggie laughed. 'I mean in Greater Houston. I just come to the MacDonald for the skiing.'

'I was beginning to wonder if you were an Indian millionaire. Time for a drink?'

She looked at the watch painted on her wrist, a one-day film of multilayer time-release paint that matched her jumpsuit, good until you took a shower. 'Well, maybe just a quick one,' she said, 'I've got to get back to Dallasworth for dinner.'

'With Mike Berry?' he asked cautiously.

'Jeeks, no!' she said, making a face. 'Mike's spending his leave with his ex and their kid. I'm singling it.'

'Me too,' Jameson said. He and Sue had no firm understanding about what would happen when he returned. She had spent her own leave visiting her parents in Denver – a grim, grey place for a holiday.

They shared a martini slush, served in little silver cryoglasses, at one of the canopied tables bordering the lake, and agreed to meet the next day.

'I'm not going to let you leave Houston without seeing some of the sights,' Maggie said firmly. 'After that, the MacDonald can have you.'

'You won't change your mind about dinner?' he said.

She glanced at the splash of paint on her wrist. Another slim wedge of green had just faded to a lighter shade. 'Can't', she said. 'I'm late now.'

She licked the last of her martini from the bottom of the cup and stood up. 'See you tomorrow,' she said. Jameson watched her slim, straight figure until it disappeared into the holiday crowds.

She was waiting for Ruiz in his room when he returned from his afternoon walk along the beach. He came in all the way, tracking sand, and closed the door behind him. He'd been burned black by the sun, but otherwise his 'vacation' hadn't done him much good. He looked gaunt and drawn and tired, and he knew it. He drew his robe more closely around his bony shanks and asked, 'How did you get in?'

'I told them at the desk that I was your daughter,' Mizz Maybury said. 'They said I could wait for you here.'

She was sitting erect on his bed, a small vulnerable figure in a short travel poncho and sandals, her hands folded in her lap. Square, competent hands, Ruiz noticed. He caught himself looking at her legs, still round and muscular despite all her months on the Moon.

'Daughter!' he snorted. 'Granddaughter, more likely!'

He shuffled over to the wall vendette in his paper slippers and punched himself an iced fruitbeer. 'Something cold to drink?'

Unexpectedly, she burst into tears. 'Oh, Dr. Ruiz, you don't know what it's been like since you left!'

He waited until she was over it, then handed her a glass. 'I can imagine,' he said dryly. 'You know you shouldn't be here.'

He noticed a small round patch on her head, about the size of a fivebuck, where her close-cropped dark hair seemed to be a little shorter. Fools, he thought. Fools and incompetents.

'Can't you do *something*?' she said angrily. 'Tell them – make them listen – come back and run things again—'

'They're not interested in my opinions,' he said. 'My opinions are an inconvenience to them.'

'I was there when one of your calls came through. Dr. Mackie wanted to talk to you, but they wouldn't let him. He *knows* what the Cygnus Object has to be, but he's afraid to come out and say so. Dr. Ruiz, he needs your help! I feel sorry for him!'

'I don't have access to any of the new data about the Cygnus Object,' Ruiz said. 'All I know is what I read in the faxes.'

'I've seen those,' she said. 'They don't say anything about the five smaller bodies. They can't pretend *those* are natural phenomena!'

'Smaller bodies?' Ruiz brought his head up sharply. 'Mizz Maybury, maybe you'd better start from the beginning.' He went over to the drawer and got his battered old pocket computer. He sat down on the bed beside her, cocking his head to listen.

She had just filled him in on the essentials when there was a heavy pounding and a harsh voice shouting 'RB!' and some-body kicked the door open.

Two large, meaty young men burst into the room. Their hands were empty, but there was the bulky shape of weapons belts under their shirttails.

Ruiz half rose from the bed.

'Hold it, Gramps!' one of the men said. He crossed the room with a bound and gave Ruiz a shove in the chest.

Maybury made a little choking sound.

'What's this about?' Ruiz asked in a steady voice.

The man looked both of them over, not bothering to answer. He was towheaded and pale, with narrow blue eyes. Maybury flushed at his scrutiny. Ruiz felt vulnerable and silly in his short robe with his knobbly knees showing through.

The second man, a thick-necked fellow with a flattened nose, was pulling out the antenna of a communicator and talking into it. 'We got 'em both. No sweat. The girl was in bed with him.'

'I wasn't—I—' Maybury began. The towhead grabbed the computer from Ruiz and tossed it to his partner.

'Evidence,' he said. The other man put the computer in a shiny black shoulder bag.

'Okay, Gramps,' the towheaded one said. 'Put on some clothes. You're taking a trip.'

'Aren't you supposed to show me some identification?' Ruiz said, sounding almost amused. 'And read me the little homily about good citizens cooperating voluntarily with the govern-ment's efforts to establish their reliability?'

The RB man sighed. 'You wanna make trouble? Come on, move it!'

Ruiz got dressed under their watchful eyes. Maybury sat on the bed, eyes downcast, her face pale. By the time Ruiz was ready, she had gotten her trembling under control. The arbee with the flat nose grasped her roughly above the elbow and hauled her to her feet.

'Hands off her!' Ruiz snapped, his eyes smouldering danger-ously. It only got Maybury a painful, bone-grating squeeze.

'Take it easy, Gramps,' the other man said. 'Awright, let's go.'

Two hours later they were sitting in a windowless office north of Washington, D.C. Somebody in authority had thought them worth the expense of a suborbital flight in a military aircraft – and worth all the broken windows and deafened vacationers in Nevada before they got above the atmosphere.

'What are we going to do with you, Dr. Ruiz?' General Harris inquired from across an acre of polished desk. 'And now you've gotten this young lady in trouble.'

His little beak of a nose was pinched and red in the sloping cliff that was his face. He drummed his fingers on the desk top.

'Trouble?' Ruiz said in a controlled voice. His eyes burned, red-rimmed, in a tired face. 'Maybury was paying a kind visit to an old friend and former associate.'

Maybury said nothing. She sat in the big chair, hands in her lap, looking around the blank walls of the office.

'Giving – or receiving – restricted information is a Federal crime,' the general said. He pressed a button, and Maybury's recorded voice came through a hidden speaker, telling Ruiz about the orbiting spark and the astonishing course change that had put the planet from Cygnus in orbit around Jupiter. Harris let it run for a minute, then switched it off.

'My Reliability Index hasn't been lowered, as far as I know,' Ruiz said. 'And Maybury has never received official notification that I've been barred from the receipt of observatory data.' He leaned back and waited.

'In security matters, a post facto determination can be made,' the general said. 'As a matter of public policy—'

'As a matter of public policy, you've decided to use me, haven't you?' Ruiz said. 'Otherwise I'd be in a cell right now. Let's stop the nonsense, General. What do you want?'

The general hemmed. Then he hawed. Then he looked at Maybury. He reached for a button.

'Maybury stays,' Ruiz growled. 'She's been bullied and harassed and braindipped. And now she's going to hear what you have to say.'

'You're a stubborn and cantankerous old man, Dr. Ruiz.'

'Never mind the flattery.'

'We want you to go along on the Jupiter expedition.'

Ruiz caught his breath. Then he said carefully, 'Want to get me out of the way, do you? So that I can't stir up any embarrassment for you while we're discovering what that thing orbiting Jupiter is?'

The general's lips tightened. 'You're determined to make things as difficult as possible, aren't you?'

'Yes.'

They locked eyes for a moment.

'We want an observer on the spot,' Harris said finally. 'Somebody with an independent turn of mind. We'll be drowning in observational data. We'll need value judgments.'

Ruiz smiled sourly. 'And I'll be conveniently away from Earth while things are turning up.'

'We don't want to lock you up, Dr. Ruiz. You're a very important man.'

'Thanks for being blunt, General,' Ruiz said dryly. 'I thought you'd never get around to that.'

'We can't risk any public unrest,' the general said blandly. 'You of all people ought to have learned that by now. If that thing out there turns out to be any danger to Earth – as you suggested when you first discovered it – there are all sorts of Rad elements ready to exploit the situation. The Chinese Coalition is just as worried about it as we are, I can assure you.'

'Why don't you just correct it?' Ruiz asked. 'If it starts giving off X-rays again, that is.'

'I'm beginning to lose my patience, Dr. Ruiz.'

Ruiz scratched his ear. He stared at the ceiling. After a while he said, 'That's quite a choice. Get locked up or go back to work.'

'You'll have full access to data,' Harris said eagerly. 'And when you get back, and policy is firmed up on this thing, you'll have your pick of options. Maybe a special project—'

'What happens to Maybury?'

The general pursed his lips. 'We won't prefer charges. Naturally, we'll have to take steps to insure reasonable security. But when this is over . . .'

'Lock her up and throw away the key, is that it?' Ruiz said.

'I can assure you that the young lady will be given every consideration.'

'I'll tell you what,' Ruiz said. 'I'll need an assistant. Somebody bright. Not one of your trained-seal brains. Send her along too. Maybury, how does that appeal to you?'

She leaned forward in her chair, eyes shining. 'Dr. Ruiz, I'd do anything to go along with you! Anything but go back to Farside. Or the kind of place they were keeping you!'

'It's all settled, then,' Ruiz declared. 'No charges, and a nice title for her on the expedition. Something that will look good on her career record.'

'Dr. Ruiz!' the general sputtered. 'I'm trying to be reasonable, but there are limits!'

'I'm sure there are,' Ruiz said. 'But we haven't reached them yet, have we?'

'Did you like it?' Maggie asked.

'It was . . . interesting,' Jameson replied delicately. He settled back in the narrow seat behind her and latched the bubble. The tricab pulled out of the lobby and into the street, the driver skilfully avoiding the beggars and Privie hawkers who clustered around each emerging vehicle before it picked up speed, pawing at the fastenings of the pods. Jameson twisted around for a last look at the Houston-Dallasworth Arts Center. The opera house, an immense iridescent egg balanced on end, had been built at the turn of the century, when architectural styles were beginning to take advantage of the new structural plastics.

'I thought you would,' Maggie said complacently. 'You don't know what I had to go through to get tickets.'

'I'm impressed,' Jameson said. 'I thought it was sold out.'

It was the cultural event of the season – a sensational revival of *Porgy and Bess* with an all-white cast and a live symphony orchestra. The critics had acclaimed the brilliance of the conception: Catfish Row could have been Privietown, and Porgy and Jasbo and Sportin' Life might have been some of the colourful characters you could find there.

'Isn't it terrible the way Privies – I mean Private Sector persons – have to live?' Maggie said earnestly.

Jameson, his pre-theatre supper still sitting comfortably in his stomach, said, 'Maggie, any PriSec citizen is free to apply for Federal employment, get the housing that goes with it, make something of himself if he wants to. Most of them just don't have the ambition.'

'You sound just like everybody else,' she flared. 'Sure, Privies are lazy and dirty and ignorant! Give them enough subsidy tickets to keep their bellies full of rice and soycorn, give them a free high on Saturday night, give them a cheap holovid to keep them quiet, bottle them up and forget them! Well, I can't be as smug about it as you! There are two hundred million Privies today – twenty per cent of the population. You can't just write them off!'

'Nobody's writing them off. The Private Sector'll be brought into the system gradually. These things can't be done overnight.'

'You sound just like a Washington stonewallah!'

'Maggie, let's not quarrel. We're supposed to be out for a good time. You're beginning to sound like a Rad.'

That stopped her. She reached back and squeezed his hand. 'You're right,' she said. 'I'm sorry.' She laughed uneasily. 'Just don't tell Caffrey.'

The cabbie's voice made an insect buzz in the battered speaker. 'Here we are, mizz.'

The trike pulled into a huge Lexiglass-enclosed courtyard with manicured lawns and dwarf trees. Jameson paid off the driver and held the lid of the passenger pod open for Maggie while she climbed out. She was wearing a layered pettiskirt with leg tubes, but she managed it with a supple grace that surprised him. She turned to him with a big freckled smile.

'Home sweet home,' she said.

Jameson looked around. Marine guards patrolled the walks, and transparent escalators rose to an elevated loggia lined with convenience shops. At either end of the court, visible through the arched roof, were twin residential towers, graceful trapezoids soaring a thousand feet into the night sky, ablaze with squandered energy. Jameson looked sharply at Maggie. It seemed rather expensive for someone with a computer tech rating. Maggie read his expression and said disarmingly, 'I splurge on my rent. The view's worth it. Otherwise, I'm disgustingly frugal.'

They passed a lobby security check, with a hard-eyed Marine studying their silhouettes on the screen of an ultrasonic mass detector, and rode a tinted transparent box up a central shaft to a floor that was very near the top. Maggie showed the holo pattern on her passbook cover to the door, and it let her in.

Jameson forgot to breathe when he saw the view. The city was a jewelled carpet spread out below. A pattern of streets stretched on forever like a spider web of glowing wires. The tall shapes of other residential towers rose out of the electric glitter like pillars of glowing coals. And there, across the silvered ribbon of a river, he could see the mile-high mirror of the Federal Tower dancing with reflected points of light.

He turned back to Maggie's living room. It was sparsely furnished, but the pieces he could see looked good. There was a couch upholstered in an expensive coarse fabric, and an antique coffee table made of glass and driftwood. There was a transparent rocking chair facing the couch, and a Lexiglass cabinet holding Maggie's collection of twentieth-century plastic bottles completely covered one wall.

'Fix yourself a drink and put some music in the slot,' she said, heading for the door at the far end. 'I'm going to peel off these tubes and put on something more comfortable.'

Jameson wandered over to the omnisound hanging on the wall. Maggie's collection of music cards was stacked untidily on a little shelf beneath it. He flipped through the plastic oblongs, reading the titles showing through the meaningless herringbone patterns of the holo imprints that held the music. It was the usual pop junk put out by the big music combines – creative-group stuff, with the words sung by whatever computer-constructed pseudovoices were the fads of the moment.

But there was a small stack of cards that didn't seem to go with the rest. They looked newer, unplayed. Bach's *Art of the Fugue*. A couple of Mozart symphonies. And – he blinked – the out-of-print collection of Farnaby virginal pieces he'd been trying to track down for years. How had Maggie managed to stumble on such a rarity?

He slipped the card into the slot of the omnisound, and the strange, otherwordly tones of 'Giles Farnaby's Dreame' began to float into the room. The Moog technician had given it a pure lutelike twang, sustained beyond what would have been possible for a real instrument, but otherwise hadn't tampered with it.

Jameson scooped some frozen martini from the nitrogen-chilled vessel on the sideboard and dropped it into a clear stemmed glass, where it caused a satisfying instant explosion of frost. He carried his drink over to the view window, and was losing himself in the glorious sparkle of the vista when Maggie entered the room, wearing a slinky green pantsgown made of some frictionless fluorocarbon material that slid over the surface of her body like oil.

'You must have been reading my mind,' she said. 'You're playing one of my favourites.'


CHAPTER EIGHT

The image faded from the screen. 'Is that all you have?' Ruiz asked.

'Yes, sir,' the NIB tech said, lifting his head from his knobs

78

and dials. 'We had less than a minute before the camera vehicle burned out. Only two frames at that rate of transmission. No time to adjust the focus – we were stuck with what was already in the memory accumulator. And as it was, we pushed computer enhancement to the point where that close-up image is ten per cent conjecture.'

'Play it again,' Ruiz said.

He was sitting comfortably in an upholstered chair in the small semicircular projection room the NIB had cleared out for him. Maybury, grave and attentive, was seated next to him, an adequate little hand-held computer resting on her lap. General Harris was sitting a few seats away with a couple of his courteous thugs.

The tech replayed the sequence in real time. First there was that puzzling cluster of bent angular shapes, distorted by the computer's efforts to achieve optimum resolution. Details were blurred, and there was a discontinuity in some of the straight lines that suggested image compromise. Thirty seconds of that, with the original zoom stopped. Then everything on the screen twitched as the second frame cut in. The things were moving, turning somehow. All the shapes were different. There was a slice of the Cygnus Object's moon for comparison. That hadn't changed at all. The third frame was nothing but a glare of red. That was when the camera vehicle had melted.

'Well?' General Harris demanded.

Ruiz pulled his chin. 'It appears that the planet from Cygnus brought some debris along with it. A moon. And now those things. They can only be artifacts.'

'Artifacts? Thirty miles across? Why not asteroids?'

Ruiz shrugged. 'Don't let the irregular shapes fool you. Don't forget we're seeing them in different planes. I'll have to write a computer programme to rotate them in three dimensions – with five different shapes, we ought to have enough input – but offhand I'll guess that they're Y-shaped or T-shaped, with a fourth axis at right angles to the other three. We never see fewer than three arms – the one at upper left was almost a perfect T – or more than four, like the one that resembled the Greek letter psi, where the long centre tine might be the oblique arm seen in perspective.'

'We'd already come to that conclusion,' the general said with grudging respect. 'We had a topology team on it.'

'So?' Ruiz lifted an eyebrow.

79

'We need an astronomer's opinion.'

'One shape like that might be a natural phenomenon. The lower limit of planetary mass would give you a body with a radius of about a hundred and twenty-five miles. That's the point at which gravitational forces tend to deform a body into a more or less spherical shape. I'm assuming a rocky body, of course. Masses smaller than that – like our friends out there – can maintain an irregular shape. But *five* of them – all out of the same bowl of Greek alphabet soup! Not a chance that it's a coincidence!'

'But thirty miles across!'

'Why not? Eurostation's a half mile in diameter. And *we've* only been in space a century.'

'Life?' the general whispered. He seemed shaken. Ruiz hadn't credited him with that much imagination.

'Life . . . tens of thousands of years ago, maybe. That blaze of X-rays would have annihilated anything moving through space with the planet. When we get out there for a closer look, I wouldn't be surprised to find that those . . . artifacts . . . have melted a bit around the edges. Museum pieces, left by some other form of life.'

'What do you find in museums, Doctor?'

'Art. Cultural clues. Knowledge . . .'

General Harris's face had turned to stone. 'And weaponry. Armour and old weapons.'

'Obsolete weapons.'

'Obsolete – to them!'

'General, you're letting your lack of imagination run away with you. This isn't another one of your security problems, like crowd control for doomsday.'

'Isn't it?' Harris looked bleak, preoccupied. 'No natural force could have slowed that planet from lightspeed. You said so yourself. No natural force could have put it into orbit around Jupiter. And what the hell melted our camera vehicle? That's one museum I don't intend to let the Chinese visit.'

Ruiz was trembling with the effort of controlling himself. 'What do you mean? What are you talking about?'

The general stood up. His two silent aides got up with him, like twin shadows. 'You have a week to get ready, Dr. Ruiz,' he said. 'You and Maybury get your gear packed and ready to be ferried to Eurostation for transfer. It'll take at least that long to sell the Chinese on the nuclear-bomb crews.'

Ruiz was half out of his chair. 'Nuclear-bomb crews!' he choked. He made an involuntary move toward Harris, and one of the general's large young men was suddenly in front of him, looking respectful.

The general was halfway to the door, his other aide trotting after him. He paused and turned a distracted face toward Ruiz. 'Calm down, Dr. Ruiz,' he said in a conciliatory tone. 'We won't destroy it unless we have to.'

'A week,' Maggie said, stretching out in the tub. 'A whole week's gone by, do you realize that? We have to report back in twenty-one days.'

Jameson turned from the mirror, razor in hand. 'You could move into my quarters – have you thought of that? I've got one of the double cabins.'

'Doc Lemieux wouldn't like that.' She laughed. 'She'd probably give us ten demerits on the psych profile. "Exclusive pair bonding is to be discouraged in the confined environment of a spaceship." Isn't that what the manual says?'

'Captain Boyle's a good guy. He won't make any trouble for us.'

Maggie stood up in the tub and began towelling her hair vigorously. There was a coltish poignance for Jameson in her spindly legs and xylophone ribs and teacup breasts dusted with freckles. She favoured him with a long examination through a fringe of orange lashes, then broke into a wide elastic smile.

'It's an indecent proposal and I accept,' she said. 'Unauthorized pair bonding and all.' She tied the towel into a turban and held out her skinny arms. Jameson put down the humming razor and kissed her. Still dripping from her bath, she pressed against him, all soft flesh and bony corrugations.

'We'll miss the giant holo ballet,' he said.

'No we won't.' She pried herself loose. 'Now get out of here and let me dress.'

Jameson went back to the living room, sealing his shirt with a thumbnail. His gear, grown to a zipbag and two duffles, was leaning against the wall where he'd dumped it. He'd had it sent over from the MacDonald Towers the night before. Maggie had argued that it was silly to go on paying for a room there when he hadn't been back for a week.

He finished dressing, then wandered over to Maggie's curio cabinet. Idly, he picked up one of the plastic bottles and turned

81

it over in his hands. It was a grimy white with a network of fine surface cracks, and he could make out the faded word CLOROX. He was putting it back when Maggie came into the room, dressed for their outing in a lizard-green dress with a little fringe of ribboned skirt that left her long legs bare.

'That's one of my most valuable pieces,' she said. 'It goes back over a hundred years. The ones I really like, though, are the ones with all the funny little pump tops that came in in the 1980s, after the fluorocarbon scare. Some of them still work.'

'What are you going to do with your collection while you're away on the mission?'

She tossed her mop of red hair. 'It's going to stay right here. I've made arrangements to put the apartment under seal.'

'That sounds expensive. Why don't you put the collection in storage and give the apartment up? We'll be gone a long time.'

'You don't understand, Tod.' She tossed her head again. 'I want to know that everything's waiting for me when I get back. Exactly the same as I left it.'

'I think I understand,' he said slowly. 'I keep a lock-coop myself near the base in Salt Lake. Store a few things there, sleep over sometimes when I want to get away from everything. Big enough for a bunk and an all-san. But it doesn't eat up my pay when I'm away.'

'No you don't!' she said impatiently. 'You're like everybody else! Most people these days don't own anything but themselves! We're all property of GovCorps!'

'Maggie, you're not going to start all that again?'

'You wouldn't be so complacent if you'd been raised in New England!'

Jameson groaned inwardly. Another argument! 'Maggie, that's all over and done with a long time ago,' he said in an attempt to soothe her.

'Is it?' she said. 'You should visit the town I grew up in and see all the old people with napalm burns and missing arms and legs.'

'Maggie, it was over before you were born.'

'The war might have been over. But not the pacification. I was six years old when that ended. I remember *that* all right!'

'That was a rebellion,' he said, unwilling to stir her up. 'The government had to put it down.'

'It was a war.' She gave him a look that dared him to challenge her.

Jameson sighed. They were on dangerous ground. Old passions, old political slogans that Maggie had learned second-hand. But they could still get her into trouble. And him too, for not reporting her. New England rebs had gained a pretty good foothold in the Congress since the agony of reunification, but they didn't get promoted too far in Federal jobs unless they demonstrated their reliability.

'It's over and done with,' Jameson repeated uncomfortably. 'Maggie, when it comes to that, I had a great grandfather who was killed in the Kansas City explosion.'

'You still don't understand.' She turned sorrowful blue eyes on him. 'You're just one of those people that GovCorp uses to fill in its blanks with.'

'Look,' he said, feeling his temper rise. 'If you're going to keep blaming me for ancient history, maybe we'd better call this whole thing off. I can always move back to the MacDonald Towers.'

'You just don't scan it, do you?' she asked. 'I feel sorry for you, Tod.'

'All right!' he said angrily. 'If that's the way you want it!' He moved to his stack of belongings against the wall and shouldered the duffle bags.

'Tod,' she began, starting toward him. The vid phone chimed. Jameson stepped aside, out of pickup. Maggie said, 'Don't go yet,' and pressed the *Who* button. No picture appeared on the screen. The set continued to chime.

'It's somebody with a Who override,' she said worriedly. 'It must be a high-priority call.' She pressed the Accept button.

The screen lit up with a picture of a jowly man holding up a Space Resources Agency dispatcher badge. 'MacInnes,' he said without preamble, 'you've been ordered to report to the Jupiter ship at once. All leaves are cancelled. A cab will be at your residence in thirty minutes to take you to the Dallas-worth shuttleport. Is Commander Jameson with you?'

'Well . . .' She looked uncertainly toward Jameson.

He took a step into pickup range. 'I'm here,' he said.

'Fine, Commander,' the dispatcher said. 'Do you have any luggage at the MacDonald?'

'No.'

'Good. You can take the cab with MacInnes.'

'What's this about?' Jameson said. 'I still have three weeks to go on my leave.'

'I can't tell you that, Commander,' the dispatcher said. 'There'll be a briefing aboard ship.'

'Can you at least tell me if—'

'That's all, Commander,' the dispatcher said, and clicked off.

Maggie had disappeared into the bedroom. He found her throwing things into a small zipbag. The green dress was crumpled carelessly in a corner. She was wearing a loose one-piece travel suit with elastic cuffs at wrist and knee.

'Need any help?' he said.

'No. I've been ready for a year. I just have to call building security before we leave and tell them to put the apartment under seal.'

'Can I leave my stuff here?'

'I suppose you'd better.' She gave him a canny look. 'We're not coming back, are we?'

'Not till we've been to Jupiter and back,' he said. 'It looks like the mission's on. And there's been some kind of change in it.'


## CHAPTER NINE

'Here they come now,' Captain Boyle said.

Jameson looked out the port. It took him a moment to focus on what the captain was peering at, and when he did, it was sharp with the clarity of space despite the quarter-mile distance. It looked like a string of widely spaced pearls stretched out horizontally, held taut by the spacesuited bosun's mates at either end. Two more attendants were riding scooters above and below the long tether.

'Good God!' Jameson said. 'Don't they have spacesuits?'

'I'm told they do,' the captain said dryly. 'But they haven't been trained to use them yet. Something to occupy us on the long outward trip, eh?'

Jameson shook his head wonderingly. 'Rescue balls! They stuffed them into rescue balls! Skipper, we can't nursemaid a bunch of beginners like those! Not when they'll be working with dangerous materials outside the ship and in zero-g conditions! It'd compromise the safety of the ship.'

'We're not going to nursemaid them, mister,' Boyle said.

'We're going to instruct them in the presence of their executive officer and stay away from them. Those are the orders.'

'Captain, that's crazy! You can't let a bunch like that wander around unsupervised! There's too much trouble they can get into!'

'Look lively now! They're here!'

There was a bump outside that sent a tiny shiver through the spinlock antechamber. Jameson, sweating in his full-dress greens, drew himself up in an approximation of a formal stance, hands clasped behind his back, feet spread, one toe hooked surreptitiously under a baseboard projection to keep himself from drifting away. The spin for the entire ship had been stopped for several days now so the additional modules could be bonded to the rim without having workers and materials fly off into space. The trim of the ship had been altered by the new, awkwardly placed mass, and the computers were working overtime to shift weights and balance the new stresses.

Kay Thorwald, the second officer, was floating in parade position just beside the captain, her large jaw set firmly, her formidable bust swollen to semiglobular shapes in the absence of gravity, her wide mannish shoulders held back squarely. Like Jameson, she'd been tapped as one of the execs to help Captain Boyle pipe the nuclear-bomb crews aboard.

Clustered against the opposite wall was the Chinese delegation, spruced up for the occasion in fashionably wrinkled blue cotton Mao jackets and baggy trousers. Captain Hsieh was in the middle, a chunky, smallish man with a round pedantic face, hands held stiffly at his sides, straining to stretch his spine. His first officer, Yeh Fei, was at his left. Yeh was a big, hulking fellow with a sloping shelf of forehead and a lantern jaw. The third member of the welcoming committee was Tu Jue-chen, the new Struggle Group leader sent up from Earth. As unacknowledged political officer, she carried more clout than Captain Hsieh. She was a terrifying harpy with hollow cheeks, malicious monkey-eyes, and a mouth crowded with big square teeth.

All three of them were wearing the round badges that showed a stylized representation of Lady Ch'ang-o ascending to the Moon with the help of the antigravity pill she'd stolen from her husband. The three-thousand-year-old legend had been the symbol of the Chinese space programme since their first manned flight, in the 1980s.

The red warning light winked out as the lock was pressurized and the latch in the centre of the door spun round. The hatch swung open. A man in Army fatigues emerged in an apish crouch that probably was his conception of how to move about in no-g conditions. He had a small round head covered with short blond stubble, and very wide shoulders. The leaf on his lapel said he was a major.

Grogan, still in his spacesuit but with his helmet off, was hovering helpfully just behind him. Behind Grogan Jameson could make out the shape of one of the bosun's mates extracting a ruffled-looking noncom from a collapsed rescue ball. There was a lot of activity inside the lock. They'd probably squeezed a third of the bomb crew inside. The rest presumably were bobbing around outside in their inflated balls while the other bosun's mate held on to the tether.

'Welcome aboard, Major,' Boyle said. Across the chamber, Captain Hsieh nodded his head just perceptibly, as protocol dictated, and echoed Boyle.

The major saluted smartly – too smartly – and got himself into trouble. Behind him, Grogan shot out a big meaty paw and grasped his upper arm to keep him in contact with the deck.

'Hollis,' the man said, flushing. 'Major Dexter B. Hollis, in command of Special Nuclear Strike Group Lambda One, reporting.'

Before one of the Chinese could object, Boyle said, 'I'm afraid I'll have to ask you for your sidearm, Major. No firearms allowed aboard.'

Hollis stared at the captain a moment. A knot of muscle worked at the hinge of his jaw. Finally he said, 'I'm under independent orders, Captain. You know that.'

Boyle held out his hand. 'And I'm in command of this ship, Major. Along with Captain Hsieh here. Your command comes under our authority in everything concerning the safety of the ship. There's no use for a handgun here. Hand it over.'

Tu Jue-chen was watching expectantly, her monkey eyes bright. Hollis glanced at her and shrugged. He unbuckled the heavy gun belt and gave it to Boyle.

'Thank you, Major,' Boyle said. 'I'll give you a receipt for that. It'll stay in my safe. You'll get it back at the end of the voyage.'

The bomb crew began to file out of the lock, big unfriendly-looking men with hard-bitten faces, shuffling awkwardly in their Velcro socks. They all had specialist ratings, patches with an eagle clutching a missile in one claw sewn to their sleeves. All of them looked miserable from their foetal confinement in the three-foot rescue balls, and one of them had a uniform covered with vomit; the trip across from Eurostation must have been pure hell for him, but he was keeping his head up and his jaw tight.

'I can have one of our officers show this group down while we're waiting for the rest of your men,' Boyle said to the major. 'They're welcome to use the crew facilities to clean up – we've got a few more amenities than in the prefab modules they've assigned to you – and we've got coffee and refreshments waiting for them in the lounge.'

'We'll go directly to our own quarters, Captain,' Hollis said tightly. 'Thanks anyway. I'll wait here until they're all inside. I'll keep them together, and I'll see that they stay out of the main part of the ship except on official business.'

'It's going to be a long trip,' the captain said. 'Those prefab modules are cramped.'

'We'll manage,' Hollis said. 'And we'll stay out of your way.'

The antechamber was filling up with the second group. A couple more of the men had been sick on the way over, and the aroma in the enclosed space was getting a little hard to take. Hollis watched through narrowed eyes as his men tried to shape up in a military manner. He'd turned his back pointedly after the initial introductions.

Grogan sidled up next to Jameson. 'What d'you think of those apes?' he said in a low tone.

'I don't like it,' Jameson said. 'Twenty-four additional men cooped up with us for a year and a half. It changes the ratio of men to women to about two to one. There's going to be trouble, you can count on it. I just hope none of those men goes prowling for Chinese women, that's all.'

'You don't have to worry, Commander,' Grogan said sardonically. 'They brought along a girl with them.'

'A girl?' Jameson said incredulously. 'One girl for the bunch of them? What the hell is the Army up to? That's right out of the dark ages, like the sort of thing they were trying after the first Mars expedition!'

'You should see her, Commander,' Grogan said. 'A real tough cookie. Wearing specialist's stripes, too. Some specialty, huh?'

Jameson tried to suppress a grin. 'Let's hope she doesn't get sick.'

'Commander, if she gets sick, they get sick too.'

The lock cycled again. Hollis waited long enough to make sure that his group was complete, then herded them in twos and threes toward the lift shaft, where a noncom stoically shepherded them to an assembly point at the rim. It took Jameson a moment to pick out the girl. She was as big and tough-looking as the men, dressed in the same shapeless fatigues, but her cheeks were shiny-smooth and she had a thick braid of blond hair hanging down her back. Then they were gone, Grogan and the bosun's mates with them, leaving nothing but a smell of sweat and stale vomit behind.

The new astronomer came aboard later that day. His name was Ruiz, and he looked a little old for space, but he handled himself well in no-g. They hadn't subjected him to the indignity of a rescue ball; he looked too brittle for that, and he was a VIP. He was ferried over from Eurostation in a small passenger gig with an assistant, a grave dark-eyed little girl named Maybury who somehow looked familiar.

She saw Jameson looking at her and said at once, 'It was the Eurostation-Texas shuttle a couple of weeks ago, Commander. We were seatmates.'

'Of course. You were wearing a poncho, and you were on your way to Nevada.' He shook hands with the two of them. Ruiz had the knack, but the girl's feet lost contact, and Jameson had to discreetly plant her again.

Boyle and Captain Hsieh were off somewhere for a meeting with the fusion engineers, making preparations for engine start-up. After Yeh Fei and Tu Jue-chen had stiffly completed their share of the formalities, and Kay Thorwald had excused herself and disappeared, Jameson volunteered to get Ruiz and Maybury settled.

'Just stay close to a wall and don't move too abruptly and you'll be all right,' he said. 'There are cords strung along the corridors, and those socks they gave you will stick to the fuzzy strips along the floors. If you *do* find yourself floating in the centre of a compartment, out of reach, don't get panicky. Air currents will eventually send you drifting up against a surface.'

'Or some friendly passerby will bounce himself off of us, eh?' Ruiz said.

Jameson smiled appreciatively. 'Oh, you've spent some time in free fall, then? I know you both were stationed on the Moon, but...'

'I put in almost two years at the old L-5 orbital observatory when I was a young man,' Ruiz said. 'They spun the living quarters, but I spent my working days in the cage. Big warehouse of a place. Even a small fraction of a g, of course, would have made the big mirror sag out of all usefulness. It was made by stretching a film of molten Merlon across a hundred-metre hoop in the first place, and it was less than a millimetre thick at the centre.'

'How about you, Mizz Maybury?' Jameson said. 'Have you spent much time in free fall?' . .

'No,' she said. 'That is, except in the Moon shuttle. But of course you spend most of your time belted in your seat, and they have the flight attendants taking care of you and everything.'

'You're doing very well,' Jameson said charitably. 'At any rate, you'll only have to put up with it for a few more days. We'll be putting on spin as soon as we're sure the new modules are fastened securely. After that, we'll have two thirds of a g all the way – except for a few hours during engine start-up, as a safety precaution.'

At that point they all had to crowd themselves against the corridor wall as one of Grogan's angels came sailing toward them, halfway between floor and ceiling, a bundle of plastic struts cradled in his hairy forearms.

'Sorry, Commander,' he said as he shot past; Jameson had to duck the end of a strut. They turned to watch the man. His line of flight was a chord that intersected the shallow upward curve of the corridor, and at the last possible moment, when his chin seemed about to scrape the floor, he gave an expert push of one foot, like the flick of a goldfish's tail, and launched himself on a new chord toward the invisible ceiling beyond.

'I'll never be able to do that,' Maybury said ruefully.

'He shouldn't be doing it either,' Jameson said. 'It's against the safety rules.'

'How long will we be accelerating?' Ruiz said as they continued walking.

'A bit over two weeks,' Jameson said. 'By that time we'll have reached about a hundred and sixty kilometres per second. Then we coast for four months, turn the ship's long axis around, and decelerate for another couple of weeks. We'll reach Jupiter in five months, thanks to the new boron engine.'

'And you're going to spin the ship during acceleration and deceleration? Won't that complicate our sense of up and down?'

'Not enough to notice,' Jameson said. 'We'll only be accelerating at about a hundredth of a g—nine point eight centimetres per second. But we'll be spinning at two-thirds of a g at right angles to the direction of thrust. That's a distortion factor of less than one to sixty-six. The floor will seem to tilt slightly, of course, but it'll be almost imperceptible.' He slapped the corridor wall. 'About enough of a tilt to start a marble rolling toward the aft bulkhead here, if you gave it a helpful push.'

'I got a good view of the ship through the porthole on the way over,' Maybury said hesitantly. 'I didn't think it would be so big. It was beautiful – like a giant toy top, with that long broomstick sticking through the centre of the circle.'

'That's a good way to think of it, except that the "broomstick" doesn't spin. It's more of an axle than a shaft. What we've really got is a space station revolving round a rocket. It's the only sensible design for very long trips. I wouldn't like to be spinning round a short radius, as they do in those glorified barrels they send to Mars, or try to apply course corrections to two weights tied to each other by a long cord.'

'Commander,' Ruiz said abruptly, 'I'd like to see Dr. Pierce first and get it over with.'

'All right,' Jameson said. 'I thought you might want to put it off till you'd had a chance to catch your breath.'

'How's he taking it?'

'I suppose,' Jameson said carefully, 'he's wondering why he's being superseded as chief astronomer just a few days before the start of the expedition.'

'I suppose you all are,' Ruiz said dryly. 'And why the powers that be have grafted a nuclear strike force onto what started out as a purely scientific mission.'

'They explained it to us at the briefing yesterday,' Jameson said in a carefully neutral tone. 'The nukes are just a precaution. Like giving an archaeologist a pistol to protect himself against snakes. But those thirty-mile-long artifacts from Cygnus have been scrubbed by radiation for thousands – maybe millions – of years, so there aren't going to be any snakes. Or so they say.'

90

'Except in this case the archaeologist's pistol has a mind of its own, eh? I don't suppose your Captain Boyle likes having an officer on board who isn't under his orders. To say nothing of the Chinese bomb crew.'

Jameson said nothing.

Ruiz sighed. 'How do *you* feel about the bomb crews, Commander?'

'As long as they don't interfere in the running of the ship or assigned missions, it's none of my concern.'

'Prudently spoken, Commander. But *I'm* going to interfere in your assignments, aren't I?'

'That's different.'

'Can you modify your Callisto lander for the Cygnus planet, Commander?' Ruiz asked.

'No. The gravitational field's too powerful – about one Earth gravity, I'm told. We could get down, but we'd never get up again. We'll have to study it from close orbit. But we can try a landing on its moon.'

'You can crash an automated probe or two on the planet's surface, though, can't you?'

'We can do better than that. We can soft-land some of the little rovers. We've got a few to spare. A planet from outside the solar system's a hell of a lot more interesting than Ganymede or Europa.'

'I'm glad you feel that way, Commander.'

Jameson permitted himself to show a little emotion. 'Hell, man, this is my *chance*! I never thought it would come in my lifetime'

Ruiz looked pleased. 'I suppose not. There'll be Centauri probes with the new boron engine, but we'll be waiting the better part of a thousand years to get any answers from *them*. Our Cygnus visitor's been masked by radiation from Cygnus X-1 for more than eighty years that we know of. It has to be from a hundred light-years' distance at the very least.'

'You were the astronomer who discovered it, weren't you, Dr. Ruiz?'

'Maybury here was the first person to notice it,' Ruiz said. Maybury bit her lip and blushed. 'But I was the nearest stuffed savant. That makes me the agreed-upon expert on the Cygnus object, and that's why the authorities sent me along to complicate your lives. I'm sure your Dr. Pierce would have done a thoroughly competent job. Well, I'll try not to interfere with him too much. He and his staff can carry out their Jupiter studies as planned. I have the greatest sympathy for him. It's going to be a dammed awkward situation.'

'Here we are,' Jameson said, stopping at the door marked ASTRONOMY. 'The observation instruments are in the no-spin axle of the ship, of course. There's an observatory near the bridge, but the readouts are down here, where the astronomy people can feel some weight on their feet.' He pushed the door open.

The meeting with Pierce went better than expected. The younger man was deferential. Fresh out of the Venusian Studies task force himself, he was awed by Ruiz's eminence as former Farside director and ingenuously respectful of Ruiz's pioneering studies on black holes and gravitational entropy. He pledged the full cooperation of himself and his staff, and managed to enlist Ruiz's help on a problem involving the Jovian atmosphere sampling scoops. All the while he kept stealing sidelong glances at Maybury, looking guilty when he was caught.

Jameson could appreciate Pierce's feelings. Maybury was a pretty little thing. He wondered if Ruiz was sleeping with her, then decided it was none of his business. He showed them to their quarters, two hastily cleaned out cabins adjoining an office with a computer terminal connected to the ship's brain and some oddball peripheral equipment Ruiz had requested. If they were sharing a bunk, the old man could stumble through the connecting room.

'Dinner's at eight, captain's mess,' Jameson said. 'Will we be seeing you?'

'I think not, Commander,' Ruiz said. 'We'll skip tonight. I'm a bit tired after the trip. I see that there's an adequate kitchenette and a good selection of self-heating instameals. Mizz Maybury and I have some observational data to go through, and then we'll have an early supper. I'm meeting with my Chinese counterpart, Dr. Chu, first thing in the morning, and I suppose I'd better be prepared.'

'Good night then, sir,' Jameson said, preparing to push himself off against the door frame.

'Good night, Commander,' Ruiz said. As Jameson launched himself down the corridor, he could see Maybury already punching something into a computer peripheral.

# CHAPTER TEN

The Jupiter ship drifted among the stars, a gigantic hoop and stick perforated with light from its blazing ports. A blast from its attitude jets had nudged it a safe distance from Eurostation's traffic and set it tumbling languidly.

On Earth, almost half the human race took a last look at the majestic image, gathered around holovids in their homes or watching the public viewplates that had been set up in communes and village schools, playing fields and places of work. Then the camera pinnace, hovering a prudent fifty miles away, zoomed in to the limit of its magnification, and the hoop became an enormous puffy doughnut, bumpy with outside structures, and the stick swelled to an immense cylindrical shaft, festooned with spherical tanks and sporting irregular bulges. Little spurts of flame flared from odd places along the shaft. Gradually the tumbling stopped. The ship held rocksteady, poised for flight.

Somewhere inside the long shaft, Chinese technicians bustled around a massive globate housing that bristled like a hedgehog with converging laser assemblies. Towering stacks of capacitors marched endlessly down the arched chamber. Pipes and cables disappeared through a thick bulkhead. On the other side of the bulkhead, a team of American technicians tended the dull bulging shapes of cryogenic storage vats and monitored a bewildering array of computer displays.

A walnut-sized pellet of boron dropped into a vat. It was hollow on the inside, and beautifully machined, with twelve precise pinholes slanting through its jacket. It was immediately stuffed with a tiny snowball made of frozen deuterium and tritium.

A computer on the American side of the bulkhead positioned the pellet to within an angstrom and fired it through a long pipe into the chamber of the Chinese device. All the lasers fired at once in a burst that lasted only a few picoseconds. They were computer-controlled by a single oscillator on the American side. This was the point that had caused so much trouble. It had taken two years of diplomatic negotiations at the highest level before a way was worked out for the sensors and timers to be slaved to the U.S. computers through a scrambler programme. The Chinese had never seen a pellet, nor was there any way they could extract the vital details of size, density, or timing from their own computer replays – though they had dismantled their own equipment many times in an attempt to gain clues from the pellet delivery pipe and the physical arrangement of the electronic interfaces.

Twelve thread-thin beams of coherent light blasted through the pellet's pinholes and converged at the centre of the snowball. A tiny volume of space turned into hell. A few cubic microns of hydrogen isotopes became ten times hotter than the interior of the Sun. The fusion reaction became self-sustaining. The pressure of the blast crushed superheated plasma to the awesome density of degenerate matter, and held the pellet together for the few picoseconds needed to initiate the next stage of the reaction.

For hydrogen fusion, a mere 200 million degrees Fahrenheit had been sufficient. For boron fission, a temperature in the billions of degrees was needed. Fusion was only the trigger. The raging nuclear fury in that tortured speck of matter stripped hot protons from surrounding hydrogen atoms and drove them with incredible energy into the now-collapsing nuclei of boron-11 atoms. The extra proton was too much for the boron nucleus to hold. Each atom split into three helium nuclei. The energy released was tremendous – far more than the controlled fusion energy that mankind had unlocked a half century before. A stream of electrically charged helium nuclei sought their mad escape rearward through the ship's nozzles.

The ship trembled and moved.

Another pellet dropped. Another chamber turned into hell. Then, three seconds later, another. And another.

The ship, shuddering, picked up speed. It was accelerating rapidly now, at one percent of a g. On Earth, an estimated seven billion people watched the ship dwindle on their screens.

They watched it until it was small and indistinct, a ghostly target pierced by a glittering arrow. A silver phi sketched against the void. A needle encircled by a wedding ring, pointing itself toward a star.

When Jameson staggered into his quarters after his first twelve-hour watch, Maggie had a mug of steaming coffee and a hot beanie waiting for him. He wolfed the crisp, paste-filled cone down gratefully. 'Thanks,' he said. 'I didn't have a chance to eat. It was wild on the bridge. The skipper's still up there. Have you had anything?'

She gestured at a half-eaten beanie, its fragile riceflour wrapping spilled out a congealing green sludge. 'I was too excited. Are we really on our way?'

He nodded. 'Everything got straightened out a couple of hours ago, when you felt us put the spin back on. The engine's working beautifully. We won't have any more trajectory corrections till tomorrow. By that time the computer should have accumulated enough data to tell us how much longer those damn bomb blisters are going to make us keep the boost on.'

'Want another beanie?'

'No, that'll hold me till mealtime.'

'Let's not go down to the mess for dinner. I'll fix us something here.'

He ruffled her red hair. 'That's fine with me. Let's put on some music and have a drink.'

She pecked him on the cheek and got up to put a music card in the slot. It was 'Giles Farnaby's Dreame' again. Jameson was getting a little tired of it, but he didn't have the heart to tell her. They had been careful with each other since making up their quarrel on the shuttle trip, and Maggie had moved in with him. Sue had taken it well. She'd been a little hurt, but she recovered quickly, and her behaviour towards Maggie had been warm and friendly.

Maggie returned with some chilled gin and one of the adulterated joints that were all anyone could get from Stores. She lit the joint and passed it to Jameson. She seemed unusually quiet.

'Something's bothering you,' he said. 'What is it?'

'It's nothing.'

'Come on. What's wrong?'

'Oh, it's just that Klein.'

'What did he do?'

'Wanted to come by my quarters tonight. Got very insistent about it. Threw rank at me. I told him I was bunking here. He started quoting regulations about pair-bonding during a mission. Said I ought to be spreading myself around. That's how he put it. Nasty man! Anyway, I've only been here about a week.'

'And you're going to stay here,' Jameson said. 'I'll have a talk with Klein.'

'He's already made trouble for Liz Becque and Omar. They're reporting for counselling sessions with Janet.'

'I'll speak to the skipper,' Jameson said. 'Nobody's complained about your work. Or mine. Klein can mind his own damned business.'

She snuggled against his chest. 'I shouldn't have mentioned it.'

The 'Dreame' came to an end on a translucent D-major chord, to be replaced by the jolly tones of 'Tower Hill'. Maggie pried the drink from Jameson's hand and pressed herself against him. There was a rapping at the door.

'Damn!' Jameson said, sitting up. Maggie picked up her drink again, and Jameson went to the door.

Mike Berry was standing there, looking tousled and exhausted. 'Could I talk to you?' he said.

'Mike! I thought you'd locked up and sacked out.'

Berry glanced over at Maggie and nodded apologetically at her. Maggie looked away and gathered her robe more closely around her. Berry turned back to Jameson.

'Yeah, I did. I left Quentin in charge, and Caffrey put a guard on the door, and Tu Jue-chen put one of her Struggle Brigade mugs on guard outside *their* door, and . . . look, could you come back to the engine room with me? I haven't said anything to Boyle yet. I don't want to make a big thing of it.'

'What's the matter?'

'Look, Po Fu-yung's techs and my techs have got to *talk* to one another, don't they? We've got a good working relationship. When something comes up, we get together in one of the nonrestricted areas off the cryo department. Now Caffrey's goon won't let Quentin out of the computer room to work with Po's man and the Struggle Brigade goon is throwing his weight around too. Could you come down and smooth things over before it develops into anything official?'

Jameson sighed and got to his feet. 'Let's go.'

He slipped a pair of stickysocks over his bare feet and followed Mike into the corridor. Maggie looked sulky and turned her face to the wall as he closed the door behind him.

'I'm sorry,' Mike said. 'But I thought we'd better stop it before it got out of hand. I didn't think we'd have this kind of a problem so soon after launch.'

Jameson nodded, 'And we've still got half a billion miles to go.'

# CHAPTER ELEVEN

They were a quarter of a billion miles beyond the orbit of Mars when the message came.

Jameson was standing on the bridge, admiring the stunning view around him through the vast comforting bulge of clear plastic that kept space outside. Jupiter hung against the night, a yellow lantern that outshone the crystal stars. It was by far the brightest light in the sky, except for the chill shrunken golf-ball of the Sun behind them, but it still showed no disc to the naked eye.

That fact alone brought home the immensity of the distances they were travelling. In the past three months they had journeyed farther and faster than any manned spacecraft before them had ever gone, but Jupiter still seemed as far away as when they had started.

Jameson indulged himself with a final long look at the brilliant dot of light, then turned reluctantly towards the command chair on the balcony above, where he could hear a buzzer sounding. He was tempted to jump for it, but he had to set an example. Some half dozen personnel of both nations were scattered among the paired consoles and the mostly empty seats rimming the circular deck. Most crewpersons preferred to serve their watches in the spin section's duplicate bridge, connected to this one by electronic ganglia, but some jobs required direct observation here in the ship's spearhead, and of course there were always one or two free-fall freaks. So Jameson dutifully clipped his jump line to the proper nylon cord in the spider web that crisscrossed the hemispherical chamber.

He soared upwards to the catwalk, his trajectory perfectly parallel to the line. It was a point of pride with him never to get a corrective yank from the safety when crew were watching. He caught the rail and swung himself easily over.

He flipped a toggle. The buzzing stopped and his screen lit up. At the horseshoe console opposite his, Yeh Fei nodded formally at him and flipped his own switch, He'd been waiting. The big, shambling Chinese second officer looked like a gorilla hacked out of a block of wood with a dull chisel, but he had a fine sense of the niceties.

Sue Jarowski and little narrow-faced Chang-ho stared out at him from the split screen. He could see a tangle of communications equipment around them. 'Commander,' Sue said, 'there's a laser message coming in.'

Beside her Jameson could see Chang-ho's thick purple lips move, saying the same thing in Chinese to Yeh Fei. This would be a joint message, in clear, for both commands, then.

'Okay,' he said. 'Put it on our screens.'

'Commander,' Sue said. 'I think you'd better get the astronomers. They won't want to wait for a replay. Something's happening on Jupiter.'

Jameson could feel the hair on the nape of his neck prickle. 'All right,' he said. 'I'll buzz Dr. Ruiz.'

Chang-ho's miniature face glared ferociously at him from the other half of the screen, 'You must to notify Dr. Chu, you must to notify Dr. Chu!' he said stridently.

'*Yi-ding*,' Jameson said soothingly. 'Of course.'

Dr. Ruiz arrived in a bathrobe. It was not an ideal garment for free fall. Maybury trailed behind him, still buttoning a man's shirt that was too large for her. Dr. Chu arrived moments later. He'd managed to get himself dressed in shorts, a blue tunic with his astronomer's rating on the collar, and a cotton cap with a Mao badge pinned to it. He was a frail, fussy man with two large chipmunk teeth peeping through a mossy moustache. When he saw Maybury, he frowned.

'Sit down, everyone,' Jameson said. 'We'll crank it back to the beginning for you.'

Data in computer script was flowing across the big display screen that Jameson and Yeh Fei had plugged in. Ruiz craned toward it with hawklike intensity until it stopped. Then he noticed that his robe had ridden up on his fleshless shanks and absent-mindedly pushed down at it. He sat down next to Dr. Chu, and Maybury handed him a lightpad that had been slaved via FM to the astronomy computer.

'They're still transmitting,' Jameson said. 'We'll play it at twice real time till it catches up.' He pressed the button that would alert Sue Jarowski.

Random flashes of light appeared on the screen. That was when the ship's laser ranging retroreflector first noticed that it was being hit by coherent light and locked in on the laser beam from the Moon transmitter. The light it bounced back served both as a ready-to-receive acknowledgment and as a guide to the sender for more accurate aim – though multiple redundancy of the digital pulses meant that the ship's computers could reconstitute even a badly scattered message. At the speed of light, the back-and-forth exchange would have taken the better part of an hour – mercifully condensed now to a few seconds by a very conservative computer that wasn't taking any chances of leaving out any information content.

Now the message itself began:

URGENT URGENT URGENT
SUBJECT JOVIAN METEOROLOGICAL PHENOMENA
SPECIFIC REFERENCE CLOUDTOP DISTURBANCE EQUATORIAL REGION
SOURCE SAGAN REFLECTOR FARSIDE
OPTICAL IMAGES BEGINNING 0019 53 07 GR STORED FOR TRANSMISSION
TO FOLLOW
ACTION ACTION ACTION
VERIFICATION REQUESTED
SPECIFIC VERIFICATION DIRECT OPTICAL OBSERVATION
MESSAGE FOLLOWS

What followed was a lot of astronomical gobbledygook to the effect that the 500-inch reflector on the Moon had observed an inexplicable vortex forming in the upper Jovian atmosphere. It was different from the usual eddies and swirls caused by high-speed turbulence in Jupiter's equatorial region. It was a whirlpool-like disturbance larger than Earth, and almost as large as the Great Red Spot. Coordinates with respect to other atmospheric features followed in lengthy detail.

Ruiz fidgeted, occasionally using his lightpad to do some figuring. He stared balefully at the screen, fingers drumming on the armrest of his chair. Finally he exploded.

'Why don't they give us the pictures instead of wasting time with all this slush? It's that jackass Kerry! "Verification requested!" What does the fool expect us to see at almost two hundred million miles with the ship's telescopes that *he* can't see at less than three times the distance with the five-hundred-inch mirror?'

'It should only be a few more minutes, Dr. Ruiz,' Maybury said timidly.

Ruiz subsided a little. 'Dammed posturing idiot,' he grumbled. 'I never should have approved his second tour of duty. I should have shipped him back to Earth when I had the chance.' He lifted a grizzled head. 'I won't tell him what I think of him, Commander. I don't want to burn out your laser sender.'

Jameson grinned. 'Mizz Maybury's right, Doctor. Nothing to do but wait it out. Your pictures are probably somewhere past the asteroid belt by now, anyway. The fellows at Farside probably knocked off for a beer a half-hour ago.'

'Here it comes now,' Dr. Chu said. They all leaned forward to look at the screen. Down below, curious faces were looking up at the balcony.

Bit by bit the computer began to assemble the first picture. At more than five hundred lines to the inch, it was quite detailed. The colour, corrected by a digital code nestled among the billions of pulses, was vivid. It began at screen left and unrolled until, seconds later, the screen was filled. The first frame was the only one they saw entire. After that, new frames were transmitted at the rate of two per second, peeling on from left, so that there was an illusion of flickering motion.

It was overwhelming.

Jameson heard Maybury sigh, 'O-o-oh!' Chu sucked in his breath sharply. Ruiz's breath came in a ragged wheeze.

Jupiter filled the screen, a great swollen luminescent ball, striped in orange-reds and yellows. The image wasn't holo – couldn't be, even with high-density laser transmission – but somehow it didn't matter. Looking at that fantastic orb, they could sense its tremendous bulk, *feel* the existence of a mass that could swallow up the entire Earth with scarcely a splash, even with nothing to scale it by.

Jupiter had a mole, a malignant black dot at rest on the rushing ochre cloudtops. The shadow of one of its moons, probably Io. That black speck was probably a couple of thousand miles across.

And there, across the cloud decks, was the Great Red Spot, a bloody egg that was twice the width of Earth. An immense eddying froth of organic molecules that had held its oval shape for the four hundred years that mankind had been looking at Jupiter through telescopes.

But no more.

It was sending out long reddish streamers, twisting threads that had to be tens of thousands of miles long, like a living thing bleeding underwater. The streamers stretched across the multicoloured cloud bands and disappeared around the curvature of the planet, forming a twisted belt at the equator.

'*Ya i!*' Chu gasped. He was half out of his chair, his hands gripping the arms. Ruiz was motionless, staring at the screen with fierce concentration.

They watched in frozen silence for long minutes. Then they saw what was causing it.

'There's our "meteorological phenomenon",' Ruiz snorted. 'Kerry's "cloudtop disturbance".'

It was sweeping around the curve of the planet, moving at what seemed a crawling pace, but actually travelling at what had to be more than a million miles per hour. At this rate it would circle Jupiter's 89,000-mile diameter in something like fifteen minutes.

It was an unimaginably huge vortex of churning clouds. As it progressed along the equator it deformed the coloured bands of clouds into an elongated eyeshape, with itself at the centre. And now they could see that it was gathering a skein of those bloody streamers from the Red Spot around itself, dragging them halfway around the planet.

'Maybury,' Ruiz said sharply. 'Is Pierce recording?'

She looked startled, 'Yes, Dr. Ruiz,' she said. 'I signalled him before we left.'

Jameson briefly considered calling Boyle, but decided not to wake the skipper up. All this had happened hours ago anyway. Boyle and Hsieh could see it in replay.

The tremendous whirling funnel was overtaking the Red Spot. It distorted the shape of the oval feature, making it bulge northward. Twisting ribbons of red stretched in a bloodshot spindle between the two loci.

A great gob of matter, the size of a continent, detached itself from the bulging Spot and was sucked into the whirlpool.

'God help us,' Ruiz breathed.

The sudden infusion of red nitriles briefly coloured the gigantic maelstrom. Jameson tried to grasp the scale of the colossal events he was witnessing, and found he couldn't. Those whipping shapes winding themselves like torn confetti around that spinning vortex were bigger than worlds, and they were covering vast distances in fractions of a second. It was a violence that would have shorn Earth in the blink of an eye and left it a polished ball, glowing with the heat of friction. Now, as

Jameson watched, the blurred spirals of cloud were turning pink, showing that ulcerous pit more clearly against the face of the planet.

Something was growing out of it.

'They're doing it to Jupiter, too,' Ruiz whispered.

Jameson had no time to reflect on what Ruiz meant. The spectacle he was seeing held all his attention. The raging vortex had marched from horizon to horizon, and he had an oblique view of it as it approached the edge of the planet.

He could make it out now against the engulfing darkness: a tenuous pillar of cloud extending thousands of miles into space in a coiling loop. The roots of that spectral rope were stained pink with coloured hydrogen. It became more transparent, insubstantial, as it ascended its twisting path, narrowing all the while until it ended as a gossamer thread somewhere inside the orbit of Jupiter V.

A thread whose tip was a glowing blue spark.

The bomb crews began their grim rehearsals the next day. Hollis drove his men hard – too hard in an environment where fatigue could be fatal. Boyle had spoken to him about it, and received an answer in advanced officialese that amounted to 'mind your own business.'

It was amazing, Jameson thought, how well Major Hollis got along with his counterpart, People's Deputy Commander Yao Hu-fang, when his relations with his fellow Americans were so distant and grudging. Hollis acted as if he were in enemy territory whenever he ventured out of his spun-foam cocoon on the inner rim of the wheel to see Boyle or confer with Liz Becque about his men's rations. He was never seen after hours in the lounge. Evidently he drank alone with his executive, a watchful, tight-lipped man named Toscano.

Standing in the observation lounge on the inner side of the rim, Jameson was getting a good view of the latest rehearsal through the overhead bubble.

The long spear of the ship's drive section, a hundred metres overhead, was aswarm with bulky spacesuited figures, scrambling around a cluster of dart-shaped missiles splayed out in their launching racks at an angle to the hull. The weapons, finned and needlenosed, obviously had been designed for atmospheric launch, and their presence on this mission showed how hasty the preparations had been.

'So they're playing with their toys, are they?' a voice said behind him.

Jameson turned. Ruiz was there, looking tired. He was dressed in shorts and sandals and a short-sleeved shirt that for once seemed to be pressed.

'They're not exactly toys,' Jameson said. 'There's a rumour that they've got a gigaton bomb with them. It's never been tested. Couldn't be, on Earth. They think it would make a fifty-mile crater, maybe even break through the Earth's crust.'

'Lunatics!' Ruiz said. 'What kind of a crater do they expect to make in space? Or Jupiter, for that matter. No solid surface.'

'The bombs are for the Cygnans, aren't they?' Jameson asked carefully.

'The Cygnans. Of course, they don't officially exist. They're not supposed to have survived ten thousand years of hard radiation.'

'That's what Dmitri keeps saying.' Jameson grinned.

'They've exhibited some remarkable activity for an extinct race, haven't they? Moving worlds about like that.'

Both men looked up through the bubble. The little space-suited figures were swarming around a piece of equipment, manoeuvring it into place on one of the launching racks. It looked as if they were hooking it into the missile guidance system.

It was late when Jameson returned to his quarters. After leaving Ruiz, he'd bumped into Li and been trapped onto a long technical discussion about using the Callisto lander to land on the Cygnus Object's moon. The moon was settling into a new orbit around Jupiter, an ellipse that crossed the orbit of its former parent world, and they would have to time their expedition for the eight-day period when the satellite would be outside Jupiter's most intense radiation zone. The orbital calculations were going to make some difficult work for Maggie and Jen Mei-mei. Jameson finally shook Li off and made his way down to the section of outer ring that held the officers' living quarters, looking forward to a drink with Maggie and a relaxed evening – or what ship's convention had defined as evening.

His cabin was dark when he let himself in. Maggie was nowhere around. Jameson frowned. She should have come off duty an hour ago. He kicked off his sandals, made himself a drink, and put on some music. With a sigh, he settled down to study some equipment-maintenance reports while he was waiting.

Maggie straggled in an hour later. She looked dispirited and bedraggled. Her orange hair hung down limply, a stray strand across her cheek, and one tail of her shirt had escaped her shorts.

'Is that a martini?' she said. 'Gawd, let me have a sip!' She flopped down on the aircouch and drained Jameson's glass. Silently he got up to mix another batch.

'Thanks,' she said as he handed her a fresh glass. 'Jeeks, what a day!'

'What happened?' he said.

She turned a tired face toward him. She looked pale and drained, and her freckles showed more prominently. 'I've been drafted,' she said. 'Me and Mei-mei. We spent the day working for Hollis.' She took a sip of her drink. 'Plotting bomb orbits.'

## CHAPTER TWELVE

From less than a quarter million miles away, the alien ship showed its form starkly through the telescopes. It swam against the luminous striations of Jupiter, an angular, many-armed silhouette. The shape was peculiar. It wasn't designed the way humans would have done it, but it made sense.

Picture a slender rod fifteen miles long – slender only by virtue of its enormous scale. It had to be at least three miles in thickness. Radar echoes had shown its cross section to be an equilateral triangle – a three-sided stick. The echoes also must have told the aliens that someone was looking at them.

From the tip of the rod, three long arms sprouted sideways making the shape of a Y. Each of the arms was fifteen miles long. Folded back along the rod, they would just about have reached its opposite end.

Each arm ended in a prism. The cross section of the prisms was the same as the rod – an equilateral triangle three miles on a side. They were in effect shorter slices of the rod, measuring four and a half miles from triangular face to triangular face.

The arms with their clubbed ends twirled lazily, a whirligig for titans.

There were five of the great ships, clustered in a pentagonal formation, revolving around a common centre of gravity. But this one, etched against Jupiter's roiling clouds, was easiest to see.

Jameson tore himself away from the eyepiece reluctantly and levered himself across the observatory to join the rest of the group. They were gathered around a large projection screen which reproduced the telescope image, but it wasn't quite the same as seeing it first hand.

'It's obvious,' Pierce was saying. The young astronomer was flushed with excitement, talking too rapidly. 'The long shaft is their drive section. In flight, those three arms fold back along the shaft like the ribs of an umbrella. Those nice flat surfaces are meant to rest against the three faces of the shaft.'

He stopped, out of breath, and glanced apologetically at Ruiz.

'Go on,' Ruiz said. 'You're doing fine.'

Pierce ran a hand over his mussed hair. 'But when they're *not* accelerating or decelerating,' he said, 'the arms open out and spin to give them artificial gravity. Those wedge-shaped modules at the ends of the arms are the environmental pods.'

'Environmental pods!' Chu exclaimed. He sucked on his wispy moustache. 'Look at the size of them! They're – they're worldlets!'

'To think of engineering on such a scale!' Li said admiringly. 'Supporting masses like that on ten-mile booms!' He flashed a disingenuous smile in Jameson's direction and said, piously, 'They must be socialists.'

That earned him a suspicious stare from Tu Jue-chen. She sucked in her pleated cheeks and fixed him with her little monkey eyes. Li met her gaze innocently. The Struggle Group leader had shown up shortly after Jameson and Li had arrived and had been glaring at everybody since then, poor Dr. Chu most of all.

Jameson couldn't imagine why she was there. It wasn't any sort of formal meeting. Ruiz had called him up when he was turning the bridge over to Kay Thorwald, and asked him if he'd like to drop by for a look at the alien ships before he went back to the spin section. The ships had just emerged from behind Jupiter in the complicated sixteen-day orbit they shared with the Cygnus Object's former moon, and Ruiz had promised him a more spectacular view than last time. On the way back to the observatory he'd bumped into Li, who'd immediately asked if he could tag along.

Jameson got Li off the hook by quickly saying, '*Djen hwa.* As you say, the engineering's on a tremendous scale. Besides swivelling the asteroid-size modules outward on the ends of those booms, they've got to manipulate them so that they're turned around.'

'Yes, yes, of course!' Pierce cried. 'My God, I didn't think of *that*!'

Tu Jue-chen looked from one to the other of them, a simian frown creasing her brow. 'I do not understand,' she said.

'What *tongzhi* Jameson means,' Dr. Chu said hastily, 'is that the pods must be *reversed* when the arms are rotating. Otherwise the centripetal force that substitutes for gravity would be in the wrong direction. The pods would be "upside down".'

'You're assuming that the booms are attached at the *rear* of the drive section?' Ruiz said.

Chu gave a little bow. 'Of course. The three arms would fold forward, to put the environmental pods as far away from the drive as possible. Fifteen miles away from it, in fact. We do not know what energies these creatures must command to travel at nearly the speed of light, but we can assume that they are dangerous.'

'And,' Pierce interrupted breathlessly, 'when the arms are extended, the pods are *still* fifteen miles from the drive – at right angles, of course. In case there's any danger from lingering radiation, I suppose.'

'Yes, yes,' Chu said, looking annoyed. 'The point is, when they're accelerating, or turned around to decelerate, their artificial gravity is in the direction of their line of flight. Otherwise, they get it from spin, just as we do.'

'Which proves,' Ruiz said, 'that if such a thing as true "artificial gravity" is possible, the aliens haven't discovered it.'

'But they're so far in advance of us—' Pierce began.

'Are they?' Ruiz said. 'They do things on a larger scale. That's all we know so far.'

'That's putting it mildly,' Jameson said. 'Moving whole worlds about! Building a fleet of ships larger than the Martian moons . . .'

Ruiz looked pensive. 'Maybe there's no other way to do it. When you're travelling between the stars, you don't go home again. Not after ten thousand years. You take your whole society with you.'

Interest flickered in Tu Jue-chen's close-set little eyes. 'How many of these creatures do you suppose there are aboard those vessels?' she asked.

Ruiz nodded at Pierce. 'Do you want to take a crack at it?'

'Hmm. Let's assume that they're roughly our size. Somewhere between twice our size and half our size. There must be an optimum size range for intelligent life. Much smaller than that and they don't pack enough brain tissue. Much larger and they become unwieldy. Specialized—'

'There are whales,' Li said mischievously. 'And elephants.'

Pierce looked disconcerted. 'Hmm, yes. But I can't see a gigantic sea creature developing into a space traveller, no matter how intelligent. The early steps would be too difficult. Besides, it's hard to imagine those pods as giant aquaria, sloshing around with liquid. The amount of mass involved, for one thing—'

'But very large land animals,' Li pressed him. 'From low-gravity planet. Space travel would be easy in early stages. And pods are rotating very slowly. At one third gravity, is it not correct?'

Maybury had joined the group unobtrusively, her arms full of stacked photographic plates. 'But when the Cygnus Object was approaching the solar system, Dr. Ruiz noticed that it was braking at nine hundred and eighty centimetres per second per second,' she said gravely. 'Approximately one g for a sustained period of time. Perhaps they spin their ships at less than normal g-force for the same reasons we do.'

Pierce nodded gratefully. 'Yes, yes,' he said. 'We're getting away from the subject. We can assume anything we like, but for the sake of convenience, let's assume that they're in a normal size range for highly evolved terrestrial animals—'

'How many creatures?' Tu Jue-chen said tartly.

'Yes, I'm getting to that,' Pierce said. 'Let me see if I remember my geometry. At three miles to a side, an equilateral triangle would have an area of approximately four and a half square miles. Now, how many levels in one of those pods? Let's be conservative and assume fifty-foot ceilings. Room for an ecology, with the equivalent of trees and so forth. That gives more than one hundred levels per mile of height . . .'

'One hundred and five,' Chu said pedantically. 'And six tenths.'

'Yes . . . I mean, *shih*,' Pierce said, flustered. He floundered a moment and went on. 'Now, I'm going to be conservative again and assume the same volumetrics as our own ship. That is to say, the Cygnans occupy only the lower three miles of their pods, and leave the top third for storage, machinery, space-intensive hydroponics, and so forth. That gives us three hundred—'

'Three hundred and sixteen point eight,' Dr. Chu said severely.

' — levels, each with an area of four and a half square miles. That works out to . . .' he floundered again.

'One thousand four hundred and twenty-five square miles per pod,' Maybury supplied. She looked straight at Chu. 'And point six,' she added.

'Thank you, Shirl,' Pierce said gratefully. It was the first time Jameson had heard of Maybury's first name. He saw her glance over at Ruiz. Ruiz was standing straight, arms folded, scorning the no-gravity crouch the rest of them had adopted, looking straight ahead at the screen.

Maybury reached around to the rear pocket of her shorts and took out a pocket lightpad, which she gave to Pierce. A few of the plates got away from her, but she corralled them with little fuss. She'd improved tremendously at handling herself in zero-g in the last few months.

Pierce scribbled on the lightpad, letting it do his sums. It kept flashing question marks at his poor handwriting, and he had to erase and write over again several times.

'Now,' he said, 'we've got three pods per ship. That's four thousand two hundred and seventy-six point eight square miles of deck space. And we've got five ships. So the Cygnans inhabit an area of twenty-one thousand three hundred and eighty-four square miles.'

Ruiz turned round with a smile. 'Fine,' he said encouragingly. 'Now who knows anything about population densities?'

'I looked up some averages in the ship's library, Dr. Ruiz,' Maybury said hesitantly.

'Go on,' he encouraged her.

She cleared her throat. 'Well, it would be densely populated, wouldn't it? You wouldn't waste space in a spaceship. No swamps or deserts. Places like England or the Netherlands have populations of over a thousand per square mile. In urban areas, like the Houston-Dallasworth megalopolis, it goes up to ten thousand. And in *really* crowded places, like Hong Kong, it can go up to two hundred thousand people per square mile.'

'Let's stick with ten thousand,' Ruiz said dryly.

Pierce stared wonderingly at his lightpad. 'That would mean that there are more than two hundred million Cygnans out there.'

They all turned instinctively to look at the silhouetted shape on the screen. With nothing to give it scale, it resembled nothing so much as a collection of jackstraws.

Ruiz nodded. 'Or, to take the lower and upper ends of Maybury's scale, anywhere from twenty-one million to four billion individuals.'

'But why?' Pierce breathed. 'What did they come here for?'

'An army!' Tu Jue-chen said, her eyes glittering. 'A—a—' She hesitated. '*Ch'in lueh che!*'

'An expeditionary force,' Jameson said helpfully.

She nodded.

'Colonists,' Pierce said. 'We *know* they're doing something to Jupiter.'

'Refugees,' Chu said, peering over his glasses. 'They left their world because it was dying.'

'Maybe they are not leave their world behind,' Li said. 'Maybe they take it with them.'

'The Cygnus Object?' Ruiz said.

Li nodded.

'Mizz Maybury,' Ruiz said, 'let's have a look.'

She moved to the instrument panel. The image on the screen shook. There was a blurry twitch as the telescope's aim swept past the alien fleet, past the kidnapped moon it was circling, to the black void a million miles to the left of Jupiter.

The blurs resolved themselves into the Cygnus planet, a sooty ball which was crowding Callisto on the elliptical orbit which intersected the path of its own former moon. Now it too was a moon of Jupiter – the biggest of them all. It was making a mess of the orbits of its stepsisters.

'Bring it up to maximum, will you?' Ruiz said.

The ball sprang toward them, filling the screen. Jameson looked down through wisps of hydrogen clouds at the face of hell.

It was a bleak, rocky desert, split with deep cracks from the tidal forces which were trying to tear it apart. The cracks steamed with noxious gases being squeezed out of the interior. Some of the cracks looked to be hundreds of miles wide, and God knew how deep – canyons that dwarfed anything on Earth. When the Cygnus planet came to its final equilibrium – if Jupiter didn't break it up first; the observatory computer was still trying to make up its mind about that – the shifts and grindings of these gravitational wounds would sculpt that world's only features.

It had no others. There were no craters, as on other airless worlds, no sea basins or continents or mountain ranges. It was a world without geology, a world that had never been born. It had come out of the cosmos as smooth as an egg, and Jupiter had cracked it.

'Rock,' Ruiz said. 'Bald rock and the traces of a hydrogen atmosphere. Nothing ever lived here.' He turned to Li and shook his head. 'This isn't the Cygnans' home planet.'

'Why did they bring it along then?' Jameson said.

'Mizz Maybury,' Ruiz called out. 'Swing the telescope back to Jupiter.'

Another million-mile twitch, and Jupiter was back on the screen, a vast marbled presence. The three-pronged shadow of an alien ship lay across it like an insect claw. The bands of coloured clouds seethed and boiled, flowing visibly towards the equator. The familiar horizontal belts of Jupiter had been gone for some weeks now, replaced by these convolving streaks. Local eddies swirled in thousand-mile curlicues, a meteorologist's nightmare. Jameson could barely make out the pale pink splotch that once had been the Great Red Spot. It had shrunk to a fifth of its former size, and it was leached of colour.

Maybury panned slowly across the cloudscape till she came to the edge of space. The bracelet that Jupiter had been wearing lately showed as a thin bright line etched against the ebony void.

'I'll tell you why they brought it along—' Ruiz began.

An alarm sounded stridently, and the ship lurched. Jameson felt his feet press against the observatory floor with about a hundredth of a g. He had weight now – about a pound and three quarters of it. Tethered objects in the room began to settle towards the floor. The ship had begun its final braking manoeuvre that would swing it past Callisto and put it in orbit around Jupiter half a million miles beyond the fringes of the radiation belt.

Ruiz opened his mouth, but before he could speak, there was a shriek from Tu Jue-chen.

'*Huo hua!*' she gasped, pointing. 'Lights!'

Jameson turned with the rest to stare out of the curved view window.

Out there in the blackness, a thousand fireflies glowed and pulsed: a swarm of small vehicles coming towards them. They were too far away for details to be seen, but they were moving fast. It was an enormous phosphorescent cloud against the deep of space.

Maybury got a telescope pointed at the swarm. Blurred shapes bounced back and forth on one of the overhead display screens. Jameson craned his neck, trying to make sense out of the irregular contours.

And then the image compensator had one of them pinned down and Jameson caught his first glimpse of a Cygnan. It quivered on the screen, a sleek many-legged shape clinging to a stick, like a lizard on a broomstraw.

Ruiz was beside him. 'They've decided to notice us,' he said.


## CHAPTER THIRTEEN

Half the crew was crowded two and three deep against the long, curving observation rail, with more men and women pouring into the bridge's lower level every minute. The Chinese and American fusion/fission teams were still at their posts in the tail of the ship, and Brough and the rest of the medical staff had elected to stay with their patients in the ring, but it seemed that everyone else who didn't have a station to tend had jammed into the ship's command centre, with Boyle's and Hsieh's tacit consent.

At a time like this, you wanted to be with other members of your species.

To the naked eye, the Cygnans were still nothing more than a cloud of campfire sparks in the void, but they were coming fast. The big observation screen forward occasionally fixed a brief glimpse of a blurred individual form; Pierce and Maybury had stayed below in the observatory to work the telescopes, and they were piping in their images.

'They're travelling a quarter million miles on those broomsticks, without a ship around them,' Ruiz said. 'They must be used to space.'

'How long will it take for them to get here?' Jameson asked.

'Three and a half hours for the trip. I don't know when they left.'

'*Three and a half hours?*'

'They're accelerating at a constant one g.'

Jameson turned back to the window in time to see the glowing patch of light suddenly flare up. A low murmur went up from the crowd along the rail.

'That was their turnover point.' Ruiz said. 'They'll be here in an hour and three quarters now.'

Jameson looked across at the big screen with its magnified image. The points of light were lengthening. They turned into lines that crosshatched the dark seemingly at random, making a net across the sky. Maybury managed to catch a fleeting close-up of one of the creatures. It was reversing itself on its stick, twirling it around in a sinuous six-handed grasp. Around it, its thousands of companions presumably were doing the same. The crosshatched lines of light shrank to points again. The glowing patch out the window faded.

Somebody tapped Jameson on the shoulder. He turned around and saw Caffrey.

'My boys and I are going to station ourselves at the main spinlock and the other locks, Commander.' Caffrey said. 'Just a precaution. The main entry points to the ship shouldn't be left unguarded.'

'Good idea,' Jameson said. 'Have you consulted with Tu Jue-chen?'

'Yeah, we settled the procedure. I'm taking three members of her Struggle Brigade with me.'

Jameson looked past Caffrey's shoulder and saw the three husky young Chinese crewmen standing there. They all wore homemade Struggle badges pinned to their singlets: cardboard discs painted with the current slogans. One of them had gone so far as to transform himself into a walking poster, with the Chinese characters for *ching hsing* – 'vigilance' – in red paint on his forehead. All three of them carried steel bars.

'Ray,' Jameson said uneasily. 'We don't know that those creatures are hostile. We can't afford to get off on the wrong foot with them.'

'Do you think I'm crazy?' Caffrey said. 'I'll keep these fellows in hand.'

'It's good to see that ship's security is keeping the ship secure instead of protecting us from the exchange of scientific information,' Ruiz said dryly.

Caffrey turned reproachful eyes on Ruiz. 'Doctor,' he said, sounding genuinely hurt.

Jameson watched the four of them shoulder their way through the crowd. They were met at the exit by Caffrey's three beetle-browed assistants, who also carried steel bars.

'God help us all,' Ruiz said. 'Slogans and steel bars. What a way for two intelligent races to meet for the first time.'

'I don't think Boyle will let any Cygnans inside anyway,' Jameson said. 'Germs. We'll send a delegation outside to meet them. Let Caffrey guard the locks. It'll keep him out of mischief.'

Ruiz looked thoughtful. 'What if—'

'Excuse me, Doctor,' Jameson said. He looked up at the balcony. Boyle was making urgent motions towards him. Jameson found a guy line and zipped up to his post. Kay Thorwald, looking worried, was sitting at a communications console while Captain Hsieh hovered over her.

'I can't get anyone in Major Hollis's territory to answer, Captain,' she said.

'Have Jarowski try to patch you through to his suit radio,' Boyle said through clenched teeth.

'What's wrong, Captain?' Jameson said.

'Look,' Boyle said.

Jameson went over to the safety rail and looked down. With the drive on, even at one per cent of g, there was the illusion of looking out of a very tall tower down towards the ballerina skirt of the ring. It was still spinning; they hadn't bothered to stop it for the braking manoeuvre.

Jameson found Hollis's pod as it swept by on its merry-go-round circuit. It was a plastic cocoon riding the inside of the wheel. Then he saw what Boyle was pointing at.

Hollis's bomb squad, silvery ants in their spacesuits, were pouring out of the pod and assembling in a small group on the inner rim of the wheel. They were all sticking close to the safety railings. They were standing at right angles to Jameson's point of view, and he knew that they, unlike he and the people on the bridge, had two thirds of their Earth weight.

The wheel swung them out of sight. When they came back into view thirty seconds later, they were marching in military formation towards the nearest spoke.

'What are they doing?' Jameson said.

'They're going to fire their nukes,' Boyle said.

'Captain Boyle,' Hsieh said in a strangled voice. 'I must insist that you put a stop to this unilateral action. The bomb crews are to work in concert. We have not yet reached a joint decision.'

'I'll do my best,' Boyle said.

'Captain,' Kay said. 'I've got him.'

'Hollis, can you hear me?' Boyle called into Kay's mike.

Hollis's voice came out of the little speaker on the console. 'I can hear you, Captain. Make it quick.'

'I order you and your men to return to quarters immediately.'

'This is a military action, Captain. You have no jurisdiction.'

'Hollis, are you crazy? You don't have the authority to commit the entire human race to a war with another civilization.'

'I have my contingency orders from Earth, Captain. I'm interpreting them as I see fit.'

'Hollis, listen to me—'

Hollis's tight, rasping voice issued from the speaker. To Jameson it sounded somehow sleepy. 'I'm locked in on all five of the alien ships,' he said 'The computer techs transferred the information from the observatory computer this morning. But first I'm going to set off a couple of gigaton bombs in the middle of that cluster coming towards us. It's only a few hundred miles across; I can drench them with enough hard radiation to cook them all. Have to eyeball it and set off the bombs by radio signal.'

Jameson snatched the microphone from Boyle. 'Listen, Major, you don't understand the situation. Those scooters are travelling at over a hundred kilometers a second at this point, and decelerating. You *can't* eyeball it. If you're off by a couple of seconds, your missiles will pass right through them or else go off too soon. All you can do is make them mad.'

'That's enough talk,' Hollis said, and switched off.

Boyle grabbed the mike back and shouted, 'Major Hollis!' but the speaker was dead.

'He's going to get his men into trouble, Captain,' Jameson said. 'They aren't proficient enough yet to—'

'Look' Kay said in a strained voice.

The last ant in the column had fallen behind and was hurrying to catch up. He must have gotten careless, or been disoriented by the star-encrusted void whirling past him, because he lost his footing and stumbled backward. Top-heavy in his gear, he toppled over the low safety rail.

The wheel hurled him out into the dark. The wriggling silver figure shrank until it was gone. There had been a sudden rush to save him, and now Hollis's men milled about aimlessly.

'Captain, can you stop the wheel?' Jameson asked.

Boyle looked at him steadily. 'No,' he said.

Hollis must have been giving orders. The confused movement of the men stopped all at once, and they all began marching again toward the base of the spoke.

They climbed the outside handles painfully, all of them being very careful now. Two thirds of the way towards the hub, they all stopped. Hollis was giving orders again. Suit jets misting, they floated at an angle toward the missile pods on the shaft. Hollis had had them do it a hundred times before when the ship was coasting, saving time by lifting off the spoke at the point where centripetal force dropped off enough.

'He just killed his men,' Jameson said between clenched teeth.

The difference in velocity was infinitesimal – less than ten centimetres per second per second. But it added up. It took Hollis and his men twenty seconds to realize that an invisible rubber band was dragging them back to the plane of the wheel. Another twenty seconds and they were there – but their starting point wasn't. The spoke swept by, tantalizingly out of reach, while they dropped past the waist of the ship at forty, then fifty and sixty centimetres per second.

Jameson's knuckles were white on the rail. 'The damned bungling Earthlubber!' he said. 'Didn't he realize he couldn't do that trick when the ship was braking?'

Only a minute had gone by. Even then, some of them might have saved themselves, but they wasted precious seconds trying to catch up to the radiating spokes of the wheel. Only one of them had the sense to aim at an efficient right angle straight toward the giant shaft that was slipping by. He caught a handhold just forward of the flaring skirt and immediately began to crawl forward, away from stray drive radiation.

The rest of them, in a panic to escape the hellish beam of the exhaust, scattered sideways. The ship plunged past them, faster with each second, They were being left behind – or, more properly, were outracing the ship, keeping their initial velocity while the ship continued to decelerate.

And then there was just a swarm of silver insects hovering against the black depths, diminishing until they were lost among the stars. The edge of the swarm had been seared by the dreadful violent flame of the drive. They were the lucky ones.

The survivor was too terrified to let go of his handhold. Grogan and one of his men had to suit up and go outside to pry him loose, They coaxed him forward towards the auxiliary air lock behind the observatory. After a while he understood that ten centimetres per second per second wasn't dangerous if you kept contact with the ship, and scrambled forward on his own.

When the bulky figure stumbled into the bridge with Grogan, there was a rush to help him out of his helmet. A long blonde braid tumbled out.

It was the girl. The only one of them who'd had the sense to save herself. People turned from the observation window to stare at her with open curiosity. In all the months of the journey only a handful of people had seen her. Hollis had kept her bottled up with his men. Jameson caught Klein eyeing her with furtive interest.

She was a big one all right, as Grogan had said. The suit peeled off to reveal a chunky thick-waisted body, heavy in the shoulders, in a bulging skintight liner that had SMITTY stitched over one flattened breast. She had a baby-fat face with a little pug nose and a mouth blurred by makeup that had been hastily scrubbed at. Smitty had a lovely, enormous black eye. Jameson wondered which of the twenty-three men in the nuclear-bomb crew had given it to her.

'You all right?' Grogan asked solicitously.

The answer was an uninflected stream of foul language that made up in repetition what it lacked in inventiveness.

Grogan nodded, 'You're all right.' He turned back to the observation window to watch with the others.

The cloud of swarming lights had grown to blot out the stars. All of a sudden, they all winked out.

# CHAPTER FOURTEEN

The three orange-ringed eyes of the creature from Cygnus stared into Jameson's face from less than a foot away. Two of them were where you'd expect eyes to be. The third, surprisingly, was under the jaw. They were extended on stubby polyps that twitched like a puppy's nose, as if the thing were trying to sniff at him rather than see him.

Jameson switched on his flashlight for a better look. The creature blinked – if that sudden reflexive puckering around the eyes could be called a blink – and then, too fast for any movement to be seen, the Cygnan was simply gone.

Almost immediately it was replaced by another. This one clung to the outside of the observation bubble for a moment, giving Jameson a brief, palpitating scrutiny, and then it too darted off, clambering across the transparent plastic in quick little fits and starts. The Cygnans moved in a sequence of disconcerting skips and then, like a stop-action film. You'd be looking at them, and then, abruptly, they'd be in a new position.

They'd been crawling all over the outside of the ship for nine or ten minutes now, like ants over a picnic ham. More were arriving every minute on their queer broomsticks. They were sleek, elongated creatures, a little smaller than men with six slender limbs. Incredibly, they weren't wearing spacesuits, just transparent sheaths stretched over their narrow heads and their clubbed tails. For the rest of it, their mottled hides were as shiny and naked as a lacquered snake.

'I feel like a goldfish in a bowl,' Ruiz said. 'Why can't we get their *attention*?'

People were lined up along the rail, waving at Cygnans, gesturing to them, trying vainly for some response. The communications teams were knocking themselves out with hand signals and easel pads. But the Cygnans didn't seem at all interested in communicating. They'd stare for a moment, then dart away.

'Maybe we're not intelligent enough for them,' Jameson said. 'Maybe they just came over to look at the animals.'

'Or maybe *they*'re not intelligent enough,' Ruiz said. 'Maybe they're just the Cygnans' equivalent of trained hounds, sent over to sniff us out. Look at those narrow heads. You couldn't fit much of a brain into them.'

Jameson squinted at the nearest alien. It squinted back at him with its three stalked eyes. He shivered, glad it was on the other side of the Lexiglass. Ruiz was right. There was something primitive about that tapering, arrowhead-shaped skull. The jaws split it down the middle in a permanent reptilian smile. There were no teeth. The inside of the mouth, when it opened, was an unpleasant-looking rasp. The Cygnan put its mouth around its food, whatever it was, and filed it down. There was a tubular, needle-spined tongue way back in the gullet to go with it.

Dmitri pushed past Jameson to take a close-up picture. He shot off a second's worth of high-speed frames on full automatic before the Cygnan twitched its body around and ran off. He was in biologist's paradise.

'You're wrong,' he burbled happily. 'The brain doesn't have to be in the head. The head may just be an extended structure for the mouth and the sense organs. Take a closer look. There's nothing like a proper, rigid braincase. Just some kind of tough cartilaginous material.'

Jameson peered up again at the undersides of scurrying Cygnans. Dmitri was right. Those long narrow heads were flexible. They tended to bend in the direction the Cygnan was looking, like an elephant's trunk.

'Where's the brain, then?' Jameson said.

'In the most sensible place, I imagine – at the top of the nerve cord. That would put it between where its shoulders would be, if it had shoulders instead of that almost-round cross section. The nerve cord probably runs through the centre of the body – not dorsally, like us vertebrates, or ventrally, like terrestrial insects. Because ...' Dmitri's face flushed in triumph. 'Because Cygnans aren't bilaterally symmetrical. They're built on a radial plan like hydras or starfish. They're descended from something like coelenterates, not flatworms.'

Ruiz looked at him sharply, then out the observation bubble again. Jameson said, 'Radial? But their limbs are paired!'

'Are they? Look again.'

Jameson tried to focus again on the scampering aliens. It was hard, because they were never still. But then he saw what

Dmitri was driving at. There was something odd about the placement of the Cygnans' limbs.

There were two arms and four legs, or four arms and two legs, depending on how you looked at it. The middle pair functioned as either arms or legs, as the Cygnans' whim dictated, so that they were continually shifting from centaurlike beings to four-armed bipeds. The three splayed fingers – or toes, if you preferred – were monkey-clever. All the joints bent in a rubbery curve, showing that evolution had provided a flexible alternative to the ball-and-socket joint.

But that wasn't where the impression of strangeness came from.

The limb arrangement was asymmetrical. When you looked closely, you saw that the limbs were staggered – one placed noticeably forward of its mate on the opposite side. The middle pair in particular were lopsided. The attaching muscles on the middle limbs seemed to be placed higher, too – Jameson would have said they were rooted near the spine, except that there was no visible spine, just rippling bands of muscle ringing the creature's body.

But once the eye got used to the asymmetry, there was no sense of wrongness. It was just . . . different.

'You see, the limbs have been displaced by evolution,' Dmitri said smugly. 'Once there were two sets of three equidistant limbs or tentacles, like a double-ended hydra. But when it became a land creature, it had to choose an up and a down. They probably evolved the same way we did – took to the trees and came down again a few million years later. Only more deft and agile than us monkeys – with a choice of four hands for making tools or four legs for running away from their enemies.'

'Or chasing their prey,' Ruiz said sourly.

'Maybe. I'll have to think about that dentition. Closest thing on Earth is a parasite – the lamprey. Rasps its way into a fish and sucks the juices.'

Jameson looked at the swarm outside and shuddered.

'Sounds unpleasant.'

Dmitri looked pleased with himself. 'The only difference between a parasite and a predator is the size of the prey. A mosquito's a parasite, a tiger's a predator. When the predator gets too big for its victim, it tends to kill it, that's all. Maybe these creatures' ancestors ate on the run, like Cape hunting dogs.'

Hastily, Jameson changed the subject. 'Would the extra limbs just atrophy? Would evolution really displace them so drastically?'

'Sure,' Dmitri said. 'Happens all the time. It doesn't even have to wait for evolution. Take the asymmetrical sole. Flounders and other flatfish on Earth start life with the usual bilateral symmetry, with an eye on either side, like free-swimming fish. When they get older and decide to lie on one side, the eye on that side moves around to the other side of the head.'

Dmitri paused to snap a picture of a Cygnan applying some instrument to the bubble. Perhaps it was taking a picture of him.

'The clincher is those three eyes,' he said after a moment. 'What's one doing under the jaw? Simple! No jaw! It's just learned to open like one. It started as three eyestalks around a central orifice.'

'So the creature's just a glorified tube?' Ruiz ventured.

'Well . . . so are we. But yes.' He frowned. 'I wonder what's so important about the other end, that the Cygnans have to wrap them up like their heads.'

'What I'd like to know,' Jameson said, 'is how they matched orbits with us. And just by eyeballing it, too!'

'And how do they manage without spacesuits?' Ruiz asked.

'Maybe a very tough outer cuticle, like nematodes,' Dmitri said.

'What are nematodes?'

'Most numerous animal on Earth. Little parasitic round-worms. Every species of higher plant or animal has at least one species of nematode living off it. Human beings have about fifty. Most you never notice. They can live in vacuum. Some even live in boiling water, in hot springs.'

'Where do you get all these nasty facts?' Ruiz said.

'My specialty was parasitology,' Dmitri said with a self-satisfied smirk. 'Good training for an exobiologist. You'd be surprised at some of the adaptations—'

'Later,' Ruiz said hastily. He turned to Jameson. 'Tod my boy, what are we going to do about out visitors? Can we let a delegation of them inside for a talk?'

'Some of us may go outside,' Jameson said. 'The skipper's talking it over with Captain Hsieh now.'

At that moment a mild sensation washed through his body, as if he were on a descending elevator. He'd suddenly lost his one per cent weight. Ruiz noticed it too. He looked up questioningly. Only Dmitri seemed oblivious. He was opening his mouth for another little lecture, his slippers hooked into the fuzzy surface of the deck.

'Drive's off,' Jameson said. 'That's odd. We still have another couple of hours of braking to do.'

'*Mister Jameson!*' Boyle was bawling his name from the control balcony.

'Excuse me,' Jameson said. He circled the nearest guideline loosely with a thumb and forefinger and kicked off into the air. He reached the balcony in a great swoop and swung himself over.

Boyle and Hsieh were hunched over a communicator screen, looking worried. Mike Berry's face looked out at them, grimy and lined. In the background a Chinese technician, illegally present in the American section, was going over a computer display with Quentin.

Boyle looked up at Jameson. 'Listen to this,' he said.

'. . . reaction just damped out,' Berry was saying. 'We can't seem to get it started again. There seems to be a strong magnetic field interfering with the shape of the field squeezing the plasma. And it's playing hell with the computers. Timing's all out of whack.'

Kay Thorwald, looking grim, was pointing through the bulge of the observation port down along the length of the hull.

'Look!' she cried.

Jameson sighted down the shaft. At the far end a dozen Cygnans were clustered together, engaged in purposeful activity. He could make out some kind of lattice attached to the ship, encircling the hull.

'That's how they did it, Captain,' he said.

Kay's hand flew to her throat. 'They'll kill us! Don't they know that? If we don't kill our momentum, we won't go into orbit around Callisto. We'll crash into Jupiter!'

'Captain!' Jameson said. 'We've got to damage that structure they've attached to the ship. I'm betting that it won't take much to do it. Smash it up with pry bars wherever the thing looks most fragile. Toss the loose parts into space. By the time they could replace it, Berry would be able to get the drive working. If we could buy a couple of hours that way, we'd have time to get into a stable orbit.'

Grogan gestured at the scurrying hordes of six-limbed creatures outside. 'We'd have to get past them.'

Jameson drew a breath. 'From the spinlock to that point on the hull is about half the length of a football field,' he said. 'If I have a dozen good people running interference for me, I think I can make it.'

'I can't risk it, Tod,' Boyle said.

'Captain, it's the only way.'

Boyle and Hsieh exchanged a glance. 'All right,' Boyle said at last. 'Let's round up some volunteers,'

Jameson kissed Maggie good-bye and gathered the volunteers around him, 'Let's go.'

There was a strangled cry from Kay. 'Look, look! What are they doing to the air lock?'

Jameson glanced out the bubble. Down at the hub of the ship, aliens were clustered all over the surface of the concentric cylinders that contained the spinlocks, thick as bees on honeysuckle. They were centring their attention on one of the outside doors.

A Cygnan with an implement that looked, at this distance, like an Easter egg at the end of a shovel handle was tracing the crack where the door was sealed. In its wake, other Cygnans were inserting toothpicks. When the eye adjusted for distance, the toothpicks became perfectly ordinary-looking crowbars. The Cygnans were already leaning on them, two or three feet hooked somehow into the surface of the hull, the remaining two or three hands bearing down on the bar.

'They're prying the damn door open!' Boyle howled.

'Let's get going' Jameson yelled, starting towards the exit. 'Caffrey'll need help.'

'Stay where you are, Commander,' Boyle ordered.

'But—'

'There's no time.'

The hatch flew off. It seemed to catch the Cygnans by surprise. They rose off the ship like a swarm of flies being disturbed. One of them appeared to have been injured by the hatch. After a moment they settled. There was a frosty explosion of air glittering against space, a white cloud growing larger. Alarms were going off all over the board.

Human bodies were floating out there. Jameson counted three.

'Caffrey must have had the inside door open, trying to get

outside to stop them in time,' Jameson said. 'The whole middle of the shaft between bulkheads'll be open to vacuum.'

Kay glanced at her instruments. 'It is.'

The Cygnan with the Easter-egg tool slithered into the opening. Its assistants oozed after it.

Grogan was beside Jameson, clutching the edge of Kay's console with raw knuckles. 'Caffrey would've had the spin matched to the shaft, then. The wheel's still safe. It'd be too hairy for them to try to get through the interface while it's grinding around. They'll come through this way first.'

He was wrong. There was another explosion of frost, a big one this time. A couple of hapless Cygnans came tumbling out of the lock, squirming round on their broomsticks to get back to the ship.

'Somebody was riding the cage, trying to get up here,' Jameson said. 'The bulkhead at the end of the spoke must have been open.'

'Who was in that section of the wheel?' Boyle asked, his voice tight.

'That was spoke number three,' Kay said, reading the board. 'Sickbay.'

'How many patients did Doc Brough and Dr. Nyi have?'

'Four, I think,' Kay said in a shaken voice.

Jameson asked, 'What about Berry and his people? And Po Fu-yung's team? Are they still alive?'

'Yes. The engine section was sealed off. But there's only enough air there to last a few hours.'

Grogan's big knuckles were working. 'We can get 'em out in spacesuits, a few at a time. Or carry enough air bottles to them to last until they finish their work.'

Kiernan was pushing his way through the crowd. 'The hydroponics section!' he said. 'Did it lose its air?'

Yeh Fei answered him. 'Yes. But the no-gravity farm is still alive. The bulkhead forward of the spinlock was sealed.'

'Can that keep us going?' Boyle asked.

Kiernan put his head together with Dmitri. After a mumbled exchange, he looked up again. 'Yes. If nothing else happens we can get some new algae tanks going. We may have to spread out into the observatory and bridge. And if we can pressurize the ring again, I can reestablish a hydroponics section there with transplants from the banks in no-g. We won't be eating well for a while, but we'll breathe.'

'Unless . . .' Everybody turned to look at Jameson. 'Unless they kill off the rest of our greenery before we can stop them.'

'All right,' Boyle said, 'We're under siege. Grogan, we're going to need all the spacesuits from the spinlock lockers. And somebody's going to have to go through vacuum to get them. How many suits can we scrape up here in the forward part of the ship?'

'Captain, there's just four. They're in the auxiliary air lock near the observatory. At least they were last time I checked. But we can't send anyone to the spinlock until I jury-rig some kind of air lock south of the no-g farm.'

'How long will that take you?'

Grogan thought it over, 'I can make it out of a water tank. A couple of hours.'

Jameson looked out the window. He could see a general movement of Cygnans towards the breached lock. Frozen air was still misting out into space.

'Skipper,' he said, 'we don't have a couple of hours.'

Boyle brooded at him from under heavy eyebrows. 'No, we don't. Once they get into the ship . . .'

He didn't need to finish the thought. Everybody there was thinking about what would happen if the Cygnans breached any more bulkheads. The humans were trapped in their own ship, in two fragile bubbles of air at either end of the long shaft that pierced the wheel. Even if they all could get into spacesuits – those unreachable suits in the spinlock – it would only prolong their death sentence.

Kiernan bit his lip. 'Come on, Wang,' he said. 'Let's get down to the farm and get as much seed stock as we can into airtight lockers.'

'Do you know how dangerous that is, Mr. Kiernan?' Boyle interrupted, 'You'll be one bulkhead closer to vacuum. Assuming we can get the ship repressurized, is there really going to be enough time to reestablish an ecology before the reserve air runs out?'

'I don't know,' Kiernan admitted, 'But we've got to try.'

'I'll go with you,' Dmitri volunteered abruptly. 'You'll need a lot of help. You'd better have a biologist along.' The boyish face didn't look weak any more. Dmitri's voice was shaking, but his self indulgent mouth was set in firm lines now. Jameson had to admire his guts.

'I go too,' a harsh voice said, 'I am biologist.' They looked up. Tu Jue-chen was there, biting her lip. Her homely face was tight and unreadable.

'Thank you, *Tongzhi* Tu,' Boyle said.

'I'd better get started,' Jameson said. 'I'll have to try to run the gauntlet with just two men. I'd better leave the fourth spacesuit here. Somebody may still be able to make it to the spinlock storage lockers for some more suits if Grogan can rig up that air lock before the Cygnans decide to come inside.' He turned to Grogan. 'You'd better get cracking, Chief.'

'The hell I will,' Grogan rumbled. 'I'm coming with you. One of my boys'll volunteer to rig the lock.' He called out over the crowd. 'Fiaccone, that's you'

'Right you are, Chief,' Fiaccone said, grinning. He headed toward the exit in a no-gravity shamble.

Yeh Fei rose from his chair, looming over the rest of them. 'I am third man,' he said. Nobody argued with him.

Jameson said good-bye to Maggie again, clasping her thin body in his arms. He felt her trembling. 'I'll be back,' he said, whispering. 'Nothing says the Cygnans have to be malicious. Maybe they're just curious.'

She was wound around him with all her strength. He broke free gently and turned to Grogan and Yeh. 'All set,' he said.

The three of them suited up in the auxiliary lock behind the observatory. Yeh had armed himself with a wicked-looking cargo hook, Grogan had his fist wrapped around the handle of a sixteen-pound sledgehammer, just behind its head. The short handle was forward. He could poke with it, or swing his fist with the heavy lump of metal in it. Jameson had a long pry bar.

Just before they spun the outer door open, there was a disconcerting moment when a Cygnan peered in at them through the small safety window. Its three orange pupils expanded from a narrow slit, like an unfolding fan. Then the creature blinked and was gone.

If Dmitri was right, there was no brain behind those three strange eyes. What unimaginable thoughts went on between what passed for a Cygnan's shoulders?

'Go!' Jameson commanded.

The hull immediately outside the airlock was a crawling carpet of mottled flesh. A sea of pikes bobbed and waved above it: the Cygnans' flying broomsticks. They held them absentmindedly, passing them from hand to middle limb to foot as they jostled one another to converge on the opening lock. The clever little toes clung to any projection or surface irregularity on the hull.

Jameson scrambled forward, Yeh and Grogan flanking him in a flying wedge. The carpet of alien life opened up ahead of them and closed again behind them. Yeh was swinging his long hook in circles to keep them at a distance. Grogan poked with his sledge handle. Cygnans skipped nimbly out of the way.

*My God, we're going to make it!* was Jameson's first thought. But then, before they had gone twenty feet, the Cygnans began closing in.

Yeh made a swipe with his hook and ripped the balloonlike sheath over a Cygnan's long snout. Vapour puffed out into space, and the Cygnan died. Jameson could see orange blood oozing out of the eyestalks.

Then, before the swing could be completed, Cygnan fingers closed on the shaft of the cargo hook. Yeh shook the grip off with his enormous strength, but the Cygnan simply shifted its grip to a middle limb. A companion came to help it and easily snatched the hook out of Yeh's grasp; Yeh's weapon passed from Cygnan to Cygnan until it was out of sight.

Grasping hands and feet were all over Jameson now. He swung out with his crowbar and felt it thud into the closely packed bodies. But dozens of three-fingered paws began tugging at it, anticipating his every move.

He could see Grogan floating belly-up above the hull beside him, being borne away by Cygnans, like a grub carried by ants. Grogan's struggles did him no good. When he shook a Cygnan claw off, two or three more were there to take its place. With their six limbs and unencumbered bodies, they just kept changing hands in a blur of motion. There was nothing to fight against.

Clumsy in his spacesuit, Jameson tried to strike out, to grab. The crowbar had been plucked away before he realized what was happening. Whenever he caught hold of a Cygnan, deft, slender fingers pried his grip loose. Dozens of hands snatched at his sleeves, keeping him from hitting hard.

Ahead of him he saw an explosion of packed bodies. Grogan had somehow broken free for a moment. Cygnans rose into the air and began to settle down again. He caught a glimpse of Grogan, writhing against a background of stars, a half dozen aliens clinging to him like terriers to a bear. Busy fingers were plucking at Grogan's hoses, at the latches of his suit. Finally came the horrible sight of Grogan's helmet being passed from Cygnan to Cygnan like a basketball, while above Grogan's collar ring a ball of oozing sludge sprayed a fine pink mist into space.

Jameson felt a moment of panic as alien fingers fumbled at his own latches. He managed to slap them away, and they didn't return. Then suddenly came a heave, like a concerted blanket-toss, and Jameson felt himself sailing into space. Tumbling end over end, he saw himself heading into the mouth of a large transparent sack that was being held open by a circle of hovering Cygnans. There was nothing he could do to change his trajectory, as he discovered when he tried to use his suit jets. Industrious little fingers had managed to disconnect them.

He was ignominiously stuffed, kicking and squirming, into the sack. The neck was drawn shut. He struck out through the tough plastic material at the smooth, shiny bodies around him. All he succeeded in doing was to work up a sweat inside his spacesuit. Can't fight my way out of a paper bag, he thought. He groped at his belt kit for something sharp. All his tools were missing.

A Cygnan with some kind of tank-and-hose arrangement floated over to him. Jameson studied the creature through the clear plastic. It was holding the tank in its middle limbs, the hose nozzle with one hand. The other hand – or what passed for a hand – began fiddling with a valve. Holding its broomstick negligently with one foot, the Cygnan started to spray him. When it had finished the job, another Cygnan floated over with a bundle of long tubes fitted with a pistol grip. His captors let go of the sack again and left Jameson hanging free. The creature vacuumed the entire surface of the sack industriously. Jameson detected a glow of purple light. Sterilizing me, he thought.

A pair of Cygnans took him then, like a sack of laundry and zoomed off with him. The creature on the right clutched its broomstick with the three right-hand limbs, like an outrigger, and the one on the left hung on to its stick with its three left limbs. They held the stack stretched safely between them, leaning inward to join hands at its neck. Jameson noticed that they kept shifting their grip. They had three choices. And there were never more than two limbs wrapped around the stick. One of them always was resting. Did Cygnans tire easily? Jameson decided that no individual Cygnan limb was as strong as a human arm or leg. But it didn't have to be.

A mile or two from the ship, he finally stopped struggling. When his air was gone, he was dead. He wanted to postpone that as long as possible. So he settled into the sack and tried to make himself relax. Ruiz had been right. Those flimsy-looking tubes the Cygnans rode stored enough power for constant acceleration. He had weight, dangling between his two captors; it felt like half a g, but it was hard to be sure.

He saw a lot of traffic going in both directions around him. The long brilliant beams of light flashing from the ends of the slender brooms made a jackstraw pattern against space.

They were heading straight toward some invisible target a quarter million miles away. There was no nonsense about trajectories, about matching orbits. The aliens simply ploughed through space as if they had all the power in the universe at their disposal. And perhaps they did, if they could move whole planets.

Jameson looked back – 'down', actually – at the Jupiter ship. It was tiny now, a double-pointed thumbtack pinned against the stars.

Then, abruptly, twin threads of light stretched across the black of space. That wasn't the boron drive. The aliens had attached some kind of propulsive units to the ship at the head and tail of the shaft. He could see it begin to move sideways, its wheel still turning, as if it were rolling through space.

The Cygnans had gone fishing. Now they were bringing home their catch.


## CHAPTER FIFTEEN

The alien ship loomed ahead, big as a world. It *was* a world, thirty miles from tip to splayed tip. From this angle it was a slender triskelion, a three-bladed pinwheel with a triangular bucket dangling from the end of each arm.

Jameson squirmed around in his transparent gamebag for a better view. He'd been cramped inside for more than six hours now, and his suit's air was almost gone.

His captors were approaching the ship head on, so he could-n't see much of the long central spar that formed the axis, except for a yawning triangular maw at the hub. That had to be the business end of the drive.

An extraordinary thought occurred to him. He had read once, in a popular book on psychotechnology, that the works of man were influenced by buried images of self. His motile surrogates of himself tended to be cross-shaped – a man with arms outstretched – like early airplanes, or four-limbed like the drive shaft and two axles of a wheeled vehicle at right angles, or, in the ultimate subconscious distillation, male symbols like rockets or female symbols like boats.

But the Cygnans – if Dmitri's morphology was to be believed – were three limbs spaced equally around a central axis. And so was their ship. There were even three stubby triangular petals – feet? – placed at the opposite end of the shaft. Jameson could make them out on another Cygnan ship hovering some dozens of miles away. They might be miles-thick radiation baffles for the life-support modules when the ship was in its folded mode. They'd be facing forward then, into a howling storm of impinging interstellar hydrogen. This all made eminent sense in engineering terms, but so did the design of their Jupiter ship. Jameson wondered what psychoanalytical innuendos the author would have found to describe *that!*

There was one more flash of insight before his mind got busy again with his predicament. Designs evolve past first solutions. Technological phylogeny, the book had called it. The cross-shaped airplane was an early effort of mankind, replaced by delta wings and various lifting bodies. Was this tremendous feat of engineering he saw looming before him a *first try* for the Cygnans?

Then he became lost in wonder. Those fifteen-mile-long jibs that held the environment pods were anchored at their roots by pins that had to be large enough and strong enough to keep a small world from flying off into space. The grooves along the flat faces of the hull that the jibs were meant to rest in were as deep as the Grand Canyon. And – he sighted along one of the arms until he came to the distant three-sided bucket – that wishbone-shaped tholepin that formed the handle of the bucket was, by itself, of a size to stagger the imagination.

He tried to visualize it – a structure four and a half miles from end to end pivoting on a pair of bearings that alone were bigger than the largest turning structure man had ever made, Eurostation itself. The bolt head he could instantly see was a bright dome the size of a small mountain.

The rotation of the arms, from Jameson's vantage point, was

almost imperceptible. Structures that size didn't have to turn very fast to provide g forces fifteen miles from the centre.

By the same token, the Cygnans seemed to have dispensed with anything resembling a docking hub. Perhaps they didn't need one at this creeping rate of rotation, depending on their own agility and the feebleness of centrifugal force so close to the spine of the ship.

Jameson shrivelled in the sack. Were they going to plunge into the miles-wide pit of the drive tube that was growing before his eyes? He saw a triangular chasm whose interior walls were blackened and pitted with the violent energies that had flung the Cygnans across ten thousand light-years.

Then with a casual flick of their broomsticks, the Cygnans altered course fractionally. The rim of the pit flashed by. Jameson, with nothing to hang on to, found himself falling past a sheer metal wall that stretched on forever.

They barely missed the outstretched arm of one of the jibs.

Resolutely, Jameson kept his eyes open, but he found his gloved hands trying to clutch at nothingness. He had a flashing glimpse of the spar's upper surface before he dropped below its horizon. This was a metal moonscape, pocked with craters and scarred with long furrows, the wounds of forgotten encounters with interstellar debris.

He looked upward as he fell below the knife edge of that strange skyline. The undersides of the spar hung above him like an axe blade fifteen miles long. These were the faces that fit into the canyon-size notch in one of the ship's flat sides. There were no pockmarks. They were smooth and shiny enough to reflect the stars.

They fell what he judged to be another four or five miles before the labouring broomsticks were able to slow them to a halt. Jameson's orientation changed. He was no longer falling down the side of an immense cliff. Now he was floating, weightless, above a vast metal plain, incised along its entire length by a triangular gorge. The landscape was tilting, moving past him. Long minutes later, the sharp edge of the landscape swam past and he was hovering above an identical plain with an identical incised groove stretching toward the vanishing point.

Jupiter dipped, then rose again above that strange, flat horizon. It was a great, reddish moon, filling the ship's sky. It *was* the sky, or most of it: a vast arch stretching from side to side, showing only a fraction of its curvature, with a band of night on its border. Here, this close, you could see the violent turmoil of the planet's atmosphere, a boiling sea of multicoloured clouds rushing toward an invisible equator.

The two creatures loafed along on their sticks, the sack stretched between them, until they found an entrance. This proved to be a squarish hatch the size of a barn door, with a perfectly ordinary-looking T-bar handle precisely in the centre. The handle was surrounded by a circle of what looked like doorknobs.

They hovered a few feet above it, dangling Jameson ignominiously between them. The sheer mass of the tremendous ship was enough to produce a minute but noticeable gravitational tug; Jameson guessed that he weighed somewhere in the neighbourhood of an ounce.

Then the Cygnans touched down, clinging lizardlike to the knobs with two or three spare feet.

Instantly, Jameson's weight was reversed. He soared upward in his sack as if he were a captive balloon, while the Cygnans kept him moored with infuriating nonchalance. Again, the spin was slow enough to keep his pseudo-weight down to a few ounces, but his stomach did a flip-flop. What if the Cygnans let go?

One of them did. The other, its toes wrapped around knobs, stretched its sleek body toward the handle in the centre. Jameson wondered how the creature proposed to open the door with the three of them clinging to it. Did it swing outward, inward, or slide open?

It did none of these. To Jameson's mild astonishment, when the Cygnan pulled on the handle, the handle got longer. Then he realized that the door was riding downward on a central shaft, of which the handle was the end. Bottom was five feet down. The creatures stepped off the door, pulling Jameson unceremoniously with them. The door flew up on its shaft, falling into place in the opening with its own weight. It settled into place in the bevelled frame. It seemed a careless way to seal a ship's air in.

Clinging upside down to what was now the ceiling, the Cygnans scurried towards a circular door in a wall. This one opened like a bank vault. It didn't go anywhere. Inside was a honeycomb of three-foot metal discs that looked like a wall of storage drums.

One of the creatures chose a lid and it popped open. Before

Jameson knew what was happening, it slithered inside. The other Cygnan stuffed the sack into the opening and followed. Jameson was being hustled down a narrow, looping tube. It was transparent, and he could see other tubes branching out on all sides, each going to some unknown destination.

It was an efficient way to travel – for Cygnans. They reverted to their six-legged mode, hardly caring which direction was up. Jameson was getting some painful bumps, even through the spacesuit.

They emerged into an enormous space – a forest, stretching as far as the eye could see. No, not quite. About a mile away was a mile-high ridge, stretching on to infinity. This had to be, he realized, the underside of that tremendous canyon-size trench he had seen on the outside of the hull. The sky was a tent – two walls converging at an apex miles above. The sky was forested too, and each had its own central ridge.

He had time for a quick look at what he had taken for trees before they hoisted him aloft. It was a tangle of thick twisting boles, intertwined like a banyan tree, with thick blue-green foliage. If there were any vertical trunks, they were accidental. The growth seemed to spread out sideways, like some enormous creeping vine. He couldn't tell if they were individual growths or one interconnected entity.

The Cygnans scurried up the nearest trunk like six-legged squirrels, taking Jameson with them. Soon they were about fifty feet up, and Jameson was getting dizzy. He knew that at his present weight a fall couldn't hurt him, but all his instincts were screaming at him. The Cygnans passed the sack back and forth to each other, and from hand to foot, as they scampered along the tremendous branches, but always there seemed to be at least one clever little paw wrapped around the neck of the sack.

After about half a mile of being towed through the branches in this offhand fashion, Jameson found himself draped over a branch, dizzy and bruised. He lay there in his bag, not daring to move. His captors had evidently stopped to catch their breath – even Cygnans had to do that, it seemed – and to tear the plastic wrappings off their heads and beaverlike tails.

They let the torn plastic flutter down to the forest floor and tossed their globular air canisters down after it. Jameson was shocked in spite of himself. In the closed economy of a spaceship, littering was a capital sin.

The Cygnans stretched and preened themselves. They groomed one another like monkeys, scratching away transparent flakes of what he took to be dead skin. Then he saw what he had taken for a tail was actually three tails, a petalled structure that folded in on itself.

For a moment, as one of the creatures turned away, he had a glimpse of the orifice the petals enclosed, a moist, tender surface that was the same bright orange as the lining of the Cygnans' mouth and the mucosa of their eyes. He had an impression of hairlike projections pointed inward, like a fish trap, and then the three petals closed up again.

Jameson studied his captors curiously. This was the first time he'd had a really good look in strong light. They were naked except for tubular harnesses festooned with soft oval pouches. Their hides were clothing enough, a mottled pattern of golds and rusts that reminded him of something between a diamondback rattlesnake and a reticulated giraffe. Under other circumstances he might have found the pattern beautiful.

He was unable to decide on their sex. They seemed to have nothing resembling external sexual organs. Hidden between the two hindmost limbs where he was unable to get a clear view of it was something that might have been a secondary sexual characteristic like a breast or a cockscomb – a soft, palpitating ovoid the colour of dried blood. It seemed squashy and vulnerable from its placement and the automatic manner in which the Cygnans seemed to shield it, and for some reason – though Jameson told himself he was being irrational – it disgusted him.

As the Cygnans continued to groom each other with their fingers and their vegetable-grater mouths, Jameson twisted in his sack to look at the life around him. He'd gradually become aware that the strange tangle of vegetation was alive with darting, twittering creatures. He could see an odd three-winged bird – or flying creature, at any rate – in brilliant, jewel-like colours. Its three petallike wings, transparent membranes through which Jameson saw shadowed supporting spines, were arranged helicopter-fashion around its stubby neck, and at the bottom of its streamlined body were three delicate clawed feet. They were about the size of hummingbirds. One of them hovered in front of his face, looking at him, then fluttered off.

There was a squirrel-size creature that strikingly vindicated Dmitri's theory. Its six limbs were definitely not paired. Instead, they were arranged in two radiating arrays, fore and aft.

It had three eyes, spaced like the Cygnans', around a central orifice. It wasn't bothered by any sense of the upright, but scampered along the branches, its body giving a quarter turn or rotating entirely from time to time as it nibbled the fat bluish leaves. In spite of its bizarre configuration, Jameson found the creature delightful, with its busy movements and its bright goldfishlike colours.

It came too close. There was a flash of movement, and one of Jameson's captors had the little creature trapped in a three-fingered hand. It chirped and twittered, squirming to get free. But the Cygnan held it out to its companion, as if offering it for inspection. The other Cygnan made an odd, nonhuman gesture – a sort of corkscrewlike drawing in of its long head. A refusal?

Then, to Jameson's horror, the first Cygnan popped the little animal into its mouth, hind end first. The snout with its rasp-like lining rotated around the tiny golden body. The creature shrieked, still alive. Inch by inch, the Cygnan sucked it in. By the time the head disappeared, the little eyes had become glassy and the circular mouth was open in a slack O. The Cygnan's spined tubular tongue came out, made a circular swipe, and was gone.

Jameson made an effort not to be sick. Being sick in a space helmet was a disaster, and every spacefarer learned how to fight down nausea. He swallowed hard, tasting the bitter bile in his throat. So much for the theory that advanced civilizations had to be morally superior!

Abruptly the Cygnans snatched up the sack again and oozed along the twisting branches, passing Jameson back and forth between them like a basketball. They were heading for the edge of the forest, that acute corner where the overgrown sky came down to meet the land.

As feeble as the pseudo-gravity was, Jameson could feel the downhill tug. Of course! The ground would only be relatively 'flat' near the central ridges. Visualize a triangle drawn inside a circle; 'up' is always the centre of the circle. It got steeper and steeper as they approached the artificial horizon. Jameson, despite the blurry motion, noticed the tendency of the vegetable growths to point towards that centre. As they advanced the gnarled trunks were leaning farther and farther backwards.

Earth blended into sky with no visible break in the forest. Everything was intergrown in thick profusion. The Cygnans made a wild leap, trailing the light puff of the sack, and caught at the wall of branches opposite. All at once, instead of plunging downhill, they were climbing towards another of the mile-high central ridges. The jungle they had just left behind became their sky.

Why hadn't the Cygnans built on a sensible circular plan, like human beings? Again, Jameson could merely guess that it simply didn't matter to them. This flat-sided plan was more convenient to them in other ways. It simplified the engineering of the folding spar arrangement. Straight lines made for easier construction. And as for the gravity gradient, perhaps the Cygnas lived in three dimensions, like monkeys or birds. Or – the thought came to him – perhaps they lived along surfaces, like so many small, clinging terrestrial creatures.

With startling suddenness, the forest ended. Jameson was looking through the branches at a flat metal prairie studded with surrealistic structures. They were placed at random along the plain: silolike cylinders of shiny metal, skyscraper-size prismoids set with gemlike facets, flaring hyperboloids with barber-pole skirts, enormous lattices of translucent coloured materials. They were connected by looping transparent tubes, like some crazy gigantic chemistry apparatus, and there were dark specks moving flittingly through the tubes.

Everything leaned.

As the geometric shapes retreated from the vast tent of the central ridge, they leaned farther and farther towards centre, until, at the knife-edge crease where ground met sloping ceiling, structures hundreds of feet high were tilting drunkenly. The mad architecture continued along the metal sky until it disappeared into the mists.

For there was a vast tubular cloud running down the spine of the empty space above. As the mists swirled and parted, Jameson could catch glimpses of a gleaming pipe stretching the length of the no-gravity centre of this artificial world. Condensation? Escaping gases? Jameson shuddered. One thing was clear. That pipe – wide as the Mississippi River – had something to do with the mighty drive that had carried the Cygnans across the universe. Humans kept such relatively feeble things as nuclear power plants out of sight, if possible! What manner of creatures were the Cygnans to live and work, unconcerned, in such proximity to *their* engine?

As the Cygnans jostled him along, he could see what supported the pipe: a row of slender metal pillars raised from the apex of the central ridge – from all three of the ridges. They didn't look half massive enough to hold up the pipe, But then, he realized, it was in zero-g up there, and the pillars need do nothing but brace it lightly in place.

Jameson found himself being stuffed through a rubbery membrane into a circular port. The membrane closed behind him – he couldn't tell how – and he was with his two keepers in a crazy rotating drum. They scuttled round its walls while a lens-shaped aperture widened into the shape made by two intersecting circles. Before it was quite a full circle they picked up Jameson's sack and heaved him through. He struck another of the rubbery membranes. He expected to bounce back in time to be snipped in half by the closing edges, but in some mysterious fashion he oozed through and settled to the floor like a toy balloon.

He found himself in an immense warehouse of a place with acres of spongy floor. The ceiling hung distant and shadowy above. The walls leaned inward. Dim shapes bulked against the walls and in random piles all over the floor. These sacks and bales and queer pyramid-shaped boxes were stencilled with odd cursive symbols that, instead of following one another in straight lines like human script, wandered in random peaks and valleys up and down.

There was a sound like a maniac trying to play Bartok on the harmonica, and Jameson realized it had been made by one of the Cygnans. The other Cygnan answered with an incredibly rapid fragment of twelve-tone solfège.

Jameson came to full attention. There had been *chords* in all that quick passage-work, transitory but unmistakable, as if the Cygnans possessed multiple larynxes.

Whatever those brief cadenzas had meant, the Cygnans picked him up again and toted him to a cluster of what looked like manholes in the spongy floor. One of them lifted a lid, apparently at random, and, legs tucked in, dropped through. Another one of those damned tubes! Jameson was tossed in next, and the other Cygnan dived through after him, head first.

They were hurtling at dizzying speed down a corkscrew spiral. Outside the transparent walls of the tube was an enormous dim void, hung round with the ghostly outlines of fantastic shapes. If they had entered one of the spars, they were plunging down a shaft fifteen miles deep, with a boxed world at the bottom.

He could feel gravity starting to take hold after a mile or two. It didn't amount to much yet, but it would be a third of an Earth g at the bottom, if Ruiz's figures on the rotation had been correct. Enough to smash him to a bloody paste if he'd gone tobogganing down the spiral by himself without the Cygnans' twelve busily pedalling legs to brake him.

His eyes were getting used to the dimness. He could see other transparent spirals in the hugeness around him, wrapped round slim silvery shafts. Other many-legged shapes were scooting up or down them. He peered down through the coils of his own tubeway and suddenly went rigid with fear.

A column of Cygnans was scurrying *up* the spiral, at the same fantastic speed. They and his own warders surely must see one another! But they weren't slowing down. They were going to collide with bone-crunching force. He had a split second to see the first shadowy shape, two coils below, flash around the shaft. He braced himself.

Nothing! Jameson looked upward. The ascending Cygnans were streaking through the tubes above. How the hell had they gotten past without a collision?

He looked across at the other tubes. The same trick was going on all around him. Ascending and descending Cygnans on a collision course in the same spiral tubeway passing one another without meeting!

Then he understood. He almost laughed, in spite of the gravity of his situation. The solution was ridiculously simple. A double spiral, like the elevators at the MacDonald. You could even find the same thing in that French château in the Loire valley with the famous double-spiral staircase. Chambord. He'd seen it in a holo travelogue. People going up never met the people coming down – a handy trick in the sixteenth century for getting out of the place.

They took more than an hour to reach bottom, an hour of being whipped round and round the central shaft at breakneck speed, while the remote walls of the murky chasm whirled dizzyingly around him and the indistinct structures that filled it blended into a tornado blur. Jameson passed out somewhere along the way. When he regained consciousness, he was out of the sack, but still in his suit, lying on a bare floor whose surface bristled with minute, rubbery villi. He was alone.

He tried to stand up and immediately lost his balance and fell down again. The blood rushed through his head and the room wheeled and tilted.

He waited until the dizziness passed, then cautiously sat up. He was in a small room with an odd shape. It was a parallelogram rather than a rectangle. It was a shape that would have made sense to Cygnans if they'd built rows of chambers along one of the three sides of an environmental pod and kept the dividing walls parallel to the bulkhead at the end.

He struggled shakily to his feet, his hands groping for support along the wall. The wall was a mass of the same rubbery projections. He cast no shadow. Light seemed to exist in the room without an apparent source. It was a dim reddish light that turned his spacesuit the colour of blood.

How long had he been unconscious? Reluctantly he lifted his eyes to the luminous squares of the helmet telltales. It was worse than he'd thought. Barely ten minutes worth of air was left.

'Are you afraid?' Maggie said.

'Terrified,' Maybury said. Her dark eyes were big. 'What's going to happen now?'

Around them the big hemispherical chamber was alive with subdued conversation and purposeless moving to and fro. The air was already beginning to taste stale. Some seventy people were crowded into the bridge and observatory areas. Everything below hydroponics was hard vacuum.

Another twenty people were trapped in the tail of the ship: the Chinese and American engine techs and the erstwhile Chinese guards. The bridge was still in communication with them. Mike Berry had reported that everything forward of them was vacuum, and presumably swarming with Cygnans. They had one spacesuit down there, but no place to go with it.

Grogan's man, Fiaccone, had managed to bring back a half-dozen spacesuits from spinlock storage before Captain Boyle had vetoed any further forays. He'd reported dead bodies floating around everywhere.

'I don't know,' Maggie said, brushing back a strand of wilted hair. It was warm and steamy in the bridge. 'It's stalemate, I guess. We're under house arrest. We can't get out, and those creatures don't seem to want to get in. God, look at them! They move like weasels! They're never still!'

Maybury followed her gaze to the glassy curve of the outside wall. It was covered with sleek six-legged shapes that stared and darted away, to be replaced by others. By this time most of the crew had moved uneasily away from the observation wall, leaving a clear space of about ten feet.

'They're afraid to come inside,' Maybury said. 'After what happened in hydroponics.'

On his last trip for spacesuits Fiaccone had been pursued by Cygnans coming through the breached spinlock. He'd barely made it through the improvised air lock into the farm. One of the Cygnans had gotten through after him before Kiernan managed to slam the lid shut. Other Cygnans were coming through, leaving the outside hatch open, but Kiernan barricaded it before too much air whooshed through. He turned to find Fiaccone hanging on to a slippery thing that was twisting and squirming in his embrace. Kiernan stabbed it with a spading fork. It writhed on the three tines, oozing an orange ichor, and expired. Its friends were rattling the inside lid of the lock. Against Dmitri's anguished protests, Kiernan and Fiaccone opened the lid and, aided by the outward explosion of air, tossed the body outside and slammed the lid shut again, leaving a Cygnan finger inside.

There had been no further attempts by the Cygnans to get through the lock. Dmitri had had to be content with the severed finger. He and Louise Phelps were dissecting it now in the observatory.

'There's something going on up on the balcony,' Maggie said.

Boyle was conferring with Hsieh. After a moment he came to the rail and rapped for attention. The bridge became silent. Everybody looked up, waiting.

'The Cygnans are through into the farm,' Boyle said without preamble. 'The instruments show vacuum there.'

There was a confusion of voices. Kiernan, just behind Maggie in the jostling crowd, said, 'The wingbeans! The algae! Everything! If only the captain had let me work down there for another half-hour I could've saved more . . .'

Boyle rapped for attention again. 'You might as well know the worst,' he said. 'The air plant's gone. We're living on reserves now.'

Maggie looked up at the ventilators. The little ribbons on the

139

grilles had stopped fluttering. Somewhere in the crowd a woman became hysterical.

'Somebody get the people out of the observatory,' Boyle went on. 'We'll have to make a last stand here. Seal off all the exits. Gifford, break out some emergency patches and stickum and get them ready.'

'Captain!' a voice boomed from the floor. One of Grogan's men. 'We've got seven suits. Let me and some of the boys get out there now. We can do it without losing too much air. We'll go through the door fast, and Gifford can slap a patch on after us. We can hold 'em off as long as our air lasts.'

Boyle conferred in whispers with Hsieh. He turned back to the rail, and said: 'It's no good. You wouldn't have a chance. You saw what happened to Jameson and Chief Grogan and Comrade Yeh. We'll use the suits in here.'

'Captain,' the man said, standing his ground. 'Seven suits aren't going to go very far with seventy people.'

'Seven people will have a chance to stay alive a little longer,' Boyle said firmly. 'We're going to draw straws. Only crewpersons are eligible.'

Beth Oliver stood up, straight and beautiful. 'Captain,' she said in a clear voice. 'Once upon a time, "crewpersons" meant people of both sexes. Well, I think I'm speaking for the rest of the "crewpersons" when I say we won't have anything to do with that sexist nonsense. The men will have an equal chance with us.'

A female murmur of agreement came from the crowd. Sue Jarowski yelled, 'Damn right!'

Boyle held up his hands for quiet. 'All right,' he said. 'I'm proud of you all. The men will be in the drawing. But of course any man who wins a suit will be free to decline it and throw his chance into the pot again.'

There was a groan from the women. Throughout the crowd, men were looking stubborn, nodding agreement with the captain. Klein stepped forward, waxy-faced. 'Captain,' he began in a strained voice.

A horrifying whistling sound came from the observation wall. Everybody fell silent and stared at the bubble. A woman screamed.

The Cygnans had cleared a twelve-foot circle at the centre of the port. Their packed bodies darkened the rest of the Lexiglass. At the fringes of the circle a dozen of the creatures were busy with glowing cutting tools. Plastic was melting and bubbling along the entire twelve-foot circumference.

There was a sudden rush toward the exits. But before anybody had gone more than a few steps, the heavy circle of plastic tumbled with nightmare slowness to the deck and a ring of long snouted Cygnan faces was around the edges of the opening, peering in at the humans.

Maggie sucked in a last desperate lungful of air before it was gone, and waited to die.

## CHAPTER SIXTEEN

There was a grating sound at the door. Jameson scrambled to his feet. He backed off to give clearance, ready for anything.

The door opened in an unexpected fashion. It was a five-foot recessed circle with a knob set low at one side. He had imagined it might swing in or out, or – in view of the recess – slide open. Instead it rolled like a cartwheel on a hidden track, the knob revolving with it until it caught against the frame, leaving an opening the shape of a circle with a bite out of it.

An alien stepped in, standing upright and holding a shotgun-sized tubular object in its middle pair of limbs. It was dressed in a crinkly transparent envelope, evidently to protect it against Earthly micro-organisms. The tubular thing was obviously an energy weapon of some sort. It had a trumpet bell at the business end with a stamenlike structure projecting from the focus. Instead of a stock or pistol grip, the weapon was equipped with a bulb adapted to the Cygnan grip.

Jameson raised his hands and took a step backward to reassure the creature. Perhaps the Cygnan didn't understand the human gesture. It squeezed the bulb, and Jameson was blind.

He was worse than blind. He was deaf, dumb, and paralyzed. He couldn't tell where his limbs were or what his body was doing. Kaleidoscopic flashes exploded through his visual pathways. There was a red – red? – roaring in his ears. His nerves jangled with an excruciating discomfort that made him want to scream, to be free of his body, as if he was experiencing some hideous magnified episode of drug withdrawal.

Worst of all, he couldn't *think*! There was a trapped knot of consciousness that *knew* he couldn't think, and that was what

141

made it a nightmare. His thoughts circled round and round uselessly, unable to track.

The sensation lasted only a moment. Or an eternity. Then, mercifully, he was himself again, He found himself sprawled on the floor, clammy with sweat in his spacesuit, He was still a little disoriented. He had lost control of his bladder during that brief hell, but the suit's plumbing had saved him from disgrace.

His cell was full of Cygnans – half a dozen of them, all dressed in the same clear protective suits. Some of them were standing erect on their hind legs, tails hanging straight down. Some were on four legs, their torsos upright so that they were shaped like little low-slung centaurs. They were jabbering at one another in a cacophony of quarter-tone scales and queer atonal chords, sounding like an orchestra of bagpipes warming up. Their actions all seemed pointless to Jameson, but then, he thought, perhaps a laboratory rat thought that the conversation of the lab workers was pointless.

The Cygnan holding the neural weapon was still there. Jameson kept very still, A Cygnan scuttled up to him, fixed him with three quivering eyes, then scuttled back. There was more bagpipe conversation.

Encouraged, he sat up, moving very slowly and keeping his hands down.

Did the Cygnans react nervously? It was hard to tell. They *always* seemed nervous. There was a lot of atonal chittering and much shuffling and twitching, but his nervous system remained unscrambled. He lifted his eyes to the helmet dials. How could he make them understand?

'Air,' he mouthed. 'Dammit, don't you understand? I've only got a couple of minutes worth of air left.'

Raising his gloved hands to his helmet, he made raking-in gestures with spread fingers, He let them see his open mouth sucking in air.

No discernible reaction came from his audience. Even on Earth, body language was different between Arabs and Japanese, Scandinavians and Mediterraneans. Maybe his pantomimes couldn't work with creatures that had six limbs, radial symmetry, brains in their torsos, and, for all he knew, no lungs.

He tried again, This time he pointed to his air tanks and traced his hoses to their gaskets in his helmet.

They seemed bored with him, A couple of them skidded

around on four legs and left the cell. The ones who were left lost interest in him entirely. Two of them had started holding hands. Another was scratching itself with a hind leg. Another had taken an object that looked like a bright yellow plastic asterisk out of a pouch and was showing it to a companion.

Jameson struggled recklessly to his feet. The trumpet bell of the weapon flicked in his direction. He ignored it. 'Your air!' he roared. 'Can I breathe your air?'

It was doubtful that they even understood his anguished cry as speech. Their own communication, Jameson had guessed, depended on the pitch of speech components rather than anything resembling consonants and vowels – and those fragments of reedy tone were too quick and transitory for even his gifted ear to follow.

His lungs heaved, and he realized with despair that he was now rebreathing the stale air in his helmet. He staggered forward, arms outspread. The Cygnans scampered out of his way. The energy weapon tracked him but didn't fire.

The Cygnans were gone, no longer in his path. Instead, they were behind him. He felt a myriad of little three-fingered hands running all over his spacesuit, hugging his legs, pinioning his arms. He was being held immobile. He struggled, but his lungs were burning and his senses were growing dim.

Then he realized that they were removing his suit.

A transparent membrane, insubstantial as a soap bubble, was stretched across the twelve-foot circle the Cygnans had opened in the hull. That's why she still could breathe.

Maggie gawked at it. A lot of gawking was going on around her. Why didn't the air pressure inside the ship bend that membrane outward? Why didn't it burst?

'Look!' Maybury said, grabbing her arm.

Not only was the membrane not bulging outward, it was bulging *inward*! Stunned, the seventy people in the control room watched it stretch, ballooning itself until it filled the centre of the chamber.

Nobody went near it. Nobody dared touch it. It looked too fragile. It looked as if it might burst at any moment.

A movement over by the row of empty spacesuits draped over a console apron caught Maggie's eye. It was Klein. He was lifting up the sleeve of one of the suits.

'Leave that alone!' Boyle's voice thundered.

'I was just—' Klein began.

'*Gwan-cha, gwan-cha!*' a Chinese voice screamed.

Five or six Cygnans had dropped lightly to the floor. They stood, quivering, inside the ship, looking alertly through the bubble at the humans. They all looked upward at the same instant and started backing away from the centre of their bubble. One of them was against the transparent skin itself, poking it outward.

The temptation was too much for one of the Struggle Brigade bullies, He snatched up a steel bar and swung it two-handed at the Cygnan's head.

'*Don't!*' Boyle yelled, but he was too late. The bar connected with a sickening impact. The Cygnan had tried to skip out of the way, but hadn't had enough warning, even with its speedy reflexes.

A gasp went up from the assembled crew, but the bubble held. The bar rested in a sagging indentation on the bubble. Slowly the indentation filled itself and the bar slid to the floor.

The injured Cygnan, incredibly was still on its feet. It writhed in evident agony, its body twisting bonelessly like some fat worm that had been stepped on. Its head was orange pulp. One stubby eyestalk waved above the mess, blinking horribly. A couple of its friends passed it up to waiting sets of hands. The other Cygnans in the inverted bubble began darting their heads like angry geese at the nearest humans. You could see the cheese-grater mouths gaping and the tubular rasp of a tongue flickering in and out inside the inflated sheaths they wore over their heads. But they all stayed well away from the boundary of the bubble.

Now there was movement above, and the Cygnans were lowering a strange device on a stand into the ship. The Cygnans inside the bubble steadied the thing and set it in place. It looked like a squat brassy pyramid with three flaring horns sprouting from its apex. One of the Cygnans did something to it, and the apex started rotating, The horns rotated with it, waving up and down like crazy semaphores.

The Cygnans jumped on one another's shoulders and scrambled out of the bubble fast. The anchoring alien stretched and flowed, becoming a foot taller, and caught the dangling hand of a living chain. Then they whisked it out of the hole.

'Smash that thing!' Boyle yelled from the balcony. 'See if you can get at it through the bubble!'

Half a dozen willing hands poked at the revolving device with bars through the resilient material, but they couldn't reach it. The blister dimpled just so far, then resisted.

'I feel so strange,' Maybury said.

Maggie, for no reason, began to feel edgy. It was like hearing a fingernail scrape along a blackboard, except that there wasn't any sound. Her teeth were on edge.

All across the bridge people were starting to behave strangely. Somebody staggered and fell. A woman with a contorted face was squeezing her head with both hands. There was a man, his mouth open, chenching his fists in front of his chest and trembling violently.

Somebody stumbled against her, as if off balance. It was Dmitri, his boyish face shiny with sweat. 'They couldn't gas us,' he said between clenched teeth. 'They don't know enough about terrestial biochemistry yet. But any kind of a nervous system can be interfered with by modulated electromagnetic fields. They must have used their gadget before on all kinds of life.'

Maggie's vision was disappearing, as if her face were swelling up in the worse allergy attack she'd ever had. There was a ringing in her ears, drowning out Dmitri's words. There was a dreadful spine-crawling sensation and the illusion of rapid flickering through her entire body. And then she was suspended in a senseless horror, while her mind scrabbled round and round trying to get out.

She was not aware of it when a horde of aliens oozed somehow through the transparent membrane without breaking it and stuffed her and the other helpless humans into airtight sacks. When her senses returned, she was floating in a giant soap bubble beside a metal cliff that seemed to stretch on forever. She was part of a chain of bubbles rising through the dark of space while a flock of shiny demons swam alongside, prodding them with broomsticks.

Jameson's ears popped. The air was thin, but rich in oxygen. It had an oily, industrial smell to it. But after what he'd been expecting, it was marvellous. He took deep, grateful breaths.

They had him pinned to the floor while they stripped off his pressure suit and skivvies. It was no good struggling. Too many of those three-fingered hands were holding him down,

145

shifting their grips with blinding speed while they pulled off sleeves, undid fasteners, shucked him out of the rest of it. By the time he realized that an arm or leg was free, they'd peeled it down and imprisoned it again. In a few brief seconds he was naked and shivering with cold.

His belongings went into a sealed sack. He guessed that he was in biological quarantine. All of the Cygnans handling him were encased in transparent envelopes. He saw nothing resembling air filters; perhaps the entire envelope was permeable to gas molecules but not subviruses.

He tried to talk, but they ignored him. They talked among themselves with all sorts of chirps and whistles and concertina humming. Once or twice, when his ear was fast enough to catch a fragment, he tried humming it back to them in perfect pitch but the effort seemed to make no impression.

Now they were probing him all over with rubbery fingers and little metal instruments that were cold on his bare skin. A three-fingered hand walked along his spine, tracing it. Another counted his ribs. Another probed elbows and kneecaps while they flexed his arms and legs.

They forced his mouth open with a bellowlike instrument and shone a light into it. He gagged as a swab poked down his throat, but then it was over and they withdrew the bellows. The swab went into a little oval container.

Next came a tray of little pipettes with suction bulbs at one end. He struggled as they inserted these into every body orifice they could find, from nostrils to urethra. His struggles didn't do him a bit of good. They got their samples and whisked them away, leaving him sneezing, itching, and smarting.

There was a tricky moment when one of the Cygnans tried to force a slim metal tube into his navel, evidently under the impression that it opened. Jameson howled in protest. He had visions of being skewered. But after a moment the Cygnan gave up and contented itself with a swab.

They took their tissue sample in direct, brutal fashion. One of the Cygnans pinched the flesh of Jameson's thigh and sliced off a piece of meat as thick as a piece of bacon. Blood welled up and ran down his leg, The Cygnans seemed excited by this. There was a chorus of harmonica music, and they siphoned off several cc's of blood with a pipette. While he lay pinioned and bleeding, a Cygnan sprayed the wound with something that burned like fire. Almost instantly the spray hardened into a rubbery, transparent skin that sealed the wound and stopped the bleeding. Jameson was thankful the Cygnan's blade hadn't severed the femoral artery.

After several more tests, including running something like a metal detector over the surface of his body, the Cygnans gathered up their paraphernalia and left. The circular door rolled in its groove and thudded shut.

They left him in his cell without food or water for what seemed to be about twenty-four hours. He spent most of that time huddled in a ball, trying to keep warm. The Cygnans seemed to like low temperatures. The door rolled open again, three plastic-wrapped Cygnans entered with their silent-movie gait. The guard with the neural scrambler was with them. Jameson tried to pantomime his need for food and water, but they ignored him. Before he knew what was happening, one of the Cygnans stabbed him in the belly.

He yelped and leaped backward. There was a raw circle about an inch in diameter just below his navel, studded with bright jewels of blood from a dozen pinpricks, He caught a glimpse of the instrument the Cygnan had used, something like half a golf ball with short needles projecting from the flat side. He'd been given injections of some kind.

The Cygnans left. An hour later he was feverish and getting sicker. He spent the next day feeling miserable. For a couple of hours he was delirious. But he had a blanket now, a square of some soft synthetic textured like overlapping orange scales that he was able to wrap around himself for warmth. Eventually his warder brought him a bowl of flat tepid water, which he lapped up eagerly, getting down on his hands and knees, not daring to lift it to his lips for fear of spilling some of the precious liquid. There were no sanitary facilities. He used the far corner of the cell, feeling humiliated. Nothing was ever done about cleaning it up.

When the fever had passed, Jameson felt ravenous. Still shaky, he pounded on the door for attention. No one came. He waited it out for another twelve hours. Then the door opened. A Cygnan skittishly set something on the floor in front of him and fled.

He pounced on it. It was a prepared meal from his own ship's galley, a thawing block of stew still in its original foil warming pan. He ignored the implications of *that* while he wolfed down the food, ice crystals and all. It was the first food he'd eaten in forty-eight hours.

He pushed the pan aside, satiated, and looked up. Two Cygnans were standing there, watching him. They were the first ones he'd seen without the transparent protective suits since he'd been taken out of his sterilized sack and isolated here. So he was at last out of quarantine They were safe from his germs now – or he from theirs.

The two aliens were holding hands, Cygnan fashion. The middle pair. One of them was carrying a foot-long implement in one of its primary limbs that resembled a two-pronged toasting fork with blunt tines.

The other Cygnan uttered a clear, chimelike sound composed of two tones. Jameson recognized it as a tetrachord: a perfect fourth. The first Cygnan let go of the other's hand and high-stepped over the rim of the door, holding the forklike object in front of it like a weapon.


# CHAPTER SEVENTEEN

Jameson looked the pair of them over. They were just inside the door, sizing him up. The taller of the two, the one with the toasting fork, came to his shoulder. The alien was roughly the size of a Russian wolfhound standing on its hind legs. The other was a couple of inches shorter and more lightly built. A male and a female? It was impossible to tell. Their bodies were smooth and without gender. Like the other Cygnans he'd seen, they wore only mottled hides, plus the ubiquitous tubular harness with the ovoid gadget bags. He could see no external sign of sex, except—

He overcame his repugnance and took a closer look at the dreadful thing attached to their bellies. It was the same palpitating horror that at first he'd taken for a secondary sex characteristic in his original captors during that dizzy hegira through the monkey-puzzle forest and across the industrial plain. He'd glimpsed a couple more of the things through the transparent suits of the Cygnans who'd done the lab workup on him. But this was the first time he'd had a clear view of one.

It was a parasite.

There was no doubt about it. It was a soft, feeble, beetle shaped creature about the size of a newborn kitten, clinging to its host like a tick with six filamentlike legs. Its tiny head was embedded in the flesh, obviously drinking blood.

Jameson shuddered in disgust. Why did a race as technologically advanced as the Cygnans tolerate the filthy things? Their biological sciences were certainly advanced enough to eradicate something as obvious as an exoparasite, as they'd just proved to him.

He furrowed his brow. Could that leechlike thing represent some exotic form of symbiosis? If so, he failed to see what possible benefit the Cygnans could derive from the creatures.

It didn't seem to be causing them any discomfort. It rode between their rearmost legs as if it belonged there, in a position designed to give it maximum protection. But then, as Dmitri once had remarked, successful parasites are always adapted to their hosts, sometimes in the most ingenious fashion – like the roundworm that lived only in the human appendix. It was the unsuccessful ones that caused discomfort.

The smaller Cygnan caught him staring and, with a gesture that he would have called modest in a human, lowered a middle limb to shield the parasite from view.

He tore his eyes away. The larger Cygnan was advancing on him. It held up the fork, showing it to him. Then it touched itself on the torso with it.

Jameson waited to see what would happen. Was this the prelude to some kind of attempt at communication? Up till now the Cygnans had treated him like a piece of meat.

Then the Cygnan touched Jameson lightly on the ribs, and he almost hit the ceiling. The pain was beyond belief – like the sting of a thousand hornets. It lasted for the merest fraction of a second. He would have fallen if it had not been so brief. As it was, he staggered for balance. He was blinded with tears.

The Cygnan had sprung back out of reach.

By God, the thing was *afraid* of him!

Its companion chirped and warbled at it – telling it to be careful. It came back, circling him with abrupt little movements.

Jameson made himself stand perfectly still. It was the hardest thing he had ever done. His heart was palpitating. He could still feel the effects of that sting.

It couldn't have been a neurotoxin like the synthetic wasp venom terrestrial police used in riot control. Alien biochemistry would be too tricky for the Cygnans. They couldn't have

149

been sure of a disabling dose. It had to have been an electric shock – thousands of volts.

The Cygnan raised the fork again. Jameson flinched, but he stood rigid, arms hanging at his sides.

The fork touched him again.

He felt only a mild tingle, nothing like the first time.

The Cygnan gestured with the fork. It waltzed halfway to the door and waited.

He was supposed to follow it.

Jameson's mouth twisted bitterly. This was human-alien communication, all right. They had managed to tell each other something. It wasn't very complicated. The Cygnan had shown him its cattle prod and told him to behave. And he had said that he would.

He shuffled obediently towards the door. His injured leg throbbed. He felt drained and lightheaded from his illness, and he longed fervently for a hot shower. The Cygnans fell in warily beside him.

He stopped. Dammit, this was no way for a man to behave. For all he knew, he was the only representative of the human race.

The Cygnans didn't like his stopping. One of them sounded the pure tetrachord he'd heard before. The other raised its electric prod.

Jameson never had to stop to think about a musical tone. They were as palpable to him as material objects, each with its own identity. These had been an F and B flat in the piccolo range. No, not quite a B flat. It was *almost* an augumented fourth, about a quarter-tone off.

He whistled it back to them. He couldn't manage both tones simultaneously the way the Cygnans did, of course, but he did the best he could, first arpeggiating it, then alternating it in a rapid tremolo.

The large Cygnan lowered its prod. It fluted a rapid scale at him.

Jameson did an imitation. There weren't too many notes for him to remember. It fell into a whole-tone pattern, like impressionistic music, with a cluster of those peculiar quarter-tones at the centre.

The Cygnan corrected him. He'd been off a fraction of a tone at the end. It didn't finish at the octave. It was a fraction sharp there, like a bagpipe scale. He repeated the sequence fairly creditably.

The two Cygnans held a brief, reedy conference. Jameson couldn't follow. It was too rapid and complicated, with all sorts of embellishments. He stood tensely waiting.

The large Cygnan turned to him again and made a sharp attention-getting sound. Then it touched itself on the mouth and the tip of its petalled tail and sounded the tetrachord again. It waited.

Jameson gave the chord back immediately, turning it into a tremolo. The Cygnans chirped at each other for a while. Then the smaller of the two came forward. It made the gestures which to a Cygnan indicated self, and trilled at him.

Jameson hesitated. The tetrachord had been easy. It was a handy, one-phoneme identification. Like, Jameson thought, a human saying 'I.' But this was more complicated.

The second Cygnan repeated it for him until he got it straight. It started with an A-major triad, only a vibration off concert pitch. Harmonics, Jameson thought, must be universal wherever there were vibrating strings – or vibrating membranes. The third was slightly flatted, like a blues note. The two top notes then exploded into a parallel glissando, up a fifth, while the A held. Then back to the original bluesy chord.

He gave it a try. He had to substitute an arpeggiated chord for the triad, then make do with just the top note of the double glissando. It sounded like a crazy bird imitation, but the Cygnan seemed to accept it. Like, Jameson thought wryly, tolerating someone with a speech defect.

But when he tried transposing the little sequence to a different key, he met the Cygnan equivalent of a blank stare – a splaying out of the three eyestalks. Evidently the sounds had no meaning when the pitch was altered.

It reminded Jameson of his early mistakes in learning Chinese – the syllables whose meaning changed drastically when you used the wrong one of the four tones. 'Chair' became 'soap'. 'Sell' became 'buy'. Except in Chinese the tones were relative, and if you got a few of them wrong your intent could usually be deduced from the syllables themselves and the context. In Cygnanese, apparently, tones were specific phonemes. Only those rare freaks like Jameson, who happened to be blessed with absolute pitch, could ever hope to communicate with Cygnans even in the most rudimentary fashion.

To Cygnans most humans would be dumb as animals. It was Jameson's turn.

He touched himself on the lips and – feeling a bit silly – on the rump, and said, slowly and distinctly: 'Ja-me-son.'

They herded him down opalescent corridors with the electric prod turned off. 'Corridors' wasn't quite the word for these cramped tubes, though the purpose was the same. It was more like a series of translucent sewer pipes snaking through decks and angled bulkheads, bridging dizzying spaces with shadowy bustling activity glimpsed tantalizingly below.

The Cygnans seemed to have no concept of rooms arranged off passageways. Enclosures simply abutted one another, opening directly from space to space in a honeycomb maze. There were no branching arteries. Each length of tube seemed to have a specific destination. It struck Jameson as a peculiar way to utilize interior space, but then, perhaps Cygnans would have found human layouts incomprehensible.

He hunched down the low tunnel, the scaled orange blanket wrapped togalike around him. Ahead of him, the two scurrying Cygnans kept having to wait for him to catch up. The curved surface made awkward footing for him. Perhaps it was more natural for Cygnans, with their limbs jutting out at an angle that way.

He hurried after them, looking up the puckered orange lips of their tailpipes. Mouth and tip of tail; the Cygnans thought of themselves as being between the two points. Perhaps it made more sense than the human gesture of pointing to oneself or tapping oneself on the chest.

They were travelling side by side horizontally, holding one and sometimes two pairs of hands, pedalling with their outward facing limbs while they kept each other braced against the lower quadrant of the walls. Every once in a while they nuzzled each other.

It would have been easier going, Jameson thought, if they'd travelled single file. But Cygnans seemed to like touching one another. He remembered the pair that had carried him through the ship.

They reached the end of the tube, a silvery disc with shadows seen through it. The Cygnans parted to let him between them, half clinging to the sides of the tube, and gave him a push.

He put out a hand involuntarily to catch himself, and it went through the centre of the disc. The Cygnans prodded him again. He pushed his way into the material. It flowed around him, sealing itself off by shaping itself around his body. It tickled. He stepped through, and it closed itself off behind him.

He turned just in time to see two long Cygnan snouts emerging from the surface. It would have looked as if they were rising from a pool of quicksilver if the surface had been horizontal instead of vertical. The Cygnans flowed through, and the silvery surface was unbroken again.

He gathered he was in some kind of work area. There were things he recognized as sinks and counter tops, and haphazard stacks of storage containers in nonhuman shapes. Against one sloping wall was an electric console studded with little pearly knobs and a keyboard-like arrangement. On closer inspection the keyboard turned out to be a row of little fretted necks, each strung with three parallel wires. Jameson tried to imagine four Cygnan forelimbs, each with three fingers, strumming it all at once. The instrument would convey information, not music. Like a computer teletype keyboard?

He saw nothing he could recognize as books, paper files, or writing instruments. How did Cygnans store data? A triangular cage with one of the little chittering creatures was balanced precariously on what Jameson took to be a Cygnan desk: a sort of oversize shoetree with a multitude of flat oval surfaces.

But Jameson had no eyes for any of it after he saw what was stacked against the far wall: a careless plunder of human artifacts from the Jupiter ship. He saw clothing, cooking utensils, upended chairs, a broken mirror, books and music cards, even an uprooted vacuum toilet. The Cygnans must have been all through the individual cabins and the recreation lounge. The lectern that doubled as a pulpit was lying on its side, and next to it was the portable Moog, its twin keyboards grinning with ivory teeth at the mess around it.

The two Cygnans had draped themselves across a pair of perches that sat in the middle of all the confusion. The perches were curving, polished hobbyhorses leaning outward from trumpet bell pedestals. Each was equipped with three sets of crossbars and a chin rest. For a Cygnan, he supposed, it was as comfortable a way of distributing weight as a chair. Another perch faced the two. Jameson gave it a dubious glance, then sat cross-legged on the floor beside it, his blanket draped Indian-fashion around him.

The Cygnans twitched on their perches. The chin rest snaked around sideways so as not to obstruct the third eyestalk mounted beneath the Cygnan approximation of a jaw. But the thick shaft of the perch concealed the revolting thing on their lower bellies, and he was grateful that he wouldn't have to look at it.

'Ja-me-son,' the larger Cygnan said.

It wasn't exactly 'Ja-me-son'. The Cygnans couldn't manage consonants – unless one wanted to call those assorted hisses and pops consonants. Furthermore, they seemed unable to grasp the idea that an arrangement of phonemes could always have the same meaning regardless of pitch. Their first attempt to repeat Jameson's name had simply mimicked his timbre and tone – a falling fourth – and they seemed puzzled when he repeated it with a different inflection. In the end they had given up and assigned him a name – the original falling fourth, with the added fillip of a rising fifth preceded by a grace note.

Jameson didn't mind. He thought of *them* privately as 'Tetrachord' and 'Triad.' He had a speech defect too. He couldn't form chords.

Finally they all got down to work. At the end of an hour, he'd figured out how the Cygnan language was formed and could manage a few words of it in a sort of babytalk.

By then, the Cygnans had accepted the convention that a hummed or whistled arpeggio was equivalent to sounding all the notes of a chord simultaneously. But Jameson could see that the concept was difficult for them. They would have to stop and think about the separate notes of the arpeggio and put them together in their heads. Then they'd try them out on each other until triumphantly, they had it – like a pair of illiterates spelling out words letter by letter – except that one letter might consist of half a dozen chords and connecting single notes, laboriously worked out one tone at a time.

It was just as difficult for Jameson. He needed constant repetition to pin down the more complex sequences, and he knew that there were subtleties – beyond the troublesome quarter-tones – that he was missing. It made for slow going.

The number of possible phonemes in the Cygnan language was staggering. They were based on the absolute pitch of a tone – not relative pitch, like the rising and falling tones of Chinese. The Cygnans had a useful range of two and a half octaves, and they could divide each twelve-tone octave into quarter-tones.

That made 120 phonemes to start with.

Just the single notes!

But a phoneme might be a single note, any combination of two notes, or any combination of three notes.

How many different two-note combinations were there? Jameson worked it out in his head.

More than seven thousand of them.

Jameson became discouraged at that point. He didn't bother to figure out how many different *three*-note combinations there were. Or what happened when you figured in all the extra little slides and turns that Cygnans seemed to use the way humans used double consonants. It was depressingly clear that the number was astronomical.

Compared with the paltry few dozen phonemes available in human languages, the richness of the Cygnan language must be beyond belief!

Perhaps, Jameson speculated with a sudden rush of awe, the Cygnans could even convey *visual* information with their language directly, in the same way dolphins could show one another the shape and depth of a bay by sonar imitation.

Actual pictures, built up of digital bits formed of sound, transmitted as naturally as breathing from Cygnan to Cygnan! Not descriptions, such as: 'I see a creature with only four limbs and no tail, about so big.' But: I see a creature that looks like *this*.'

In human terms, Jameson thought, how many thousands of words would it take to teach someone, say, a tune by Beethoven? How much simpler just to hum it. And a tune, compared with visual material, was a straightforward linear piece of information containing relatively few bits.

He tried not to worry about it. The most rudimentary sort of pidgin Cygnan would have to do. After all, he consoled himself, South Sea islanders had managed to trade with the first British mariners using a few dozen basic nouns and modifiers. It hadn't been necessary for them to learn the language of Shakespeare.

Slowly, painfully, tone by tone, hoping the two Cygnans' patience would last, Jameson acquired the first dozen words of

155

a vocabulary that consisted mostly of parts of the body and a few objects in the room.

Next he tried an abstraction. What did the Cygnans call their race? What class of creatures, he asked them, included both Tetrachord and Triad?

He made the sounds of their names, followed by the Cygnan-style inclusive gesture, and ending with the little trill he had come to recognize as a Cygnan interrogative. He was rewarded with a burst of harmony. In five minutes he learned to repeat this as arpeggios, and the Cygnans warbled their approval.

An aproned assistant arrived at that point to put another of the pyramidal cages on the desk. It was a Cygnan apron, worn lengthwise, anchored by a loop over head and tail, with a scalloped leathery flap hung down either side.

Jameson thought he'd clinch it. Before the assistant could leave, he made the inclusive gesture for all three of the Cygnans and repeated his question.

There was a lot of agitated chirping. Then Tetrachord and Triad both turned to him and gave him an entirely different word.

Jameson wiped the sweat off his forehead with a forearm. What was going wrong? He decided to attack it from a different angle. What did the Cygnans call humans?

'Ja-me-son,' he said in the three-note figure that signified his name. Then he made the inclusive gesture and whistled, 'Ja-me-son, Ja-me-son,' followed by the interrogative trill.

*What are many Jamesons called?* He waited.

He got his own name back firmly, once. *There is no such thing as a class of Jamesons.* He tried again, and got his name back with the cascade of dropping thirds that they always used to correct him with. *A mistake.* Evidently such a thing as many Jamesons was a conceptual impossibility.

Doggedly he tried again. Numbers, then. Numbers were basic. He held up a finger. 'One.' He extended another. 'Two.' He added a third. 'Three.' Then he trilled the Cygnan interrogative.

He waited. Nothing.

He tried again. 'One . . .'

The smaller Cygnan, Triad, was showing signs of becoming restless. She – why did he think of this one as she? –turned to Tetrachord and tootled at him. Tetrachord tootled back.

Then he slithered off his perch and picked up the electric prod. He gestured towards the door with it.

It was time for Jameson to go back to his cage.

He rose to his feet reluctantly. He hadn't made much progress. Would he get another chance? Cygnans didn't seem to be long on patience. Or curiosity.

If only he could speed up the process of communication.

He allowed them to herd him halfway to the door before he stopped. Then he became stubborn, earning himself a mild tingle from the prod.

Moving slowly so as not to alarm them, he started towards the untidy stack of human goods over at the far wall. They did nothing to stop him. He was able to reach the Moog.

He turned it on. The little red light glowed. There were still a couple of dozen hours left in the batteries. Quickly he pulled out the stops, trying for an approximation of the Cygnan voice. A touch of oboe. A flute. A bassoon with its wave frequency moved up to the treble range. A synthetic soprano voice saying '*ah*.'

The preparation took him a few seconds. He glanced over his shoulder. How much time would they allow him? Not enough time to reprogramme the little computer that was the heart of the Moog; that would take hours. But he didn't have to do anything very complicated to start with. He altered the tuning of the A to shift it slightly from concert pitch, and the Moog obligingly shifted the rest of the scale to go with it. Then he lowered all the C sharps a trifle and retuned a couple of the notes he wouldn't be using for the demonstration, to provide the quarter-tone notes he *would* need.

He turned. Triad was coming toward him, hissing. Her rasplike tongue flickered in and out. His time was up.

Jameson put his hands on the keyboard and said her name in perfect Cygnanese. With, he hoped, hardly a trace of an accent.

He worked on the Moog while the assistant brought in their lunch. He didn't care to think about the Cygnans' lunch except to note that it didn't seem to enjoy being eaten. His own lunch was another half-thawed block of food from his own ship's freezer – this time a pie-sized portion of mincemeat stuffing intended for Christmas dinner.

The Moog had two five-octave keyboards. He compressed them into a single compass of two and one half octaves composed of quarter-tones. It fit the Cygnan vocal range perfectly.

He fiddled individually with what seemed to be some of the more important tones in the Cygnan vocabulary – the off-key B flat in Tetrachord's name and the wrong-note bagpipe tone that finished off the octave, among others. But for most of it he simply had the computer chop up the normal equal-temperament octave into forty-eight pieces instead of twelve. He could retune other crucial notes one at a time as they came up while he was learning to talk Cygnan.

It took him another hour to alter the Moog's memory so that it would replay some of the standard Cygnan sequences at the touch of a button – the interrogative trill and the cascade of minor thirds, and some of the turns and arabesques he'd been able to pin down so far. He had only to play them once through and tell the Moog to remember them. They were plugged into the bank of cheater buttons that were meant for slip beat rhythms and computer-generated contrapuntal voices.

When he'd finished, not even Johann Sebastian Bach could have played recognizable human music on the Moog. It was a Cygnan speech synthesizer now, with lots of unused learning capacity.

His accomplishment earned him a reprieve. It made conversing a lot easier for the Cygnans, for one thing, and that rekindled their interest. They didn't have to stop to figure out what Jameson meant when he interpolated a broken chord, and they didn't have to repeat things for him endlessly; the Moog's play-along attachment taped them the first time, and the Cygnans could go about their business while Jameson devoted himself to memorizing word lists.

They didn't even make him return to his cage. Instead, they let him sleep in a small storage room adjacent to their office or workshop, or whatever it was, and work on his vocabulary while they were busy. During their frequent absences, he was allowed to wander through the workshop, as if he were a trusted pet. Among the looted human artifacts he found clothing and toilet articles, and soon he was able to get warm again and clean himself up. The aproned assistant brought him his meals at regular intervals: more frozen food from the freezer and, as time went on, unfamiliar stuff that the Cygnans evidently had learned to synthesize. Most of it was an unappetizing mush, but it didn't make him sick. At least he wouldn't starve when human supplies ran out.

To Jameson's immense relief, the Cygnan language turned out to be easy. The structure, such as it was, was positional. He was able to get along fairly well simply by piling words on top of one another, as you could do in Chinese.

He remembered something one of his language teachers on Earth had told him: Sophisticated languages tend to dispense with grammar. Languages of primitive cultures, like Eskimo or Hottentot, have far more complex a structure than highly evolved languages like English or Chinese. The Cygnans, who had been wandering through space for untold millennia, must have a far older civilization than man.

Their language had been simplified. Given time, Jameson could have taught Mike Berry or any other competent amateur musician to play back Cygnan 'words' by rote on the Moog's modified keyboard, or punch in his programmed phrases. But Mike didn't have absolute pitch, so he could never have understood the Cygnan's replies.

The Cygnan language was simple, all right. But nobody in the crew except Jameson could possibly have understood it.

## CHAPTER EIGHTEEN

'Is this a little Jameson?'

At least Jameson assumed the word was 'little' or something close to it. It fit the context and contained, within a cloud of embellishments, the set of phonemes that denoted something that was small in size or a model for something larger.

'No,' Jameson said, his fingers flashing over the keyboards of the Moog. 'It is an animal.'

He had gotten to that point of fluency where his fingers thought for him in Cygnanese. It must be the same, he imagined, for people who habitually communicated in deaf-and-dumb signals: language without vocalization, but language nevertheless.

'Yes, but is this the animal that (*tootle-tootle-peep-peep-peep*) Jamesons?'

His mind had automatically translated the piping sounds into idiomatic English – all but the (*tootle-tootle-peep-peep-peep*) It sounded a little like the word for 'produce' and a little like the word for 'consume' and a little like the ideogram for putting together the parts of something. It was another of those Cygnan ambiguities that Jameson could never seem to get the hang of.

The animal in question was a small bedraggled kitten that crouched on one of the oval pads of Triad's desk, almost too weak to move and certainly too frightened to jump down. It was tiny and featherlight, with matted grey fur, and its ribs showed pitifully. It had spunk, though. It hissed at Jameson or the Cygnans when they got too close, showing a pink tongue and little needle teeth. Where the animal had come from was a mystery. Tetrachord and Triad had disappeared for about twelve hours and had returned in a state of high excitement, lugging triangular containers. The kitten came out of one of the containers.

'I do not understand,' Jameson said cautiously. His fingers hammered away at the keys. 'What is (*tootle-tootle-peep-peep-peep*)?'

He hoped he'd got that right. Sometimes the tiniest transposition of a tone led to wild misunderstandings, which had caused his problem with the concept of many Jamesons. The Cygnans still vehemently denied that there was a class of Jamesons, but they freely used the idea of a Jameson to refer to humans. Jameson couldn't understand the distinction.

He received no reply. The Cygnans acted displeased with him. But all he'd done was repeat the word that Triad had used. Or had he? He felt like a small boy who has unwittingly used a dirty word.

He thought furiously. He didn't dare risk having the Cygnans break off the conversation, as they frequently did when things got difficult. What had Triad asked him? One component of the ideogram was 'to consume'. Was she asking him if kittens were parasitic on man? They were obviously too small to be predators.

He risked it. He pointed at the swollen parasite that swung between Triad's hind legs.

'Is this the animal that (*tootle-tootle-peep-peep-peep*) Triads?' he asked.

The reaction was swift and startling. Tetrachord untwined himself from his perch and made a savage rush at Jameson. Jameson shrank back, alarmed. These mock rushes seemed to be a Cygnan reflex to anything threatening – either physical or intellectual – but they were scary nevertheless. Tetrachord darted a long neck at Jameson, making hissing sounds. The spiked tongue flicked in his direction.

Triad's reaction was different. The smaller Cygnan shielded the parasite from view with two hands. The orange orifice at the end of the tail, which often revealed itself partially when the Cygnans were relaxed or doing something pleasurable like eating, closed itself up purse-tight. Triad assumed the posture which seemed to signify self-protection or embarrassment.

Desperately Jameson assumed the submissive posture. It was the Cygnan form of apology. He turned his back to Tetrachord and crouched, holding himself perfectly still.

Mollified, Tetrachord returned to his perch. When Jameson thought it was safe he stood up again and went to the desk. He picked up the grey kitten. It vibrated against his chest, all skin and bones.

He walked over to the locker containing the supplies of human food that he'd scrounged from the Cygnan's loot. He rationed it out to himself whenever he needed a change from the synthetic mush the aproned assistant dished out to him.

He found a can of condensed milk and poured some of it in a bowl. He set the kitten down on the floor in front of it. The kitten began avidly to lap it up.

The two Cygnans watched with mounting interest. 'The animal would not eat the human food we gave it,' Triad reported. 'It would only drink the water.'

A few circumspect questions got Jameson the information that the kitten had refused offerings of rice and wingbean paste from the ship's stores. They hadn't tried giving it meat.

'How long,' he asked carefully, 'has it been since this animal has eaten?'

He got an answer that it was equal to the length of one of the Cygnan's active periods. It was the only unit of time he had succeeded in establishing so far. The kitten hadn't eaten for eight or nine days; that was the closest he could figure.

'Where did you find the animal?' he asked.

He wondered who in the crew had managed to smuggle a kitten on board ship and keep it hidden for all those months. No – not a kitten. A mother cat. Pregnant. Wait a minute! What was the gestation period of a cat? Only a couple of months! That was impossible. The trip to Jupiter had taken five months, and the kitten couldn't be more than a few weeks old.

An awful suspicion began to dawn on Jameson.

Triad gestured toward the triangular containers. 'We found the animal on your planet,' the creature said.

Tetrachord and Triad were indulgent. They let Jameson hang around while they unpacked the containers, though they hissed at him if he got too close.

Soil samples in little transparent bags. A dead beetle. Some dessicated samples of vegetation that was indisputably terrestrial. To Jameson the stuff looked tropical. South America or Southeast Asia? And – sinister import – a preserved human hand and forearm with the shredded remnants of a cotton sleeve sticking to it. The kitten's owner?

They took out two more dead kittens and part of a third. The grey one had been the only one to survive the trip. Eight days, if he could believe the Cygnans.

Eight days from Earth. Was that possible?

Jameson didn't even have to do the arithmetic. This was a favourite spaceman's pipe dream, one that came up during every bull session.

Halfway from Earth to Jupiter at a constant acceleration of one gravity. The second half of the trip at constant one gravity deceleration. Eight or nine days was about right. If he needed confirmation, the kitten was proof enough. He looked at it sitting next to the empty bowl, contentedly giving itself a wash. Perhaps there had been water in the capsule it had travelled in – condensation or even a water supply. But it couldn't have survived without food for much longer than that.

Brute force. Unlimited power. That's what it would take. Never mind about vectors or the finer points of space navigation. But if those puny-looking Cygnan broomsticks could manage constant acceleration at one g, then certainly they could mail a package from earth in eight days.

'Are there Cygnans on Earth now?' Jameson asked.

Tetrachord and Triad were preoccupied. Jameson had to ask several times before he got a reply.

'No. That is a wrong question. A Cygnan on Earth is a not-Cygnan, so that what you say has not-meaning.' While Jameson wrestled with that, Tetrachord went on: 'We have caused to be sent to Earth a (number?) of *tweetle-tweetle-chirp-trill*.'

'What is a *tweetle-tweetle-chirp-trill*?'

Impatiently, Tetrachord glided over to the queer console at

the far wall, still clutching a soil-sample bag in one middle claw. The fingers of three hands blurred over the pearly knobs and flicked over the rows of wires on their fretted necks. A picture formed on the three clustered circular screens – all the same picture, but with subtle differences. The Cygnans didn't use holo images. Their three eyes evidently focused separately on each of the three images and their brain translated them into a picture they could use.

Jameson concentrated on whatever picture seemed clearest at the moment. What he saw was a hangerlike interior occupied by a narrow flat-sided needle in the shape of an elongated pyramid. Twenty or thirty Cygnans were bustling around it, giving it scale. The object was about ten metres long, he guessed . Three flaring nozzles stuck out of the corners of the blunt end. The pointed end was broken away, and Cygnans were removing odd-shaped containers from the interior. All the Cygnans wore transparent protective suits.

A probe. An automated probe.

How the hell had the Cygnans slipped their probes through Earth's radar defences without precipitating a world war?

'How long have you been studying Earth?'

The answer was indefinite, as answers involving duration or measurement always were. Jameson gathered that it hadn't been for very long, though. Not until after the human ship had entered the Jovian system.

That was odd. They must have picked up radio signals from Earth and Mars long before they themselves went into orbit around Jupiter. And picked up the com laser flashes to the ship. It seemed to Jameson that when you had travelled more than ten thousand light-years, having a look at an indigenous intelligent life form would have a high degree of priority. But evidently the Cygnans had just now gotten around to being curious about people.

'Why are you studying us now?'

'You are too puny to interfere with our purpose. But the mother-within-herself is prudent.'

More Cygnan gobbledegook. He'd run into the 'mother-within-herself' reference before and had pinned its literal meaning, if not its import. He wished he could pass on these clues to Janet Lemieux or someone else more qualified than he. But the thrust of Tetrachord's answer became clear when the Cygnan plucked some wires on the console and another scene

163

took shape on the three circular screens. They showed a film or a tape or a sound-picture of the Jupiter ship after it had been evacuated. Cygnan technicians had removed the protective blisters over the nuclear missile racks. They were taking lots of pictures, or whatever happened when light from those glittering little boxes they carried bathed the missiles, but they weren't touching the launching racks. They acted somewhat skittish, and were staying well clear of them.

The Cygnans were miffed about the nuclear bombs, and Jameson couldn't blame them.

'We wish you no harm,' Jameson said. 'But humans also are prudent.'

'Humans cannot harm us,' Tetrachord said flatly. His heart pounding, Jameson said, 'What do you want with Earth?'

'Want?' The two Cygnans tossed the word back and forth, like shrikes calling to each other in counterpoint. 'The Earth is a wrong thing. It is not a thing that we want. We have no need to take it.'

That took Jameson's breath away. Tetrachord hadn't used 'take' in the sense of possessing something. He had used the idiom for carrying something away.

Could he keep the Cygnans talking? They became bored easily. For a moment, they were intently watching the kitten. Its bath finished, it was clawing its way up his trouser leg. It settled in his lap, purring. There was an excited chirping from the Cygnans. Desperately Jameson ran his fingers over the keyboards of the Moog.

'Why have you come here then?' he asked. 'What do you want in this star system?'

The Cygnans seemed at a loss to reply to him. They went into a hand-holding huddle, fluting at each other for a long time. Finally Tetrachord went over to the console again. An outside view sprang to life on the triple viewscreens: the tremendous disc of the planet Jupiter, repeated three times.

Jupiter had changed. Jameson stared in wonder at its seething bulk. The bands and the Red Spot were completely gone. The process the aliens had started had advanced considerably since the last time he had seen the planet. The atmosphere had churned itself into a boiling porridge, a uniform dirty yellow in colour. It heaved violently, popping world-sized bubbles that burst through the surface and were sucked into the billowing chasm that divided the planet in half.

'This is what we want,' Tetrachord cheeped at him. 'We'll take it with us.'

## CHAPTER NINETEEN

Jameson sat there, too stunned to move. The kitten purred in his lap, its sharp little claws digging into him rhythmically. Over on the triple screens, Jupiter continued to boil away.

*If you're going to steal a planet*, he thought insanely, *why settle for anything except the biggest?* Smash and run, with the brightest bauble the solar system has to offer!

Jupiter!

A mere bagatelle, massing three times the rest of all the planets and moons in the solar system combined! A giant among worlds – eleven times the diameter of Earth and more than three hundred times its weight. A melon next to a grape! He supposed it was fortunate for the human race that the Cygnans thought big.

He patted the kitten absently. Under the soft fur it was all bones. The Cygnans were still watching him with their triangulated eyes. He flipped switches and pulled stops on the Moog. He was finally getting somewhere; every nuance had to be right.

'Why?' Jameson typed. 'Why do you need the large planet?'

The two Cygnans hesitated. Their stumpy eye polyps twitched. They were facing a problem about vocabulary.

'Jameson eats the green food made from growing things,' Triad skirled. 'The small animal from Earth eats the white liquid. Then Jameson has the power to move. Then the animal has the power to move. Does Jameson understand?'

'Jameson understands,' he tapped out on the keys.

'An engine must eat. Then this place may move.'

Fuel. They were talking about fuel. A couple of quick exchanges and he had the Cygnan word for it.

Tetrachord spoke up. 'The fuel which our engines eat is the mother-of-matter.'

He got it right away. Hydrogen!

They were using Jupiter for fuel. To the Cygnans, that was all Jupiter was good for. They'd simply dropped in on a handy solar system to tank up.

Gas giants were common throughout the universe. They were a necessary consequence of planetary formation. Most of those that had been detected, like the superjovian companions of 61 Cygni and CIN 2347, were considerably more massive than Jupiter itself. Using them for refuelling stops must be a convenient way to star-hop.

Mother-of-matter – that was as good a description as any for the most basic of the elements. Rather poetic, in fact.

Jupiter was composed almost entirely of hydrogen. The giant planets, with their tremendous gravitational strength, were able to hang on to the light gases that had given them birth. Oh, the atmosphere was laced with helium and with such impurities as water, methane, and ammonia. And somewhere at the centre of that vast slush ball, like a cherry pit, was a small rocky core about the size of the planet Earth.

But mostly it was hydrogen – an atmosphere hundreds of miles deep, squeezed gradually by its own unsupportable weight until it began to behave like a liquid. There was no clear boundary. It became an ocean without a surface, some twelve thousand miles deep, an ocean in which the planet Earth could have sunk without trace. It was also an ocean without a bottom. At that depth, under pressure of three million Earth atmospheres, the thickening syrup of molecular hydrogen underwent another transformation. Its molecules dissociated into atoms. It turned into a metallic form never seen on Earth: a dense fluid that could conduct electricity.

It would make a bottomless reservoir of hydrogen fuel. Siphon off the upper atmosphere and the lower layers, released from pressure, would boil up into a gas again. Drain the oceans that weighed on that strange ball of metallic hydrogen and the viscid stuff would turn into the molecular form, in turn boiling off as a gas at its surface.

Jupiter would make a great fuel tank. How close to the speed of light could you get before you used it up?

Jameson looked over at the triple image of Jupiter on the circular screens. How much of Jupiter was gone already? It was impossible to guess. The Cygnans could have stolen a mass equal to several Earths without making an appreciable dent in it. And as the surface pressure let up, what was left of Jupiter would expand. To Jameson's naked eye there was no difference in Jupiter's size.

Jameson's fingers rippled over the keys. The Moog cleared

its electronic throats and said, 'How? How is it possible for you to do this thing?'

'The planet you call Jupiter will fall,' Tetrachord repeated for the fourth time. 'And we will fall after it.'

'Yes, but what will it fall *towards?*' Jameson asked, getting desperate. It wasn't easy discussing orbital mechanics in baby-talk.

'It will fall to that-which-pulls,' the Cygnan tweeted, 'when that-which-pulls grows heavy enough.'

Jameson clenched his big fists in frustration. They were going around in circles. Any more of this and the Cygnans would give up on him, as they always did when the going got tough. He might never have another chance to reopen the subject.

He composed his thoughts and ran his hands over the keys again.

'Where is that-which-pulls?'

Tetrachord gestured vaguely toward the bulk of Jupiter on the screens. 'You see it,' he said.

What did that mean? Was Jupiter supposed to fall towards itself? 'Give me a closer look,' Jameson said.

Tetrachord twisted a serpentine neck towards the triple screens and warbled at them. The console evidently could be voice-activated as well as manually controlled by the little tuned wires.

The view of Jupiter enlarged. The screens zoomed in on a segment of the hoop of glowing wire that circled the giant planet above the cloudtops. A rim of clouds stretched from Jupiter to the hoop like a hat brim.

The zoom stopped. Jameson was looking at a sash of light stretching in triplicate across the screens.

The close-up of a piece of halo told him nothing. 'I see that the light draws hydrogen ('mother-of-matter') from Jupiter. But where does the hydrogen *go*? How is it stored?

That earned him a lot of disconcerted whistling. 'To store hydrogen has not-meaning. It is to be eaten by that-which-pulls.'

Back to square one. Exasperated, Jameson said, 'I don't see anything there except light.'

They seemed puzzled that Jameson couldn't see what they were showing him. They held a bagpipy conference about it.

Then Tetrachord made some adjustment at the keyboardlike row of fretted miniature guitar necks.

As Jameson watched, the glowing bracelet that circled Jupiter began to flicker. It became a series of fireballs chasing one another's tails. The fireballs finally slowed so that he could see them. What he saw was a herringbone frieze of overlapping shapes. Through the ghost images he could make out the basic form of the thing.

It was a strobe effect. Jameson was looking at a frozen frame of the object that circled Jupiter at a blurring speed that by now must be an appreciable fraction of the speed of light.

The Cygnans needed no such visual coddling, he suddenly realized. The neurons in their visual pathways must be able to fire selectively, at millions of times per second, as naturally as a human being might squint for better focus. They carried their own built-in strobe flash.

'That-which-pulls,' Triad hummed.

It was one of their probes – an elongated pyramid like a flat-sided spike. It was doing nothing but circle Jupiter, again and again, picking up speed with each circuit.

'Does Jameson know that as a thing goes faster, it grows heavier?' Tetrachord asked.

By God, the creature was quoting the theory of relativity at him! What Cygnan Einstein, thousands of years in the past, had arrived at the great keystone equation governing the increase of mass with velocity? Jameson dug into his memory for what he had learned at his Academy classes long ago.

'Jameson knows that if a thing would go as fast as light is fast, its weight would be ...'

Damn! What was the Cygnan word for infinite'? He'd never learned it. Perhaps there wasn't one. And did they understand 'weight' to mean 'mass'? And how did you express the concept of a square root in Cygnanese? The square root of one minus the square velocity divided by the square of the speed of light – how did you go about saying a thing like *that* in pidgin? Maybe the Cygnans didn't use square roots, either. Perhaps they arrived at their results in an entirely different fashion – like Russian multiplication.

He stared at the little triangular probe on the screens. Could a thing that small really move the biggest planet in the solar system? His instincts said no. Einstein said yes.

What was its mass by now? Enough to make the outer fringes

of the Jovian atmosphere fall into it. Jameson could see the threadlike stem of a whirling tornado sucked into the needle craft – a tornado that was whipped round the circumference of Jupiter at thousands of miles per second, unwinding the giant planet like a ball of twine.

The probe couldn't be more than a few dozen metres in length. But its speed made it legion; it zipped around the planet like a horde of hydrogen-sucking vampires, bleeding Jupiter's substance from the great continuous wound at the equator.

Faster and faster, squandering that bottomless reservoir of hydrogen to push itself fractionally close to the unattainable speed of light, this one tiny gnat could unpeel Jupiter layer by layer. Then, pregnant with stolen mass, it would reach a point on the curve where it outweighed Jupiter itself – or what was left of Jupiter.

Long before that point, Jupiter would begin to respond to its gravitational tug. The two bodies would be revolving around a common centre of gravity, rising through Jupiter, then outside it. Some of the energy could be diverted to form a vector.

The giant planet would then follow the little robot ship like an elephant on a tether. The gigantic alien ships, in turn, would be drawn along in Jupiter's wake, using its bulk as a convenient shield against the inferno of X-rays and gamma radiation sparking off the planet's forward face.

Jameson scratched the stubble on his chin. The mysterious Earth-sized planet that the Cygnans had deposited in orbit around Jupiter was – he guessed – the discarded core of another gas giant. The sheer extravagance of it took away his breath. The Cygnans had to be the wastrels of the universe.

Maybe it was the only way to travel between the stars at relativistic speeds. Take along a gas giant for a fuel tank. Or, more accurately, have it take *you* along. A fuel supply – and protection against the hellish storm of radiation that happened when you collided with interstellar hydrogen at a speed approaching that of light.

The scale of it was staggering. But after all, he told himself reasonably, the principle wasn't too different from that of an early chemical rocket burning tons of fuel to put a few pounds into orbit. As the fuel was burned up it imparted its energy to what was left of the payload – a point that had been lost on some of the early critics of space travel, who insisted that not even the most powerful known fuels contained enough energy to boost themselves to escape velocity.

His mind raced. Think of Jupiter, then, as being a series of fuel tanks which are progressively discarded as they are used up. The point at which the little probe gained enough mass to move Jupiter and Jupiter lost enough mass to be moved didn't really matter; it could be expressed as a differential equation. Half a Jovian mass – or a tenth of it – was still plenty of mass left to play around with.

The Cygnans could afford to be profligate with their stolen planets. Suppose, Jameson thought feverishly, they burned 90 per cent of Jupiter to attain a velocity of, say, 98 per cent of the speed of light for their strange caravan. Ninety-eight per cent, he guessed, would be about the point where a law of diminishing returns set in and the implacable equations of relativity demanded the expenditure of impossible amounts of energy to attain infinitesimal increments of velocity. So what? They'd coast at .98c. That would still leave them more than thirty Earth masses to brake with. Burning 90 per cent of *that* would still leave them with three Earth masses at the end of their journey.

Be generous. Assume some inefficiency in their system. Surely they couldn't *totally* convert matter to energy. Throw away a couple of Earth masses. That would still leave them with an Earth-sized rocky core.

Like the one that was now in orbit around Jupiter.

But wait a minute. Assume even *more* inefficiency!

Once they got going, they might pick up enough interstellar hydrogen to make up the difference. After all, why waste that manna of hydrogen infall as they ploughed through interstellar gas clouds?

A twentieth-century scientist named Bussard once had calculated that an intake area of about 80 miles in diameter would be a sufficient-sized scoop for an interstellar ramjet feeding on clouds of ionized hydrogen. True, he was talking about a 1,000-ton spaceship, but he was also talking about ordinary hydrogen fusion.

Even at the final stages of their journey, with their Jovian giant shrunk to Earth size, they'd have a scoop with a diameter of 8,000 miles. And that was just the small end of a truncated cone – the impact area. The size of the large end would be anybody's guess. It would depend on such things as gravitational attraction and the rate of ionization induced by the planet's magnetic field. It could sweep an area hundreds of thousands of miles in diameter.

Jameson felt his cheeks burning with excitement. He wished he had Ruiz to talk this over with. Ruiz would be able to work out the maths. But he was sure that he was right in his assumptions. It *felt* right! Hell, he could be wrong by a factor of ten and the principle would be the same. Burn 99 per cent of a gas giant to get the remaining 1 per cent – plus your piddling fifteen-mile ships – up to velocity. Then brake by burning 99 per cent of the remaining 1 per cent. Maybe they'd ridden here on a superjovian, ten or twenty times Jupiter's mass. Maybe they'd have to limp out of the solar system at a mere 90 or 95 per cent of the speed of light.

'The word is infinite,' Tetrachord said. He sounded like a cageful of twittering birds, all except the sound for 'infinite', which was a single sweeping glissando spanning two octaves, with a little turn at the top. Was it Jameson's imagination, or was there an overtone of approval in the Cygnan's voice. like a person patting a smart puppy on the head for doing a trick?

'But an infinite weight can never be reached,' Jameson responded quickly.

'No.' Again Jameson thought he heard approval. 'But that-which-pulls will be heavy enough in . . .' There was a phrase for a unit of time.

That was the sticky point. The Cygnans, in their arrogance or self-sufficiency, had never bothered to give Jameson a scale involving Earth's year or period of rotation. Perhaps they simply didn't care to study the planets encountered during their transient pit stops. They used a Cygnan time scale, and to understand the timetable for this cosmic theft he was going to have to find out something about the Cygnan home planet. Perhaps it didn't even exist any more, but it was still part of their cultural baggage.

Just how close to the speed of light could the little probe itself get in its flashing circuit, and how long would it take it to gain enough mass to move Jupiter? The probe didn't have to accelerate any mass except itself; its fuel tank was external – Jupiter's atmosphere. He frowned, trying to recall some of the theoretical scuttlebutt that had come out of the abandoned studies for a Centaurus probe. A twentieth-century rocket expert named Sanger had estimated that a respectable-sized spacecraft could attain 99.999,999,999,999,999,996 per cent of the speed of light by annihilating a mass the size of the Moon. You could get there in a year at one g, in less than four days at 100 g's.

The probe the Cygnans called 'that-which-pulls' had been at it for more than six months. It must have brushed the speed of light within a few days. Now it was nibbling away at the remaining fraction, fighting an uphill battle against relativistic imperatives. The efficiency of its engines would be diminishing, from an outside observer's viewpoint, by the penalty of an enormous time-dilation effect. But it was certainly getting there.

Now how the hell did the Cygnans keep the probe from flying off into space? At that speed, with its abnormal mass, and with its tight turns around Jupiter, the centrifugal force must be . . . unthinkable!

He was about to ask Tetrachord when he realized that the question was without meaning. What did it matter *how* much energy was diverted to tie the probe down in orbit? Just take *whatever was needed* out of all that kinetic energy stolen from Jupiter's mass, no matter how mind-boggling the sum. Blow it out in a direction perpendicular to the orbit. Or change the attitude of the robot craft to provide a vector that would balance the enormous forces. The method didn't even have to be particularly complicated. A simple feedback mechanism would do.

He took a closer squint at the cascade of repeated shapes frozen on the screens. There! He could make it out! A plume of light sprouting from the waist of the ship, driving it inward toward its primary.

He shuddered. What was that spray of light? A waste product of the drive, as heat is the byproduct of the work done by a mechanical engine? He suspected that the Cygnan exhaust was something akin to pure gamma rays. It wouldn't do to let *that* stuff get too close to an inhabited planet, to say nothing of that terrible bow wave!

'How will you remain in the shadow of the light-that-kills?' he asked impulsively, improvising words and hoping his meaning was getting across.

The two of them twittered happily. They were proud of their puppy. It had done another trick.

Tetrachord plucked at the console, wiping the viewscreens. The picture was replaced by a triptych of bright toylike geometric shapes rotating and counter-rotating in intricate patterns like the mechanism of a transparent clock. The moving parts ticked away in tiny jumps in sequence around the three identical screens.

A model of their system! Here was a planetarium for Cygnan schoolchildren, showing them how their convoy of artificial worldlets travelled through space! He'd hit the jackpot again. He didn't need any maths to grasp the basics of what was being shown to him.

At the centre was a glowing red ball, moving against an abstract background of stars. That was the gas giant. The one they had already used up, soon to be replaced by Jupiter.

Around its waist was a string of tiny chips that pulsed in sequence to indicate motion. An abstraction of the robot probe, tailored to Cygnan perceptions. He squinted more closely. On one of the three screens he could see a fan of light directed outward – the lethal spray of radiation.

Enclosing the two-body system in a wider, polar orbit was a smaller sphere of opalescent grey. One of the gas giant's moons, dragged along by its kidnapped parent. It rotated in a plane that was almost vertical to the loop described by the probe. It put Jameson in mind of a gyroscope configuration, or perhaps one of the simplified representations of an atom that used to be popular in his schoolboy days.

Then, in orbit around the moon – again in another plane – he saw five glittering mites, three-armed asterisks spinning on stems. The Cygnan ships.

The ships, in turn, were rotating around a common centre of gravity, chasing one another around in a circle. It was the system of five ships, considered as a single body, that rotated around the moon.

It was beautiful.

He sat watching the show, transfixed, like a boy mesmerized by a complicated set of electric trains. Everything had its own motion. Nothing collided.

He watched it for a long time to be sure how it meshed.

To keep from being flung into space, the little probe, that-which-pulls, had to keep blowing off energy all the time the intricate procession was travelling, even when it had stopped accelerating. It was a worm, draining away the substance of the planet. There could be no such thing as coasting without consuming fuel.

The Cygnans would have to drop in periodically on star systems close to their line of flight to refuel. Otherwise they would find themselves without enough mass to brake and be doomed to go flying forever through the universe.

How many stars had they plundered of gas giants during their long hegira?

Each shanghaied planet, of course, would have cost the Cygnans at least a year's braking time, plus another year to boost up to relativistic speeds again. For the rest of it, how long would it have taken, ship's time, to travel the 10,000 light-years that Ruiz had postulated? At 98 per cent of the speed of light, Jameson knew, the time-dilation effect would be approximately fivefold. The Cygnans had been cooped up in their triangular cans for more than two thousand years of subjective time. They had managed to maintain a technological civilization, but he guessed things were getting a little stale.

Triad was tootling at him. 'Does Jameson see how we are always in the shadow of the moon?'

Jameson returned his attention to the screens. He tried to keep track of the separate motions.

The pilfered moon, despite appearances, wasn't revolving around its parent. It was orbiting around the common centre of gravity shared by the gas giant and the probe that was in tight orbit around it. But since the centre of gravity was so close to the planet's surface, of course, it made no practical difference to what he was seeing.

The moon, from his point of view above the system, was rotating counterclockwise around the gas planet. The direction of motion of the whole system was upward, towards twelve o'clock.

The mitelike ships, in orbit around the moon, were travelling clockwise.

Their orbit had the same period as the moon's orbit around its primary. They were always in a trailing position, shielded from impact with interstellar hydrogen by three thousand miles of rock. At every point of the opposing orbits, the ships were in the lee of the radiation.

He watched the clockwork simplicity of it.

With the moon in six-o'clock position, the rosette of ships was also in six o'clock in its elliptical lunar orbit. It was shielded by both the moon and the bulk of the giant planet itself.

When the moon emerged from that cone of safety, to three-o'clock position, the ships were at the moon's nine o'clock. But since the moon was by that time tilting its twelve inward towards the giant, the ships were still in a trailing position.

With the moon at twelve o'clock, leading the whole procession, the cluster of ships was safely behind it, at the moon's twelve o'clock. Another quarter turn for both orbiting systems put the moon at nine and the ships at three – still in the moon's radiation shadow.

The ships' orbits, he suspected, would have to be adjusted continually to match their period to the moon's rotation – especially as the mass of the primary shrank. But surely, manoeuvring the five ships would require only a fraction of the total energy expenditure eaten up by moving a Jovian or superjovian!

It was beautifully simple and elegant! Jameson watched in admiration for long moments.

Even the deadly probe, with its radiation backlash, was never at the crossroads of the moon's orbit at the two points where their paths intersected. Everything ticked along beautifully.

'I see,' Jameson said. 'Your ships are safe.'

The two Cygnans whistled their approval. Tetrachord wiped the screens and dropped down on four legs. One of his upper limbs twined around Triad in an almost-human gesture of affection.

Jameson blared the sharp fanfare for attention. Startled, the Cygnans jerked their heads in his direction.

'What about Earth? My planet. Will *it* be safe when you leave this system?'

Consternation. Much twittering back and forth. Jameson had the impression that they had never thought about it, that it hadn't occurred to them to care.

Finally Tetrachord punched in an inquiry to the ship's computer or whatever passed for one aboard the Cygnan vessel. There were flashing images that made no sense to Jameson. They hadn't bothered to adjust the screen for human vision this time.

Tetrachord twisted around. His eyestalks stretched like taffy in Jameson's direction.

'Jameson,' the creature said. 'We will cross the orbit of your planet when we leave. We will pass close to your sun and swing around it to change direction.'

Jameson got a crawly sensation down his spine. The Cygnan caravan would cross the Earth's orbit twice.

'Just how close to Earth will you pass?' he asked.

There was no answer for a while. Jameson found he was holding his breath.

The Cygnans wouldn't have reached anything near light-speed by the time they crossed Earth's path, of course, so the deadly shower of X-rays that had announced their approach to the solar system would be no danger. But the probe's deadly drive would be on. That in itself might be enough to sterilize a hemisphere if it got too close and was pointed in the wrong direction. Then, too, there was Jupiter's own radiation belt, extending millions of miles into space. The Cygnans themselves would be safe from charged particles in the zone swept clean by their moon, but Earth might not be so fortunate.

And there certainly would be tidal effects.

Jameson trembled at the thought of what might happen if a Jupiter-sized mass passed too close to Earth. Earthquakes, floods, perhaps even the breakup of the Earth's crust.

What if the Earth's orbit were changed, moved a couple of million miles closer to the sun? Or pulled farther away? Or changed, like Pluto's, to a more elliptical orbit? Earth's climate could be permanently altered – an eternal ice age, with much of terrestrial life obliterated, or a water world, steaming under the melted polar caps!

Earth might even be plucked out of orbit to fall into the Sun.

'How close?' he repeated urgently.

'Jameson will be safe,' Triad hummed soothingly. 'We will take Jameson with us.'

'Dammit!' he exploded. 'That's not what I asked! What about the *Earth*?'

He stopped. He'd unthinkingly used human speech. They didn't understand the words, but the violence of his outburst had startled them.

Triad pressed herself against her larger companion. The soft, rat-sized thing plastered to her abdomen reacted to her distress by digging in more firmly with its insectlike legs.

Tetrachord hissed reflectively at Jameson. His upper body stretched to become a foot taller.

Jameson stood facing the alien pair, fists clenched. The kitten had dropped off his lap and scurried away. After a moment,

Jameson's fists fell to his sides. The tension in the bodies of the two Cygnans gradually relaxed.

Jameson stooped over the keyboard of the Moog again and played out his question. 'Where will the Earth be when you pass?'

There was a pause while they digested his query. Finally Tetrachord said, 'We do not know.'

'Find out,' Jameson said. There was no Cygnan word for 'please'.

They exchanged some running cadenzas, too fast for Jameson to follow. Then Tetrachord, still with a couple of arms around Triad, turned to his electronic zither and twisted some frets. A rapid chirping came out of the console. Tetrachord chirped back at it. For some reason the Cygnan had not encoded the question to the ship's computer. He'd asked someone.

Jameson couldn't understand the reply. Colloquial Cygnan would always be beyond him.

After a delay, a picture formed on the tripartite screen – another nursery diagram, like the one he'd been shown of the Cygnan travel arrangements. This one showed a series of concentric triangles with a glowing yellow triangle in the centre. The Sun and the orbits of the planets! Jameson gulped. Was that how the Cygnans saw circles? It hadn't been so in the previous projection, but perhaps this was someone's shorthand sketch or working diagram.

An irritated shrilling came from the console. A small green triangle appeared at the third place from the sun and moved back and forth along its track until it found a place and settled down. The orange triangle representing Jupiter jumped out of its orbit and moved jerkily Sunward. It dragged the yellow line of its orbit with it, opening the triangle into a four-sided evolute of ellipse. The evolute stretched as Jupiter intersected the inner solar system, traced a sharp V around the Sun, and headed out into the depths of space again.

Mercury and Venus jumped in their orbits. The white triangle representing Venus had been set spinning. But Earth had been spared.

'Your planet will be on the other side of the Sun,' Tetrachord said, unnecessarily.

Jameson eased himself down on the Moog's stool. His knees were trembling. He became aware that he was drenched with sweat.

If he could believe the Cygnans – and if they didn't decide, from some incomprehensible alien motive, to recompute their line of flight – Earth would be allowed to live.

As long as nothing delayed the Cygnans' departure.


## CHAPTER TWENTY

The attendant was old. If it had been a human being, Jameson would have said it shuffled. By this time he was familiar enough with Cygnans to know that this one's characteristic darting body movements were stiffer and slower than Tetrachord's or Triad's. Its mottled hide was duller, drier, less glossy. Did older Cygnans outlive their parasites, as terrestrial animals sometimes did? At any rate, there was no sluglike pest hanging from its belly, though Jameson thought he detected an old cicatrix where a tiny bloodsucking head might once have been embedded.

Its name – or at least the sound by which the other Cygnans addressed it – was a buzzing alteration of augmented fourths, so Jameson thought of the creature as Augie.

Augie was sidling warily into the room now on three legs, carrying a pan of greenish gruel in its forward pair of limbs and clutching a two-pronged electric prod in its free middle claw. Augie had never gotten over being afraid of Jameson.

Jameson backed off a little so as not to frighten the little creature. Augie set the pan down on the floor, back arched stiffly and eyestalks scanning in ragged circles. Retreating, the Cygnan got a foot tangled in the leathery double-ended poncho it wore for an apron. It hastily disentangled itself and skittered backward through the rolling disc that served as a door. The crescent opening closed with a thud.

Jameson could almost feel sympathy for the attendant. The poor creature had been saddled with responsibility for the monster from Earth for several days now. Triad and Tetrachord were off on one of their incomprehensible errands. Whenever they were gone, Jameson was kept locked up in a small adjoining chamber.

He looked sourly around at his surroundings. His cell was a narrow wedge crammed with Cygnan junk: dusty oddly shaped containers emptied of their original contents, heaps of pretzel-shaped transparent tubing, a broken three-armed perch. He'd dragged in as much of the looted human stores as was useful: clothing, packaged food, bedding, some miscellaneous furniture and utensils. He was dressed in clean coveralls that were too small for him; the name stitched over the breast pocket said *Gifford*. He had improvised a shower and sanitary facilities in the narrow corner, and when he was able to get into the main chamber he refilled his perforated jerrycans with water and emptied his makeshift chamber pots into the waste-disposal system. Augie wasn't much on cleaning up.

Jameson was mute, too, without access to the Moog. Augie made no attempt to understand his whistled arpeggios.

Jameson sighed and took the pan of gruel over to the salvaged table he ate on. It seemed to be mostly shredded wing-bean pods and undercooked hamster meat embedded in a starchy mush that the Cygnans had synthesized or adapted from their own chemistry. Sugars and starches must be as basic as DNA. He spooned it into himself as rapidly as possible. The stuff had practically no taste, for which he was grateful.

He was gulping the last few spoonfuls of the bland, glutinous mess when the kitten came over to rub against his leg and miaow. He scratched its ears and crossed to the locker where he kept his dwindling supply of human foodstuffs. There was only one can of condensed milk left. With a sigh he opened it and poured some into a saucer.

The kitten lapped the milk up eagerly. It had filled out a little and its fur was no longer so ratty, but it was still pathetically thin. It was going to have to learn how to eat bits of hamster meat and the Cygnans' synthetic concoctions. It at least had a name now: Mao – Chinese for 'cat'.

He fished a fragment of pink flesh out of what was left of the gruel and extended it on a finger to Mao. The kitten took it into its mouth and chewed it ineffectually with needle teeth, then let it drop on the floor. Jameson massaged its nape, feeling the little fragile neck bones through the fur, then let it go back to its milk.

He was washing up – he'd found that if he didn't wash the pan himself, Augie gave him his next meal with food still caked to it – when he noticed a crack at one side of the door.

He went over to inspect it, and found that Augie had been careless. The locking mechanism had failed to engage. Cautiously he rolled the door back a couple of inches and peered through.

The cluttered main chamber was silent. Augie was nowhere in sight.

Jameson didn't even stop to think. He had been cooped up in his pen too long now. The Cygnans didn't like him wandering around unsupervised. From watching his captors, he had some notion of how to tap the ship's library through the computer console.

He rolled the door all the way back and stepped through. Mao hopped over the rim after him.

The place smelled musty. Little furry insect-creatures twittered in their cages. Jameson prowled to the far door and satisfied himself that it was shut tight. Out there, hundreds of Cygnans dashed about their obscure duties. Augie must be in one of the adjoining chambers, packing up. Lately Tetrachord and Triad had been moving equipment and cages elsewhere. The shelves of caged snacks were almost empty now.

He went over to the fretted console and studied the wires and studs, trying to remember what Tetrachord had done to activate it. This was the first time he had been this close to it. Usually if he aproached to within ten feet the Cygnans hissed at him and made threatening gestures.

He pressed the pearly stud that turned it on, then strummed one of the finger boards at random. The screens lit up, and he was looking at a vast silvery hall where thousands of six-legged aliens clung to a piperack forest of perches, watching an egg-shaped niche where a lone Cygnan, mirrored on all sides by a reflecting surface, twirled round on its hind legs, holding up four objects that looked like dumbbells with skeletal pyramids for weights. A couple of Cygnans in the foreground started to twist around toward the screen. Jameson hastily shut the console off.

What had he tuned into? A classroom lecture? A religious service? A performance of some sort? Had there been a monitor pickup of any kind? Could anyone in the audience have seen him?

He waited until his heart stopped pounding, then cautiously tried strumming the metal strings with the console off. If he put his ear to the frets, he found he could hear a faint twang, like elfin tuning forks. The tuning system wasn't anything so simple as a chromatic scale in quarter-tones. The triple strands of wires seemed to be arranged for Cygnan convenience, probably reflecting frequency of use, like a typewriter keyboard.

By trial and error he found the combination that he thought would get him into the children's section of the library. It was a simple succession of Cygnan phonemes incorporating an interrogative and a sound meaning something like 'young' or 'new'. He'd heard Tetrachord vocalize it while trying to make some point clear to him. It had always got some nursery pictures or diagrams.

He practised till he thought he had it right, Then, holding his breath, he turned on the machine and plucked the strings.

He was looking at a row of purple globes, glossy as eggplants, set in grooves along a floor littered with something that resembled green popcorn. The globes were plugged into the faces of an endless sawtooth partition that ran the length of a hall that dwindled to infinity.

He saw miniature Cygnans clinging to the enormous fruits, six or seven to a globe, their rasplike snouts buried in the skins, sucking out the juices. Adult Cygnans, aproned like Jameson's own attendant, scurried up and down the aisle, rearranging the tiny creatures and occasionally pulling them free to tend to them. The adults gave Jameson the scale of what he was seeing. The miniature Cygnans were about the size of weasels. The purple things were as big as hippopotami.

Then one of the eggplants quivered and shifted its position. Jameson for the first time noticed the vestigial limbs, six flipperlike stumps, that sprawled out uselessly from their bloated bulks. The heads must be on the other side of the sawtooth partition, feeding mindlessly at an endless trough . . .

He managed to switch off the console before being sick on the floor.

A nursery! He'd tuned in a Cygnan nursery! Those non-sentient hulks must have been bred through countless generations to give blood and body fluids, the way humans had bred milk cows. They were nothing but brainless food factories.

Jameson tried to put his discovery in a rational light. He told himself that laying hens and feed-lot cattle and beef hamsters were practically vegetables, some of them barely ambulant. He reminded himself that people once had swallowed oysters alive, back in the days when it was still safe to eat oysters. But the sour taste in his mouth wouldn't go away. He kept seeing an image of the oozing, abraded wound in the hide of one of the purple creatures when a Cygnan nurse had yanked a feeding tyke away.

When his stomach settled down, Jameson tried again. This time he got it right. The three-ring cluster of screens displayed what appeared to be a library index in simplified visual terms suitable for a being who had asked for information in babytalk.

On one screen a wheel of tiny glittering images rotated slowly against darkness. No, it wasn't a wheel, it was a spiral, pulling bright little midges out of infinity.

A second screen showed the unwinding spiral edge-on. The little pictures marched on from the side of the screen in a widening funnel, feeding the outer rim.

The third screen was close-ups, one by one, of each image as it reached the point on the spiral where it disappeared.

Evidently even Cygnan children could look at all three screens at once and make sense out of the procession. The principle of organization was incomprehensible to Jameson. It all seemed random, in no particular order. But then, he told himself, a Cygnan would say the same thing about an alphabetized listing in a human dictionary.

Helplessly Jameson watched the images flow past. The subject headings were fascinating in themselves, but he was all too aware that he might be interrupted at any moment. There was a generalized botanical representation of fat blue leaves and salmon-coloured fruits that would have driven Dmitri wild. It gave way to a disembodied Cygnan eye with the spiral galaxy in Andromeda, exactly as it was seen from Earth, reflected in its depths. Then there was a construction of shiny metal rods working away like a model steam engine. And a length of green rope patiently tying and untying itself into a recognizable square knot.

Jameson tried strumming the word Tetrachord had given him for 'planet'. Immediately the spiral flow of midges speeded into a streaking blur and came to a stop. On the close-up screen was a swollen red ball against a background of unfamiliar constellations.

The screen asked him a question.

Jameson almost jumped out of his skin. Then he realized that the Cygnan voice had to be mechanical: recorded or computer-generated.

After a pause, the artificial voice queried him again. Crestfallen, Jameson realized that he couldn't understand. He was used to talking to Tetrachord and Triad, period.

On a hunch, he strummed the word for 'yes'.

The spiralling midges disappeared. He was peering at a strange landscape, identical on all three screens.

In the foreground was a city. Soaring towers reached into a lemon sky, stark shapes that no human mind had conceived. There were jagged shards of shiny black stone traced with networks of white threadlike exterior paths for climbing. There were angular shafts with jutting cantilevered branches. Three knife-edged spires leaned towards one another to meet at a common apex, their bases enclosing a triangular park landscaped with blue vegetation. Traffic moved in a thick stream around the buildings, three-wheeled vehicles shaped like upright eggs, changing direction without turning, The drivers, visible through the transparent bubbles, were Cygnans, clinging to a central pole, with passengers and baggage disposed around them in a circle.

Jameson's breath quickened. This was no spaceship interior landscape. He was looking at what could only be the Cygnans' home planet.

He stared greedily, trying to absorb details,

The buildings cast complicated shadows, washed-out fingers of colour that stretched in all directions. It was day, but that yellow sky was almost filled with an enormous ruddy moon, a squashed moon that ballooned from horizon to zenith. There was a slice out of one side. Its outline was fuzzy, its face marbled.

The Cygnan observer panned across the landscape.

There were two suns, low on the horizon. The smaller of the two was a fiercely glaring blue-white hole in the sky. The other was a swollen red giant. But something was wrong with it. It bulged on one side.

As Jameson watched, the traffic in the roadways speeded up, like an animated cartoon. Soon he could see nothing but a blur. The shadows grew like spilled dye. Time-lapse.

The smaller sun moved toward its bloated companion. The red sun swallowed it with a gulp. The shadows merged and deepened.

A Cygnan voice was giving a commentary. Jameson strained to make sense out of the calliope squawks. There were too many abstractions. He caught the word for 'mother' – at any

183

rate, the generalized phrase for 'progenitor' that seemed to figure so pervasively in Cygnan thought. Something about the Great Mother that swallows her . . . damn, what was that word? It had the root signifying a relationship. Offspring? No.

The scene changed. The white sun was emerging from the rim of the giant. But the giant itself was moving towards the darkening moon.

The scene changed again. It was night in that strange city. The moon hadn't moved. It had gone dark, but you could see it as a monstrous silhouette, blotting out the stars. It was outlined by a rim of red fire.

The Cygnan commentator said someting incomprehensible that contained the word for 'eat'. The red sun emerged from the rim of fire, spilling blood across the moon. As it rose, it disgorged the white sun. The white sun fled from it, widening the gap, casting a brilliant light as it rose higher in the sky.

Jameson drew in his breath. The Cygnans, it seemed, had evolved on a satellite world that always kept the same face turned toward the gas giant that was its primary – a primary that itself circled a double star.

The Cygnan voice trilled ecstatically. Jameson couldn't follow it. What strange sacraments of eucharist and resurrection would beings like the Cygnans have devised for themselves while they were struggling towards a scientific society?

He grinned wryly. Probably he was just listening to a straightforward astronomical commentary. The Cygnans, after all, called hydrogen something that translated as 'mother-of-matter'.

The red sun ate the white sun again, and spat it out. Both rose higher in the sky. Now, as Jameson watched, they merged. The white sun moved across the swollen red disc, its radiance almost wiping it out, flooding the city with cheerful light.

The scene changed – night again, but a different sort of night. The moon was lit. Its monstrous presence loomed over the twisted towers, glowing like hot coals. But now it had a hole precisely in its centre, the shadow of the Cygnan world, like the pupil of an enormous eye brooding at its creation.

Jameson was so riveted to the screen that he didn't notice Augie enter the room. He realized it, too late, when the kitten sprang spitting from his lap and streaked for cover under a low fixture across the room.

The Cygnan attendant advanced on him, belly-low on five

184

legs, holding an electric prod. It hissed at him, motioning him away from the console.

With despair, Jameson glanced at the unfolding scenes on the triple screen. Now a Cygnan lecturer was juggling coloured balls in four of its splayed hands. Two of the balls glowed like Japanese lanterns: a big red one and a blue one. The voice was going to explain all about multiple eclipses to the kiddies. And Jameson was going to miss it. *Damn!*

He slid off the seat and edged along the console wall, trying to put space between himself and the prod. If it touched him, he knew, he was done for.

The Cygnan prowled sideways, keeping parallel with him. It seemed to move sideways as easily and naturally as it moved forward. He'd often seen them move backward for short distances, too, without bothering to turn round, their eyestalks pointed rearward. That gave Augie a decided advantage in the stalking game.

Augie darted at him, feinting with the prod at Jameson's legs, then darted backward again. The hexapodal creature was holding itself so low that its leathery poncho, half unlaced as usual, dragged on the floor.

Jameson scrambled backward, out of the way, tripping over a low pedestal. Augie immediately pressed the attack. The long sleek alligator-shape launched itself at him like a harpoon. Desperately Jameson flung himself sideways. Perhaps human reflexes were a match for a Cygnan's blurring speed after all – at least an elderly Cygnan like Augie. Jameson knew he would have stood no chance whatsoever if there had been more than one of them. But the electric fork just missed contact.

There was a sizzling sound and the smell of scorched plastic. The fork had embedded itself in the padded cushion of a perch. Without stopping to think, Jameson grabbed the handle of the prod just forward of Augie's grip.

Instantly four or five rubbery paws were grabbing at him. Jameson ignored them. He yanked with all his strength. The Cygnan's grip was as weak as a child's. Jameson had the prod. No time to figure out how to use it He flung it away as hard as he could.

The Cygnan twisted away like an eel, going after the prod. Jameson made a grab for the clubbed tail and yanked the creature back. Augie uttered a strangled klaxonlike squawk. It turned sinuously, bending double, and struck at him with its long head.

He felt a pain that burned like fire. The creature had managed to get the tip of its abrasive tongue into the meat of his upper arm. Jameson, still keeping a grip on the tail, grabbed with his free hand for one of the fleshy eyestalks and forced the Cygnan's head back.

Augie was thrashing around. Millions of gristly fingers were pawing indiscriminately at Jameson's wrists and ankles, doing no harm. Jameson shifted position and knelt on the Cygnan's thick tail. Augie gave a terrible squawk again and shuddered convulsively before going limp.

Jameson had it by two eyestalks now, with his weight on its tail. He seemed to have injured the creature or made it sick. The petals at the tip of the tail were parted slightly, and there was a thick yellow exudate oozing out.

Augie was trembling. It was being careful not to move, to avoid damage to its eyes. Jameson gave a little tug to emphasize the point, then let go with one hand. He reached down, feeling for the poncho's laces, and pulled a length off. Working quickly, he muzzled the Cygnan, winding the cord around its snout. It was harder than he expected. The Cygnan didn't have a normal jaw that could be clamped shut, like a terrestrial animal. It could still peel back the edges of its mouth at any point past the encircling cord. Jameson had to do the whole snout up like a mummy, and even then the Cygnan was able to spread the tip apart like a rosebud and show a half inch of that rasplike tongue.

Jameson's arm was bleeding. There was a little round pit in it about a quarter inch deep. He had a feeling that if he hadn't jerked away so quickly, it would have gone all the way through to the bone.

With the Cygnan's head trussed up, Jameson moved swiftly to immobilize the rest of it. Still keeping a grip on an eyestalk with one hand, he pulled the creature's leathery poncho around backward, trappings its limbs. Then, two-handed, he laced it up in back like a straitjacket.

The Cygnan squirmed helplessly in its wrappings, making angry sounds. Jameson dragged the writhing bundle to a corner out of the way. Even then it tried to strike at him with its half inch of protruding tongue, but Jameson was able to keep himself out of reach. He took a moment to rip the sleeve off his borrowed coveralls and bandage his arm.

The show was still going on in the trifolium viewer. How much had he missed? The part about the complicated eclipses might have told him something useful about the Cygnans' abandoned home. Ruiz would have been able to do wonders with a few clues about the nature of the double-star system they had emerged from. But Jameson didn't dare try to turn the sequence back. He was afraid he'd lose it altogether and never find it again.

He was looking at a vast panorama of industrial effort. On a barren plain lit by the baleful light of that sky-filled moon, hundreds of thousands of Cygnans were toiling like ants. Great mining machines like thousand-foot metallic earthworms burrowed into the soil. On the arched horizon there was the bright flare of a rocket taking off.

With a start, Jameson recognized what he had taken at first for a squat pyramid sticking up out of the soil. It was the peak of those three skyscrapers that leaned together. Cygnans with barrel-wheeled bulldozers and beetlelike backhoes were digging them out. Other Cygnans were cutting away the metal framework and bearing it off. Jameson caught his breath. How many thousands of years had it taken for that city to be buried?

Now, almost like an intercut in a human film, he saw the Cygnans' tremendous fleet being assembled in space. In the foreground was the triangular base of one of the environmental pods, miles across, with a swarm of service vehicles hovering around it. Perhaps a hundred miles farther out was the half-folded frame of an uncompleted ship, looking like the claw-print of an immense bird stamped against the curve of the gas giant that had been the Cygnans' moon.

The scene spun to let him see the paired suns. They overlapped. The red sun was moving across the face of the white sun, so he knew that what he saw was not a trick of perspective.

The white sun was bigger.

During the ages it had taken for the Cygnan city to be buried, that sun had grown to perhaps twice its former size. Or else the red giant had shrunk. Or both.

This time the white sun was giving the red giant a bad case of indigestion. At what would have been full eclipse, Jameson saw a blinding white halo around the dull red disc of the giant.

They began to pull apart. The red sun extruded a nipple. It swelled toward its brilliant companion. Skeins of fire stretched between the two.

The red giant shrank like a leaky balloon. The Cygnan observer had speeded things up again. How many Cygnan observers, over how many lifetimes?

Hanging motionless beside it, the white sun bloated. It puffed up as he watched, dwarfing its diminishing mate.

Momentarily Jameson wondered how it was possible for him to see the stars in the same relative positions. If the screen was showing him a time-lapse version of eons of stellar evolution, then their minuet around each other would have speeded up to a whizzing blur, streaks of light across the void.

Then he realized that – of course – the Cygnans were using their strobe trick to stop unwanted motion. The wobble must have been too rapid at this speed for even Cygnan synapses to handle, so the computer was doing it for the kiddies.

The process of engorgement seemed to have stopped. The glowing balls hung side by side against raw space, a cherry next to a peach.

The suns receded. He was looking out into deep space now. A profusion of stars burned against blackness. The Cygnans' double star stayed in the mathematical centre of the screen. Soon his eye could not separate them.

The migration had begun.

At what had to be at least a couple of light-years out, he began to wonder why the stars in his field of view weren't changing colour. Either the Cygnans weren't yet travelling at anywhere near the speed of light, or the computer was compensating for red shift.

He was wrestling with that problem when the screen exploded.

A dazzling flash of light left him blinded. For an instant, through the haze, he saw a brilliant glare in the centre of the screen.

Supernova!

When his vision came back, the stars were rushing towards him as the screen zoomed to the limits of magnification. The library was about to show him something interesting.

The light went out like a dying light bulb and there was nothing except the engorged white star shining in space. The image must have been computer-enhanced. He could see a disc the size of a cotton ball.

The cotton ball began to wobble. The computer was manipulating the strobe effect – at a ratio of thousands of images to one – to show that it was dancing with . . . *something!*

Something invisible.

A background star became a smear of light and winked off. An instant later it reappeared and shrank to a point again. The stars immediately nearby were rippling, like objects seen through heat waves. By looking closely, Jameson could see that the rippling stars were lapping around a fairly well-defined circle where no background stars shone.

Something was bending light, swallowing it. The invisible something that was whirling in dervish circles around the white star that had fed on its substance.

There was only one thing in the universe that swallowed light.

Jameson watched in awe, hardly daring to blink, until his eyes were burning. The circling dance went on a long time – as long, it seemed to him, as the entire stellar sequence leading up to it had taken. He wished fervently that he had a watch so that he could time the relative duration. His eyes began to play tricks on him. The moving boundary where light splattered and disappeared seemed to become tangible: a black blot in the blackness of space. It was an illusion, he knew. The thing – the *nothing* – in the centre of that blot could never be seen.

Now, with startling suddenness, the white star began to grow again. Its colour changed to blue. It inflated to enormous size, bigger even than the red giant had been.

Blue supergiant! It had exhausted its hydrogen and become a helium star.

Now, in a blink, the black hole became visible – not the hole itself, but the terrible events in its accretion disc. For a moment of cosmic time there was a flash of hideous light as the Cygnan computer selectively shifted an X-ray source burning with the power of ten thousand suns to the visible spectrum.

The screens went blank.

Before Jameson could move, the room was filled with hissing Cygnans. Triad and Tetrachord were among them. They saw the trussed-up Augie and set up a din that sounded like the shrill of a roomful of teakettles. There was a blur of flashing movement in Jameson's direction. He flung up an arm to protect his face, then felt a searing flash of pain what wiped him out of existence.

# CHAPTER TWENTY-ONE

Tetrachord tugged gently at the leash. Jameson gagged as the loop of cord, threaded through his nostrils and dangling down his throat, tickled his pharynx. Then the moment of nausea passed, and he ambled obediently down the concave sidewalk after the two aliens.

The kitten was in his arms. He'd managed to scoop it up before they led him off in disgrace. He damn well wasn't going to leave it to Augie's tender mercies.

The tether wasn't too uncomfortable once he got used to it. Jameson once had been fed by a tube through his nose in the hospital, and he'd found that it looked worse than it felt. It made the back of his throat feel sore, that was all, and he didn't want to think about what would happen to his septum if he resisted the tug of the leash. But all the same, he was glad he hadn't been conscious when the cord was inserted. And he dreaded its removal.

Perhaps it was the usual practice for Cygnans, with the peculiar anatomy of their planet's life forms, to fetter their domestic animals through some analagous body cavity. It was a damned effective way to lead a human being around.

They had decided Jameson could no longer be trusted. He'd proved to be a dangerous animal, no longer fit to be a house pet. As with a puppy gone bad, they might feel some lingering affection for him, but they were regretfully taking him away all the same.

He trudged along behind the hand-holding pair, trying to keep the cord slack as much as possible. Augie, sans poncho, was slithering along behind him at a safe distance, holding the electric prod.

Around him the Cygnan city swarmed with mottled life. He was being led through something akin to a commercial district, with the Cygnan equivalent of shops and restaurants and perhaps theatres. Vividly coloured angular structures soared crazily up to a luminescent approximation of a sky a quarter mile above. The faces of the buildings were alive with thousands of busy Cygnans, clinging to latticework perches that extended all the way up. The long tubular snouts turned in Jameson's direction as he passed, and the twittering noise level went up as they caught sight of him and paused in their activities. The scurrying crowds parted to make way for the dangerous procession, and a swarm of the curious trailed in Jameson's wake, keeping a respectful distance and piping questions at a sullenly silent Augie.

A little Cygnan the size of a beagle skittered up to him and was pulled back out of harm's way by an adult, exactly as a human parent might snatch a curious child out of the way of a circus animal. Jameson lost his step, trying to avoid tripping over the thing, and was rewarded by a painful yank of the cord snubbed around his septum. There was a sickening sensation inside his head as a loop of the tether scraped the walls of the nasal cavity, and he had a fit of coughing and choking.

His feet stumbled along automatically. When the tears cleared from his eyes the path was emerging from the overhanging cliffsides of the vertical structures into a parklike stretch with pale blue lawns of packed fuzzballs and contorted shrubs like tangles of red spaghetti on either side.

They skirted a picture-book lake with manicured borders. Odd-looking sailing craft bobbed on the turquoise waves: brightly coloured round bowls, curved gooseneck masts with cheerful windsock sails to catch the breezes generated by spin and temperature differentials. The bowls were just big enough to hold courting couples – if that's what the paired Cygnans were. One of the little sailboats skimmed past, near shore, and Jameson caught sight of a slithery duo necking passionately. Necking was the only way to describe all that six-handed stroking and fondling.

The Cygnans had made a pleasant life for themselves in this hollow worldlet that hurtled between the stars. There would be holiday visits to the other two worldlets attached to the ship, and visits from ship to ship. A society of upwards of two hundred million Cygnans – perhaps as many as four billion – on perpetual holiday in their cosy bubbles of warmth and air rising through a stern darkness.

Perhaps, Jameson thought, after having witnessed the extinction of their own two suns, the Cygnans were disposed to avoid solar systems like the plague. Stars were dangerous neighbourhoods to be in. You stayed just long enough to steal a planet and run.

Jameson looked across an open plaza spoked with transparent travel tubes clogged with Cygnans entering or leaving the area. The tubes snaked at every level through walls, through enormous aquarium tanks, through enclosed habitats, through cages.

Cages.

A frightful stench was in the air, a fetid compound of rotting straw and halogens, of barnyard odours and ammonia, as if a menagerie had been set down in a chemical factory. The place was noisy, too – a hubbub of screeches and bellows and clicks and yaps and howls.

Jameson could make out some of the creatures in the nearby cages. He saw a tall insectoid thing like a cluster of milky bubbles on a tripod. And a thing like a fluffy dishrag that flapped miserably along a filthy cage floor. A pair of tendrilled sacs that dangled like hanging baskets from the wire roof of their enclosure. A shaggy pear-shaped cyclops that scratched itself with its single long arm.

Here and there across the plaza random groups of Cygnan sightseers paused to stare in Jameson's direction, then turned their attention to the more interesting exhibits. Tetrachord made encouraging noises. When Jameson didn't move, the Cygnan pulled gently at the nose tether and urged him like a trained bear across the gravelled plaza into the main body of the zoo.

They crossed an acre-size quad where a lot of methane breathers had been grouped together. Jameson caught a lung-searing whiff through leaks in some of the sealed tanks they passed. Through frosty glass he glimpsed a segmented blocky worm that moved with nightmare slowness by pulling off the rearmost section of its body with a pair of cranelike arms, then setting it at its head, where apparently it merged and joined again at the interface. Jameson wanted to stay and see what happened when the segment with the arms reached the caboose, but the Cygnans were urging him along again.

The methane section petered out into a hodgepodge of insulated tanks that obviously contained high-temperature beings. Jameson could feel the heat on his face as he loped past. The tanks were filled with a clear fluid that might have been liquid sulphur. Inside he saw rippling ribbon worms and torpedo-like fish things. The arrangement of exhibits seemed completely random. Jameson had the impression that the zoo simply had been allowed to grow by accretion.

They stopped at what must have been Tetrachord and Triad's living quarters at the back of a warehouse area. They rated an apartment all to themselves, a musty cubical – if 'cubical' was the word for an interior space shaped like a crazily leaning polyhedron – crammed with peculiar objects on spoon-shaped shelves. Jameson recognized a couple of resting perches, side by side beneath – *beneath?* – a hanging trifoliate screen. On a raised platform nearby was a graduated set of what looked like miniature resting perches. It made Jameson think of doll furniture.

They made him wait in the centre of the room. Tetrachord went to a cupboard and came back with three of the bulb-handled, shotgun-size neural weapons with the flaring muzzles. He handed two of them to Triad and Augie and kept the third for himself.

Jameson found that not at all comforting.

They left by the back way, and now they were in an exhibition hall, a huge place with interior spaces like a space-shuttle hangar. Everything looked newer and fresher here. A few Cygnan workers were applying shiny orange paint two- and three-handed with bulb-handled brushes, or caulking glass tanks. Most of the cages were empty. There was no Cygnan traffic in the surrounding travel tubes.

A small scuttling creature in one of the nearer cages caught his attention. He managed to vector his armed escort over for a closer look, despite the drag at the back of his septum. He saw a little horny many-legged creature with one enormous claw almost as big as it was.

Jameson almost wept. A crab. A perfectly ordinary fiddler crab. One of the Cygnan probes must have scooped it up. It was the only link with Earth he had, except for the struggling kitten in his arms.

They hurried him past the cage, and then he was in a dim, cavernous hall whose walls were thick glass cliffsides, ten stories high. For some reason the Cygnans stopped. Whatever was in the tremendous tanks was unusual enough to interest even them.

The cloudy liquid within was obviously under enormous pressure. The air in the hall was noticeably chilly. Jameson strained his eyes in the murky red light.

Shapes were swimming about in the depths of the tank, great shadowed shapes as large as whales. Jameson felt a chill that was not due to the temperature.

Triad rapped on the glass with the bell of her weapon. There was a vast stirring within.

The gigantic creatures emerged from the depths of the tank, crowding the glass. Jameson had the impression of flat, pancake shapes, more than a hundred feet across, undulating lazily to keep their trim. They were aware of him and the Cygnans. He felt them looking at him through the glass.

With a shock, Jameson realized that the creature filling his field of view was wearing some kind of harness, shiny leathery straps that were as broad as a roadway. It had limbs of sorts, too, scalloped projections of its outer rim, like the billowing shroud points of a parachute. It had them curled around a barb-tipped bone spear that was a hundred feet long.

With a shudder, Jameson wondered about the size of the animal whose skeleton had provided a one-piece artifact that long. It had to be some kind of a floating island with a kite framework of flexible bone.

There was a bone dagger, too, a honed triangular blade the size of a whaleboat with squiggly symbols inscribed on its flat side. And some kind of a pouch dangling from the harness, a catchall the size of a small barn.

Whatever this looming colossus was, it was intelligent. Primitive, but intelligent.

A hunter. A hunter whose quarry was bigger than it was.

It pressed against the glass, obviously looking him over. Jameson saw no evidence of anything resembling sense organs. No eyes, no flaps or tendrils. Perhaps it sensed with the surface of its entire mountainous body. Chemical senses. But what was it seeing him through the glass with? It could scarcely be infrared under the circumstances. Radar waves? Jameson supposed that even at the extremes of the electromagnetic spectrum an organism could provide definition by rapid and continuous scanning. Hunters needed keen senses.

'Where in the universe . . .?' Jameson breathed.

The Cygnans could not have understood him, but perhaps they were thinking their own thoughts. At his elbow, Tetrachord said: 'So near. And now the Jameson will never meet them.'

This time Jameson whistled it in his imitation Cygnan.

'Where?'

They turned abruptly toward him, as if surprised that their pet was talking again.

'This animal is from the planet you call Jupiter,' Tetrachord offered with careful enunciation.

Jameson stared at the undulating disc of flesh. So there *was* life in Jupiter's planetwide ocean after all. The speculations had been correct. Under that crushing atmosphere, in a sea that was twelve thousand miles deep before it turned to something else, there was plenty of room for life to develop. A sea of hydrogen laced with organic molecules, with a volume at least 300,000 times the volume of all Earth's oceans For an instant Jameson's imagination ran riot. He saw vast herds of dirigible-like grazers browsing at the rich nitrile pastures that welled up to become the Great Red Spot and the lesser spots, while these leviathans of the hydrogen deeps stalked them with hundred-foot bone spears.

Then he felt a dawning horror. The Cygnans must have scooped up their Jovian specimens *before* their Einsteinian siphon had churned Jupiter's atmosphere into a homogenized maelstrom. They'd *known* there was intelligent life there. Yet they'd gone on to make all life on Jupiter extinct.

The thought was all the more horrifying because there was no malice involved. Just selfishness. Thoughtlessness. Lack of empathy. In that respect they were no different from humans, in the mad century that had forever wiped out the humpbacks and the great blue whales.

They prodded him to move again. He took a last backward look at the Jovians before the massive creatures flapped off into the depths of their tank. He felt a pang of overwhelming sympathy for them. They were, after all, his brothers under the Sun.

They seemed to be in some sort of Hall of Bipeds now. Rows of cages along a curving corridor apparently formed the narrow ends of habitats that widened out in a fan beyond. The creatures that Jameson glimpsed as they led him down the corridor were obviously animals, not intelligent beings. He saw a little green bearded creature like a misshapen troll gravely pacing its cage with its knuckles dragging on the ground, and a hulking spiny-skinned thing with a little bullet head growing directly out of a barrel chest. Then there was a pair of delightful feathery humanoids, elfin pink creatures who stared at him with great sad eyes as he passed.

The three Cygnans gave a wide berth to the feathery humanoids' cage. Augie skittered nervously past it, skipping ahead momentarily and twisting a long neck to look back. There was a wire mesh arrangement in front of the bars to keep anyone from getting too close, with its own locked gate. Jameson couldn't see the reason for the extreme security precautions. The humanoids looked harmless enough. They were delicate, attenuated creatures who certainly would be no match for a Cygnan.

They reached the end of the hall, where he saw another locked cage. Beyond, Jameson could see a stark, garishly lit enclosure with wide bare terraces sloping down to a shallow pool filled with brownish water. Figures moved among the branched metal uprights set around the water's edge. They were obviously human.

Jameson strained toward the bars, trying to see. Tetrachord held him back by the tether while Triad unlocked the cage door with one of her cylindrical keys.

Figures were bounding up the terraces toward him whooping and yelling. Jameson recognized Mike Berry, gaunt, long-haired, and bearded, wearing only a pair of tattered denim shorts. And one of the Chinese crewmen, a young probe tech.

The three Cygnans jerked their neural weapons upwards, fanning them back and forth. The humans skidded to a stop, staying a respectful distance from the bars, New arrivals bumped into them from behind and stayed where they were. The noise died down. They stood silently watching.

Tetrachord unfastened the tether, leaving a foot-long loop of cord dangling from Jameson's nostrils. Augie backed away, keeping the weapon trained on him. The Cygnans gave him a shove, and he stumbled into the cage, the kitten cradled in his arms.

Mike Berry stepped forward, his face grim. 'Welcome to the zoo.'

## CHAPTER TWENTY-TWO

'This won't hurt,' Janet Lemieux said. 'Sit still.'

With a deft yank she pulled the severed cord out of Jameson's nose. There was about a foot of it, crusted with dried blood.

Jameson swallowed experimentally. The back of his throat

still felt sore, but it was an immense relief to have the cord out.

'Thanks, Doc,' he said. He put his arm back around Maggie and pulled her close to him on the step. She was painfully thin, even for her. He could feel her ribs through the threadbare cotton shirt she wore. All of the eighty-odd crewmen and crewpersons gathered around him on the terraced slope had lost weight. Jameson had lost weight too, but he was painfully conscious of the fact that he was in better condition than the rest of them.

They were scattered in a loose semicircle, waiting expectantly, sitting on the edges of the terraces or leaning against the iron trees, a bunch of ragged scarecrows in scraps of clothing. The Chinese remained a little apart, sticking together.

Jameson's eyes fell on Ruiz, looking like a bearded death's head, a collection of raw bones, in faded shorts. Like the rest of the men, he'd given his shirt to the women. Maybury was standing unobtrusively near him, her pretty little face marred by dark circles beneath the eyes. Further back, Omar Tuttle was looking Jameson's way, unsmiling, a starved bear with his arm around a gaunt and straggly-haired Liz Becque. Liz was pregnant. Jameson caught Sue Jarowski's eye She gave him a wan smile. Mike Berry stepped up beside her and put a hand on her shoulder.

The surroundings were bleak under the glaring yellow light grounds of a depressing grey substance like hardened oatmeal, the stagnant brown pool, a dusty sky that hadn't been washed for centuries. Across the pool some dispirited greenery was struggling for existence; Kiernan and Wang seemed to have coaxed some wingbean vines to grow in a shallow depression filled with coarse earth.

Captain Boyle pushed his way to the front of the crowd. He was still wearing his cap, but otherwise he'd stripped to shorts. His bare torso was as red as a boiled lobster, but a lot of the meat had gone, and his once florid face was blotchy. He looked a decade older.

He looked Jameson up and down. 'Where've you been, Tod?' he said mildly.

'I've been talking to Cygnans,' Jameson said.

There was a stirring at the fringes of the Chinese group. Tu Jue-chen stepped forward, her waxen face angry. 'Impossible,' she snapped. 'No one can talk to them. They tried to communicate with Comrade Yeh. They kept him in a cell for days before putting him here with the rest of us. Isn't that so, Comrade?'

Yeh shuffled uncomfortably. 'It's true. They tried to make me copy their whistles. I thought I had a word or two at first, but they meant something different every time.'

Jameson nodded at the big man. He was surprised that Yeh had survived. When he'd seen him borne off by a horde of Cygnans, he was sure they'd killed him, as they had Grogan.

'That's because you were whistling in different keys, Comrade,' he said. 'It depends on absolute pitch.'

Boyle's square head came up alertly. 'You found a way to talk to them?'

'That's right, Captain,' Jameson said.

'You are a traitor, admit it!' Tu Jue-chen said in a fury. 'Otherwise they would not have pampered you so! Now they've sent you here to spy on us'

Boyle's face hardened as he spoke to the Struggle Group leader. 'You can't have it both ways, Comrade Tu,' he said. 'If he doesn't know how to talk to Cygnans, then he can't be a spy for them,' He turned back to Jameson. 'You better tell us about it,' he said.

Patiently Jameson explained about how Cygnan phonemes were formed, and how he'd programmed the Moog synthesizer to imitate them.

'Can you still communicate with them?' Boyle asked urgently.

'Without the Moog, it's hard, Captain. But I can get a few primitive ideas across . . . if they bother to pay attention. And I can understand most of what they say directly to me – again, if they bother to try. When they talk to one another, I miss a lot.'

'Commander, we're in bad shape here. We could use some of the stuff from the ship. Clothing, soap. Razors. Birth-control pills. And we could stand an improvement in our rations. Kiernan and Wang are trying to get an ecology going. The Cygnans gave us some plants from hydroponics, some hamsters and fish and so forth. But it'll be some time till we can feed ourselves entirely – if ever. In the meantime we depend on the synthetic slop they dish out to us, and Dr. Lemieux and Dr. Phelps say it isn't adequate. Wrong balance of amino acids, vitamin deficiencies, and so on.'

'I'll see what I can do, Captain. At least I know where

they've stockpiled our stuff. But I don't know if I can get them to listen to me.'

'You've got to, boy! Those damned walking eels are trying to take care of us, I suppose. But it doesn't seem to occur to them that we're trying to communicate. When I think of how—' He broke off. 'We're just curiosities to them. Zoo animals.'

Jameson's gaze strayed to the branching transparent pipes overhead. There were a few shadowy six-legged shapes moving through them. 'I know what you mean, Captain,' he said.

'Dammit, they *know* we're intelligent beings!'

'We know porpoises are intelligent beings, Captain. Known it for fifty years. That doesn't stop us from putting them in aquariums.'

'Or killing them when they get in the way of our fishing remotes,' Janet Lemieux put in.

Boyle had command of himself again. Jameson was pleased to see the Old Man's spine straighten. 'Did you see any spacesuits, Tod?' the captain said.

Jameson was startled. 'Captain, you're not thinking about an escape?'

'It's my responsibility to think about it, Commander. Captain Hsieh and I have talked it over. We're keeping our options open.'

'Captain, what if we get out of our cage, even out of this zoo enclosure? It'd be like those porpoises getting out of their tanks. In an inland aquarium at that! Where do we go?'

'Our ship has to be parked somewhere nearby. Some of the crew members regained consciousness soon enough to see the Cygnans pushing it along behind us.'

'Captain, I saw the ship.'

'You *saw*—' Boyle swallowed, then went on more quietly. 'You saw the ship? What kind of shape is it in?'

'I don't know what the interior's like, Captain. I didn't see any evidence that they'd ripped out any essential equipment. Just carted away some of the loose stuff. I'd guess that the power plant and the controls are intact ... and maybe even enough frozen seed stock in hydroponics to get an air plant going again. The outside of the ship's okay, though. The missile racks are still in place, if that's any indication – they hadn't even gone near them. And the pod for the Callisto lander is intact. I suppose it could be used to nudge—'

'I beg your pardon, Commander,' a voice said. Jameson turned to see People's Deputy Commander Yao Hu-fang emerging from the knot of Chinese. The bomb-crew officer was a lean, ascetic man who had managed to keep his beard plucked and his head closely cropped despite his incarceration. He'd donated his shirt, but retained a cotton singlet with a huge puckered ridge that indicated that he'd somehow contrived to darn the frayed edges of a hole together.

'Yes, Comrade,' Jameson said politely.

'Did I hear you say that the nuclear missiles are intact?'

'They seem to be, but I hope ... There's nothing we could do with them except annoy the Cygnans ... Oh, I see what you're getting at! You think we might be able to use the propulsive units to manoeuvre the ship if we have to.'

'Perhaps.'

Boyle broke in briskly. 'Well, we can talk about all that later. The first step is to inject some morale into the crew, get them properly fed and cleaned up, whip things into shape around here. We're human beings, not animals. I don't know if we can ever be entirely self-supporting, even with our hamsters and fish and vegetables, but we're damn well going to control our own destiny to the extent we're able.'

Then everybody was crowding around Jameson, asking breathless questions about his sojourn with the Cygnans, clapping him on the shoulder, welcoming him, while Maggie snuggled up to him. Even the Chinese broke through their reserve and, forgetting ideology, pestered him with questions.

The kitten, Mao, was popular with both factions. He was passed from hand to hand, fussed over, coaxed to eat titbits that had been saved from human rations. Jameson got a lump in his throat when he saw how pathetically starved eveyone was for this little furry link with Earth and the human race. He couldn't help thinking of the Jovians, swimming forlornly in their tank of liquid hydrogen in the next exhibition hall.

The normally standoffish Klein surprised Jameson by making an awkward effort to be sociable. Jameson, a little ashamed of his dislike of the man, did his best to answer Klein's persistent questions about the sights he'd seen through the walls of the travel tube leading down the ship's arm, the layout of the zoo and the surrounding Cygnan country, and the like.

Klein still looked fit, compared to most of the crew; he'd made an effort to take care of himself. His sleek seal's head was combed and plastered down, his sloping shoulders and thick upper arms showed knots of hard muscle, his shorts were mended and looked pressed.

'You mean you were in the place where those snakes *live*, Commander?' Klein was saying. 'When they went to get those nervous system guns of theirs—'

He was interrupted by Mike Berry, who wanted to hear Jameson's theory about the three-armed design of the Cygnan vessels.

'Technology follows morphology,' Mike said sententiously. 'But if their designs got frozen all those thousands of years ago, they must have a frozen society, too. Maybe they're not all that intelligent. Just got the jump on us, that's all. Take this drive of theirs that squirts them around at close to the speed of light, for example. Maybe it's not all that far beyond us. Take an ordinary photon. Like the ones that are letting you see how sexy Maggie is. Now, you pump it full of energy – a billion times as much. Know what happens? That proletarian photon of yours takes on airs. It starts to behave like a hadron. It thinks it's a massive particle like a proton. Now you generate a beam of high-energy photons—'

'Now wait a minute, Mike,' his assistant, Quentin, interrupted, his peach-fuzz face alight with combat. 'First tell the man about vector mesons with zero strangeness. Yeah, I'm talking about the rho. You measure those two pions . . .'

Jameson left them babbling at each other and elbowed his way through the crowds with Maggie in tow. He was stopped by Dmitri.

'How did it feel to have a team of alien biologists study you, Tod?' Dmitri said. 'God, I wish it had been me! What an opportunity! The specimen studying them back! I can't get a close look at them through those tubes, and when they feed us they make us keep back. Look, you've got to sit down with me and tell me everything you saw.'

'They weren't biologists, Dmitri,' Jameson said. 'Just zookeepers. They brought me in the staff veterinarians to make sure they kept me healthy . . . probably used my own tissue cultures to treat the rest of you and get a line on synthesizing human food. That's their job. But I don't think the Cygnans have any great abstract interest in human beings.'

Dmitri's face fell. 'But they've *got* to be interested in us!' he said.

Jameson took the younger man by the arm. 'Let me tell you about the Jovians,' he said.

He was able to pry himself away from Dmitri a half-hour later and look for Ruiz. The crowd had scattered by then, breaking up into smaller groups. Kiernan had some recruits working in his garden. Some of the Chinese were having a meeting, with guards posted to keep eavesdroppers away. A couple of women were washing clothes in the pool, scrubbing them against the concretelike brim. Jameson tried not to notice a few furtive couples who had retreated to more-or-less-isolated spots on the perimeter of the terraced arena; the Cygnans hadn't provided much in the way of screening materials.

He found Ruiz squatting on his heels at the base of one of the iron trees. He was contriving some sort of little square frame by lashing together four plastic strips that might have been braces ripped off a hamster cage. Beside him, Maybury was threading dried beans on cotton unravelled from her shirt.

'Ah, Commander Jameson, Mizz MacInnes. Sit down, both of you. We're just making an abacus. We've got a pen, too, and some precious scraps of paper we're hoarding. Begged shamelessly for the contents of people's pockets. *Por Dios*, what I wouldn't give for a light-pad!'

Jameson squatted down beside him. 'I wish you had one too, Doctor. I've got some orbits for you to compute.'

Ruiz put down the frame. 'You managed to find out a few things, did you?'

'Yes.'

'Did you find out where the Cygnans came from?'

'I got some information that might help you figure it out. I also think I found out how they keep from getting fried by their own X-rays while they're travelling. I'd like you to verify it.'

'All right. Let's get to it.'

'I've got something more important to tell you first.'

'More important than *that*?'

'Do you have any idea how much time has elapsed since the Cygnans picked us up?'

'A very good idea. Some of our people managed to keep their watches.'

'Do you know where Earth is in its orbit in relation to Jupiter right now?'

202

Ruiz gave him a penetrating look. 'I don't keep planetary tables in my head. But yes, I can give you a rough notion.'

'Tod, what's this all about?' Maggie said.

Jameson spoke without taking his eyes off Ruiz. 'I want Dr. Ruiz to figure out how long we've got before the Cygnans leave this system and take us with them.'

Ruiz raised his eyebrows. 'They're leaving, then?' he said.

'That's what they told me. If you'll let me have one of those scraps of paper, I can draw you a diagram of the relative positions of all the inner planets as they'll be when the Cygnans cross Earth's orbit.'

Ruiz was excited. 'Including Mercury?'

'Yes.'

Ruiz handed him a pen and a page torn from a book. It was from a pocket Bible – the first page of Genesis. 'Go ahead, Commander. Try to be as accurate as possible.'

Jameson contrived a crude compass by tying a piece of Maybury's thread to the pen. He drew the orbits as he remembered them from the Cygnan's animated diagram, translating the triangular format to circles. When he finished, Ruiz and Maybury went into a huddle. They bisected and quadrisected angles with thread and a straight edge made from the cover of the Bible. They scratched figures in the cementlike surface of the terrace. Ruiz finally raised his head.

'I can pin it down fairly close, Commander,' he said. 'I'll assume an error of no more than four degrees in your planetary positions. But Mercury's our second hand. That's only about one day's travel for Mercury. I'm also assuming that the Cygnans will stay true to form and accelerate at a constant one gravity. That's less than a day till they intersect Earth's orbit.'

'How long till they leave?' Jameson said.

'About nine days. Give or take a couple of days.'

Maggie drew her breath in sharply. Jameson didn't look at her. He turned to Maybury. The girl's face was pale and drained under a dark cap of hacked-off hair. Her eyes were huge. He could see her narrow shoulders trembling.

'Is that right?' he demanded.

She bit her lip. 'That's right. If your diagram's anywhere near right, the Cygnans expect to begin to move Jupiter out of orbit in about nine days.'

'Tod!' Maggie said urgently. 'We'd better tell Captain

Boyle right away! That leaves practically no time at all for his escape plans!'

'We're not going to tell the captain.'

'*What?*' Maggie sat suddenly erect.

'We're not telling the captain. Or anybody. Maggie, I want you to keep quiet about this.'

'But, Tod—'

'Nine days isn't time enough to do anything. A lot of people would just get hurt. Even if we got loose in the ship for a while, we couldn't go anywhere. We'd just get the Cygnans stirred up, get in their way.'

'I don't believe what I'm hearing!' she said. There was an edge of contempt in her voice. 'Maybe it *is* hopeless. But Captain Boyle says it's our duty to try to escape.'

'Under ordinary circumstances, sure. But our duty now is to the entire human race. And we're all they've got.'

Maggie shook her mop of red hair. 'Tod, what *are* you talking about?'

Ruiz shifted on his haunches. With his starved bony body and the rags around his loins, he looked like some Indian sadhu. 'He means that we've got to be sacrificial lambs.'

'Maggie,' Jameson said urgently, 'in nine days a Jupiter-sized mass is going to sail across Earth's orbit and past the Sun on its way out again. What's left of Jupiter plus the virtual mass of the probe they're using to move it. Most of the mass will still be there – they won't have used up all that much at a speed of only . . .' He floundered.

'Less than four hundred kilometres a second,' Ruiz supplied.

'They'll miss Earth itself by a wide margin both times,' Jameson continued. 'Even so, there'll be gravitational effects, but they'll be mild.'

'A slight increase in our normal earthquake activity,' Ruiz said sardonically. 'Some bad weather. No more than a few hundred thousand people killed. A fractional adjustment in Earth's orbit, of interest chiefly to astronomers and farmers.'

Jameson took Maggie by the shoulders. 'But if we do anything to delay the Cygnans – by a month, a week, maybe even a few days – they'll have to find a new exit slot. And that time, Earth might not be so lucky.'

'We're going to squeak by,' Ruiz said bleakly. 'But it might interest you to know that a difference of a month would get us brushed by Jupiter's radiation belt, among other things. Of course, at a distance like that, death by radiation would be academic. Gravitational effects would do the job – break up the crust, scour the continents with the oceans, and tumble us toward the sun.'

'If Jupiter still *has* a radiation belt,' Maybury said shyly.

'Oh, it'll still be there. There'll still be a forty-thousand-mile ball of metallic hydrogen inside to generate a magnetic field. And the wind from the Sun will be a lot stronger.'

Jameson said, 'So you see, Maggie, we don't want to precipitate anything. Like it or not, we leave with the Cygnans.' He gave her a lopsided grin. 'We'll have plenty of time later to think about how to take over the ship, all eighty or ninety of us.'

She shook off his grip. 'Maybe you're right,' she said. 'But it's not up to the two of you to make that kind of decision. Captain Boyle's in charge.'

'And Captain Hsieh,' he reminded her.

She flushed. 'And we ought to put it in *his* hands.'

Jameson was losing patience with Maggie. He'd had a lot of practice at it on Earth and during the trip out. 'I thought you were the one who was always lecturing me about being a good little Guvie robot, kowtowing to authority Maybe you got through to me, Maggie This is too important to take chances with. Dr. Ruiz and I are taking the responsibility.'

Maggie's manner softened. 'All right,' she said. 'But Boyle's not one of those brainless government stonewallahs. Maybe he's all spit and polish, but he's human. You can trust him.'

'I trust him. I trusted him with my life. But I'm not going to lay this one in his lap.'

'Tod—'

'There are too many crazies in the command structure. Did you hear what Yao asked me about the nukes? My God, what if they got it into their heads to try to take some kind of action against the Cygnans? They couldn't succeed, of course, but they might get the Cygnans annoyed with Homo sapiens. One little fly-by with that drive of theirs on, and they could cook the whole Earth down to the bottom of the lithosphere.'

Ruiz said, 'If they succeed in getting one of their bombs off, it would be worse. They couldn't destroy a whole ship, of course – it's thirty miles between components. But they could kill a couple of million Cygnans and damage one of the ships. It would take them months to repair damage, transfer population. Delay the Cygnans' departure.' He shrugged. 'Good-bye Earth.'

'So you see, Maggie,' Jameson said, 'it's up to us.'

'No,' Ruiz said. He looked straight at Maggie. 'It's up to Mizz MacInnes.'

Maggie bit her lip. 'I can't help thinking about all these people.' She waved a thin arm at the scattered figures on the artificial landscape. 'Condemned to spend the rest of their lives as exhibits in a . . . a menagerie. Without even a chance to have any say about it.'

'Think about fourteen billion people on Earth without any say in it, M-Maggie,' Maybury said in a very small voice.

Maggie was silent. 'We're being very arrogant about all this, aren't we,' she said finally.

'Yes,' said Jameson.

She gave him one of the blinding smiles that made him love her. 'God help the four of us if our cagemates ever find out,' she said.


After the Cygnans turned the sky off, Jameson and Maggie lay side by side on their strawlike bedding for a long time without speaking, holding hands across the intervening space but otherwise not touching. They were a little apart from the others, in a shallow angle where one of the terrace shelves bent around the outer wall of the enclosure. The people who were still moving around tacitly gave them a wide berth, as they did all the other scattered couples. It was dim but not dark, with a pale luminescence that was a fair imitation of starlight. The Cygnans had instituted a terrestrial day-night cycle here. Some hundred yards away, somebody had built a small fire, probably with dried vines, and there was a small group around it softly singing folk songs. Somewhere in the dimness Jameson heard a woman moan as if in pain.

'Some of them are pretty shameless about it,' Maggie said. 'Klein and that Smitty girl from the bomb crew. As soon as the lights are out – bang! Ugh, disgusting! I'll say this for your friend Ruiz and his little assistant – nobody's ever caught them at it.'

'Maggie!'

'All right, I'm a cat. But I hope you can persuade the Cygnans to let us have our birth-control pills. We're starting to have pregnancies. Four so far.'

'I know. I saw Liz Becque.'

'Oh, that. That one got started in the ship. The others don't show yet. Want to know who they are?'

'No.'

She squeezed his hand. 'I know, Tod. Life in the zoo's going to be hard enough. When you talk to the Cygnans, tell them humans need privacy.'


## CHAPTER TWENTY-THREE

Three days passed before Jameson managed to talk to his keepers.

The first morning, in the artificial dawn before the human section of the zoo opened up to Cygnan visitors, the steaming basins of slop were wheeled in by Augie and an unfamiliar Cygnan who limped along tripod-fashion on what looked like a half-regenerated leg. Augie held the silent ring of humans at bay with a wide-mouthed neural gun while the crippled Cygnan unloaded. When they finished, they backed off warily and locked the barred gate after them. Jameson, in the fore-front of the crowd, a space cleared around him, warbled his fractured Cygnan in vain. Augie didn't appear to notice that he was trying to communicate. Jameson wondered if Augie could even tell him apart from the other humans.

'Nice try, Commander,' Captain Boyle said. 'Don't get discouraged. We'll have another chance later.'

Jameson got in line with the rest while the distribution committee, supervised by Liz Becque and her Chinese counter-part, ladled the stuff out. When it was his turn, Liz said cheerfully: 'There'll be an ounce of fish with supper tonight. Kiernan says there's enough to go around. If the Cygnans give you access to our stores, see if you can bring back some spices, will you? And some of the canned fruit.'

The next day went no better. Augie was absent. The lame Cygnan assisting Triad seemed preoccupied. Jameson whistled and gestured in vain. Finally he took a chance and moved forward a few steps. The lame Cygnan shrilled a warning. Triad swivelled a serpentine head around, the three eye polyps around her mouth pointed in his direction. Encour-aged, he took another few steps. The next thing he knew was the agony of sensory dissociation. When things swam back into focus, the Cygnans were gone. Boyle and Gifford were helping him to his feet. He was shaking with reaction and with a residual jangle of the nerves. He felt like an old man. Several other people who had been too close to him had been caught by the modulated field generated by the crippled Cygnan's weapon. Jameson wasn't too popular with them the rest of the day.

The third day, Triad and Tetrachord served the rations together. They both wore aprons. Jameson revised his assessment of them. They weren't even the head zookeepers, just the ones in charge of the sector that included humans and humanoids and Jovians and other creatures the Cygnans lumped together. They had Augie for an assistant, but they had a help problem.

Jameson whistled for their attention. Surprisingly, he got it at once. They whistled a few meaningless phrases back at him and went about their business. Jameson persisted. He repeated over and over again that he wanted to talk. The Cygnans had an argument. Triad won, and the next thing Jameson knew, they were motioning him away from the other humans.

As he passed through the gate, a cheer went up from the crowd. He could hear jolly voices behind him.

'Hey, Commander, bring back some booze if you can ...'

'How about a load of frozen steaks?'

'Don't forget toilet paper ...'

Back in the Cygnans' cluttered quarters, Jameson was made to wait in the centre of the floor while they sent the lame assistant out for the Moog. The place seemed more disorganized than last time. It was stuffy, and there was a strange sour odour hanging in the air.

Jameson looked at his keepers hanging from their perches. Tetrachord seemed sluggish. The parasite dug into his belly was more bloated, like an engorged tick. Triad didn't look too well either. She kept twitching her budlike tail nervously. Were the Cygnans sick?

The Moog was brought in by a couple of straining Cygnan labourers who dumped it on the floor and left, giving Jameson a wide berth. Jameson went eagerly to it. He opened the telescoping legs and turned on the power supply. The instrument looked battered. Some of the keys weren't working, and the power was low.

It took fifteen minutes of effort to make the Cygnans understand. He told them that the health of the humans depended on their having access to food supplements till they got a garden growing in the enclosure. He clinched it by saying that with a few human artifacts to work with, they could give zoo visitors a more approximate view of terran life.

When they returned Jameson to the enclosure, a reception committee was waiting. Boyle said, 'Well?'

Jameson looked at the ring of faces: Boyle, Hsieh, Kay Thorwald, Tu Jue-chen. Beyond, a ragged assortment of men and women were straining to hear.

'I can bring two people with me to load up. They can't spare the personnel. The Cygnans will check each item. Nothing that can be used as a weapon or for escape attempts, nothing dangerous to the ecology of the spaceship, like yeasts or algae. We get food, clothing, limited building materials, some personal items. They pretty well stripped the ship.'

Tu Jue-chen sucked an invisible lemon. 'Two people – no good.'

'One Chinese, one American,' Boyle said.

'With Jameson, two Americans. Must have two Chinese.'

Jameson said, 'They won't let me take three people. They were clear about that. And we'd better get moving before they change their mind. I don't know how many trips we'll be allowed.'

'Two Chinese,' Tu Jue-chen insisted.

Jameson left her arguing with Boyle and went to eat the breakfast that Liz Becque had saved for him. Liz hovered over him while he was eating it. She had a list of foodstuffs to give him. She saw him looking at her belly.

'Two months to go, Tod,' she said ruefully. 'Omar and I were careless. Then I kept it a secret until it was too late for one of Doc Brough's retrogenesis pills. God, I wanted that child! I knew it would be the end of my career in the Space Resources Agency, but I didn't care! Now it's going to be the first baby born in a Cygnan zoo.'

'Born among the stars, Liz,' Jameson said. 'We've got a human society going in this starship. Ninety of us, with our own personal ecology. Neolithic man got started in commun-

209

ities far smaller than that. There's eternity ahead of us. Anything can happen.'

Liz gave him a brave smile. 'A primitive tribe, are we? *Homo dum anima* ...'

He looked at her blankly. 'Dumb animals? Now, Liz ...'

'It's a stupid pun. A Latin proverb: *Dum anima est, spes esse* ... while there's life, there's hope.' Abruptly she burst into tears and walked away.

Boyle was climbing down the grey steps toward him, Kay and the two Chinese following. They had Klein and Chia Lan-ying, the Chinese stores exec, in tow.

'Here's your two porters, Commander,' Boyle said. 'You'd better get moving.'

Jameson looked doubtfully at Chia Lan-ying. She was a lovely thing, with rosy cheeks and huge eyes almost hidden by dense bangs. She looked tiny and frail next to Klein.

'Maybe you'd want to send comrade Yeh or one of the men,' he said. 'We want to move stuff as fast as possible.'

Tu Jue-chen drew her simian brow into a network of angry Vs and said, 'You will not fool me. Comrade Chia is in charge of supplies.'

Jameson sighed and gave it up.

Chia proved to be a deft and efficient worker, darting through the mouldering piles of goods and finding useful items and helping Klein and Jameson load them on the circular dolly with three ball-bearing wheels that the Cygnans had provided. Jameson had to admit that she was a better choice than Yeh; muscles weren't that important in the low gravity anyway.

Klein tried his patience, though. He kept goofing off to prowl through the scattered stuff from the cabins when he was supposed to be helping Jameson wrestle the heavy stuff like food lockers and fish tanks onto the dolly. Jameson was about to say something when he saw Klein stiffen, then pounce on something in one of the jumbled piles.

'My duffle,' he said sullenly when Jameson came up behind him. 'And some of my other stuff.'

'Show it to the Cygnans before you load it,' Jameson said. He wasn't going to make an issue about Klein's personal possessions; maybe the man would get down to work now that he had found them. 'We can't take a chance on trying to sneak contraband past them.'

He'd already caught Klein attempting to pocket somebody's jack-knife. The Cygnans frowned on anything that might be used as a weapon, though Jameson had gained a dispensation for safety razors when he explained their use.

'Just some clothes and toilet articles,' Klein said, his sallow face closed.

Jameson saw brushes, a shaving kit, Klein's heavy gum-soled boots, some crumpled garments, a pocket chess set, some fancy bottles. He gestured at a silver flask.

'All the liquor goes into the common store,' he said.

'Just aftershave lotion,' Klein said. He unscrewed the cap. 'Here, take a sniff.'

'That's not necessary,' Jameson began, but Klein was already holding the flask under his nose. 'Okay, come on, let's get those blankets loaded.'

A cheer went up every time they pushed a loaded dolly through the gate. There were lots of willing hands to help them unload and send them back again. They worked steadily for almost two hours before the Cygnans put a stop to it.

Visiting hours were about to begin.


There was a celebration that night after the sky went dark and the observation tubes had emptied of their flitting six-legged shapes. Boyle and Hsieh had agreed that some of the liquor and joints could be doled out for a party. They could hardly have stopped it. A boost in morale was badly needed.

Jameson sat with his back against a slab of terrace, his belly comfortably full of the meal Liz Becque and the Chinese nutritionist had served up from the precious store of packaged foodstuffs he'd brought back. It had been a brilliant approximation of a *man han* feast, complete with green noodles pressed from Cygnan mash. There had been reconstituted beer and wine, and a joint for every five people, and there was a great tub of punch contrived from fruit-juice concentrates and five squandered gallons of grain alcohol. It would be back to synthetic rations tomorrow, Jameson knew, but for now everybody was happy.

Maggie's head stirred on his shoulder. 'Look at them,' she said lazily. 'I wonder if they'd be having such a good time if they knew the Cygnans were going to start moving Jupiter in six days.'

Jameson looked around uneasily, but nobody was within earshot.

'I know,' Maggie said. 'It's our guilty little secret.'

'Let 'em be happy while they can,' he said, squeezing her hand.

In the dilute silver light, the great terraced bowl of the enclosure had lost its drabness. He could see the pale outlined figures standing around or sprawled in conversational groups, Chinese and Americans mingling. Over by the bar, a tank cover on trestles, Liz and Chia were ladling out the punch. Behind a subdued babble of voices there was the dreadful wail of a harmonica and the easy accompaniment of the guitar he'd managed to bring back for Mike Berry. Across, on the upper slope, he saw an unsteady couple heading toward a makeshift pup tent devised from a sheet and cordage, early as it still was. A number of such improvised privacy screens had been set up throughout the enclosure since they had brought back bedding.

Ruiz was holding forth a couple of levels down. He'd been giving an informal briefing to Boyle and Hsieh of what he'd deduced since Jameson had found him a lightpad with stored mathematical tables and astronomical data. A small crowd had grown around him. It now numbered about twenty.

'Hi, Tod, can you come over here for a minute?' They were waving for him.

Jameson groaned and got to his feet. He'd been through it all a dozen times already.

'Give the man a drink.' Somebody put a cup of warm beer into his hand. There was a friendly thump on his back as he pushed his way through the crowd, dragging Maggie.

'Is Dr. Ruiz kidding, Tod? Is this really what those walking worms showed you?'

Ruiz's lightpad was passed hand to hand until it reached Jameson. A glowing blue diagram had been scratched on its obsidian surface.

Jameson studied the sketch. At the centre was a circle with a narrow ellipse around it, like a sketch of Saturn and its rings seen almost head on. It was the Jovian planet at the centre of the Cygnans' travel arrangements, with a representation of the orbit of the robot probe that siphoned off hydrogen and turned it into kinetic energy. The Jovian's battle-scarred moon was sketched in directly above the Jovian-probe system. Ruiz had drawn a lopsided circle to indicate its orbit. Below the moon, between the moon and the Jovian, was a circle of five small dots representing the Cygnan spaceships rotating around *their* common centre of gravity. Their common orbit around the moon was indicated by an oval outline.

'That's about it,' he said.

'Run through it again, Doc,' somebody said.

'All right,' Ruiz said good-naturedly. 'Hold that up, Commander, so everybody can see. First we have the robot in a powered orbit around the gas giant. It's travelling at very nearly the speed of light, using up the planet's mass without having to accelerate it, until its own Einsteinian mass outweighs what's left of the planet.'

'Wait a minute, Doc!' a boisterous voice said. 'The centrifugal force would be tremendous!'

'You weren't listening, Gifford. I said a *powered* orbit.'

'Yeah, but did you figure out the centrifugal force?'

'It doesn't matter,' Ruiz said with rare patience. '*Whatever* percentage of the total kinetic energy is needed to maintain a tight circle is progressively diverted to a thrust perpendicular to the orbit. The Cygnans aren't concerned with efficiency. They've got a whole planet to use up. By the same token, a percentage of the total kinetic energy is used to provide a vector, so the Cygnans can get the whole system moving in whatever direction they want.'

Mike Berry had stopped playing the guitar and had moved into the circle. 'That's right,' he said. 'All it means is that the Cygnans strip their Jovian gas tank of mass faster – or longer – before they can move what's left.'

'Yeah,' somebody gibed. 'Shut up, Giff!'

Ruiz straightened creakily. Like most of the others, he was wearing one of the crisp new uniforms Jameson had retrieved that morning, but it hung loosely on his emaciated frame.

'If we've got that settled,' Ruiz said, 'would you flip the store-and-recall button for us, Commander? Keep doing it. Thank you.'

Jameson watched the pictures change on the black surface. Ruiz had painstakingly drawn a four-step animated diagram showing the multiple orbits. The moon jumped in its circle around the Jovian planet, moving counterclockwise. The rosette of dots jumped in its egg-shaped orbit around the moon, moving clockwise.

'The orbit of the ships around the moon has the same period as the moon's orbit around the planet,' Ruiz went on. 'Doubtless the ships' orbits are continuously adjusted to keep them synchronized as the planet shrinks and the moon's orbit changes. But as you can see, the ships are *always* sheltered from the radiation caused by collision with interstellar hydrogen.'

'Beautiful, beautiful,' Mike murmured.

'Commander Jameson thinks – and I agree with him – that a significant portion of that impacting hydrogen also becomes grist for the Cygnans' mill. After all, it's already been ionized. It becomes an energy bonus to partially offset the inefficiency inherent in the Cygnan method of travel.'

'Can I quit?' Jameson said. 'My thumb's getting tired.' He passed the lightpad back to Ruiz.

'It seems kinda complicated,' the Giff said, being a bad boy again.

'It wasn't complicated for the Cygnans,' Ruiz said. 'Don't forget, they started with the components of the system already in place. That moon they use for a shield was the world they evolved on . . . I wonder how they feel about travelling with its corpse. The gas giant they used for fuel was the primary that their world revolved around. It would have been natural for them to start building their fleet in orbit around their world. They had a whole population to transfer, a shipboard ecology to establish, a technology to develop. It might have taken millennia. They had the time. Perhaps they didn't develop the technology for that Einsteinian siphon of theirs until the work was well under way. They might not have travelled at relativistic speeds for the first few centuries, while they completed the shakedown for those synchronized orbits. It wouldn't have happened all at once.'

Jameson was the first to pick up on it. 'You said . . . they had the time. What do you mean?'

Ruiz was fiddling with his lightpad. He had more of his day's work stored there. He looked up, almost absently.

'One of their suns was going to go supernova. And they had half a million years to get ready for it.'

The crowd around Ruiz had grown. Word had gotten about that something lively was going on. Jameson could see Liz

Becque nestled against Omar, her arm around his thick waist, her post at the punchbowl deserted. Even Klein had joined the group. He was at the fringes of the crowd, his knotted arms folded, standing next to Yeh and Chia, so intent on the discussion that he'd forgotten his aversion to his Chinese shipmates.

'The Cygnans are the children of a binary system that now consists of a black hole and a blue super-giant,' Ruiz said. 'They spent twenty thousand years watching one of their suns swallow the other.'

Beside Ruiz, Captain Boyle nodded gravely. 'We can begin to understand something about the Cygnans' motives now. We knew that they came from the *direction* of the X-ray source known as Cygnus X-1, about ten thousand light-years away. What Commander Jameson managed to see on the Cygnan computer display confirmed that it was their *origin*, incredible as that seems.'

Mike Berry was itchy with questions. 'Twenty thousand years. That's longer than all human history. You sure of that figure?'

Ruiz swung his narrow beak toward him. 'We can calculate the timetable for the evolution of an X-ray binary system from the mass of its components. And we get that from their dynamical behaviour.'

Jameson spoke up. 'The Cygnan commentary got eloquent about a "Great Mother" that swallows her . . . not "children" . . . maybe something like "little brother". I assumed it had something to do with eclipses in a double-star system. I saw some spectacular ones.'

'It was more literal than that,' Ruiz said. 'One of their suns *was* swallowing the other. And the mass exchange took place fast enough to be noticeable over the generations. It must have been a key part of the Cygnan race consciousness since they first crawled out of the ooze and became civilized beings.'

Liz Becque shuddered and drew closer to Omar. 'You mean they actually would have *seen* one of their suns getting bigger and the other getting smaller?'

'As their suns evolved, yes.'

'Think of it!' Dmitri blurted. 'To live under such a sky! When you think of the burden of myth and theology we humans have invented from our own simple sunrises and sunsets and seasons . . .'

'The myths would have turned into scientific knowledge,'

215

Ruiz said dryly. 'When they got to the point where they knew what we know about close binaries and mass exchange, they would have known exactly what the fate of their suns would be. And exactly when it would happen.'

Dimitri sucked in his breath. 'A race spending its entire history with the foreknowledge of doom – first as myth, then as certain knowledge.'

Jameson squeezed Maggie's hand for comfort. It was no wonder that the Cygnans had no empathy left over for other life forms.

Out of a babble of voices, someone asked: 'The black hole swallows the supergiant, is that it?'

'No,' Ruiz said. 'It's the other way around – at first. And they hadn't got to be a black hole and a blue supergiant yet. You start with two ordinary, healthy stars. But they're big. That's important. One is about twenty solar masses, the other about six.'

He sketched two circles in the air. Such was the force of Ruiz's personality that Jameson could imagine that he saw them hanging there.

'They're in a close binary system. Very close. They circle each other in only four and a half days. There's a gas giant farther out, in their common ecosphere.' He sketched another imaginary circle. 'It's many times bigger than Jupiter, but not quite big enough to have been kindled into a star. It's got its own family of satellites. One of them's the Cygnan home world. It's about the size of Mercury.'

'The smaller of the two bodies now in orbit around Jupiter!' Maggie said brightly.

Ruiz gave her a hooded look. 'It's very likely,' he said. 'They had to kill their world to escape a murderous sun. I wouldn't be surprised if they had a sentimental attachment to the coffin.'

'Wait a minute,' Mike Berry objected. 'The Cygnans boosted at one gravity. Doesn't that imply that they evolved on an Earth-size planet?'

Unexpectedly, it was Dmitri who came to Ruiz's rescue. 'Takes only a year to boost up or down from light speed at one g,' he pointed out. 'The Cygnans could take that easily, with their body structures – six legs, low profile, no rigid bones. Besides, they're spinning this ship at one third g now.'

Ruiz inclined his head in acknowledgment.

'You were telling us about the timetable for the evolution of an X-ray binary system,' Jameson prompted.

'Just so,' Ruiz said. 'All right. We start with two healthy stars. Big stars burn out quicker. Right? So the twenty-sol star uses up its hydrogen first. It becomes a supergiant, hundreds of times larger than our own Sun. It's a helium star now ... '

'Without wiping out all life in the system, Cygnans included?' Gifford said incredulously.

'It's part of a close binary system,' Ruiz said. 'It can only expand to the limits of its Roche lobe.'

'That's why the big star looked pear-shaped!' Jameson said.

'Correct, Commander. When the star overflows its Roche lobe, the surplus mass is transferred to the companion star. The mass exchange takes only about twenty thousand years. Perhaps less. When it's finished, the twenty-sol star is down to less than six solar masses. The six-sol star has grown to somewhat more than twenty. It adds up to about the same.'

'So their joint ecosphere isn't affected,' Dmitri put in. 'The Cygnans survive.'

'They survive, yes,' Ruiz said. 'But they'd have had a difficult twenty thousand years. Helium stars burn *hot*. The Cygnans must already have started thinking about moving from the neighbourhood. They knew that worse was to come.'

'The supernova?'

'Yes. The star that ate its companion's mass is in good shape. It has a new lease of life. It can burn its stolen hydrogen for another six million years. But the other star is doomed. It can burn its helium only for about half a million years. Then the carbon core explodes.'

'So the Cygnans had half a million years' warning?' Mike Berry said.

'That's right. But evidently they didn't wait around that long. It's not very healthy to be in the vicinity of a supernova. From what Commander Jameson observed, it looks as if the Cygnans mobilized their society and got out within the first few thousand years.'

Dmitri was trembling with excitement. 'But Jameson *saw* the supernova explosion! The Cygnans left a few thousand years after the mass exchange, then kept a watch on the stars they'd left.'

'Correct, Mr. Galkin.' Ruiz looked as if he was enjoying himself.

'But – but that means that the Cygnans have been evolving in an artificial enviroment for *half a million years*!'

There was a rush of excited voices. Ruiz waited it out. He held up a hand, and the noise died down.

'It took longer than that,' Ruiz said. 'The Cygnans have been travelling for six million years.'

## CHAPTER TWENTY-FOUR

There was a commotion within the crowd, and Tu Jue-chen came pushing her way through. They parted to make way for her, the Americans with somewhat more alacrity than the Chinese. She stood panting on the step below Ruiz and the ship's officers, shaking a liver-spotted fist at him.

'You are lie!' she shrilled. 'You are lie!'

Beside Jameson, Maggie whispered, 'What's this all about?'

'I don't know,' Jameson said. 'She's got some ideological bee in her bonnet.'

Ruiz's expression was absolutely correct. 'Why do you say that, Comrade Tu?' he said.

She showed her horse's teeth. 'Because,' she said triumphantly, 'after six million years they would be socialists!'

Ruiz appeared to ponder the matter. 'How do you know they're not?' he said finally.

'No!' she spat. 'They are degenerate society!'

'I should think so,' Ruiz said, 'after six million years in their circumstances.'

'Six million years is impossible!' Tu insisted.

Maggie nudged Jameson. 'I don't follow her logic. Either they've been around long enough to become degenerate, or they've been around long enough to be socialists.'

'Don't bother about the logic, Maggie,' Jameson said. 'It's just her way of getting across to the troops that the Cygnans are no longer their socialist buddies from the stars. We're having a change of line.'

'But why?'

'Comrades don't lock the chosen up in a cage. They can't communicate with the Cygnans, and they know it now.' He frowned. 'I wonder if they're planning some kind of action.'

'They are not travel for six million years,' Tu was screaming. 'You tell them, Comrade Chu!'

The Chinese astronomer had been standing off to one side, going over figures on the lightpad with Maybury. He stirred uneasily and said: 'You see, Comrade Tu, the interval of time—'

'Tell them, tell them!'

Dr. Chu looked unhappy. 'Of course there is always the possibility of error in Dr. Ruiz's computations, but—'

Unexpectedly, Captain Hsieh broke in. His round face was stern, his short stocky body stretched to full height. 'We must listen to Dr. Ruiz,' he said. 'He has learned an important thing about the *hsing-ch'ung*.' The word he'd chosen meant literally, 'star-worms'. 'We must try to understand, so that we may act correctly.'

'What's happening?' Maggie whispered.

Jameson said, 'There's some kind of shift in power going on. We're a long way from New Peking. I think Captain Hsieh and his supporters have decided they're never going to see it again.'

People's Deputy Commander Yao Hu-fang spoke out from the crowd. 'Go ahead, Dr. Ruiz. We would like to hear you.'

Ruiz nodded at him. He waited until the tumult died down. Tu Jue-chen wormed her way through the milling crowd and went off to sulk.

'Comrade Tu is right, in a sense,' Ruiz said, watching her go. 'The Cygnans haven't been *travelling* six million years. They *left* six million years ago.'

Dr. Chu put down the lightpad, took a nervous glance at Captain Hsieh for reassurance, and said: 'We can be sure about the figures. You see, after the supernova explosion it would have taken the system another six million years to become an X-ray source. The X-ray stage is brief. It could not last more than fifty thousand years. But we know that Cygnus X-1 is an X-ray source *now*!'

'Or *has* been within the last ten thousand years.' Ruiz said.

'Of course,' Chu said apologetically. 'It is ten thousand light-years away.'

'Go on, Dr. Chu,' Ruiz said. 'You're doing fine.'

'When the helium star exploded, its remnant collapsed. It became a black hole. Cygnus X-1, in fact, was the first black hole to be positively identified, back in the twentieth century. Now, the black hole continued to circle its companion – waiting, as Dr. Ruiz might say, for a chance to take back its stolen mass.

'It must wait for six million years, till its companion burns up its ill-gotten hydrogen and becomes a blue supergiant. Blue supergiants are almost always associated with such X-ray sources. A blue supergiant some – oh, twenty times larger than the sun will begin to lose mass in the form of a solar wind, at the rate of about a millionth of a solar mass per year. Some of the mass falls back into the black hole. It disappears from the universe forever. But during that fall to infinity, the gas accelerates to tremendous speed, and is heated to a temperature of millions of degrees Kelvin. It is this envelope of falling gas that generates X-rays. For a brief period – not more than fifty thousand years – it will shed X-rays burning with the radiance of ten thousand suns.'

Chu stopped and mopped his brow. His eyes roved toward Hsieh, then to the Peoples' Deputy Commander.

'After that,' Ruiz said, 'the newly formed blue supergiant overflows *its* Roche lobe and pours its mass down the black hole at a rate that extinguishes it as an X-ray source.'

Mike Berry was facing the two astronomers, hands on hips. 'So you say our six-legged friends left home six million years ago, before all this happened?'

'There's no doubt of it,' Ruiz said.

'Then tell me this – if Cygnus X-1 is ten thousand light-years away, and they've been travelling at the speed of light, *where have they been all this time?*'

Ruiz looked pleased at the question.

'That's obvious,' he said. 'Making stops.'

Mike was a very bright person. He chewed it over a few moments, then said: 'Dr. Ruiz. You've deduced a hell of a lot about our little buddies from the mass of a star and the mass of a black hole. Now this ought to give us a clue about how long—'

'It does,' Ruiz said.

Boyle got to his feet. 'Dr. Ruiz, I think—'

'Let him go on,' Hsieh said. 'Our people have a right to know.'

'You're right,' Boyle said. 'Go on, Dr. Ruiz.' He sat down.

Ruiz looked round the crowd. Almost the whole human colony was there now. In the artificial starlight their faces were a pointillist cobble of silver blobs. Here and there a firefly darted as a glowing joint was passed from hand to hand.

'The average distance between stars in our part of the galaxy is about six light-years,' he said. 'If the Cygnans travelled a more or less straight line getting here, zigzagging from star to star, they encountered sixteen or seventeen hundred of them. If they stopped to refuel at *every* star, they would have stayed for an average of three thousand six hundred years each time.' He paused. 'If they stopped at, let us say, every tenth star, each visit would have lasted some thirty-six thousand years.'

'But *why*?' Mike pushed away the joint that someone offered him. 'Tod Jameson says the Cygnans aren't *interested* in the systems they visit! They never make planetfall. Even granting that they'd have to do some robot mining from time to time, refurbish their ships, they ought to be able to travel more than six light-years on a gas giant! Once they got coasting at close to light-speed, they ought to be able to reach another *galaxy*, for God's sake, without refuelling – even with the inefficiency you mentioned before. Just shut off their robot siphon and let it career away into infinity. Make another one when they want to brake. Why waste two years out of six accelerating and braking if they're going somewhere—'

'They're not going anywhere,' Ruiz said.

'What do you mean?'

'They've forgotten. After six million years, they've forgotten. Their pattern of travel – hopping from star to star – made sense when they started out. They were looking for a new home. They didn't find one they liked soon enough. So after a few thousand years, I imagine, they got used to living in ships. They were safe in the ships. A real world might not be safe. But their pattern of travel persisted. Degenerate societies cling to old habits, just like degenerate organisms.'

'Okay,' Mike said. 'Maybe you're right. But I'm still asking why they hang around a system they're not interested in for three thousand years.'

Ruiz looked around at the dappled faces. He sighed. He turned back to Mike. 'Maybe they're getting up their courage for the next jump.'

There was a growing murmur in the crowd. Ruiz held up a hand.

'We don't know what it's like to travel between the stars,' he said. 'All that empty space must be a terrifying thing. Our own mariners in the ancient world and Middle Ages never braved the open sea, even when they knew their destination. They island-hopped, stayed within sight of land, travelled coastwise from point to point.'

'Scared? After six million years in space?' Mike said. 'Minus – how much time for time dilation? You figure it out, but even if they'd come nonstop, it couldn't have saved them more than ten thousand years.'

'That's the point exactly,' Ruiz said. 'If they'd covered the ten thousand light-years at – let's say – ninety-eight per cent of the speed of light, then time is slowed . . . hmm . . . fivefold, and they have to spend two thousand years in the empty space between the stars. Even at ninety-nine point ninety-nine per cent of light-speed, the jump takes them a hundred years. *Lifetimes* for millions of Cygnans who never get to come in out of the dark! But if they star-hop, then with a year to boost, a year to brake, hmm, a few weeks or months to cover the intervening light-years, than they never have to spend more than three years adrift. Then they spend the next three thousand years or more getting brave enough to do it again.'

A tremulous voice came out of the silver dark: Liz Becque. 'Dr. Ruiz, are you saying that we're – that the Cygnans are going to remain *here*, in *this* solar system, that long?'

Ruiz shrugged. 'There's no reason to assume anything different.'

Maggie turned quickly to Jameson. 'I thought you said—'

'*Shhh* – the old fox knows what he's doing.'

'But—'

Jameson leaned to whisper in her ear. 'Something's up with the Chinese. I don't think Ruiz believes they'll do anything precipitous, but he's taking the pressure off anyway. This buys time for the Cygnans.'

Maggie looked around, made sure no one was listening. Everybody was intent on Ruiz. 'But what he said about their stopping and staying at almost every star – that's true?'

'It has to be,' he said with an uneasy glance around. 'Either that or they parked somewhere for the whole six million years.'

Maggie wouldn't let go. She seemed agitated. She tugged at his hand. 'But you *said* they're leaving in a few days. Why is *this* solar system any different?'

Jameson said, 'Maybe the Cygnans have finally got their courage back.'

'Tod, *answer* me!'

'All right. Maybe they're afraid of people. Maybe every once in a while, when they run across a system that looks unhealthy, they grab their hydrogen planet and hightail it out of there.'

'The nuclear bombs we brought with us?'

Jameson glanced around again. 'Yeah. And whatever else the human race might dream up in the next few thousand years.'

Up on his platform, Ruiz was still talking. ' . . . So perhaps the Cygnans aren't the formidable civilization we thought they were. As Dr. Berry pointed out, even their mass conversion engine might not be beyond our own capabilities in a century or two. We're still developing. They stopped, long ago. They're beginning to look like timid, fearful creatures. But fear can be more dangerous than confidence. We mustn't forget that the Cygnans have great powers, the capacity to do great mischief. So I'd urge us all not to do anything to panic them. Earth is still in a vulnerable position.'

Maggie was nodding in agreement. 'Their orbit out of here . . . ' she began

'Maggie, shut up,' Jameson said. He gave her hand a warning squeeze. Klein was shouldering his way through the crowd, about to pass close to them. There was movement in other parts of the crowd as three or four people tried to manoeuvre themselves to the forefront to get closer to Ruiz. There was the sound of good-natured protest as people got shoved.

Ruiz had a debate going with young Dmitri Galkin. Dmitri was going on ponderously about fear and aggression in grey lag geese. 'The mechanism of redirected behaviour . . . ' he was saying.

Klein had reached the front of the crowd. With a lithe movement he vaulted the final terrace and sprang to his feet in front of Ruiz.

'That's enough talk,' Klein said. He faced the crowd. 'Everybody listen to me!'

Dmitri started forward. 'Now just a minute,' he began.

'I said shut up!' Klein said. He gave Dmitri a shove that sent him sprawling. Dmitri was saved from toppling over the edge of the step by two or three people who caught him and propped him on his feet. There was a growl from Omar Tuttle, who let go of Liz and started forward. Omar stopped in mid-stride.

Klein was standing in a little cleared space where Ruiz and the ship's officers had backed off from him. He was waving a flat, ugly object whose silhouette was unmistakable, even in the dim light. How he had obtained it was a puzzle.

It was a gun.

'All right,' Klein said. 'Everybody calmed down?'

He stood rocking on the balls of his feet, the gun held dangling at his side. He looked remote and feral, with the narrow face and the sleek ferret head and the oversize arms, meaty as thighs, sticking out of the chopped-off sleeves.

The packed throng was silent except for the whisper of shuffling feet. Nobody moved.

'Better,' Klein said. 'I'm taking command of all American personnel here under the provisions of the National Security Act and the authority vested in me by Articles 42b, 46a, and subsections C and D.' He delivered the words in a mechanical, singsong tone. 'I am officially identifying myself as a special surveillance officer of the Reliability Board, with full authority over all SRA employees for the duration of this emergency.'

'An arbee fink!' Omar spat. A murmur went through the crowd.

Klein flinched, but stood his ground. 'Full compliance with my lawful orders is enjoined on this group under penalties of the Act. I will deputize such persons as I deem suitable. I will be assisted in these endeavours by security personnel attached to the Chinese crew under treaty provisions between the United States and the People's Republic.'

Little Chia Lan-ying was making her way to Klein's side, followed by the hulking form of Yeh Fei.

'Hear me,' she said stridently. 'I am cultural officer of *She-hui pu*, the Social Affairs Department, and chief loyalty fighter here. Comrade Yeh knows this. Remember the Four Bigs! Grasp the Revolution! Obey the People!'

The Chinese contingent looked at one another uneasily and began to draw together in little groups. One of Tu Jue-chen's people nodded vigorously and shouted, 'Grasp the Revolution! Obey the People!' The cry was taken up by others.

Jameson said angrily to Maggie: 'Caffrey and Tu weren't enough. They had to send types like those to keep an eye on us!'

He started forward. Maggie grabbed his sleeve. 'Wait.'

Several more people emerged from the boundary of the crowd and formed a loose phalanx around Klein and Chia. Jameson recognized the spare, lean form of Yao Hu-fang and one of the members of his bomb crew. One of the maintenance engineers, Fiaccone, was there with some kind of pipe in his hand. Gifford took his place with the group, bouncing and clowning around, his clasped hands raised above his head like a boxer.

'The Giff?' Jameson said. 'I don't believe it!'

'He's a true-blue,' Maggie said. 'If Klein told him the government wanted him to lift both feet at once, he'd hang there in the air until he was told to come down.'

Captain Boyle stepped forward. 'Where did you get that gun?' he said gruffly to Klein.

Klein looked him over coolly. 'All right, Captain, I'll tell you,' he said. 'The chamber was inside the heel of a pair of my boots. The grip was in the other heel. The barrel was the handle of my safety razor. The spare clips were stacked in the bottom two thirds of a bottle of aftershave lotion, under a false reservoir. I was able to retrieve it this morning, thanks to Commander Jameson, along with the rest of the equipment concealed in my kit.'

Boyle stuck out a big hand. 'Give it here, mister,' he said.

Klein lifted the gun slightly, not pointing it anywhere in particular. 'It's a very compact piece of ordnance,' he said conversationally, 'barely three eighths of an inch through the grip, but it's fully automatic. It's designed for riot control. It fires a stream of explosive microflechettes, one hundred rounds to a clip. It could cut a man in half.'

'You'd have to be crazy to take a thing like that aboard a spacecraft,' Boyle rumbled. 'Hand it over.'

'Captain Boyle,' Klein said. 'You are hereby directed to render all assistance and cooperation to an authorized agent of the Reliability Board under the directive governing the conduct of officials in the employ of GovCorp.'

Boyle continued to look Klein in the eye until Klein averted his gaze slightly. Then, with a contemptuous glance at the slim, squarish weapon, he dropped his outstretched hand and stood, legs apart, with his hands clasped behind his back.

'What is it you have in mind?' Boyle said.

Klein looked around at the group clustered on the broad ledge behind Boyle: Kay Thorwald and Captain Hsieh, Ruiz and Maybury and Dr. Chu, with Mike Berry pressing forward to hear. He looked over at the silent and attentive crowd. Then he said, 'Captain, perhaps we'd better go to the far side of the enclosure with one of the Chinese representatives and discuss it there.'

'Spit it out, mister,' Boyle said. 'We're all waiting to hear.' He stood fast, solid as a rock.

Chia said, 'We will need volunteers. Go on, you say it.'

Reluctantly Klein said, 'We're going to carry out our contingency orders.'

'What are you talking about?' Boyle said.

'Major Hollis and his men are dead – in the line of duty. But Deputy Commander Yao's men are capable of carrying out the mission. It coincides with their own orders.'

'Nuke the Cygnan ships? You're insane. You'd never even make it to the air lock of this tin can we're in, let alone cross empty space to our own ship!'

'You're wrong, Captain. Loyalty Officer Chia and I have worked it out very carefully. We've reconnoitered the immediate area personally, on our outing with Commander Jameson. We've spent weeks interrogating every member of the crew as to their recollections of the layout of the enemy ship – many of them were conscious or semiconscious when they were brought in – and we've pieced together an escape route. You yourself drew such a map, if you recall. We'll want that too, by the way.'

Jameson flinched as he listened to Klein. So that was why the man had been so friendly, so inquisitive about his experiences in Cygnan territory!

Boyle growled, 'There's fifteen miles to cover – uphill – before you even get to the hub of the ship. And the area is as densely populated as Hong Kong.'

'The Cyngans don't like to travel across open spaces. There are service routes. If we encounter any of the enemy, we're armed. Captain, it's no different from crossing any other enemy territory. I was a counterguerrilla during the Baja uprising—'

'A fine piece of butchery that was,' Boyle said curtly.

'I don't like your attitude, Captain,' Klein said.

'You're not required to, Mister Klein. You were giving me the information I'll need to evaluate your plans. Get on with it.'

The encircling crowd listened neutrally to the exchange, jockeying for position. Jameson managed to force his way to the forefront, Maggie at his back. His further progress was blocked by a grinning Gifford.

'Sorry, Commander,' Gifford said. A muscular young Chinese from the Struggle Brigade was backing him up with a fist wrapped around a chunk of the cementlike terrace material.

'You're flirting with mutiny, Giff,' Jameson said.

'Nothin's happened yet,' Gifford said. 'In the meantime, why don't you just stay put.' He gave Jameson a friendly wink.

Up on the next ledge Klein was **saying**: 'I don't have to do this, Captain, but I could use your help, so I'll tell you. Our chances are reasonable. We've got weapons and we can get more. Between Chia and me, we've got a full range of electronic surveillance equipment we brought aboard as buttons, zippers, uniform tabs, and the like. We can drop spy-eyes and acoustic detectors to guard our rear, and we have subminiaturized mobile probes we can send ahead for reconnaissance.' He was holding something invisibly small out in his palm to show Boyle.

'And then?' Boyle said. 'How do you get across to our ship?'

'It's less than a hundred miles away, according to Yeh. He got a look through an outside port when they had him sequestered. We can make it on suit jets, and our suits are right outside in that warehouse section.'

'What's to keep the Cygnans from coming after us?'

Jameson heard the 'us 'and didn't like it. Was Boyle starting to take all this seriously? 'Captain,' he called out.

Boyle paid him no attention. Gifford and the Chinese strongarm made a warning gesture.

Klein waved his flat little pistol. 'We'll keep them busy with a few nuclear bombs. They won't have time to worry about us.'

Boyle shook his head authoritatively. 'We'd be sitting ducks. It would take hours to get the boron reaction going, even if our engines are still undamaged, and in the meantime – '

Chia leaned past Klein. 'We have thought of that. We will have comrade Li with us. He can use the Callisto lander to get us moving. The chemical engines will fire immediately.'

Klein nodded. 'And the automatic probes by themselves provide enough thrust to break us out of Jupiter orbit and start us coasting sunward. We checked with Gifford.'

Boyle stared at his feet for a while, his hands clasped behind his back. Finally he lifted his head. 'You seem to have thought it all out. I don't think the odds are good, but we're duty bound to escape if we can. Captain Hsieh and I will be in command, of course. I'll take your weapon. We can't order everyone to go with us – it's going to be a farfetched gamble – but I imagine a majority of the crew will elect to take the chance—'

'Hsieh will not go,' Chia hissed. 'He is a traitor. Comrade Yeh can operate ship with you.'

'Captain,' Klein said softly. 'You don't understand the situation. We can only take essential personnel. The bomb crew and a minimum number to get the ship back in operation. Any more will slow us down.'

From the crowd, Omar Tuttle shouted: 'What happens to the rest of us? Scientific personnel and the like? We stay here and get nuked with the Cygnans?'

Klein's otter head jerked around, trying to identify the speaker. 'We won't bomb this pod of the ship,' he said smoothly. 'We can cripple the ship with a low-yield bomb in drive section, placed fifteen or more miles down the shaft. With any luck you can stay alive until Earth can rescue you. In the meantime you'll all be no worse off than you are now.'

'Crud!' a peppery voice yelled. 'It'd take years to get up another Jupiter expedition. What the hell do you think the Cygnans will be doing all that time? And then what? You think the crew is going to fight a billion Cygnans hand to hand and get us out alive? We're stuck here and we'd better make the best of it!'

Klein located the voice. 'You're one of the ones who's coming with us, Kiernan. You'll be needed to reestablish a shipboard ecology.'

'The hell I am! I'm needed right here!'

'You'll shut up and obey orders!' Klein snapped. 'Or I'll have you up on Reliability Board charges when we get back!'

Kiernan started to say something, then thought better of it as Fiaccone appeared next to him with a length of pipe. People had started to edge away from Kiernan, leaving a clear space around him, Jameson noted wryly. They didn't want to get involved. Mention of the Reliability Board had done that, though Earth was half a billion miles away. You had that kind of prudence embedded in your bones when you grew up working for Gov-Corp.

Not Boyle, though. 'Mr. Kiernan has a point,' he said deliberately. 'Let's not raise any false hopes. Those who stay behind will stay for good, unless Earth gets some kind of communication going with the Cygnans.'

He turned to Klein. 'And we're not going to jeopardize their safety by initiating hostile action. I want that clearly understood. This is an escape attempt, not a military action. The decision to attack these aliens with nuclear weapons is one that can only be made on Earth. You couldn't do anything except antagonize

228

the creatures. How many missiles do you think you could get off before they retaliated? And how many missiles do you think would get to their targets when they can match velocities freehand on those broomsticks of theirs?'

'I don't know,' Klein admitted. 'But we can inflict as much damage on the enemy as possible before we leave.'

Jameson had heard enough. Before Gifford realized what he was up to, Jameson gave him a shove that bowled him over. The Chinese strongarm made a swipe with his fistful of artificial rock, but missed. In the low gravity, Jameson vaulted to the ledge and ended up standing beside Boyle.

'Captain,' he said. 'Before you go along with this, you'd better listen to what Dr. Ruiz has to say.'

'Shut up,' Klein said.

Yeh made a move toward Ruiz, but Boyle said sharply, 'Hold it right there. I think we all better hear this.'

Yeh halted and Klein lost the chance to control the situation. The crowd had started rustling again, straining to get close. Klein evidently was nervous about the impression that rough stuff might make.

'The Cygnans are going to leave this system in about six days,' Ruiz said.

There was a moment of shocked silence; then pandemonium broke out. When it died down, Mike Berry shouted, 'You told us they'd be here for over three thousand years!'

Ruiz passed a hand wearily over his eyes. 'That was the averaged figure,' he said. 'It still holds. But Earth seems to be one of the exceptions.'

'You withheld this information?' Boyle asked in a hard voice.

'Yes. I had very good reasons.'

'Captain, this was my doing,' Jameson began.

'We'll discuss that later,' Boyle said. 'You said you had reasons. Go on.'

'Discussion's ended,' Klein said, raising his little gun. 'I already know all about it.'

Ruiz looked at the gun with pointed contempt. 'How do you know?' he said. 'Have the two of you been planting your eavesdropping devices around this enclosure?'

Chia broke in breathlessly, half addressing the crowd. 'Six days, sure! Means we must hurry! No time left!'

'Shoot if you're going to,' Ruiz snapped. 'Otherwise put the silly thing down.'

'I'm giving you the benefit of the doubt for the moment, Dr. Ruiz,' Boyle said harshly, 'but don't try my patience. We're all waiting to hear your explanation.'

Ruiz took his time about it. He ran through his computations in a dry lecture-hall voice. 'So we can be reasonably certain,' he finished, 'that if the Cygnan fleet is allowed to leave on schedule, Earth will escape with no more than a bad case of the surface hiccups. But if Mr. Klein and his overzealous friends manage to delay the Cygnan departure by as much as a month, the human race stands a good chance of being seriously depleted, or entirely wiped out. In the worst case, the Earth would fall into the sun.'

'You don't know,' Boyle temporized. 'You're only guessing. There's no way of predicting how long the Cygnans might be delayed. Earth could be at the other side of its orbit.'

'The Cygnan route crosses Earth's orbit twice – on opposite sides of it. The combined strike zone adds up to at least one hundred and twenty degrees out of three hundred and sixty. *At least!* Are you a gambling man, Captain? Do you want to bet that the human race has a two-to-one chance of staying alive?'

Boyle was silent a long time. He stood in his bulldog position, his lower lip thrust out, a frown on his wide forehead.

'We're wasting time,' Klein said. 'In about six hours that overhead plumbing's going to be filled with those vermin-ridden snakes.'

Heads swivelled involuntarily to fix on the darkened tubes that twisted through the zooscape. Some of them looped down almost to ground level. They'd been pried and hammered and hacked at by some of the more belligerent younger men, but nobody had been able to do so much as scratch them.

So many people in the crowd missed Boyle's first step toward Klein. The captain's hand was extended. 'We're not going anywhere,' Boyle said in a level voice. 'That's an order. I'll take that gun now.'

Klein actually began backing away. 'Don't make waves, Captain,' he said. 'We can get along without you if we have to.'

Jameson tensed, gauging his distance from Klein, from Yeh and Chia. The others were too far away to bother about. A few yards away he could see Mike Berry stirring uneasily.

'Hand it over,' Boyle said, and lunged forward, making a grab for it.

There was a fluttering sound in the thin air, like someone riffling the pages of a book, and Boyle was suddenly writhing on the ground, his leg almost severed at the knee.

A woman screamed, and there was a general scramble among the spectators to get out of the way. Jameson, off balance, fought to stay still.

Klein swung the tiny gun around in an arc. 'Anybody else?' he said.

Boyle was still conscious, but looked as if he were going into shock. The silver-sized microflechettes had stitched across his leg, almost blowing it off. Blood spurted from the pulpy mess, black in the chalky light.

Down in the struggling throng, the voice of Janet Lemieux sounded, high, clear, and indignant. 'You get out of my way, Jack Gifford! *Move!*' In a moment she was kneeling next to the captain, taking off her blouse and making a tourniquet out of it. She looked up impatiently. 'Somebody get me my medical bag,' she ordered. *'Hurry!'* The kit had been among the priority items Jameson had managed to bring back with him that morning.

Klein and his gang had drawn into a tight, cohesive group and were edging their way from the scene along the broad apron of the terrace. They'd made a mess of it, and they knew it. People got out of their way hastily, parting to let them through. Jameson watched them go, along the rim of the stepped bowl, all the way to the opposite side, toward the entrance. He could see their forms, tiny and dim, gathered in a circle, having some kind of conference.

Maggie had found him again. She hung on to his arm. 'Tod, what's going to happen?'

'I don't know,' he said

Janet was thumbing back one of Boyle's eyelids, looking at it with a coldlight stick. She'd got Maybury to help her. The little astronomy tech was elevating a plastic bag with a tube leading down to a needle in Boyle's arm.

'Is he going to lose the leg?' Jameson said, bending over.

Janet gave him a look of tight fury. 'Probably,' she said. 'And there's no way to clone a new one for him here.'

Maybury said, her voice shaking, 'Isn't there anything you can *do*, Commander?'

Jameson shook his head. 'I could rally some of the men. We could arm ourselves with the garden tools and pipes from the hydroponics equipment. But Klein has the upper hand. We can't get near him with that automatic weapon of his. Those things have a range of a couple of hundred yards in this gravity, and aim doesn't count.'

'But you've got to stop them! They're crazy!'

Ruiz limped over and rested a hand on Maybury's shoulder. She looked up at him with quick gratitude.

'Commander Jameson's right,' Ruiz said. 'Chia has a hand-laser, too. I saw it. And the devil knows what other weapons they smuggled in here.'

People had started to drift across to the gateway to see what Klein and his friends were doing there. There was quite a respectable crowd now, keeping a wary distance, watching silently. Then there was the sound of a scuffle, and some angry shouting. The crowd started to disperse, then changed its mind and came uncertainly together again.

'Something's going on,' Jameson said to Maggie. 'I'd better . . .'

He stopped and strained to see in the dim light. Somebody was running towards him, bouncing in huge swoops in the one third gravity down the shelved bowl. As the figure drew closer he saw that it was Beth Oliver, her blond hair dishevelled and flying.

'Tod!' she panted, drawing near. 'They're taking people with them! By force! They've got Kiernan, and Kay Thorwald – they say she can handle the ship with Yeh! And Sue Jarowski!'

'I'd better see what I can do,' Jameson said. He turned and started to go. Maggie hung on to his arm, trying to drag him back.

'Tod,' she said. 'Don't go.'

He disentangled her gently. 'With Boyle out of it, and if Kay's being held, then I'm in charge. I'd better see—'

'You can't do anything,' she cried, oddly agitated for someone as usually self-assured as Maggie was. 'You said so yourself. You'll only get hurt.'

'I'll be all right,' he said, turning again.

'You don't know what Klein and that – that Chia are capable of!'

'I'm afraid I do,' he said, nodding toward where Boyle lay sprawled. Janet had the bleeding under control, and she had a rolled-up blanket under Boyle's head. Dmitri and Kiernan's opposite number. Wang, had taken over from Maybury and had set up a tripod of garden tools to hold the drip bag. The leg hung by shreds, and Janet was removing pieces of bone with a pair of tweezers.

'I'll go with you,' Mike Berry said, falling in beside him.

'All right, Mike, but keep out of trouble. Where's Ruiz? Maybe he can try and talk to Klein again.'

'He went over there a few minutes ago,' Mike said. 'Mayb's with him. You aren't going to get anywhere with that bastard, Tod. You know that type. If he blew up the world, he'd say he did it to keep America free.'

Jameson nodded grimly. He ascended the tiers of synthetic stone, past the metal trees and the random tumbled blocks the Cygnans had put there for variety. To his left a miniature waterfall was sluicing down the steps towards the murky pool at the bottom. Mike hopped along beside him, trying to keep up, bouncing too high in the low gravity and then having to take another giant step when his foot touched bottom.

As Jameson drew close, he could see people milling around uncertainly, keeping well beyond an invisible line. On the other side of the line were the people in Klein's party. Most of Yao's bomb crew were there – a score of powerfully built young men and bandy-legged girls who had armed themselves with a miscellany of slats, garden shears and trowels, and what must have been branches of the iron trees, clandestinely filed to the snapping-off point during weeks of captivity. Only one of Tu Jue-chen's Struggle Group fighters was there – the one who'd helped Gifford. The rest must have been dismissed as unreliable, despite their attempt to switch sides. Jameson's own partner, Li, was in the party, apparently voluntarily, as was Maggie's opposite number from the computer section, Jen Mei-mei. They were talking to three Chinese fusion techs.

Kay, Kiernan, and Sue were backed up against the inward-leaning wall of the zoo enclosure, guarded by Gifford and Fiaccone. Gifford was holding Kiernan, pinioning the smaller man's arms behind his back. Kiernan looked dazed, as if he'd been hit on the head. Mike's young assistant, Quentin, under no apparent restraint, was talking volubly at Sue, who averted her head, refusing to look at him.

Chia and Yao were on their knees, doing something to the lock mechanism of the massive barred door. It was an armour-plated disc, big as a wagon wheel, half buried in a slot in the metallic sill. There was a neat array of tiny electronic instruments and miniature tools spread out on a quilted jacket whose cotton stuffing oozed from a dozen slashes. Jameson made out the flickering blue glow of a CRT display no larger than a thumbnail, and then, from beneath Chia's hand on the lock, a flash of laser light. Klein was standing over them, negligently facing the crowd, the wicked little gun in his hand.

'Quent!' Mike bellowed as they approached. 'What the hell are you doing there?'

The boy broke off his recitation to Sue and turned to face Mike and Jameson. 'Jeez, Mike, I mean what was I supposed to do? Klein, he told me I *hadda* obey orders.'

Klein's sleek head quested in Mike's direction, then paused to examine Jameson. 'Thanks for bringing him over, Commander,' he said. 'It saves me from having to send someone to get him.'

'Listen, Klein,' Jameson began, fighting down anger.

'We're going to need him to activate the boron reaction. Quentin says he can't do it by himself.'

'Berry's not going. And neither are those other people.'

Klein lifted the gun and pointed it at Mike. 'He's going. Berry, get over there with the others. That's an order.'

'The hell I'm going!' Mike said.

Klein said, 'If you don't get over there in about three seconds, you'll take the consequences.'

'Yeah? When you get back to earth, tell them to come on out here and arrest me.'

'You're a traitorous son of a bitch,' Klein said tightly, 'and if I can't use you, I'm going to—'

Jameson stepped quickly between Mike and the gun.

'This has gone far enough,' he said, with as much force as he could muster. 'Klein, didn't you understand a word Dr. Ruiz said? If you interfere with the Cygnans – if you *succeed* in interfering with them – you're going to endanger the whole human species.'

Klein's voice cracked, showing the strain he must have been under. 'I've had it with you, Jameson! You and Ruiz keeping essential data from me, and then interfering – Step away from that man before I give you the whole clip right in your—'

Mike stepped from behind Jameson. 'Hold it,' he said. 'Don't get yeasty. I'm going.' He gave Jameson a ghastly grin. 'Say good-bye to our lovely hosts for me, and try to drop a line

234

now and then.' He moved over to the group huddled against the wall. Quentin immediately began haranguing him, gesturing with both hands.

There was the screech of protesting ratchets, and the huge circular lock rolled in its slot, mounting an incline. '*Wan pi te.*' Chia said, and gathered up her tools. Yao, with the help of a couple of muscular missile men, slid the great barred door open.

'Hurry,' Yao called over his shoulder. He and Chia were pushing their people through the gate into the vast empty exhibition hall outside.

Klein looked thoughtful. 'Just a minute,' he said. 'We'd better have an astronomer.'


# CHAPTER TWENTY-FIVE

'You can go straight to hell,' Ruiz said, 'if you can find the place. I don't intend to give you the slightest help.'

He stood facing Klein, his back stiff and straight and his stubbled chin thrust out, looking like an immensely dignified scarecrow. He was bad news now, and people were beginning to edge away from his vicinity.

Some of Klein's muscle, four or five husky missile men, had drifted over to fan out on either side of him, hefting their makeshift weapons. The girl, Smitty, was among them. Jameson had taken her for one of the men at first, with her broad shoulders and big frame, but now he could see her breasts like flat dinner plates under the man's undershirt she wore, solid as the meat of arm and shoulder. There was no question of Klein's leaving without *her*.

'Don't make us drag you,' Klein said. 'You could get damaged and slow us up.'

'Then get on with it and damage me,' Ruiz said. 'But I won't lift a finger to help you put Earth in jeopardy.'

Klein lifted his gun. 'I've seen your file, Ruiz,' he said, his voice rising. 'With your Reliability Index, I'm at a loss to understand why they trusted you on this mission in the first place. I'd give you summary termination right now if I felt like wasting ammunition.'

Beefy hands closed on Ruiz's arms. Smitty was behind him,

an arm crooked around his throat. Ruiz tried to scuffle with them. Klein looked around at the crowd with worried eyes.

Gifford, hauling a limp Kiernan through the gate, said, 'We don't need the old crock. Maybury does all his figuring for him anyway.'

'Leave her out of it!' Ruiz cried. He actually broke free for a moment, and then a lead pipe came down on his head. He crumpled to the ground. Smitty and one of the Chinese began methodically to kick him in the ribs.

'Stop it!' It was Maybury. She ran to Ruiz and cradled his battered head. 'Dr. Ruiz, Dr. Ruiz, say something!' Ruiz's head lolled. He was as limp as an empty pressure suit.

They dragged her off him and hustled her through the gate, her feet off the ground. Jameson knelt beside Ruiz. 'He's alive,' he said. 'Somebody go get Janet, quickly!'

Klein's troops and their prisoners filed through the opening in the gate, weighed down with their improvised weapons and bundles of supplies. Somewhere nearby, Jameson heard Liz say bitterly, 'They took practically all the food we got from the ship's stores.'

The delay with Ruiz had been a mistake for Klein. As the last couple of Chinese got through the gate, backing up and brandishing their weapons warningly at the people left inside, somebody up front piercingly yelled: '*Liu hsin, liu hsin!*'

Dmitri was shaking Jameson by the shoulder. 'An alarm,' he said. 'They must have set off some kind of alarm when they opened the door. The Cygnans are coming.'

Jameson heaved himself to his feet and ran to the gate. Ignoring the threatening gestures of the Chinese in the rear guard, he sprang to the bars and hauled himself up for a better look.

Two Cygnans were skittering down the curving corridor of the hall of bipeds. One of them was down, snake low, on all sixes, the long tubular snout aimed like an arrowhead. The other trotted on four legs like some nightmare centaur, cradling a gleaming blunderbuss in its flexible arms.

It was Tetrachord and Triad, come to put the animals back in their cages.

The neural weapon had a short range, a cone of modulated microwaves that lost its efficiency at twenty or thirty feet. But when Tetrachord fanned it over the twenty-odd people in Klein's party, the floor was going to be covered with blind,

236

writing bundles of short-circuited nerves who would be kept that way until they could be hauled back to the cage.

Klein's group split in two and scurried to opposite sides of the hall. Basic military tactics. A pair of zookeepers wouldn't be much on strategy.

Jameson clung to the bars, taking in the scene. In the cusped vestibule that formed the intersection of the narrow ends of the five major habitats, the fleeing humans had spread out in two broken arcs that bent towards each other like pincers, some fifty feet apart. No matter which angle the Cygnans approached from, the neural weapon was not going to be able to sweep the nearer half of one of the two lines.

As if realizing this, Tetrachord veered first to the right, then to the left. Triad failed to change direction fast enough, and that was what saved her.

At a distance of about ten yards, Tetrachord, still running, reared up and shouldered his blunderbuss – or, rather, deployed it with the bulb-shaped grip braced in one rubbery claw. Jameson, seeing the whole thing in the slow-motion vision of stimulated adrenals, irrelevantly admired the unbroken rhythm of the Cygnan running pattern as it shifted from four legs to three to two.

And then the creature's long flexible head disappeared in an explosion of orange gore.

Jameson caught a frozen glimpse of Klein picking himself off the floor, where he'd thrown himself for a prone shot. Then he realized that Tetrachord's headless body was still running, and he remembered that a Cygnan's brain was somewhere below the neck, a swelling of the central ganglia. He shuddered, wondering what thoughts might be going on within the blind, deaf isolation of the body. Klein was in no hurry to fire his explosive darts again; perhaps he enjoyed watching the creature's agony. Tetrachord dropped to four legs, then six, the neural weapon clattering to the floor, running more and more jerkily, then lowering the long sleek body almost deliberately, the legs still twitching. A great gout of orange fluid, thick as syrup, was spurting from the tattered stem of the neck.

A sound like a steam whistle split the sudden hush, and Jameson saw a golden flash streak between the two lines of humans toward the safety of the cage. It was Triad, chittering with fear, her six legs pedalling in a feathery blur.

Klein had lost his chance to fire at her. He swivelled around, his gun held stiff-armed, and for a moment Jameson feared that the man was insane enough to hose down the humans clustered at the cagefront, and some of his own people, with a stream of microflechettes. The moment passed, and Klein lowered the gun as the Cygnan oozed past the open gate and, flinching away from the humans, cowered against the wall, afraid to go farther.

Klein laughed. He strode to the cage and looked in. Jameson dropped to the ground. His eyes met Klein's.

'Stupid snakes!' Klein said. 'Ruiz was right about one thing – their brains must have gotten frozen six million years ago. They don't look so tough now. We're going to make it, Jameson.'

'Listen, Klein,' Jameson said. 'All right, escape if you can. But don't use the nukes.'

Klein didn't bother to reply. He motioned Jameson and the others away from the door with his gun, then rolled it shut all the way. There was a solid-sounding thunk, then a series of clicks as ratchets fell into place. Klein tried the door with a tug of his powerful arms. It held firm. He turned on his heel and walked away.

Jameson followed him with his eyes as he walked the length of the vestibule toward the headless Cygnan body. It had stopped twitching. Klein bent and picked up the neural weapon. He handed it to Chia, and the little procession, with its herded prisoners, moved past the rows of cages down the hall and disappeared round a bend.

A circle of people were gawking at the huddled Triad, keeping well out of reach of the rasping snout. It hadn't occurred to anybody to try to harm her. Jameson went over to her. It was up to him to try to retrieve the situation.

The other people let him through. They looked at him expectantly. Perhaps they were wondering what the Cygnans would do to them in the morning. He bent over. 'Careful, Tod,' somebody said.

The Cygnan was shivering violently and uncontrollably. Her three eyestalks waved purposelessly around the central orifice at the tip of the flexible snout, like the tentacles of a sea anemone. Jameson doubted that the creature had distinguished him from the other suddenly dangerous animals that surrounded her.

He tried her name three times before he got her attention.

Then her long head quested towards him like an elephant's trunk and she whistled the three tones that meant 'Ja-me-son.' It sounded a little like the call of a whippoorwill, and for some reason Jameson read pathos into it.

He looked her over carefully. She didn't appear to be hurt, but she was behaving strangely. A human being in the grip of some powerful and uncontrollable emotion might writhe the way she was now doing. Was it grief over the loss of her mate? Fear? What the hell was it that a Cygnan felt?

The rings of muscles were contracting in sequence down the whole length of her tubular body, like a species of peristalsis. She coiled and twisted with each successive wave, so that he was able to see her form all the way around.

The parasite was missing.

There was a lighter patch on her skin where it had clung, and he could see the six little wounds where it had dug in its feet. At the top of the oval patch, where the tiny head had been embedded, was an ulcerated sore.

Dmitri was kneeling beside him. 'Is the creature sick?' he said. He cast a professional eye over the Cygnan. 'Do you notice – there's a slight turgidity of surface tissue, especially around the mucosa of the eyes and mouth. That can't be normal.'

Jameson took a closer look and saw that Dmitri was right. There were other changes. The gold-and-russet pattern of her reticulated hide seemed brighter, more vivid in colour. Jameson had the nagging feeling that some important datum was just beyond his grasp. Why, when the alarm went off, had the Cygnan run off helter skelter after her mate without thinking to arm herself?

'Triad,' he tried again, but the Cygnan was warbling to herself. The swollen eye polyps were waving at random again.

'Oh God, look!' a woman's voice said over by the bars.

'Go get a hoe or something,' someone else said, and there was the sound of running feet heading toward Kiernan's vegetable garden on the other side of the enclosure.

Jameson straightened up and went over to the gate. A dozen men and women were staring, fascinated, at something in the hall beyond.

'What's going on?' Jameson said.

'Look!' Beth Oliver said, her voice filled with loathing.

Jameson peered through the bars. A soft pulpy thing the size

239

of a large frog was crawling painfully across the floor towards the cage. It was one of the Cygnan parasites. It had detached itself from Tetrachord's cooling body and was inching along blindly on its weak little legs.

'Its host is dead,' Hsieh said to Jameson. 'It senses the presence of another Cygnan in here with us – like lice deserting a dead rat for the nearest warm body.'

The thing pulled itself along with snail slowness. Jameson could see that it had no head to speak of – just a long thin sucking tube that probed the air like an antenna.

'My father told stories of the prison camp in Khabarovsk, where they kept him after the Yakut liberation, before the Americans agreed to take in Russian refugees,' Dmitri said softly. 'The prisoners were plagued by bedbugs – Siberian bedbugs, the size of dog ticks. When spring came, after the first thaw, they got permission from the guards to leave their infested bedding and sleep on the bare ground, fifty feet from their huts. They settled down – it was still light – and they saw a horrible brown tide spilling out of the huts and covering the ground like a carpet, coming toward them. It was the bedbugs. They can sense the presence of human blood even at that distance. In jungle warfare in the last century, American troops used them to detect guerrillas. They carried bedbugs in a special box, open to the air on one side, and when the bedbugs smelled blood – only human blood – they made excited little cries that could be picked up by sensitive microphones in the boxes . . .'

Jameson looked over at the writhing Triad. 'Dmitri, could that be some sort of toxic reaction?'

Dmitri thought it over. 'Maybe. We know too little about Cygnan physiology. It's possible immune reaction could rid host of parasite, leave host sick with its own antibodies.'

The parasite had covered the distance to the bars. Everybody involuntarily pulled back out of its way as it squeezed itself through the bars.

'Ugh, disgusting!' Beth said.

'Too big to step on.' Omar laughed in his bass voice. 'In bare feet, anyway.'

Up close you could see the russet-and-gold diamond pattern on the pulsating oval of the thing's body. 'Protective colouration,' Dmitri said. 'It evolved with its host. Beautiful adaptation!'

'Beautiful?' Beth said, sounding sick.

Despite its apparent lack of eyes or other sense organs, the parasite was making a beeline for the shivering Triad, who stared at it as if mesmerized. It dragged itself along on its threadlike legs, the obscene sucking tube extended.

'Here's the hoe!' somebody yelled. Wang came puffing up with the garden tool and handed it to Omar.

'I can't watch,' Beth said, turning away.

Omar raised the hoe to strike, when suddenly an ear-splitting whistle came from Triad, like the one she'd emitted when Tetrachord died.

Everybody turned to stare. Omar paused at the top of his swing to look around, then braced his thick legs to bring the hoe down.

All at once everything clicked for Jameson. 'Stop!' he yelled.

He hurled himself forward, one shoulder low, and caught Omar behind the knees. The two of them went tumbling end over end in the low gravity. The hoe went spinning out of Omar's grip.

Jameson picked himself up. 'Sorry,' he said, and extended a hand to help Omar to his feet.

Omar dusted himself off. 'What the hell was that all about?' he rumbled from somewhere inside his massive chest. He seemed more puzzled than angry.

Jameson turned to make sure the parasite was all right. It had covered another ten inches in its grublike progress towards Triad, who shrank against the cage wall in a shivering paralysis.

Overcoming his repugnance, he bent and scooped it up in his hand. It was not slimy, as he had expected. It was warm and dry to the touch. It writhed and contracted in his palm, its threadlike legs clinging.

Triad made a faint wheezing sound. The others looked at Jameson with incomprehension or revulsion, except for Dmitri, whose face was expectant.

'This isn't a parasite,' Jameson told them. 'It's the other half of the Cygnan race.'

'A parasitic male!' Dmitri said, turning the squirming creature over in his hand. 'Of course! Why didn't I think of it?'

Over at the sloping wall, a few of the braver young men were restraining Triad, who was making weak, uncoordinated attempts to get to Jameson and Dmitri. Most of the diminished human colony was there, including Janet Lemieux, who had left a sedated Boyle in the care of a couple of volunteers. Ruiz had already regained consciousness with the help of a stimulant she'd given him, and though he hadn't yet tried to sit up, he was watching with lively interest.

'The Cygnans are all females,' Jameson said. 'The ones we've been thinking of as Cygnans, I mean. What fooled me was the way they behave like courting couples. And the personality differences, and the fact that one was bigger and stronger than the other. If they've got to pair off to reproduce, I suppose it's natural that a weaker would tend to gravitate towards a stronger.'

Dmitri nodded in agreement. 'Not only natural – it's a survival mechanism for the species.'

'What are you two *talking* about?' Liz cried plaintively.

Dmitri laughed with sheer enjoyment. 'These little males are just nonsentient vegetables,' he said. 'The Cygnans exchange them like engagement rings. Why didn't I see it? It took a rocket jockey like Tod here to point it out to me.'

'But that thing in your hand doesn't look anything like a Cygnan,' Omar objected. 'It's more like an insect.'

'Ah, but it *does!*' Dmitri said. 'Same body structure – but the legs have atrophied because it needs them only for clinging, and the "head" has regressed to its only function: to suck blood. No eyes, because a parasite doesn't need them, and if I dissected it I would find no digestive organs, because it gets its meals predigested. But the gonads, you can be sure, are well developed, as they are in all parasites. It is perfectly adapted to its way of life.'

'What a filthy thing!' Beth said.

'Filthy?' Dmitri said, in genuine puzzlement. 'Perhaps to us. To the Cygnans, perfectly natural. Nature always provides rewards to encourage reproduction – rewards in the form of pleasure, or at least release from compulsion.' He nodded towards the struggling Triad, whose body contractions had grown rhythmic and violent. 'That poor creature is in torment.'

'But a parasitic mate!' Liz said. 'Isn't that a bit far-fetched?'

'There are any number of terrestrial examples,' Dmitri said. '*Trichosomoides crassicauda*. It's a parasitic worm, like the Cygnans' distant ancestors. The male lives as a parasite within the uterus of its own mate. *Edryolychnus*. It's a deep-sea fish, very ugly. The male's a tiny appendage that attaches itself to

242

the female early in life. Its eyes and other sense organs atrophy. Its blood vessels fuse with hers. I could go on.'

'Strange way to perpetuate a species,' Omar said.

'No stranger than ours. Males aren't very important in the scheme of things. They're just a mechanism for exchanging gametes. Female spiders *eat* their mates when they've finished their job. This thing in my hand is a gene package, not a lover. A Cygnan's emotional equivalent of a mate is the other female she trades males with.'

Jameson became thoughtful. 'Dmitri, how would it work biologically?'

Dmitri looked around happily. 'There's an almost precise terrestrial analogy. A mite that's parasitic on moths: *Lasioseuis lacunosus*. About one egg in twenty hatches as a male. The male is born first. That's so it can be an obstetrician for its sisters. It helps in the birth of the females by pulling them out of the mother's body. It lives as an ecoparasite with the mother for a brief time – it can't survive removal itself. But before its sisters leave home, it impregnates them.'

'But the Cygnan male doesn't impregnate its *own* sister?' Jameson said.

'No, it simply becomes a parasite on her. Let's say it works like this. Suppose the Cygnans have multiple births, or hatchings, or buddings, or whatever. The male can't survive on its own, any more than *Lasioseius lacunosus* can. It must immediately hook itself into the bloodstream of one of its much larger sisters or die. The attachment of a first male probably stimulates production of a hormone or chemical trigger that prevents the other male siblings from implanting themselves –'

'The way an ovum becomes impervious to other sperm after the first one reaches it,' Janet said, looking up from her work of bandaging Ruiz's head.

'Yes, yes,' Dmitri said impatiently. 'At any rate, it's the fittest that tend to survive.'

'The courtship mechanism . . .' Jameson prompted.

'Dmitri nodded. 'What you call "courtship" is two females pairing off and eventually exchanging their parasitic males. It must be as charged with emotion for them as sex is for humans. The exchange is an evolutionary survival mechanism which prevents inbreeding. Presumably there's a hormone or body-chemistry block which ordinarily prevents a parasite from impregnating its sister-host. The courtship ritual, on the other hand, must release pheromones – prepare the endocrine systems of both the hosts and the parasites to accept the switch, just as a foreplay prepares both human sexes for sex.'

Jameson's eyes strayed toward Triad. The involuntary contractions of her body looked as if they were causing her physical pain. With each wave her rubbery body compressed by a third, then stretched out again like taffy. He was unable to imagine what she was feeling but clearly she was in the grip of a powerful biological imperative.

Her own tiny brother was already within the body of the dead Tetrachord, presumably dead or dying itself. The other half of the exchange must have been interrupted by the alarm. The squirming thing in Dmitri's hand was animated by its own biological imperative. If it failed to make contact with Triad soon, then the union of Tetrachord and Triad would produce no young.

Did Cygnans mate for life?'

One of the Struggle Brigade stalwarts, a sinewy fellow with close-set eyes and bristly black hair brushed forward over his forehead, had retrieved the hoe and was prodding Triad with the handle. Jameson reached him in three swift strides.

'Stop that!' he said, and snatched the hoe from the startled man. He tossed it down the slope as far as he could throw it. The Cygnan, in her private misery, shuddered. The sounds she was making were nonhuman, but to Jameson's acclimatized ears they were piteous nevertheless.

Hating himself for what he was doing, he got down on one knee and said, in his broken-chord Cygnanese, 'Triad, I talk. Do you hear?'

Dmitri broke off his lecture. He started forward. 'Stay where you are,' Jameson said sharply. Dmitri stopped. The other people fell silent and watched Jameson.

The clustered eye polyps quivered and stretched in Jameson's direction. It was like looking into three orange-rimmed inkwells.

'I hear, Ja-me-son,' the Cygnan trilled. 'Give me the little brother.'

'Not yet. You must help me leave this place.'

'Jameson and his sisters are a wrongness in the sight of the mother-within-herself. You have stopped Tetrachord at the time of her (?)'

Jameson didn't recognize the last ideogram, but Triad,

244

despite her distress, had made an effort to put the rest of her message in terms he could understand. 'Stopped' was the term for a damaged piece of machinery. 'Wrongness' was the word for 'mistake' that had cropped up so frequently during his language lessons.

'What is she saying?' Dmitri asked eagerly.

'She's saying that we're abominations in the sight of her deity because we murdered her mate,' Jameson said.

Beth made an indignant noise. 'What about the people *they* killed? And the Jovians and the other life forms they've exterminated? I suppose that if we don't have six legs, we don't count!'

'No,' Jameson said. 'We don't.' He turned back to Triad. 'The sisters who ... stopped ... Tetrachord are a wrongness to Jameson and his other sisters too.'

Another contractile spasm squeezed the Cygnan, squashing her. When it passed, the three eyestalks fixed on Jameson again, and the mouth centred among them opened like a pitcher plant. 'Give me the little brother.'

'No. You must help me leave.'

'You are a wrongness. Like the other two-legs.'

Jameson had no time to decide what that meant, because the Cygnan was fumbling among her pouches. She extracted a short curving instrument that looked like a section of thick gold bracelet with little wheels set along its edges.

'Watch out!' Somebody yelled. 'It may be a weapon.'

'I don't think so,' Jameson said. 'I think it's a key.'

Triad dragged herself over to the gate. The humans made way for her. She clamped the gold bangle on the thick disc that contained the lock mechanism. The curves matched, and the wheels fit into a pair of grooves that ran around the outer rim.

She whistled, a complex roulade of chromatic phrases, and the section of bracelet crept along the grooves under its own power, or power provided from within the lock mechanism. It disappeared under the edge of the disc, and the whole wagon-wheel-sized assembly lifted. The gate slid open smoothly.

Jameson reached underneath and retrieved the device. 'For opening cages from the inside,' he said. 'The animals could never figure out how to use it.'

Everybody had shrunk away from the opening as if it were dangerous. Nobody seemed anxious to leave. Jameson turned to Dmitri. 'Put it down. Gently.'

Dmitri set the squamous little creature down on the floor of the cage. It humped its broad back. The sucking tube that was its head waved from side to side, seeking. It homed in on Triad and pulled itself along on its feeble legs, like an injured beetle.

Ruiz spoke up for the first time. Under the bandaged head, some colour had returned to his lined face. 'They couldn't reproduce at their one-gravity acceleration, could they? No population growth until their ships are coasting or parked.'

Jameson nodded at him. 'No. And if we ever get back home, we can tell them the Cygnans won't be interested in settling on Earth, either.'

The tiny male had reached Triad. It crawled blindly over the surface of her body. Her hide twitched. As Jameson watched, the tightly wrapped petals of the structure that looked like her tail parted and unpeeled. They spread all the way open like a blooming orchid. The little parasite crept inside like a bee looking for nectar, squeezing past the inward-pointing spines that, like a lobster trap, would prevent it from ever leaving again.

Cygnans *did* mate for life. Even when their inamorata was dead.

The petals of the tail closed tight again. There was only a drop of thin orange serum trembling at the tip. The rippling contractions of Triad's tubular body died away and stopped. The rings of muscle relaxed. She lay limp and unmoving.

Jameson rubbed his knuckles over his eyes. He felt tired. It had been a long day for everybody.

'Some of you pick her up and get her out of sight in one of those tents,' he said. 'Go easy with her. And I'll want a detail to get the body of the other Cygnan out of sight. I don't know how long it will be before other Cygnans come to check, but if they don't see anything obvious, it may buy us some time.'

Captain Hsieh drafted some volunteers and got Tetrachord's headless body inside the compound. They wrapped it in one of the precious blankets and covered it with rubble.

Jameson looked up at the winding observation tubes, frosty in the subdued light. In not too many hours, they would be filled with sightseeing Cygnans.

He turned to face the others. 'All right,' he said. 'Who's going with me?'

# CHAPTER TWENTY-SIX

'Here's all the food I could get together,' Liz Becque said apologetically. 'And there's about three gallons of drinking water in those cans and jugs. You couldn't carry much more than that. You'll have to depend on finding water along the way.'

Jameson examined the supplies spread out across the pokes that Liz had improvised from squares of sheeting. It included all the canned and packaged food that Klein had overlooked, and some pressed bars of a fish-and-wingbean pemmican that she'd made from the leftover supper rations.

'You may not get fed in the morning,' he warned. 'Triad won't be in any shape to get the zoo routine back to normal.'

'It's all right. We'll go hungry tomorrow. It's the least we can do.'

Jameson began to tie up the bundles. He became aware of Omar Tuttle standing nearby, shuffling his big feet.

'I'm sorry, Tod,' Omar said. 'I'd go with you, but I'd better stay and look after Liz. The baby could come on at any time.' He avoided meeting Jameson's eyes.

'Okay,' Jameson said. 'Don't worry about it.' He went on tying up the bundles, and after a while Omar went away.

He couldn't blame Omar. He'd told them all himself that there was little chance of catching up with Klein before the alerted Cygnans intercepted him, or of doing anything useful if he did. Klein had a small army with him. Armed.

'Don't go, then,' Beth Oliver had said reasonably. 'Let the Cygnans catch them. You'll only be making things worse for us.'

Pierce had said: 'All you'll accomplish is to be brought back here anyway, and that's if you're *lucky*. Nobody shoots zoo animals. But you shoot mad dogs that are running around loose.'

Janet Lemieux had said: 'We need you here, Tod, Captain Boyle's going to need somebody to back him up. Otherwise the Chinese will control things. And you're the only one who can talk to the Cygnans.'

What it all boiled down to was that everybody had an excuse

for not going. Pierce, sheepishly displaying the arm broken during the capture. Liz with her indisputable pregnancy. Omar with his surrogate pregnancy. Janet, who was needed by Boyle and who soon would be needed by Liz ...

But dammit, he could have used some *help*!

None of the Chinese, of course, would even consider going along. Chia had made herself unquestioned authority of the Chinese contingent for as long as she was aboard the Cygnan ship. Bring her back, and you'd committed an act of lèse majesté for which you'd suffer when she started running things again. And back here at the zoo, two factions were already shaping up: Captain Hsieh's followers and the regrouped forces of Tu Jue-chen. Neither of the principals would willingly leave the field to the other, and none of the followers would desert the standard; it was important to be on the winning side early in the game.

For that matter, if Klein were brought back alive there could be a clash about constituted authority among the Americans. Klein carried the baton of the Reliability Board, and all of them, Jameson included, to some degree had been conditioned to its touch.

Except perhaps Ruiz.

Jameson looked across to where Ruiz was waiting for him. The old man was standing straight and tall, too proud to let anyone see him leaning against the wall. The bandage around his head was already askew where he had been fooling with it. His fierce hawklike profile was turned away. He'd bullied Janet into giving him stimulants he'd need to keep him going.

'Medical supplies are short, Dr. Ruiz,' she had told him.

'Boyle and I are your only patients at the moment, and Boyle doesn't need them.'

Janet had bit her lip. 'You ought not to be doing anything strenuous. You certainly have a concussion, and you *may* even have a fracture under that cut scalp.'

In the end she'd given in. Then it had been Jameson's turn.

'You'll slow me up, Doctor,' he said bluntly.

'I'll keep up with you. If I don't, you can leave me behind. You'll be no worse off.'

'How long do you think you can keep going on those things Janet gave you?'

'Long enough.'

'All right. I need all the help I can get. But you'll kill yourself.'

'Commander,' Ruiz said, his eyes bright with speed, 'that madman took Maybury with him because of me! *Estupido!* I had to make speeches! Why didn't I just go along quietly and try to slow him down?' He shook his head and immediately winced with pain.

Ruiz had been Jameson's first recruit.

Dmitri was his second. The young biologist had impulsively followed Ruiz's example. He admired the old man. And perhaps he wanted to prove to Jameson that he was a man of action. Jameson hid his misgivings and thanked him.

Then Maggie had thrown her arms around him and announced that she was going too.

'I thought you were trying to talk me out of it, like Janet.'

'That was before I knew you were *really* going! You're not going to leave me behind!'

'Good girl, but –'

'I *won't* stay behind with all those *sheep*!' she said fiercely.

That hadn't endeared her to the others. But Jameson had to admire her independent spirit. He felt a little ashamed of himself. He'd been one of the sheep himself, for too long. It was Maggie's example, with her rebellious heritage from the New England Secessionists, that had opened his eyes and given him the resolve to resist the Kleins and the authority they represented.

He finished tying up the bundles and handed them out, giving the lightest one to Ruiz. 'Just a moment,' he said. 'I just want to say good-bye to Boyle.'

Boyle was breathing deeply and rhythmically. He looked somehow shrunken between the two blankets. There was a makeshift screen around him: sheets hung from ropes that were strung between the abstract branches of the iron trees.

'He doesn't know you're here,' Janet said. 'I put him under.'

'When are you going to operate?'

'Soon. I'm boiling the instruments now. I'll have to make do with what was in the medical bag.' She laughed uneasily. 'I've never performed an amputation before. In fact, I haven't practised medicine since my internship. Just administrative psychiatry. Qing-yi's going to help me. Did you know that she was a *chijiao yisheng* – what they call a barefoot doctor – in Kweichow Province before she qualified for the space programme? She doesn't have a medical degree, but she's performed more operations than I have.'

'Is he going to be all right?'

'He'll be fine. He has the constitution of an ox. And lots of willpower; he'll make himself a crutch and be hopping around in no time. Maybe some day . . .' She hesitated. 'The Cygnans must know about regeneration – you saw that assistant. If we can get a dialogue going with them . . . Tod, won't you stay?'

'Chances are, I'll be back before you know it. If not . . .' He shrugged. 'Look, you can't depend on one man with absolute pitch. We humans are ingenious creatures. It can be done with computer-generated sound and translating interfaces. There are some good electronics people here, and if you can actively enlist the Cygnans' interest . . . Do it for the captain, Janet. And for your children.'

He turned toward Boyle. 'So long, Skipper,' he said. 'Good luck.'

Incredibly, from some iron resource of will, Boyle's eyes flicked open. Jameson sensed that he was fighting the drug. 'Good luck, boy,' he whispered. 'It's up to you.' His eyes closed, and he was breathing deeply again.

'He didn't know what he was saying,' Janet said.

'Yes he did,' said Jameson, and walked away quickly. Ruiz, Dmitri, and Maggie picked up their bundles when they saw him coming. Jameson shouldered his own parcel, slipping one arm through the loop at the knot, and moved past the clustered people at the gate without looking at their faces.

A dozen yards past the thick bars, he paused to look back. They were already pushing at the gate, sliding it shut. It fell into place with a solid thunk. The animals had locked themselves back in their cage.

'Wait a minute,' Dmitri said.

'Come on!' Jameson said. 'There isn't time for you to stop and look at specimens.'

'They're trying to attract our attention,' Dmitri said.

Ruiz looked at the cage behind the wire mesh barrier. 'He's right,' he said. 'Those creatures are intelligent.'

Jameson turned around and went up to the barrier for a closer look. It was the cage that held the feathery humanoids. The pixieish little creatures were swarming frantically over

250

the bars, making urgent gestures with their delicate four-fingered hands.

'They're cute,' Maggie said.

'They're carnivores,' Dmitri said. 'Look at those little pointed teeth.'

'Like a kitten's!' Maggie said indignantly.

'We're carnivores too,' Ruiz said. 'Gives us something in common with them.'

Jameson looked the creatures over. They were fluffy and flamingo-pink, with huge round violet eyes that gave them an astonished expression, like a tarsier. They had button noses and dainty underslung jaws that, head on, gave them an appealingly chinless appearance, like pink teddy bears. They sported tufted tails, which they kept winding around their waists or necks like feather boas.

And they had stacked a little pile of artifacts against the bars for demonstration purposes. A pair of little felt boots, too short for their feet until you noticed the four holes for toes to protrude through and rest on the projecting sole. A filigreed cup that could not have held anything, and seemed to have no purpose except to be beautiful. A miniature rake that was obviously a grooming comb.

'They had those ready to show us,' Ruiz said. 'They were waiting.'

As if on cue, the two elfin beings went through a swift and well-organized pantomime. They became Klein murdering Tetrachord, and Triad streaking for the safety of the human compound. Then they took turns becoming Jameson and his three companions emerging, imitating posture and body language with amazing accuracy despite the differences in body structure. Finally, with unmistakable gestures, they begged to be taken along.

Jameson looked sorrowfully at the sheet of clear, almost invisible glass that sealed off the cage, between mesh and bars. There was no telling what kind of atmosphere the creatures breathed.

Feeling clumsy by comparison, he made a series of gestures to tell them that it would be fatal for them to breathe the Cygnan air.

The fuzzy little beings gestured back, more urgently, pantomiming the idea that they could breathe outside the glass case.

'What do you think?' Jameson said.

'They're bright,' Ruiz said. 'Bright and quick. They want out, and they seem to know what they're doing. I feel sorry for them. Too bad we can't help them.'

Jameson made up his mind. 'I have a hunch they'll be useful,' he said. 'They've been prisoners of the Cygnans a lot longer than we have. They may know a thing or two.'

Ruiz was doing arithmetic in his head. He nodded agreement. 'They've been on this ship a minimum of ten years subjective time, even assuming that the Cygnans picked them up on their last stop. And that their last stop was during the mid-twentieth century, when Cygnus X-1 was discovered – and the Cygnans would have been detected as well, if Cyg X-1 weren't masking the final leg of their approach.'

Dmitri was looking worriedly at the extra gate and the glass. 'The security precautions are extraordinary,' he said. 'The Cygnans must consider them to be dangerous beasts.'

'They're intelligent beings,' Jameson said, 'who wear shoes and who while away the time while they're locked up by carving ornamental cups.'

He pried at the wire mesh with his bare hands. The mesh was a warning, not a barrier, and it was intended for one-third-g strength of Cygnans, not human muscles. With Ruiz and Dmitri helping him, he was able to tear an opening wide enough to squeeze through.

The glass was unbreakable. After a moment's examination of its perimeter, Jameson found the round opening of a Cygnan keyhole. He fished in his pocket for the cylindrical key he'd taken from one of Triad's pouches.

'Tod,' Maggie said quickly, 'that glass is there for a reason. What if they're not oxygen breathers You'll kill them.'

'It's their decision,' Jameson said. 'They say no.'

He pushed the cylinder into the hole. It twanged and jumped back into his hand. The glass panel slid aside.

They all held their breath, half expecting the smell of ammonia or methane. The two feathery humanoids regarded them gravely through the bars, unharmed. Jameson took a cautious sniff. There was a spicy smell, like cloves or cinnamon, but the cage seemed to contain the basic Cygnan atmosphere. There wasn't even a pressure differential.

Why had they been glassed in?

'Germs,' Maggie said suddenly.

'Too late to worry about that now,' Jameson said. He found the lock, and the bars retreated into overhead sockets.

Before he knew it, two gossamer sprites were crowding round him, looking up at him with enormous violet eyes and jabbering at him in squeaky voices. They were no taller than twelve-year-olds. The spicy scent was stronger and rather nice.

'They're thanking you,' Maggie said.

Up close, the rosy plumage turned out to be a silky nap of cobweb-fine hairs that split and branched at the tips, like dandelion down. There was an almost irresistible impulse to plunge your hands into it and feel the softness. It was the down that fluffed them out to give an illusion of even moderate bulk. Underneath there was nothing to them – just a pliant, willowy frame with hardly any flesh on it. Wherever the fairy silk rippled and parted in response to stray air currents, they were all skin and fine bones and tendon. On Earth they wouldn't have weighed more than fifty pounds apiece.

They bounded ahead like mischievous children, then stopped and looked back to see if the humans were following. Jameson grinned and picked up his bundle.

'Nocturnal species,' Dmitri said. 'Notice the eyes? And it gets cold at night where they come from. The divaricated follicles of their coats provide good insulation, with a layer of trapped air next to the skin. I wouldn't be surprised if the tips open and close to regulate temperature – much more efficient than the erectile follicles of terrestrial mammals.'

'They look so *human*!' Maggie squealed. 'Like little elves!'

'Only superficially,' Dmitri said, watching the two beings scamper ahead of them. 'See those butterfly hips? And the articulation of the shoulder joints? And they're not mammals.'

'Even so,' Jameson said, 'their resemblance to people is amazing. A coincidence . . .'

'Not amazing,' Dmitri said. 'And no coincidence. There's a limited number of efficient forms available to quadrupeds who become bipeds. The Cygnans must have collected thousands of life forms. They lumped their handful of humanoids together.'

He nodded toward the cage they were passing. The squat green troll within, with its knee-length beard and arms hanging to the ground, was obviously not intelligent. As it caught sight of them, the top of its head lifted like a lid and emitted a bellow; then it scampered away, upright but on all fours.

253

They were out of the Hall of Bipeds and beside the towering glass cliff that contained the Jovians. Maggie gasped, and Dmitri lagged behind like a small boy.

There was a vast churning within the cloudy liquid, and one of the enormous pancake shapes came hurtling toward them to flatten its quarter acre of surface against the glass. The floor beneath their feet shook with the impact.

'One crack in the glass and it would be all over – for them and for us,' Ruiz said. 'If the liquid hydrogen didn't instantly freeze us solid, the explosion when a creature that size depressurized would blow us to bits.'

'Let's get out of here,' Maggie said nervously.

The Jovian, its scalloped outer mantle curled around the shaft of its hundred-foot harpoon, was hammering on the glass with the butt.

'It's angry,' Jameson said. 'I don't blame it. It can't imagine how it ended up in this – goldfish bowl.'

'This goldfish bowl is all there is in the universe for them now,' Ruiz said gruffly. 'I wonder if it thinks we're responsible.'

Dmitri was staring entranced at the living mountain of flesh. 'No skeleton – very sensible for a creature that lives at a pressure of a hundred thousand atmospheres. And the ratio of surface area to volume –'

Jameson pushed him along and got him, still talking, out of the mammoth aquarium. The two humanoids waited impatiently for them ahead. They seemed to know where they were going. They threaded their way among the empty cages and drained tanks of the empty exhibition hall towards the warehouse section that Jameson had intended to head for. Had they been to the zookeepers' living quarters too?

They set up a shrill chattering, and Jameson hurried to catch up. He stopped when he saw what they were excited about.

A dead Cygnan lay sprawled in a pool of orange blood next to the tank it had been caulking. The back end of its body was a glistening hash. It must have been trying to run away when the stream of explosive splinters caught it.

Some of Klein's handiwork.

'When the Cygnans find this corpse, they'll be hunting us down like vermin,' Jameson said.

'That's what we are, aren't we?' Ruiz said. 'Rats in the walls.'

The door to Tetrachord and Triad's quarters had been blown open. Jameson sniffed the air.

'They must have had plastic explosive,' Jameson said.'

'They did,' Dimitri said. 'I heard Gifford say that Klein had it moulded to look like the soles of his boots.'

'Those heavy boots that were so out of place in space,' Jameson said. 'Nobody ever thought to question them.'

'How could you?' Maggie said. 'I mean, something like that is too far out.'

The cramped interior of the zookeepers' apartment had been torn apart. Objects had been swept off the spoon-shaped shelves and trampled underfoot. The graduated set of miniature resting perches had been wantonly smashed. Jameson recognized their special poignance now. Nursery furniture.

The Moog was still where he'd left it, but it had been hammered into junk. 'The son of a bitch!' Jameson flared. 'He didn't want anyone talking to the Cygnans after he was gone!'

He searched the litter. The cupboard that had held the little arsenal of neural weapons was empty. Klein's party was armed to the teeth now.

'If we *do* catch up with Klein, what do you expect to do?' Ruiz asked tartly.

'We'll worry about that when we catch him,' Jameson said and kept on looking.

He found what he wanted among the litter on the floor. Klein had overlooked it, or hadn't realized what it was.

One of the two-pronged electric prods the Cygnans had herded him with.

'It doesn't have any reach,' Maggie said. 'It's no better than a knife or a club. You can't get near someone with a gun.'

'It's better than nothing,' Jameson said, sticking the implement in the waistband of his shorts.

He poked his head out the other door to make sure there were no Cygnans in the warehouse section, then led his troops outside. The two little humanoids scampered along beside them, their silky fur bouncing.

He knew the worst even before he reached the stacks of looted human artifacts. Why had he ever led Klein here?

The junkpile had been thoroughly picked over for anything useful. Spacesuits, of course – enough to outfit Klein's whole party. The ones that hadn't been taken were slashed, faceplates smashed, hoses pulled out.

Maggie held up a slashed suit, tears running down her face.

'Why? Why didn't they leave the rest of us a chance? Just a *chance*!'

'They don't want us to have a chance,' Ruiz said, his face grim. 'The people they left behind are a complication in their plans. I'll tell you what I think. I think the first missile they intend to fire will be targeted for this pod.'

'No!' Jameson cried. 'Not even Klein or Chia would do a thing like that! Disable the spine of the ship, they said! They wouldn't slaughter their own people!'

'Types like that always *start* with their own people,' Ruiz said.

Dmitri was rummaging in the piles of goods. He came up with a fire axe that had been overlooked and stuck it in his belt. Maggie collected a bottle of alcohol and some cotton and, after she had explained their use, then said: 'Don't look shocked. I come from a family of rebs.' Ruiz found a kitchen knife and tied it to the end of a fibreglass pole that had been part of a stretcher. Jameson armed himself with an eighteen-inch crescent wrench and then, in the same tool locker, found a six-pound maul and an assortment of chisels. After some thought he tied a nylon cord around the handle of the maul and stuffed a coil of twenty or thirty feet of line inside his shirt.

'Something's moving!' Maggie cried. 'Over there!'

Jameson whipped around and saw a tiny glittering thing emerge from a pile of castoff clothing and begin to climb the slanting wall. Before he could do anything there was a blur of pink motion as one of the diminutive humanoids streaked for the thing. It trapped it in a dainty four-fingered hand and presented it to Jameson.

Jameson looked it over and immediately smashed it beneath his heel.

'What ... was it?' Dmitri said.

'Piece of electronics,' Jameson said. 'One of Klein's motile probes. Pinhead lens, rice-grain mike, little magnetized ball-bearing wheels, trailing a spider-thread antenna. It must have been activated by our movements or body heat. Klein's watching his rear.'

'So now he knows we're after him,' Ruiz mused.

'Probably. I don't know what the range of a thing like that is.'

'How do we find them?'

'Good question. He's got those miniature probes to scout out a safe route for him. Wish we had the same. Or at least a bloodhound. Now, which direction did he go in?'

He looked around the expanse of floor, frowning.

'What's got into them?' Maggie said.

The two humanoids were behaving oddly. They were prowling the area on all fours – not on hands and knees, as people would have done, but bent double in an impossible arch, walking on the tips of their toes and the backs of their little hands, with their fingers curled up. The position seemed entirely natural for them. They moved with a supple, spidery grace, their faces casting back and forth a half inch from the floor.

Dmitri watched them intently as they worked in widening circles, then turned to Jameson.

'I think you've got your bloodhounds,' he said.


CHAPTER TWENTY-SEVEN

They climbed more than a mile before they saw their first live Cygnan. Klein had been correct in his assumption: Even in an artificial environment that was more crowded than Hong Kong or Dallasworth there were service and utilities routes that were untravelled and almost unvisited.

'It's like sneaking through the sewers of Paris in a novel by Victor Hugo,' Ruiz said, 'while thousands of Parisians are walking around a few feet overhead.' Then he had to explain who Victor Hugo was.

The route they followed was a tangled confusion of pipes, enormous three-sided ducts and twisting cables as thick around as oak trees. They passed through narrow chimneys of metal that they had to squeeze through inch by inch, and yawning spaces that seemed to have been wasted in the design of the ship. Jameson was reminded of just how old the ship must be; some of the chambers they traversed had been used for various purposes and abandoned by past generations of Cygnans. The dust of centuries lay on the crumbling artifacts that loomed in the flickering dimness provided by skeins of leaking optical fibres.

'Cygnans are sloppy housekeepers,' Jameson said at one

point, looking at an electrical cable that had been gnawed clean through by some small animal. 'They never repaired this.'

'The function it served might have disappeared a thousand years ago,' Ruiz said. 'Do we maintain the Roman aqueducts, or the transatlantic cables?'

There was life all around them in the unused spaces – little furry things that fled chittering as they approached. Mosslike fungus grew near damp spots where pipes had burst or condensation beaded the walls. Once they saw a small flying thing – a podlike shape suspended from a crown of furiously beating transparent wings.

The ducts and conduits branched off like some immense fossil vine to disappear through bulkheads or snake their way through side tunnels and adjacent chambers. Once Jameson put his eye to a rent that showed light and saw a horde of Cygnans slithering across a floor to crowd around a dozen raised perches where other Cygnans dispensed tiny pea-green cubes from wide-mouthed baskets slung around them. Another time the feathery humanoids stopped Dmitri just in time to prevent him from stepping through an opening where Cygnans disembarked from a travel tube to a platform that debouched to a multibranched artery.

It was the humanoids that kept them out of trouble. They darted ahead and then back like coursing gazehounds, sniffing out danger and herding Jameson and the others into side tunnels, or by example making them hide behind ducts and bulkheads till stray Cygnans passed. And all the time, the two elvish beings followed the trail of Klein and his group, selecting trails from among alternate routes with utter certainty.

'Butyric acid,' Dmitri said suddenly.

'What?' Jameson said.

'Butyric acid. It's a constituent of human sweat. Every time you take a step, something like two hundred and fifty billion molecules of butyric acid pass through the sole of your shoe. A good bloodhound or German shepherd can detect a millionth of that amount and follow a trail a week old. These two fluff-balls of ours seem to live by scent.'

'Very interesting. But we haven't time to—'

'There's something else.'

'What are you talking about?'

Ruiz and Maggie stopped to listen. The two humanoids were twenty feet farther on, dancing impatiently up and down.

'How do they make us hide when there are Cygnans nearby?' Dmitri said.

Jameson wrinkled his brow. 'Why ... they make a lot of gestures, and they act excited, and then they hide behind something ...'

'Think again. We don't wait around and stop to think. We act very quickly. They *tell* us Cygnans are around.'

Maggie said, 'Well, we seem to *sense* what they mean. I can almost *feel* us getting close to Cygnans ... Oh!'

Dmitri grinned with triumph. 'Exactly. It's the most evocative of the senses. Human beings use it every day without being aware of it. It makes us like people or dislike them, triggers sexual behaviour, evaluates our surroundings on a subconscious level, makes us nostalgic without knowing why—'

'Slow down,' Jameson said.

'He's too much of an ox to notice,' Maggie said. She turned to Jameson and said: '*Smell!* They tell us by *smell!* When they want to warn us that there are Cygnans around, they lose that nice spicy aroma and they suddenly smell sort of *musty*, the way Cygnans do.'

Dmitri nodded vigorously. 'They *manufacture* smells as well as detect them. They probably can imitate any smell they encounter. Make up new ones, too.' He laughed delightedly. 'Odours to order!'

'Maybe,' Jameson said. 'Come on, we're wasting time.'

'I'll *show* you,' Dmitri said.

He hurried to catch up to the humanoids, the others following. The two creatures were at a division in the metallic gorge where two narrow flumes diverged, making motions to go right. Dmitri ignored them and turned left.

'What—' Jameson began.

'Watch,' Dmitri said. 'Or I should say, smell.'

The little creatures squeaked with distress. After a couple more attempts to turn Dmitri around, they planted themselves at the right, waving their pink tails in agitation.

It hit Jameson with full force. A smell like old socks. A locker room with a million sweaty feet. The lemur-like creatures were fanning it toward the three humans with their bushy tails.

'I'm convinced,' Jameson said. To the evident relief of the humanoids, the humans began following them up the metal flume, climbing the thick vinelike cables. In the low gravity, it was easy.

Ruiz, his jury-rigged spear slung across his back, said between puffing breaths: 'Why would a critter develop an ability like that?'

'Any number of biological reasons,' Dmitri said happily. 'Carnivorous plants make themselves smell like rotten meat to attract flies. Moths generate pheromones to attract mates. Deer deposit scents to warn other deer of danger. Rabbits mark their territories with scent glands to keep other rabbits out. Skunks protect themselves with odours. All different ways of using scents to communicate or modify the behaviour of other creatures.' He stopped. 'I just had a thought.'

'What?'

'Why do we like them?'

'Because they're *cute!*' Maggie called from above.

'What if that nice spicy smell you like so much isn't their natural aroma? What if it's tailor-made to influence our attitude towards them?'

Ruiz said, 'How could they know what appeals to us? Different life form, different planet, entirely out of their biological spectrum.'

'Feedback,' Dmitri said. 'They respond to all the billions of scent molecules we're putting out from our skin, our mouths, our gonads, our intestinal tracts. Their olfactory organs analyse them as naturally as our own eyes put together a lot of data and give us the shape of the world around us. Then their scent glands mix up a brew that gets the response they want.'

Jameson grunted. 'Scents couldn't affect us that powerfully.'

'Couldn't they? The smell of a baby can bring on a maternal response in a nonlactating female. The presence of menstruating females in a group living situation can bring on a woman's period. A man can make you want to fight him by the smell of his fear, or back down by the smell of his rage. Do you know that a cat has a scent gland on its forehead that –'

'All right!' Jameson said. 'I give up!'

'It doesn't have to be sinister, you know,' Dmitri said, mollified. 'They needed our help, and they instinctively tried to make themselves pleasing.'

Up above, the two pink forms were swinging themselves up the braided cables and optical fibres like a pair of cotton-candy monkeys. The vertical crevice twisted and widened into a dim grotto filled with the shrouded shapes of corroded machines that resembled rusty twelve-foot-high beehives. The dust, thick on the floor, showed the tracks of many humans. There was a litter of empty cans to show where they'd stopped to camp, and from somewhere behind the hives came the unmistakable smell of human waste.

'Watch it!' Ruiz cried as he pulled himself up into the chamber, and Jameson whirled to see one of Klein's little glittering bugs scurry across the floor. He pounced and scooped it up, and with one smooth unbroken motion flung it back down the metal chasm they'd climbed from.

The two humanoids had disappeared. Jameson looked around, trying to locate them among the tall domelike shapes. He stepped round one of the hives and came face to three-eyed, long-snouted face with a Cygnan who seemed to be as startled as he was.

Jameson made a dive for it. At the back of his mind was the thought that if he could grab hold of a leg and manage to keep himself from getting drilled through by that rasping tongue until the others rushed up and helped him pin the alien down, he could tie it up with some of the rope he carried, just as he'd tied Augie.

'Kill it!' Maggie shouted behind him.

That gave him a jolt, but the advice was academic. The Cygnan reared up like an ocean wave and oozed backward along itself until it was running away, *upside down* on its queerly articulated legs. It was already a dozen feet away and rotating on its axis to put itself right side up, without missing a beat, before Jameson could react. Ruiz threw his spear, which clattered harmlessly off one of the metal hives.

Jameson pounded after it futilely. He watched helplessly as it skidded around a dome and streaked for a crack in the grotto wall.

'Let's get out of here!' Ruiz said, gasping.

The Cygnan rounded another dome, its flexible head raised like the trunk of a charging elephant. Jameson changed course, knowing he could not head it off.

He circled around, a mouse lost amid an acre of overturned bowls. He had lost track of the Cygnan. Ruiz, his spear retrieved, was circling in the opposite direction. Dmitri and Maggie were doing their best to flank him. But the Cygnan didn't emerge anywhere.

261

'Here!' he heard Ruiz gasp.

He ran in fifteen-foot leaps toward Ruiz's voice, Dmitri bringing up the rear. When he saw Ruiz, spear braced, fixed on something behind a dome, he approached from the opposite side. Maggie was coming up behind Ruiz, a kitchen knife in her hand.

'Look,' Ruiz said.

The Cygnan was stretched out on its back, writhing voluptuously like a puppy on a deliciously scratchy rug. The two humanoids squatted peaceably on their furry haunches beside it, looking like great big jolly pink nursery spiders.

There was an overpowering musty odour hanging like a miasma over the scene, too powerful to be coming from the one Cygnan. It was overlaid by a pungent, sour smell that tugged at Jameson's memory until he realized that it reminded him of the scent in the zookeepers' quarters the time Tetrachord had behaved so sluggishly.

'They've got it mesmerized,' Dmitri said wonderingly.

'Help me tie it up,' Jameson said.

He trussed the Cygnan's legs together with the nylon line, in two groups of three limbs each. He'd found that one of the middle legs stretched naturally to join the front limbs, while the other middle leg wanted to fold rearward. The Cygnan offered no resistance. It was alive and moving, but uncoordinated. The fan-shaped irises of its eyes had contracted to slits, despite the dimness, and the three eyestalks were limp.

'Now we know why the pink beasties developed the ability to mimic odours ' Dmitri said. 'Their ancestors used to hypnotize their prey.'

'What was their prey, Dmitri?' Ruiz said. 'The ancestors of the Cygnans?'

'No, I don't think they could have evolved on the same planet.'

'How ... how could they do a thing like that with *smells*?' Maggie asked, motioning toward the hogtied Cygnan, whose whole body was pulsating, lengthening and contracting like an accordion.

Dmitri shrugged. 'How does the *Pesis* wasp mesmerize a tarantula, get the tarantula to stand still while the wasp digs its grave, cooperate while the wasp walks under its fangs, paralyses it, and lays an egg on its abdomen? I don't know. Maybe these pink teddy bears release super-pheromones, thousands of times more powerful than the natural variety, the way synthetic analogs of morphine like etorphine are thousands of times more powerful than morphine itself. Maybe synthetic pheromones initiate powerful endocrine reactions that cause exaggerated versions of normal Cygnan syndromes – pleasure, fear, torpor, docility, autointoxication, *anything!*'

'In a creature that evolved on a different planet?' Jameson said.

Dmitri shrugged again. 'The humanoids seem to be virtuoso scent-producers. And they've been around Cygnans a long time. No wonder they were kept behind glass.'

Jameson wound nylon cord around the Cygnan's snout to keep it from sawing away at its bonds when it recovered from its trance. The two humanoids watched him with huge intelligent eyes.

'They ought to find it in a day or two,' he said. 'By that time we'll have made it, or we'll have been too late.'

'Do you really think leaving that individual alive is going to make a difference in what the Cygnans think about human beings?' Ruiz asked wearily.

'I don't know,' Jameson said. 'Probably not.'

He picked up his duffle and got to his feet. The humanoids seemed reluctant to follow suit. They kept trying to drift back to the helpless Cygnan.

'Tod,' Maggie said. 'Do you think . . . ?'

'I don't know,' Jameson said. 'And I don't want to know.'

'They didn't take any food with them.'

Jameson gestured violently for the humanoids to get away from the Cygnan. Their spicy aroma was irresistible. They smelled like a bakery. He was suffused by a feeling of tenderness and warmth towards the little creatures.

'Stop that!' he barked.

'Tod,' Maggie said hesitantly. 'I have the weirdest feelings in my breasts, as if they were full . . .'

Jameson advanced on the humanoids, making threatening gestures. They cowered and backed away, jabbering unhappily. The bakery smell diminished. After a longing, saucer-eyed look at the trussed Cygnan, they scampered off, leading the way to an exit.

'Cute little fellers,' Ruiz said.

They crawled across the sky, looking down at the queer land-scape below with its little manicured parks and gardens, and straight-edged lakes with their bright wind-sock sailboats, and the crowded city streets squeezed between the latticed towers.

'How high up are we?' Maggie said.

'About five miles,' Jameson told her. 'But the top layer that we're looking at now is probably only a quarter mile down.'

'I'd hate to fall just the same,' she said. 'Even at this low gravity.'

The sky had been poorly maintained over the centuries. What looked like unbroken luminescence from below was a tangled spaghetti of stained and broken transparent plumbing, supported by a girderlike framework. A glowing liquid gurgled through the pipes, pulsing with brilliant white light. Suspended beneath the girders were sheets of a frosty, translucent material that diffused light. Some of the panels were missing or torn, and it was through these gaps that Jameson was able to get his bird's-eye view of the landscape as he crawled along the supports. He wasn't worried about being seen from below; distance made them specks, and the specks were masked by the glare.

'Bioluminescence,' Dmitri said. 'Some kind of microscopic fluorescent plants being pumped through these pipes. The Cygnans have had a long time to select for brightness – maybe even do a little genetic engineering. I wouldn't be surprised if it doubles as their air plant.'

Jameson managed to restrain him from breaking a pipe to collect a sample. The last thing they needed was a fiery rain calling attention to them. The already-broken sections of pipe were dark; probably a computer turned off little pumping stations by the hundreds when pipes lost pressure.

Crawling was easy in the low gravity. Their weight, low to begin with, had diminished considerably during their long climb to the roof of the mini-world. But none of them could match the ease with which the humanoids travelled. They prowled ahead on all fours, maintaining the pliant arch-shape that kept their noses close to the girders, sniffing out Klein's trail.

From up here, Jameson was able to get a feeling for the over-all layout of the environmental pod – one of the three pods swinging round the shaft of the ship. For a moment he felt a pang of regret that he would never get to see the other pods. Were they identical to this one? Or had history and jerrybuilt

264

growth over six million years turned them into different countries?

In the centre of the harlequin expanse was a triangular canyon that plunged to the floor of the world, its sides alive with golden movement. Spanning it, half-way down, was the colossal pin on which the world turned. At the bottom was a rusty floor with a small riddled patch of grey, which he knew to be the honeycomb enclosures of the zoo.

They had come a long way.

And somewhere ahead, in this labyrinth of pipes and struts squeezed between the layers of sky, was the round shadow he'd seen overhead – the convergence of the gigantic wishbone that gripped the turning pin, and an entrance to the miles of hollow shaft that led to the central axis of the ship. Somewhere in that airtight interface would be forgotten ways to get into the shaft. At least, Klein seemed to have found one.

There it was! The low overhead had begun to climb at a shallow angle, and through the forest of eye-dazzling plumbing he could see a curving black wall that had to be the outer boundary of the interchange. Behind the wall would be the reception area where the spiral tubes had dumped him and his captors when he'd first been brought to the ship. He'd never seen it, having lost consciousness before reaching bottom. The Cygnan circulatory system must be immune to merry-go-rounds. But he knew it would be crawling with Cygnan traffic. Surely within that enormous vertical void they would find bypaths and crooked ways.

The humanoids had given up trying to get any closer to the wall. They were ranging back and forth along the perimeter, like good hunting dogs.

Ruiz drew abreast of him, clutching his spear. His face was a sickly grey. The effort was taking its toll. There was crusted blood on the bandage around his head.

'It'll get easier,' Jameson said. 'By the time we get up to the top, we won't weigh anything.'

'Don't worry about me,' Ruiz snapped peevishly. 'I'll keep up.'

Jameson looked him over. 'How's the head, Hernando?'

Ruiz grimaced. 'Terrible. Like a galloping hangover. The uppers will keep me going for another forty-eight hours.'

'You're going to come down hard. You're burning yourself up.'

'It won't matter after that. There'll be all the time in the universe to rest.'

Dmitri called: 'They've found something.'

The four of them wriggled forward on their bellies. The humanoids were hovering over something huddled on a catwalk leading to the black wall.

'More of Klein's work,' Ruiz said.

It was the body of a Cygnan, almost split apart by gunfire. A mass of wetly glistening organs spilled out of the hole torn in its body, egg-shaped nodes clinging to a spongy mass of coral-branched tissue. The creature once had mated; the pulped remains of a parasitic male showed within the body cavity. She'd been a maintenance worker; there was a toolbox lying near her, a kind of basket with bulbous grips around the edges instead of a handle.

'Still warm,' Dmitri said. 'We're not far behind them.'

'Help me drag the body out of sight,' Jameson said. They wedged it deep within a tangle of pipes.

The humanoids already were sniffing out Klein's traces near the body. They found a trail and followed it, walking on their knuckles and toes. It led to an unobtrusive opening at the base of the wall. The humanoids made certain there were no Cygnans nearby; then they all made a dash for it.

Inside was what looked like a small repair station. They found lengths of plastic pipe, braces, and odd-looking fasteners stacked haphazardly around the chamber with characteristic Cygnan carelessness. There were also more Cygnan bodies strewn around the place – three of them, their orange blood splattering the walls.

Maggie looked pale. The freckles stood out on her white face. 'They'll be discovered next shift – whenever a Cygnan shift begins,' she said. 'There'll be a hunt, if one hasn't started already.'

'Easy,' Ruiz said. 'There may still be time. It may not dawn on them for a while that Klein's headed for the hub. He's just a very dangerous animal loose in the city. And they may not put it all together for a while. How many violent deaths take place in a twenty-four-hour period in a place the size of Dallasworth? The police look at it on a case-by-case basis at first, until somebody decides a maniac is loose.'

'It's morning back at the zoo,' Dmitri said thoughtfully.

'And the zookeepers are missing,' Ruiz said firmly. 'That's all. There are a lot of exhibits to search – if anybody's interested in searching right at the start. And the Cygnan sightseers will see an exhibit of these strange creatures called humans, and none of them will know how many are supposed to be in the cage.'

Jameson said, 'You're very comforting, Hernando.'

'What other choice do I have?' Ruiz said impatiently. 'Let's go.'

It took them another two days to reach the hub. They were able to climb an average of half a mile per hour in the rapidly diminishing gravity, but they had to stop to hide frequently, whenever the humanoids' sensitive noses sniffed out the presence of Cygnans. They stopped to sleep twice; Ruiz slept fitfully, hopped up by the stimulants Janet had given him. Jameson scrupulously called a halt for ten minutes every hour to let them rest, and every four hours he made them eat some of their rations and drink some water. They were able to refill their jugs at any number of places where condensation caused by the chill outer walls of the shaft had run into hollows, making respectable pools. Once there was a rainstorm that lasted a half-hour; the interior spaces of the arm were vast enough to cause weather.

Jameson never saw the humanoids eat or drink. During the humans' rest periods they frequently disappeared, coming back when it was time to play bloodhound again. Jameson never inquired into the reason for the humanoids' little side expeditions. He prayed fervently that humanoid and Cygnan biochemistry were incompatible, and that the humanoids' incredible sense of smell was leading them to stores of synthetics they could snack on. If there was anything edible within miles, Dmitri assured him, they would be able to home in on it.

The spaces they traversed were between the outer skin of the folding arm and the yawning central well that contained the corkscrew tubeways. From time to time, with the humanoids to warn him of danger, he cautiously checked their progress by poking a head out of an inner compartment and peering into the dim abyss beyond, where the flashing shapes of Cygnans whizzed through the transparent spirals. They were too far away and moving too quickly to notice him; what he was afraid of was being seen by a Cygnan on one of the nearby adjacent

267

ledges that overhung the chasm. But the humanoids' sense of smell was infallible.

The Cygnans used the spaces around the core of the arm – but mostly for storage. It could hardly be otherwise, when down became up and up became down every few years. They wouldn't have wanted to go to the trouble of refurbishing every single cubby and cell. But every mile or two Jameson and his party came across clusters of gimballed containers that were as big as houses. What were they? Low-gravity luxury housing? Factories or biological laboratories? Slums? It was impossible to tell. But some of them had windows, and Jameson gave them a wide berth.

They avoided open spaces like the plague, climbing the pipeline beanstalk as it wound its way through the niches and flues and chambers that riddled the outer layers of the shaft, and leaving it for alternate routes whenever it emerged into some roomy expanse.

Twice more they came upon dead Cygnans. One had been turned into orange hamburger by Klein's automatic weapon. The other had been burned – perhaps by Chia's lazer – and hacked apart needlessly by an axe. Klein had left a trail of miniscule spy instruments, but the humanoids were adept at finding these by the scent of the human oils that had been left on them. Jameson destroyed them as fast as they were found and tried not to worry about them.

'They'll be terrified if they see us coming after them,' Ruiz grunted. 'Kitchen knives and wrenches and a couple of pink mascots.'

'They might not have seen us,' Jameson said. 'They won't be monitoring their bugs continuously – just spot-checking them.'

They were bobbing around like balloons by this time, in gravity that was too weak to notice, launching themselves upward in giant swoops. For the vertical ascents, the humanoids changed their mode of travel, boosting themselves along the ducts and cables, their faces never far from the surface.

Eventually they found themselves in a small, crazily shaped room whose ceiling was a doughy substance that dimpled when Jameson experimentally poked a finger into it. The dimple began, slowly, to fill itself as he watched. Around them was the terrifying hiss of escaping air. The whole chamber was part of a huge gasket – a gasket with a faulty seal, as it happened – and Jameson knew that the leviathan bulk of the starship's main body hung above, with its three-sided forests and leaning turrets and the inconceivable energies of the interstellar drive sleeping within its spine.

There was a puckered area in the centre of the ceiling. Without hesitation, one of the humanoids leaped straight upward. Its head and shoulders sank into the navel-like depression. It wriggled briefly, and its legs disappeared from view. The second humanoid gibbered encouragingly, exuding an odour of perspiring feet.

'I'll go first,' Jameson said. 'Then you, Hernando – careful not to stab me with that spear. Maggie, you're next. Dmitri, you bring up the rear.'

He sprang for the dimpled spot, and it swallowed him up. He fought his way upward through the doughy sphincter, all his senses muffled. After he'd forced his way through it for what seemed an inordinate distance, he had a moment of panic. What if he was simply burrowing into a thousand feet of insulation, to smother deep within its yielding mass? But common sense told him that the humanoids must have picked up traces of human scent. This was a definite passage, perhaps an emergency route. He could breathe in the spaces his head and shoulders opened up, though the air was stale. After what seemed hours, the spongy stuff disgorged him into an echoing void that smelled of metal and lubricants.

He was clinging to a metal slope that tilted to a dim gorge beneath. Across an intervening space a tentlike wall of metal leaned massively inward, its angle matched to the cliff he clung to.

To his right the view stopped at what he first took to be mountain ridges, until he realized that he was looking at the edge of a great toothed wheel half a mile across. There was a gargantuan jumble of machinery – ratchets and pawls and pinions on a scale that made him feel like a flea in a tower clock. To his left the enormous metal cavern stretched on for miles, and he knew that he had finally reached the axis of the ship.

The ancient metal of the cliff was scarred and pitted, its face pocked with handholds and even places to stand. He eased off to one side and helped Ruiz through, then Maggie and Dmitri. The other humanoid wriggled through last.

The feathery beings motioned him to silence and pointed up toward the peak of the metal mountain. Their gestures told him to be cautious.

He climbed the rusty slope and reached the top, another fifty feet up. He peeked over the edge. Down at the bottom of that toboggan-slide incline was another gorge, rising to another inward-leaning cliff.

Figures were moving around down there.

Human figures, tiny with distance. They milled around a projecting housing that had to be an air lock. It had a round door, pulled out like a drawer front on three shafts. Some of the figures, bulkier than the others, were either wearing spacesuits or being helped into them.

There was no way he could slide down the metal toboggan slope without being seen a long way off. Was there a way around the end of the ridge, where those gigantic gears meshed?

He eased himself cautiously down a foot and sighted along the crest.

And froze.

A mob of dark shapes was pouring out of the shadowed spaces behind the titan's gears and swarming purposefully along the ridge towards him. Jameson fumbled for his rope and hammer. He had just time enough to glance down the slope, and see that the humanoids had disappeared, when the dark shapes halted a couple of yards away. They started to deploy themselves down the two sides of the ridge to encircle him.

The one straddling the ridge, keeping his feet planted to keep from drifting off in the almost nonexistent gravity, was Gifford. He was hefting an axe. The others, wielding axes and crowbars, were members of the Chinese missile crew, six men and a chunky, muscular-looking girl.

Across the intervening space, Gifford grinned at him like a crew-cut ape. With his snub nose and flat boyish features he looked as open and friendly and uncomplicated as he always had. He shifted his grip on the axe.

'Too bad, Commander,' he said. 'You overlooked a couple of the bugs.'


# CHAPTER TWENTY-EIGHT

Jameson threw the hammer. He threw it a couple of yards to the side of Gifford, reining in the cord that was tied to it as he did so. The six-pound maul caught Gifford in the ribs, knock-

270

ing him sideways off the ridge. He began his long, slow tumble to the floor of the gorge, helpless to arrest his fall.

Jameson continued hauling in on the cord, imparting further momentum to the hammer. Next it caught one of the Chinese missile men in the side of the head, sending him rolling in slow motion down the steep slope, his crowbar clattering and bouncing along with him.

Jameson kept the hammer twirling like a lariat. It whizzed full circle around him and knocked the girl's legs out from under her. She toppled backwards and floated towards the floor of the metal canyon. Her head hit the cliffside about a hundred feet down. She'd gathered enough inertia by then for a broken skull, despite the low gravity.

Out of the corner of his eye, Jameson saw Ruiz scrambling up the slope with his spear, Dmitri and Maggie behind him. One of the Chinese stepped inside the whirling arc of the hammer. As he raised an axe, the rope twanged into him from the other side and the hammer, its pendulum swing shortened, wrapped him round in a cocoon of rope. Jameson tugged sharply, and the man went sprawling down the slope, taking rope and hammer with him.

In a split second glance, Jameson saw that Gifford's feet had made contact with the slope about two hundred feet down. He was running desperately, trying to keep on his feet, unable to stop because of his momentum. He'd have to keep running, faster and faster, all the way to the bottom, hoping that he wouldn't take a tumble. If he survived without broken bones, he wouldn't be back up here in a hurry.

With the whirling hammer gone, the other Chinese were closing in on Jameson. One of them was almost on top of him, raising an axe over his head with both hands. Jameson reached for the wrench in his belt, with the sickening realization that he wasn't going to get it out in time, wasn't going to be able to dodge out of the way, before the axe blade came crashing down on him.

But then, in a slow motion dream that was partially pumping adrenalin and partially low gravity, he saw Ruiz scrambling the last few feet to the top and thrusting with his spear. The Chinese screamed as the lashed butcher knife slid into his liver, and the axe went spinning out of his grip.

Then Dmitri was there, wading into the fray with the fire axe. His face looked white and determined. Chopping people up wasn't in his temperament, but he'd made himself realize that any hesitation, any flinching, could be fatal. He swung the axe two-handed at the nearest Chinese, his eyes closed. The Chinese dodged the axe easily, and one of his friends brought a steel bar crunching down on Dmitri's shoulder with a force that lifted his feet off the ridge. Probably he'd been aiming at Dmitri's head, but the blow disabled Dmitri anyway, smashing his clavicle. Dimtri, with a surprised expression on his face, slowly crumpled. He landed in a sitting position on the metal slope and began a toboggan slide back down where he'd started from.

Ruiz was trying to fend off an angry looking opponent with his fibreglass pole. The knife had broke off in his victim's body. Jameson crouched, the wrench in his fist, keeping his eye on the other two surviving Chinese.

Where was Maggie?

The question was answered a moment later when a Molotov cocktail came soaring up from the cliffside below. She'd aimed too high. Instead of shattering at the feet of the Chinese, the bottle, trailing a flaming wick, arced high over their heads and began to fall slowly down on the other side of the ridge. It hit about a hundred feet down and exploded in a puff of bright flame. Fiery rivulets coursed their way down the incline.

Shouts and movements came from below. All she had succeeded in doing was to attract attention. Jameson caught sight of her, clambering up the cliff with a knife in her teeth, her red hair billowing, her skinny knees scraped and bloody. And then he was ducking under a blur of metal as a bandy-legged fellow with an earnestly murderous expression swung a pry bar at him. Jameson thrust with his crescent wrench and caught the man under the chin. There was a sickening crunch, and the man folded, choking to death on a crushed larynx.

Ruiz's opponent got past the fibreglass pole, club raised, Ruiz was still tough and smart, despite his age. He was a graduate – or survivor – of the duck-board streets of the New Manhattan refugee camp, after all. He resisted the natural impulse to back away and give his enemy a clear swing at him, and instead got under the club and started hugging him. The man struggled to stay on his feet as Ruiz began gleefully to bite, gouge, and use a bony knee where it would be most painful.

The remaining Chinese had frozen, club in hand, to look at

his dying friend. His image had a snapshot clarity to Jameson as he crouched there with the bloodied spanner still in his hand. The missile man was a big fellow, with a jaw like a pelican's pouch and a spare tyre around his waist. Perhaps they'd chosen him for his size. He didn't seem to have much stomach for fighting. Jameson reached under his shirt and threw a handful of chisels at the man's face. The man threw up a thick forearm to protect himself. Jameson unfolded like a jacknife and pushed him heartily in the chest. The man yelled, '*Aii!*' and lost his balance. He rolled like a barrel down the slope towards his comrades. He was going to be a mass of bruises when he reached bottom.

A couple of people were coming up, scaling the slope. Jumping did no good; you were likely to find no handhold and have to start all over again at the bottom. It would be a while before they got here. There was a movement of blue ants towards the colossal clockwork down at the end of the cave; there must be an alternative route there.

He hurried to Ruiz on one hand and two feet. Ruiz and the missile man were doing their best to strangle each other. The Chinese had dropped his weapons; Ruiz had given him no choice with his gouging and biting. Ruiz was getting the worst of it now. The man was pressing his thumbs into Ruiz's larynx. Ruiz lost his grip and weakly tried to break the man's little finger – an old New Manhattan trick. Jameson laid his wrench along the missile man's skull. Ruiz got up, rubbing his throat. Together they tumbled the stunned Chinese down into the metal valley.

Ruiz tottered unsteadily on his feet. He turned to face Jameson.

'Thanks, I—'

He never finished. There was a spluttering sound from the Shadows at the end of the ridge, and Jameson was spattered with Ruiz's blood.

Ruiz's body began its nightmare drift down the slope. Jameson went flat and with a convulsive twist levered himself below the opposite side of the ridge. A stream of angry mosquitoes zzzz'd overhead.

'*Get down!*' he yelled to Maggie, just in time to keep her from sticking her head over the peak.

Before he could do anything, Klein's thin face rose above the metal rim, about twenty feet away, where the shadowed

273

hugeness of the Cygnan machinery overhung the cliff. Klein aimed his nasty little gun at him.

'Stay where you are, Jameson,' Klein called. 'Stay alive a minute. McInnes, move away from him.'

'Do what he says, Maggie,' Jameson said.

Jameson weighed the situation. He could launch himself in a hopeless scramble toward Klein as soon as Maggie was out of the line of fire. He might as well die trying. Or he could stay where he was and wait for Klein to rake him with automatic fire. There was no cover on that featureless metal slope.

He threw the wrench at Klein, not too fast.

Klein unhurriedly moved aside a couple of inches, and the wrench went sailing lazily past him. The aim hadn't been good.

Klein seemed to be enjoying himself. 'Got anything left to throw, Jameson?' he asked.

'As a matter of fact, I have,' Jameson said. 'Here, you can have it.'

He reached around to the back of his waistband and drew out the Cygnan cattle prod. His thumb found the recessed stud in the bulbous handle and, with a metal-bending strength impossible to Cygnan fingers, jammed it full on.

He tossed the instrument in a slow underhand pitch towards Klein, setting it spinning. His aim was better this time. Klein, with a ferret's grin, batted it aside contemptuously.

The prod's centre of gravity was somewhere in its three inches of bulbous grip. The slender prongs spun round it with a radius of fifteen inches. Naturally, whatever it was going to hit, it would hit prong end first.

Klein howled as a thousand wasps stung him. The hand holding the gun jerked upwards spasmodically, sending the weapon flying towards the shadows. Klein's senses were gone, erased by fifty thousand volts.

Jameson launched himself along the ridge in a flat dive and caught Klein's twitching body before it could fall. '*Maggie*!' he yelled. 'Get the gun!'

Klein was moaning in his arms. He was limp, paralysed. Jameson could appreciate the pain the man was feeling. He had felt it himself. It was like sticking your finger into a light socket.

He saw Maggie working her way along the rooflike slope towards the looming shapes of machinery. There was a service platform there; the gun would be somewhere on it. With the gun to hold off Chia's gang, and with Klein as hostage, there would be a chance to throw a monkey wrench into the mad plan to bomb the starship. Eventually a Cygnan would happen along, even in this uninhabited housing for the gigantic mechanism that folded the arm of the ship.

'Maggie, hurry up!' he called.

He could see the little forms of Klein's reinforcements, halfway up the slope now. Klein stirred in his arms. He'd require another touch of the prod soon. Jameson could see it, just a few feet away. Klein's convulsive spasm had slammed it against the slope, where it rested in a shallow corroded groove.

'You . . . bastard,' Klein said weakly.

There was a movement in the shadows. Jameson turned his head to see Maggie standing there under the fifty-foot teeth of the gears. She had the gun.

She pointed it at him.

'Let him go, Tod,' she said.


'Good work, McInnes,' Klein said.

Maggie stood where she was, very sensibly not coming any closer to Jameson. 'Are you going to take me with you?' she said.

Klein moved away from Jameson to leave Maggie a clear field of fire along the ridge. 'Yes,' he said. 'I promise you.'

'What about a suit?'

'You can have Mei-mei's suit. I'll fix it up with Chia. You can run a computer as well as Mei-mei can.'

'What's this all about, Maggie?' Jameson said.

'Go on, tell him,' Klein said.

Maggie faced Jameson defiantly, her knuckles white on the gun. 'I work for the Reliability Board too,' she said. 'You were my assignment.'

Jameson's knees felt weak. 'I don't believe it,' he whispered.

'That's right,' Klein said, amused. 'Her first assignment was your friend Berry. She turned in a good report on him – I don't know why they let him stay on the mission. Then she was told to watch you. You were a tough nut to crack, Jameson. She couldn't get you to make any Unreliable statements. You were a good little government boy. I told her to keep working on you. I knew you'd slip sometime. And you did. You were a Rad all along, weren't you?'.

'You're crazy,' Jameson said. He turned to Maggie. 'Maggie, how could you do a thing like that?'

She tossed her head. 'You wouldn't know!' she said bitterly. 'You've had it all, right from the start. Government family, government education, the right friends and the right opinions. How would you like to have a New England code in your pass-book, a grandfather who fought in the Secession, and a father who always got you into trouble by talking like a Rad?'

'She turned him in when she was sixteen, Jameson,' Klein said. 'That was what got her on our books. We okayed her for the Space Resources Agency training programme after that. She's worked for us ever since.'

'That apartment!' Jameson said. 'And the ski weekends at the MacDonald, and the concert tickets, and the collection of antique plastic bottles! No wonder you could afford them!'

The gun never wavered, but her eyes begged him. 'You don't understand! You were *born* Government! I had to *fight* for it! It was get into a government programme or be a dirty Privie all my life!'

Almost, Jameson was moved. But then he remembered Ruiz's body tumbling down out of sight, and Boyle, crippled.

'You're right, Maggie,' he said. 'I don't understand.'

Maggie's face had gone ugly. 'I'll tell you something!' she spat. 'You're a bore and a fool, and you're lousy in bed, and I'm glad I'll never have to listen to that stupid Giles Farnaby music again!'

'Maggie,' Jameson said steadily. 'They left you behind. They wrote you off. Don't you realize that? Give me the gun.'

Klein stooped and picked up the Cygnan prod. 'Good-bye, Jameson,' he said. There was a dreadful searing pain, and then Jameson, blind, deaf, and paralysed, was falling into an endless abyss.

There was a red darkness with bright sparks of pain drifting through it. There was a hollow silence with the sound of distant surf booming behind it, and over that, the sound of a woman sobbing.

He stirred, and hurts stabbed all through a body that was monstrously stiff and swollen and raw-edged. Presently he became aware that the sound of surf was within his skull, and the woman sobbing was outside it.

His eyes flicked open. He was sprawled, half sitting and half reclining, against the base of the metal slope. Through blurred vision he saw dim figures busily moving about on the floor of a metal plain that bulged with odd protuberances as big as glacial boulders.

The sobbing came from Maybury, a dozen yards to his left. She was huddled over the body of Dr. Ruiz, cradling his broken head. 'Dr. Ruiz, Dr. Ruiz,' she whimpered, She gulped air. 'Her – Hernando . . .'

Chia was standing a little beyond, looking down at Maybury impatiently. Her smooth, exquisite face was smudged, dark hair straggling around it. She was wearing a quilted blue spacesuit and had one of the cylindrical Chinese helmets tucked under her arm. In her ungloved hand she held a hand-laser.

'Get her into a suit,' Chia said.

Numbly Maybury allowed herself to be led away and stuffed into a spacesuit. Jameson's vision was clearing. He could see that almost everybody was suited up.

He tried to move, and discovered that he was tied up, wrists and ankles. He wriggled a bit. It hurt a lot, but nothing seemed to be broken.

Gifford came limping over, bent like an old man. 'Awake now, you son of a bitch?' he said admiringly. 'I'll bet you have a sore backside. You slid down it like a playground slide and never bounced your head once. That's more than I can say for a couple of the poor bastards you shoved over the edge. Five dead, all together. Chia wants to burn you, slow. She and Klein are still arguing about it.'

'Why am I still alive?' Jameson said.

'You can thank Maggie. She told Klein there wasn't any reason to kill you now that it's over. Said it wouldn't look good on the report. Ruiz and Boyle – that's another story. They were shot while attempting to interfere with an arbee officer in the performance of his duty.' He grinned. 'Anyway, chum, there are too many witnesses.'

He limped away to join the crowd of spacesuited figures clustered around the air lock. Was one of those bulky blue dolls Maggie? She'd have had a time squeezing into Mei-mei's suit, even with all the slack that a Chinese spacesuit provided. The Chinese, egalitarians all, didn't believe in custom fitting, but there were limits.

Jameson tested his bonds. There was no give to them. But what was the use of getting loose anyway? He felt close to despair. They'd be gone – in minutes now. They'd already got through the hardest part of their obstacle course. The Cygnans, even if searching for them, had no idea precisely where they were. Now all they had to do was cross fifty miles of space on their suit jets. How long would it take them? An hour? They'd be spotted, of course. With luck they'd be halfway across by then. Then it would take time for the Cygnans to organize a pursuit. It wouldn't take long to get the missiles in firing order. They wouldn't even bother to compute orbits, probably. Just aim them, with a proximity fuse or a radio signal. The Cygnans would snuff them out in short order, of course. But the damage would be done. How long would it take the Cygnans to repair the damage done by just one 100-megaton bomb? They'd have to jettison what was left of a pod, maybe even evacuate a whole ship if the central drive was damaged, and resettle a population of millions.

What had Ruiz said? A delay of a month in the Cygnans' departure would surely break up Earth's crust, flood it with radiation, tear it out of its orbit, as the Cygnans sailed past with their Jovian trophy. And *that* would be by mere oversight! With ten million of their sisters murdered, they might decide to do that very thing on purpose!

Jameson watched helplessly as the first group filed into the air lock, which could hold four or five people at a time.

The air lock was simplicity itself. The Cygnans were profligate with their air, just as they were with other people's hydrogen. There was no lock mechanism, no vacuum pump. You grabbed a handle on that round door and pulled it towards you manually. It slid forward like a desk drawer on three greased shafts. You had to duck under one of the shafts to get inside, but that didn't bother Cygnans. Attached to the back end of the shafts was another circular door. Once you were inside the lock, you pushed on it and squeezed through the outer opening into space. When the outside door was projecting out into vacuum, the inner disk sealed the cylindrical lock. When the inner door was pulled inward, as it was now, the outer door stopped up the shaft.

Nobody could possibly goof and leave both doors open at once. If you were polite, you pushed the door shut when you were outside. But, knowing Cygnans, Jameson doubted that they bothered. They just left it for the next fellow.

One of the Chinese was pushing on the door now, sealing

the people inside. He kept going, another six feet into the round metal tunnel, waited a minute, then pulled the door back out. It didn't seem to take much effort.

The next load included a couple of prisoners in American spacesuits. Jameson wondered who they were. Kiernan was one of them, from the bantam size of the suit. The other was a woman – Sue Jarowski or Kay Thorwald. It wasn't Maybury. She was being half supported by Klein's girl friend, Smitty, while Fiaccone screwed her helmet on.

Jameson struggled for a better position. Nobody paid any attention to him. He felt a faint breeze on his face and the nape of his neck; there was a movement of air towards the lock. It probably leaked around the edges – more Cygnan sloppiness. He was sitting more or less facing the lock, a little beyond the place where it stuck out of the bulkhead, obliquely facing the rearward jumble of gigantic clockwork and the shadowed ramp up over the ridge that had allowed Klein to take him by surprise. All he could hope for was that some Cygnan maintenance worker might come through there, past the boulderlike protuberances embedded in the floor, in time to set off an alarm.

But it was already too late for that. They were all gone now, except for a final group of five and Klein, who was just getting into his spacesuit. He evidently was going to leave last so that he could guard the rear with his machine pistol. If a Cygnan *were* to happen along, Klein would simply cut her down and be out the lock a minute later.

Mei-mei was pleading with them. She'd been stripped to her underwear. Her low-slung figure looked dumpier than usual in a coarse cotton singlet and baggy drawers. Maggie had taken the long-john liner the Chinese wore under their quilted spacesuits; Jameson couldn't help thinking that she was going to have cold wrists and ankles out there.

'No!' Jameson heard Chia say loudly. 'Go and wait with the Jameson person and do not bother me any more. You are ordered to stay here. The People's Coalition will rescue you in due course.'

'*Wo p'a te!*' the girl wailed. 'I am afraid!'

'You are stupid and counterrevolutionary!' Chia said. 'The star-worms will not hurt you. They will take you back and put you with the others.'

Mei-mei started whimpering again. Chia raised a dainty

279

hand and gave her a ringing slap across the face. 'Go! Do you want to be punished for social contradiction?'

Tears running down her pudgy face, Mei-mei slunk towards him and squatted down a few feet away. She shot him a venomous glance. Her underwear wasn't very clean. Jameson didn't envy Maggie her hour in the commandeered spacesuit and liner.

Chia and the four in her party filed into the cylindrical barrel of the air lock, stooping under the extended shafts. One of them was an American – Smitty. Klein shoved on the round manhole cover and sealed the barrel. A moment later, as somebody inside pushed the outer lid, the thick disc slid inward another six feet and stayed there.

Klein sauntered over, his helmet tucked under his arm and the machine pistol dangling at his side. He surveyed Jameson, ignoring the Chinese girl.

'I'm going to enjoy this, Jameson,' he said. 'You've given me a lot of trouble.'

'I thought you promised Maggie you'd let me stay alive.'

'That Privie bitch! I had to keep her quiet. She'll be making out her own report when we get back. And they'll be debriefing the rest of them for months.'

'But now there aren't any witnesses.'

'Right. Except Butterball here.'

'You don't have to shoot her. Nobody on this ship is ever going to see Earth again.'

'She's just a slimy ChiCom. I wish I could kill them all.'

Mei-mei had just figured out what they were talking about. She began backing away on all fours. 'No, no!' she wailed. 'Comrade Chia say—'

'Shut up!' Klein ordered.

Jameson raised himself on one elbow. 'Listen, Klein—'

'You shut up too. I don't like you, Jameson. You know you got me a reprimand on my record when you complained to Boyle at the beginning of the mission? When I get back I'm going to be a hero. The man who saved Earth from the Cygnans. I've got it all figured out. You and Ruiz say the Cygnans are planning to leave the solar system. I believe you. But not about it being dangerous if they're delayed. You just want to protect your slimy worm friends. Well, when they start moving out of the system, everybody is going to think it was because they got a taste of a couple of nukes. And I'll be the man who did it!'

'You'll never see Earth, you damned fool! It won't be there when you get there!'

Klein wasn't bothering to listen. He raised his flat little weapon and moved back about ten feet so he wouldn't get his suit splattered with blood.

Jameson wanted to sneeze.

While he was making up his mind about it, Klein *did* sneeze, a huge explosive spasm that jerked his otter-slick head back and made his little eyes water. He rubbed a sleeve across his nose and aimed the gun again.

Jameson felt awful. His throat was sore, and there was a weight like cement on his chest. His eyes itched. Behind him he heard Mei-mei coughing.

Klein staggered backwards, still trying to aim the gun. In the space of a few seconds, his face had gone puffy and splotched. His nose was running. His eyes were squeezed to tight slits.

Jameson hardly noticed. He was hacking away, and his vision was blurred by tears. His head felt like a balloon.

Klein dropped his helmet. He clawed at his throat and eyes. He seemed to be having some kind of massive histamine reaction. His swollen tongue protruded like a red rubber ball. He made choking sounds. The skin stretched tight across a face that was so distended as to be unrecognizable. He fell over on his back. The dreadful whooping sounds stopped. The hand that had been clawing at his throat went limp. It too was swollen, looking like a blown-up rubber glove.

Jameson's vision began to clear. The sneezing fits died down. He felt awful. He looked past Klein's body towards the shadow of the machinery. He detected movement there. The two pink humanoids stepped out from where they had been hiding.

Behind him, Mei-mei gasped. Then he heard her snuffling. Her head sounded as stuffed as his own.

The elfin beings bounced towards him, their silky coats lifting and falling dreamily in the weak gravity. When at last they stood before him, he could see that the pink gossamer was being ruffled by a breeze. They exuded a cool mintlike smell. He immediately began to feel better.

They plucked at his bonds with clever fingers. He got shakily to his feet and went over to look at Klein's body.

The skin had stretched so tight over Klein's face that it had split like an overripe melon. A straw-coloured serum oozed out of the cracks. Klein's features were invisible, buried in the bloated mass.

'Acute anaphylactic shock,' a voice said. 'He died of an allergic reaction.'

Jameson looked up. Dmitri was emerging from behind one of the bulky metal boulders. His right arm dangled limply from his shattered shoulder. His eyes were red-rimmed, and he was sniffling. He approached Jameson in a low-gravity shuffle.

'The humanoids?' Jameson asked.

Dmitri nodded. 'Evidently they've been around us long enough to manufacture human allergens. A whiff of some exotic protein, probably. Unstable molecular structure that breaks down in seconds – just time enough to make the human body go wild activating chymotrypsin enzymes. You were lucky to be ten feet upwind of him. It was just enough to save you.'

'How about you?'

'I was upwind too – and a good deal farther away from our pink friends. The movement of air must have been towards that lock Klein was standing in front of. These little pixies tested the wind first. So that's what those feathers are good for. They may be cute as kittens, but they're dangerous carnivores – or their ancestors were. They not only can tranquillize their prey, they can kill it at a distance, with something a lot more deadly than fang or claw.'

'Why didn't they help us before Ruiz got killed, then?' Jameson said bitterly.

Dmitri tried to shrug, then went white with pain from his shattered shoulder. When he recovered, he said, 'We were out in the open. Nothing to hide behind. And there were probably too many of them.'

'Can you stay on your feet a while longer?'

Dmitri nodded. 'I took a couple of Hernando's pep pills. His stuff was at the bottom at the other side, where I fell. They got me all the way here. It was a hell of a climb with one arm, even if I *do* weigh only a couple of pounds.'

'Can you use your good arm to help me get Klein out of his suit? Time's running out.'

Dmitri was aghast. 'You're going after them?'

'I'll have Klein's machine pistol.'

Jameson tried to pry the gun out of Klein's bloated hand.

The finger was swollen in the trigger guard. Jameson closed his eyes and pulled, but it was no use. The humanoids saw his problem. One of them made excited chipmunk noises and bit the finger off with its needle teeth. It handed the gun to Jameson.

Dmitri was being sick. When he was finally able to talk he said: 'I don't think we're going to be able to get Klein out of that suit, Tod.'

The humanoids were trying to be helpful. One of them ran and got a butcher knife that Chia's party had left behind. It cocked its head and stared at Jameson with its enormous violet eyes, then gravely offered him the knife.

Dmitri, his face ashen, said: 'You *could* butcher him inside the suit, take him out in little pieces.'

Jameson said savagely, 'And I'd *do* it if it would get me through that air lock. But the suit would be unusable.' He sniffed the stench leaking from Klein's neck ring. 'In fact, it's probably unusable now.'

The humanoids had disappeared while they were talking. When Jameson realized that fact, despair hit him like a fist. They'd probably sensed the proximity of Cygnans. It was going to be all over, any minute now. Chia and Yao's bomb crew must be miles away by now, jetting towards the Jupiter ship. Without hope or purpose, he continued to try to shoehorn the body out of the spacesuit.

Ten minutes later, Dmitri cried, 'Look!'

The humanoids were emerging from the recesses of the machinery again. They were herding a single Cygnan between them. The Cygnan acted drunk. It wobbled towards them on rubbery legs, its tail and head raised in a shallow U-shape, waving in befuddled fashion.

'Oh, fine!' Jameson said.

'Wait a minute,' Dmitri said. 'They must have something in mind. They're very bright – brighter than us, I'll bet – and they want to get off this ship in the worst way.'

They watched the humanoids put the Cygnan through some incomprehensible exercises. The Cygnan seemed very anxious to please.

'Appeasement syndrome,' Dmitri said. 'Every social species has them. Baby-biting inhibitions, submissiveness to the pack leader, food-offering to the young or the helpless. Who knows what the Cygnan equivalent is? But our feathered friends know how to trigger the hormones that cause it. And they've doped that creature up to the eyestalks, too. All it wants to do is make us all happy.'

The humanoids walked the Cygnan up to the airlock, pulled it open and hopped inside. They showed her Jameson, trying to pry Klein's body out of the suit. They patted her and caressed her and ran their feathery fingers over her snout and tail, and chattered at her in their piping voices. They weren't using any approximation of Cygnan language, Jameson could tell, but somehow they were communicating.

The Cygnan, stumbling and falling, managed to get to one of the bulbous housings near the lock. Jameson had assumed they contained some kind of machinery. But at her manipulations, the whole face of the thing opened up.

'A tool locker!' Jameson breathed. 'Look, Dmitri, some of those plastic sacks they ferried us here in. And those globular air canisters. And a rack of those broomstick scooters. And the plastic sheaths they wore over their heads and tails.'

'How are you going to use them?' Dmitri said. 'You still need a spacesuit.'

One of the little pink creatures was urging Jameson over to the locker. It plucked at his clothing with little quick movements. In a moment of shock, he realized that it was undressing him.

'Don't be shy,' Dmitri urged. 'It has something in mind. Go along with it.'

Jameson turned his back to Mei-mei and dropped his shorts. The humanoid was peeling off his shirt. When he was stripped to the buff, the Cygnan waddled over to him on four unsteady legs, carrying an object shaped like two cones, one large and one small, joined at their narrow ends. It pointed the open end of the small cone at him.

'What's it going to do?' Jameson said uneasily.

'Don't worry,' Dmitri said. 'It *loves* you.'

There was a violent hiss, and Jameson felt the shock of something cold on his body. The Cygnan was spraying him with some foaming liquid.

It scooted round and round him, spraying every square inch of his body methodically, all the way up to his chin. It made him lift both feet, one after the other, and did the soles. It paid special attention to the crevices between the toes. Then it sprayed him all over again, with more personal attentions that would have made him blush if the Cygnan had been human. The stuff made all his cuts and scrapes sting. He stood there, feeling foolish, covered with bubbles from neck to foot. In seconds, the bubbles began to collapse. He felt unpleasantly sticky for a few moments, as if he'd been coated with molasses. Then the stings and hurts on his back faded and disappeared. The stuff hardened on the surface of his body, forming a transparent rubbery membrane that showed every mole and freckle. You couldn't tell the film was there, except for the fact that it gave his skin a silvery cast, like scar tissue, and plastered down his body hair. On a Cygnan's mottled hide, it would have been entirely invisible.

'So this is why the Cygnans didn't need spacesuits,' he said.

'A spray-on spacesuit?' Dmitri said.

'Why not? What's the function of a spacesuit, except to seal in an atmosphere, regulate temperature, and pressurize the surface of the body so that blood vessels won't rupture? If Cygnan skin works anything like ours, it's already a gas-tight membrane and an efficient temperature-regulating system. Except for a breathing mask, all you really need is a kind of support hose for the entire body.'

'Why didn't the Space Resources Agency ever develop some kind of a stretch suit, then?'

'Too hard to get into. It would have to be some kind of shrink plastic that could only be used once. A spray-on's the perfect disposable!'

'Tod, that thing could kill you! You don't know if that membrane's permeable to moisture! I don't even know if Cygnans sweat!'

'I'll have to take that chance, Dmitri.' Jameson flexed his arms and legs. The membrane stretched over his joints like a second skin. 'I don't *feel* overheated. I'm going to trust the Cygnans. I'm betting that the stuff conserves just the right amount of body heat and transmits the rest to maintain a balance.'

The Cygnan was earnestly trying to fit a plastic bag over his head. He waved her off while he stepped back into his shorts, less for modesty than for the built-in support they provided. Human anatomy needed a bit more help than the Cygnan's smooth contours did.

Jameson turned to Dmitri. 'Dmitri, I—'

'I know. I'd only be in the way. Don't worry about me, Tod.

I'll stay here with Mei-mei until the Cygnans come along and put us back in the zoo. It won't be a bad life for an exobiologist. It's a fascinating opportunity, actually.'

He grimaced, then carefully sat down. The pain of his smashed bones was getting through to him, despite the pills.

'Janet will set that for you when you get back. Can you hold on till then?'

Dmitri nodded. 'Sorry I can't help. Sorry I flubbed it up on the ridge with my little hatchet, too.'

Jameson laughed. 'You've more than made up for it. Thanks.'

Dmitri looked thoughtful. 'There'll be a lot for me to do here. We're going to have to learn how to get along with the Cygnans. If they don't have the empathy, we'll make up for it. They're going to learn a thing or two about human beings, too. We won't stay zoo animals forever. We'll breed – we've always been good at that. Too good. In another six million years, who knows? Maybe there'll be a new partnership out there among the stars – the descendants of free-living flatworms existing side by side in technological symbiosis with the descendants of parasitic roundworms.'

The tranquillized Cygnan finally put the plastic sheath over Jameson's head and inflated it from one of the globular canisters. It was a tight fit, rather like a stocking mask, but it stretched. The canister stuck between his shoulder blades with an adhesive disc. A simple transparent hose connection, part of the sheath, plugged in to it. There was no provision for removal of wastes; Jameson suspected that the sheath was selectively permeable to heavier gas molecules. A careful squirt around the neck of the sheath sealed it to him.

Jameson sniffed the air. It smelled good.

The two pink pixies were urging the Cygnan into a sack. It crawled inside and curled up peaceably. The two humanoids crawled in after it, with a collection of air canisters.

They wanted to take it along!

After half a minute of futile gestures, Jameson gave in. He sealed the neck of the sack and turned to Dmitri. Dmitri's lips were forming the words 'Good luck.' Mei-mei was huddled next to him, big-eyed.

Jameson looked over at where Ruiz's crumpled body lay. The gaunt profile, skin stretched like parchment over the sharp cheeks and the beak of a nose, stared past the metal ceiling, perhaps a mile overhead, to something unseeable beyond.

'So long, Hernando,' Jameson said. 'You tried.'

With Klein's gun in his belt and a Cygnan broomstick in his hand, he picked up the transparent balloon with its two or three pounds of alien life inside, and stepped through the lock into the dark.

## CHAPTER TWENTY-NINE

A necklace of people stretched across the stars. Jameson counted: twenty-seven of them, all holding hands. They'd turned off their thrusters long since. They were falling raggedly toward the spoked wheel of the Jupiter ship a couple of miles away – a circle drawn round a Y, shining with reflected Jupiter light.

He was riding the Cygnan broomstick backward, braking at a reckless quarter g, gripping it with both hands and clamped thighs to keep from sliding down the slender shaft toward the deadly beam of light that fanned out from its business end. The four-foot bubble with the Cygnan and the two humanoids curled inside was snubbed securely to the shaft.

The necklace was mostly blue, with nine white human trinkets spaced along it. Six of them would be the American prisoners, each sandwiched between two guards. That left twenty-one of them to deal with – including Maggie.

He eased down the thrust, matching velocities. The broomstick had only one control, a sliding stud that turned it on and graduated the thrust all the way up to one g. You pointed it where you wanted to go, and you judged your turnover point by eyeball and by the seat of your pants.

The necklace broke up as he approached, turning into a random swarm of blue and white manikins. Jameson slid the little flat pistol out of the waistband of his shorts.

He wondered what he looked like to them. He must be a startling figure, bare-chested in airless space, straddling a metal staff with a rainbow bubble shimmering at his back.

Suit jets flared, quick diamond sparkles against blackness, as the drifting shapes used their suit radios to organize themselves. Jameson was acutely aware of his nakedness.

At a quarter mile, Jameson switched off that frightening beam of raw energy. The prisoners were mixed up in the jumble of stuffed figures. He might have drawn his finger of light across his enemies, but the others would have sizzled and fried too. He was going to have to get in amongst them.

He twisted around, climbing the stick like a firepole, one leg twined and one hand gripping to give him maximum freedom of movement. His agility in the skintight sheath would be an advantage. He hadn't realized it was possible to feel this free in space.

Slowly, slowly, the figures became more distinct, seeming not to move closer but to grow before his eyes. They were a complicated frieze against a speckle of frosty stars, sharp and harshly lit in the clarity of vacuum. He could pick out faces behind faceplates: Chia, her rosebud lips curled, holding Maybury's upper arm with one hand and with the other fumbling in her toolbelt. Yeh with his big jaw and sloping shelf of brow. A young Chinese fusion tech, looking frightened. Gifford, staring popeyed at him, one mittened hand closing on a screwdriver.

And then he was among them, one bare foot lashing out to kick Gifford away before Gifford, clumsy in his suit, could slash with the screwdriver. A Chinese missile man was swinging at him with a barbed hook, like something moving in a dream. He dodged easily and fired a burst at close range into the broad chest. Klein's ugly little gun twitched in his hand. He was appalled at what happened then: The spacesuit shredded and bits of the living man inside exploded outward. Jameson's momentum kept him going. He crashed into Yeh, and instantly the man's big mitts were closing on the plastic balloon around his head. Jameson ducked out of the way, and before Yeh could grab, a thrust of Jameson's shoulder had sent him spinning out of the fight.

Another man from the missile crew collided with him. Something gleamed in a mittened fist. Jameson let go of the broomstick, and his left hand found the safety latch at the man's airhose connection. He gave a yank. The stuffed suit twitched and the mittened fist opened up. A sharp little awl drifted away. The body tumbled lazily backward, horror behind its faceplate.

Jameson then found himself in a clear space, a flock of people wheeling around him like gulls. Suit jets puffed out their glittering motes, and four blue shapes were converging on him. He had time to recognize Yao's face behind glass, the lean ascetic features drawn back in a rictus. He fired, and the missile

288

officer ran into a hail of little bees that plucked at the material of his suit and turned him into a rag doll. Jameson swivelled and cut the two men flanking Yao into ribbons. Still rotating on his axis, he aimed the machine pistol at the fourth man, coming at him with a glowing soldering iron fed by a cable from a belt pack.

He pulled the trigger, but nothing happened.

*Empty!*

He flung the pistol at the man's helmet. It bounced off. The man kept coming. The tip of the soldering iron shone orange. Jameson wriggled helplessly in emptiness. The broomstick with its vacuole of alien life hung out of reach, slowly twisting. Jameson had no reaction mass, no way to move. He hovered there, waiting for the searing touch of the iron.

And then there was a flash of brilliant light, brief as lightening. The Chinese disappeared below the waist. The torso came tumbling on, the gloved hands clenching and unclenching reflexively in the brain's last memory of pain. When the half of a man bumped Jameson, the soldering iron was swinging on its tether and he was able to snare it without getting burned.

He twisted his head around and saw the Cygnan broomstick sailing away under the impetus of the burst of light. One of the humanoids must have managed to reach the sliding stud through the yielding membrane and switch it on for the fraction of a second that it was lined up with the attacking Chinese.

They'd chosen sides, all right!

Nobody else seemed to have been touched by the finger of light, but now the broomstick was a hundred yards away and still retreating. The humanoids might be able to turn it on, but they couldn't aim it. There was another flash of light that only worsened their vector, and then they were falling into endless night.

There was a sparkle of a suit jet, and one of the white suits that had been hanging against the flamboyant backdrop of Jupiter took off after the broomstick. It wasn't Gifford; Jameson could see him hovering next to one of his Chinese friends. Was it Fiaccone?

He located Chia's small blue suit in the starry space around him. Aiming himself carefully, he shoved as hard as he could at the dreadful thing that was bumping against him. The dismantled torso floated off, and Jameson was coasting with nightmare slowness towards Chia.

Chia let go her grip on Maybury and pointed something at Jameson – the corkscrew-wrapped barrel of a hand-laser. He could see it pulsating with faint light as its flash tubes pumped photons. It would take only a couple of seconds until photon excitation reached the critical point; then a spurt of energetic light was going to drill him clean through.

He floated relentlessly towards her, powerless to change direction. With the light of Jupiter on her, she was limned sharp and clean in his vision. Behind the square visor her face was a blushing peach, distorted by fury. The half-naked apparition before her had ruined her plans, probably beyond salvage. Only five members of the bomb crew were left, without Yao to direct them.

Jameson was only a dozen feet from her now. He wondered if it would hurt.

A thread of violet light stretched past him and winked off. Maybury, floating forgotten behind Chia, had come out of her daze of grief. Or perhaps she had only been waiting. She had Chia's wrist in a small gloved hand. The laser flashed again. Then Maybury's other hand in its stubby-fingered gloves was spread over Chia's faceplate, unscrewing the fastenings. Chia struggled, like an overstuffed doll in her spacesuit, but she couldn't get her arm back far enough to dislodge Maybury. The faceplate blew off and the peachlike face behind it burst with running juices.

Jameson collided with the tangled bodies. Gently he pried Maybury's hands loose and pried the laser from Chia's grasp. He gave the body a little push to disengage it, and made Maybury understand that he wanted to keep holding on to her for the use of her suit jets.

No more than fifty feet away, Gifford's wide form blocked the stars, the screwdriver still clasped in a mittened fist. He was conferring, helmet to helmet, with one of his Chinese allies, his other hand gripping the man's sleeve. Jameson tensed, waiting to see what the two of them would do. The laser in his hand was very comforting.

The helmets came apart. Gifford still was steadying himself with a grip on his friend's arm. Then, with a swift, savage motion, he plunged the screwdriver into the belly of the man's suit. Jameson couldn't tell immediately if it had penetrated. Gifford reversed his grip and smashed the weighted handle of the screwdriver into the Chinese faceplate. He kept hammering until the visor went frosty. The blue suit had become floppy. Gifford held the screwdriver up, letting Jameson see it, then tossed it away.

Jameson nodded.

Gifford swam over to another white suit, which had to be Fiaccone, and the two of them went over to get Smitty. Jameson could tell that it was Smitty because he could see a glint of golden hair inside the helmet; it had come undone, filling the bowl. They all put their helmets together for a minute, conferring. Then they waved their hands outward toward Jameson in the universal gesture.

Other white suits were drifting towards Jameson on short bursts of thruster: the prisoners; nobody among the remaining ten Chinese was bothering to keep any of them under guard. One of the Americans – an undersized suit that had to contain Kiernan – had gotten hold of some kind of floating tool, and he was shaking it threateningly in the direction of the Chinese. It must have massed considerable, because Kiernan was bobbing up and down at the end of the handle almost as much as the tool was.

The clustered Chinese had turned to watch something. Jameson looked in the same direction.

A pencil of light was drawn against the frosty void – the broomstick coming back. The American who had chased it was bringing it back. Jameson could see the white doll-like figure hunched over the shaft. The bubble with its curled-up Cygnan and foetal humanoids was still snubbed in place.

The figure swung the shaft under, climbing for a moment on a pillar of fire, then did a complete backflip, rising on arms and legs like a jockey. The searing beam of light traced a large circle around the scattered swarm of people, then died out as most of the rider's forward velocity was cancelled.

It had been an expert braking manoeuvre.

It had also been an object lesson.

The Chinese went into a quick conference by radio. Jameson could tell they were talking by the amount of nodding and gesturing that went on.

The broomstick rider drifted in Jameson's direction, using suit jets to damp out the remaining momentum. As he came close, Jameson saw that it was Mike Berry, with a big grin on his face.

The Chinese finished their discussion. They made ostentatious palms-outward gestures and floated over to join the Americans. What was left of the Jupiter expedition was united again.

A last blue-clad figure, awkward in a spacesuit that was too small a fit, had been left behind. That would be Maggie in her borrowed suit. After a moment, she followed. She had nowhere else to go.

## CHAPTER THIRTY

'Where are the six-legs?' Li said, sweating inside his helmet. He'd removed his faceplate and mittens so that he could work faster, even though the Callisto landing module wasn't fully pressurized yet. 'They must know for long time now that we here in ship.'

'I don't know,' Jameson said tightly. 'I just hope that they don't come after us for at least a couple of hours. By then we ought to be far enough away and moving fast enough so they'll figure it isn't worth the bother of chasing us.'

He continued working with his screwdriver on the guts of the dismantled control panel. He'd torn the plastic bag off his head as soon as he safely could. The Cygnan spray-on spacesuit already was starting to flake away in white scales that looked like dead skin – evidently a consequence of being exposed to atmosphere after being in vacuum. When his job in the lander was finished, somebody was going to have to come out with a spare spacesuit to ferry him back to the ship.

Maybury was wedged uncomfortably against him, crouching in front of the luminous squiggles of the lander's computer console. The cockpit wasn't really big enough for three people. She had been plotting escape orbits through a radio link to the Jupiter ship's data banks, but now she was looking through a telescope out the bowl-shaped port.

'Commander, you'd better have a look,' she said.

He took the telescope from her. Jupiter overflowed the port. a billowing globe that now had a distinct rim around it. The sticklike Cygnan ships were black hieroglyphs against its face. They were arranged in a five-pointed figure rotating around a common centre of gravity.

Looking at those forked shapes, it was hard to believe they contained worlds.

Jameson lifted the eyepiece to his face. He saw that Maybury had programmed the telescope's pea brain to damp out most of the light on Jupiter's chaotic wavelengths. The tortured planet was a dim ghost among the stars. The five ships were no longer silhouettes. They took on proper three-dimensional shapes, chisel-edged constructions illumined by the amplified light of the distant Sun.

A ruby thread of light stretched between two of the crouched forms. Laser light. Jameson wondered if one of the ships was the one he had been on; he'd lost track of their positions.

Now another thread of light stabbed out, linking with a third ship. From the tips of the inverted V, two more beams joined themselves to ships at the lower points.

'What is it?' Li said, sweat rolling down his face.

'They're communicating,' Jameson said. 'Keep working.'

Cursing in Chinese, Li continued to trace circuits. He ripped out a tiny wire and respliced it elsewhere.

The Cygnan ships had to be shedding a lot of dust and molecular debris to make the laser light that distinct. The invisible cloud that surrounded the fleet must have grown to a radius of thousands of miles in the months they'd been parked here.

'Sloppy housekeeping,' Jameson muttered.

'What?' Maybury said. 'Oh, you mean whatever's scattering light. Cygnan ships are leaky, aren't they?'

Jameson continued watching. The lines traced a pentagram across Jupiter's spectral face in filaments of red fire. The angle of vision foreshortened it a little, giving it depth. He knew it was rotating, though he'd have to wait a long time before he saw movement.

An astonishing thing happened next. A perfect five-pointed star etched itself within the pentagram.

Of course, it was a geometric accident, the consequence of every ship being linked up with every other ship, but it was a strange and spellbinding sight all the same.

A pentacle within a pentagram.

He gasped just as the sign erased itself.

'What happened?' Li said.

'They've stopped talking. We haven't much time.'

He handed the telescope back to Maybury and took up his screwdriver again. There was a clipboard of checklists for powering and firing the landing vehicle in an assortment of circumstances, but they were of limited value. None of them included the problem of using the craft's engines while it was still clamped to the mother ship. Before Jameson dared cut in the engines, he and Li had to disconnect the safety circuits and improvise an entirely new firing sequence.

'What do you think?' he asked Li.

'Another half-hour.'

Jameson punched through to the bridge. Kay Thorwald's plain, pleasant face showed up on the little screen.

'Ready to blast in a half-hour, Kay,' he said. 'What's the condition of the ship?'

'We've finished a preliminary damage survey, Tod. There's nothing we can't fix – in time. We're not going to try to make the whole ring airtight. We'll all just have to live in close quarters in a few of the compartments. Kiernan says he can get the air plant going – enough frozen seed stock survived.'

'How about the attitude controls? Can we get this ship pointed in the right direction?' He glanced down at the slip of paper Maybury was shoving under his nose. 'Maybury says that if we fire in thirty minutes, you've got to line the ship up with Vega and keep correcting for the angle of my push.'

'Just a minute.'

She turned away from the screen towards a work table where Yeh was going over some diagrams with Fiaccone. She and Yeh talked a moment.

'Comrade Yeh says that he can do it. Some of our attitude jets are gone, but we can lock the ring and use the thrusters that normally set it spinning. There's a good distribution of workable ones around the circumference. We're feeding the problem to the computer now.'

'Thanks, Kay.'

He switched off and got the engine room. A harried-looking Chinese fusion tech said, '*Dong-yi-dong*, I'll get him.'

Mike appeared on the screen, his hair and beard dishevelled.

'How long?' Jameson said.

Mike scratched his head. 'The Cygnans didn't touch much,' he said. 'But they bollixed things up just looking. Quentin will have the boron part of the cycle fixed in a couple of hours. But we can't get a fusion reaction going for at least a day.'

'It's up to Li and me, then,' Jameson said.

'You and the Giff,' Mike said and signed off.

Jameson looked out a port at the long shaft of the ship. Gifford's white spacesuit was visible among the blue-clad Chinese strapping down a scoop-nosed drone that Jameson recognized as one of the Jupiter's cloud top orbiters. Just over the curve of the hull was the stubby shape of the vehicle that contained the radiation-shielded crawler that had been destined for a soft landing on Io. They had represented a bold ambition of the human race. Now, he thought sadly, neither of them would ever be used. Their increment of thrust – that's all they were good for now.

He tried to attract Gifford's attention through the port, but failed. He called Communications and got Sue Jarowski. 'Sue,' he said, 'can you patch me through to Gifford's suit radio?'

'Right away.' He watched her face as she pushed buttons. The long Cygnan captivity had melted flesh from her wide Slavic cheekbones, making them even more prominent. Her full, bold mouth and strong chin were set in concentration. Absent-mindedly she pushed back a curtain of thick dark hair. Jameson was thinking how striking she looked when Gifford's voice crackled from the speaker.

'Yeah?'

Outside, Gifford was looking in his direction. He raised a gloved hand and waved toward the window of the Callisto lander.

'How's it coming?' Jameson said.

Gifford's voice came over the sound of frying eggs. 'Give us another couple of hours and we can get one more drone out of its cocoon, pointed in the right direction, and bolted down. Then we gotta come inside. These boys can't work under acceleration. It ought to be enough to start the push. When we run out of juice, we'll come out again and strap on a cluster of rocket engines from the missiles.'

'A couple of hours?' Jameson said. 'Can you cut that in half?'

'Commander,' Gifford said, sounding aggrieved, 'I've got only five of these boys to work with, plus Smitty. And she's still under your boat, bolting on the braces.'

'Can we break out of orbit with just the vehicles you've got ready now?'

'Maggie says no. If you want me to, I'll ask her to run the figures through the computer again.'

Jameson's face turned to stone. 'Don't bother,' he said. 'I'll take her word for it. Just work as fast as you can.'

Maybury made a small choking sound behind him. 'They're coming,' she said.

Jameson looked out the other port. Space was filled with a sudden hail of fire. Over a front that must have been a hundred miles across, streaks of light lengthened and shrank to points again, like golden straws tumbling among the stars.

'That was their turnover point,' Jameson said. 'They're half-way across. Decelerating at one g, they'll be here in minutes.'

Li looked up from the console, his blunt peasant face smeared with grime where he'd wiped away sweat with stained fingers. 'All through now,' he said. 'Safety override is off. Now we should put it through test sequence.'

'No time,' Jameson said. 'We'll have to take our chances.' He spoke into the mike pickup. 'Gifford, hear this. Tell the men they have thirty seconds to find something to grab on to. We're moving.'

He switched off before Gifford could object. Some of the men must have been listening through their own circuits. There was a scramble as stuffed blue dolls wrapped themselves around stanchions, hooked themselves onto safety rails. Immediately under the port, Jameson saw Smitty wriggle out from beneath the lander and glide belly-down along the hull until she found a grip.

He settled down in the pilot's seat beside Li, and the two of them began to run through the newly edited checklist for powering the vehicle. Maybury crouched behind them, light pad in hand, helping them keep track of all the changes.

It felt strange to be doing it this way, after all the months of training. He and Li had honed themselves for one purpose: to land the spidery craft on the surface of Jupiter's second-largest moon. The lockers behind them were crammed with geological equipment. The little boxy hovercraft for exploring Callisto's surface was still folded in its bay. Now the lander would never touch down. It had been turned into a tugboat.

The main engine fired, and the cabin shook with unplanned stresses. A few seconds later, Jameson saw through the port that Gifford had ignited the strapped probes by radio signal. Little jets flared along the shaft of the main ship and along the circumference of the ring, as Kay and Yeh compensated for the irregularities in direction of the thrust.

There was no sensation of movement yet. The buildup was going to be slow, slow.

Maybury's voice came hesitantly. 'Maggie's calculations were correct, you know. This won't break us out of orbit.'

Without turning his head, Jameson said, 'You checked her figures, then?'

'Yes,' Maybury said in a small voice.

'It doesn't matter,' Jameson said. 'We'll get ourselves into a return trajectory later. All I want to do now is get us moving!'

Slowly, like a freight train being pushed along the tracks by an elephant, the great wheel-and-axle of the Jupiter ship responded. Jameson could feel the first faint suggestion of weight on the seat of his pants. There was visible movement against the grid of stars, some of it lateral as the ungainly mass shuddered to align itself.

It wasn't good enough.

Outside the port, space was alive with beams of light, flashing on and off as thousands of Cygnans made their final correction manoeuvres. They were close enough to be visible through the port, little squirming golden worms clinging to matchsticks.

'Tod, *p'eng yu*,' Li said, staring straight ahead. He'd used the word for 'friend', not 'comrade'. 'I want you to know I'm sorry. None of it was my idea.'

Outside, trapped on the hull, one of the Chinese missile men lost his nerve and threw a wrench at the naked creatures swarming on their broomsticks. It tumbled harmlessly past one of the nearer Cygnans, who oozed sidewise to avoid it.

'What will they do?' Maybury said in a strained voice.

Jameson shifted in his seat. 'We've got nukes aboard,' he said. 'We ran through their ship like weasels in a chicken house, killing. What would you do?'

Maybury's hand, small as a child's, was clutching his, the nails digging into his palm. Li stared out the window, saying nothing. Outside, Gifford's work party had drawn together in a small defensive group, their movements hampered by the necessity of using a hand to keep from drifting away under the ship's gentle acceleration. The Cygnans had no such problem. Some of them had already touched down, anchored to anything handy by whatever hand or foot was convenient, like sea polyps swaying in the current. At the head of the ship they were crawling like maggots all over the observation bubble.

'*Oh!*' Maybury gasped.

Jameson jerked his head around to see what had startled her.

She was staring, wide-eyed, toward the Cygnan fleet in the distance. At this angle it could be seen against the dark. They'd moved far enough by now so that it hung like a cluster of shiny grapnel hooks above the raw and bloody carcass of Jupiter.

The laser light was flashing between them again. The figure of the five-pointed star within the pentagram did not appear again. Instead there was a shifting play of spiky forms as each ship in turn sent out brief tendrils of light to all its companions. A succession of clawed figures, looking like Greek or Hebrew letters, flamed red against the face of night.

Jameson could not guess at the message content. But the flashing signals galvanized the Cygnan horde. Like shiny midges, they rose by the hundreds off the crippled ship and wheeled and darted in a forming swarm. A thousand beacons lit the night, and then they were vanishing, a cloud of distant sparks heading with incredible velocity toward the ships beyond.

'They're gone!' Maybury said wonderingly.

Jameson looked across at the barbed shapes of the ships hovering over Jupiter's ripe and swollen orb, still semaphoring their sins and psis and lambdas, drawing fiery scratches in the void.

'Not quite yet,' he said.

They were four million miles out, well past the orbit of Callisto, when it happened. The feeble engines of the probes and missiles had not yet set them free, but had put them in a loose elliptical orbit that would carry them outside the orbit of Jupiter VII. Mike, Quentin, and the three Chinese fusion techs were working round the clock. Everybody pitched in to help: Maggie and Maybury on the engine-room computers, Jameson and Li and Fiaccone unplugging the damaged outside structures. Jameson had passed Maggie a couple of times in the corridors without speaking to her.

Now Jameson slumped, exhausted, in a contour seat on the ship's bridge. Mike had promised boron fission within a couple of hours. The last missile rocket engine had been expended.

'What if they come back?' Kay Thorwald said, looking at him with red-rimmed eyes through a strand of straggling hair. 'Even when we get going, we can only accelerate at a hundredth of a g. They can catch up to us in a few hours, any time they feel like it.'

Jameson looked out through the big bubble at Jupiter's bright sphere. Io, or the sodium glow that surrounded it, was visible as a fuzzy yellow golfball that from this angle seemed to be poised just above Jupiter's eastern edge. The Cygnan ships were invisible, but they could be seen through a telescope as a glowing pentad hovering close to Io, keeping its bulk between them and the giant planet. They had transferred their orbit from their own moon, the one they had brought with them, to Io with its closer position, a bit over a quarter of a million miles from Jupiter. The pentacle of laser light was evidently a calibrating device as the five ships fine-tuned their new joint orbit.

'That's not what I'm worried about,' Jameson said. 'They're ready to move, all right. Those ships started changing their orbit about three seconds after the boarding party got back to them. What worries me is being this close to Jupiter. If we're still in orbit around it when they start moving, we'll go right along with them. And we don't have Io to shield us from radiation once they start moving through interstellar hydrogen at close to light speed.'

'We be dead long before that time,' Yeh grunted from his console. His lumpy acromegalic face was lined with fatigue. He had worked without rest since reaching the ship.

Jameson nodded. 'If we didn't get torn loose by the sun and fry to death, it would be hunger, decompression, or systems failure. Take your pick. We'll be lucky to nurse this wreck back to Earth in one piece.'

'*Bye dzwe na-yang!*' Yeh suddenly bellowed. 'Don't touch that!'

The feathery humanoid snatched its hand away from the control board, its teddy-bear face looking somehow hurt. It rewarded Yeh with a bad smell, something like rotten eggs, and pranced off to join its friend over at one of the scattered monitor screens on the floor.

'Mischievous little devils, aren't they,' Kay said.

Jameson watched the rosy-furred creatures fiddle with the console. They had somehow managed to conjure up a star chart. Now one of them was making peeping field-mouse noises, rolling the display, while the other one danced around in front of the view window, pointing at constellations.

'They aren't the simple hunters they seemed to be, any more than we still are,' Jameson said. 'They come from a techno-

299

logically advanced civilization. They were trying to show Mike something about how the Cygnan broomstick worked until he threw them out of the engine room. I think that before we get back home they'll be helping us man this ship.'

The pink bipeds had been an invaluable help with the Cygnan prisoner, keeping it tranquillized and getting it settled in a cage – a cage, Jameson reflected, that was probably less comfortable than the one he'd been confined in aboard the Cygnan vessel. The Cygnan was in Kiernan's care now. It would have a lot of hamsters for company if Kiernan could get a few of the frozen ova in his files to start dividing. The humanoids had painstakingly sniffed every food and biological sample that Kiernan had shown them to try to improvise a diet that would keep the Cygnan alive until they got back to Earth. One of the things it could eat, surprisingly, was turkey, so it was going to get everybody's portion of frozen Christmas dinner – if everybody lived that long. The humanoids themselves had rejected all terrestrial animal protein, and were putting together a combination of spun vegetable protein that evidently added up to the right balance of amino acids. With the superbly analytical laboratories in their noses, they were in no danger of starving.

The Cygnan prisoner, the humanoids had given Jameson to understand, was not just some run-of-the-mill technician, but was an important person they had taken some pains to select. They seemed desperately to want to keep it alive.

The humanoid looking at the stars suddenly bounced into the air and tumbled weightlessly toward Jameson like a giant ball of pink milkweed. Its fluffy tail whipped around the guardrail to anchor it, and it plucked at Jameson's sleeve, making urgent piping sounds. When it finally had Jameson's attention, it struck itself on its little chest and flung a slender arm toward the constellation Cygnus.

'What in the world,' Kay said.

'He's telling us where his home is,' Jameson said.

'Of course. It would have to be somewhere in the volume of space between here and Cygnus, along the Cygnans' line of flight. But which star? It might not even be visible to the naked eye.'

'It's not Deneb or Albireo. They're too far away from the line of sight toward Cyg X-1, and we know the Cygnans came in more or less under its X-ray umbrella. Wait a minute! I think it's trying to tell me that it's 61 Cygni! But if *that's* so, then—'

Jameson didn't get a chance to finish. Yeh had risen from his seat so abruptly that he had to grasp an armrest to keep from floating off.

'*K'an, K'an!*' he said excitedly. 'Look! It happens!'

In a moment the three of them were crowding the observation rail, looking out into the dark. An awesome event was taking place out there.

Against the burning stars, Jupiter moved!

Jameson could only gape. The scale of what he was witnessing was almost beyond human grasp.

Slowly, ponderously, the colossal bulk of the planet stirred.

It sloshed.

Across its seething face, a great sluggish tidal wave of thickened hydrogen brimmed over hundreds of miles of atmosphere and lapped in an advancing wall that would have tumbled Earth like a cork.

It stretched.

It no longer was the oblate sphere that man had known since he started looking at it through telescopes. The thing spinning around its waist had given it a flying-saucer shape, a hatbrim of raging hydrogen fighting to pour itself into the circling maw of a gnat.

The gnat had strained and swallowed an elephant. By now, zipping around the captive giant at very nearly the speed of light, the robot probe had converted enough of the stolen hydrogen into Einsteinian mass to tug at the remainder of that tremendous corpse.

How much of Jupiter was left? To Jameson, it looked no smaller than before. Perhaps it had lost a few thousand miles of diameter, perhaps not. As its outer layers were stripped away, the rest of that compressed hydrogen, relieved of pressure, would tend to boil and swell. And even with half its bulk gone, Jupiter would still be the most massive object in the solar system other than the sun itself.

'It won't be there!' Kay said suddenly. 'I just realized that from now on when we look up in the sky at night to find Jupiter, it won't be there!'

Jameson looked around and was amazed to see tears running down the mannish cheeks. 'Sorry,' Kay said. 'I'm just tired.'

'It'll be our turn some day, Kay,' he said. 'When we've used up everything else, we'll start using up the planets.'

With trembling hands he swung one of the stubby ship's telescopes around in its gimbals and turned on the magnetic lens. The computer-controlled fields flexed transparent plastic, shaped a pool of mercury into a reflecting curve. A picture stirred itself into being on the photoplastic plate behind the eyepiece, held steady by the electronic image compensator.

A Cygnan ship stretched toward him like a claw. It had stopped rotating. The three long spars, with their buckets of life at the ends, spread motionless from the tip of the notched beam of the drive section. As Jameson watched, the buckets swivelled in their wishbone cradles and snapped into place, reversed. He tried to imagine what was happening inside those worldlets. Had the lakes with their queer bright sailboats been drained? Were the animals hushed in their cages, waiting for gravity to resume?

The spars folded inwards, swinging through their fifteen-mile arcs. Jameson could see how their triangular cross sections and the three-sided buckets fit into the grooved sides of the starship, just as Pierce had said they would.

He lifted his face from the eyepiece. Jupiter was picking up momentum, like a stone rolling downhill. It moved past the stars, dragging its moons with it.

And us too, if we don't fire our engines soon, he thought.

He called the observatory and got Maybury. She'd finished her work in the engine room a couple of hours ago.

'Are you recording?' he asked.

'Yes, Commander.'

'How fast are they accelerating?'

'One gravity, same as before.'

'Their trajectory. Is it going to be what we figured?'

In the screen, Maybury bit her lip. 'It's too early to tell, Commander.'

'Keep tracking them.' He switched off.

Kay had returned to her console, taking instrument readings with Yeh and feeding questions to the ship's computer. She looked up as Jameson returned to his seat.

'We're going to have a lot of borrowed momentum when we break loose from Jupiter,' she said. 'We may reach Earth in less than four months.'

Jameson nodded. 'The astronomers are going to have a

merry time figuring out what all that gravitational displacement will do to the balance of the solar system.'

Kay hesitated. 'Tod, will ... will the Earth be safe?'

Jameson drew a long breath. 'We'll know for sure in just a couple of days. That's all the time it will take for them to cross Earth's orbit.'

Before returning to his cabin to collapse in his bunk, Jameson sought out Maybury in the observatory.

The ship's engines had been firing steadily for a couple of hours now; Mike and Quent, and the three Chinese fusion techs, were taking turns staying awake to monitor the boron-11 fusion/fission cycle. Maggie had calculated an escape orbit from the death-grip of Jupiter, which was now falling towards the Sun at more than a thousand kilometres a second. Enough manoeuvring jets had been unplugged so that Kay had even been able to put some spin on the ring. The ship would live until it got back to Earth.

Provided Earth was still there.

Maybury looked up from a computer console as he entered. Her face looked dreadful: a wan porcelain mask with two great dark holes in it. Her head moved as though her neck had gone stiff.

'Still working?' he said.

'I thought I'd just set up some hypothetical programmes to calculate gravitational stresses for Earth using various trajectories for Jupiter.'

'You don't have to stay awake for that. There's not a damn thing anybody can do to change things.'

'I know. It's just something to do.'

He settled down in a seat next to her. With the engines firing, he had almost two pounds of weight.

'I found out where the two humanoids came from.'

She was all attention. 'Where?'

'61 Cygni.'

She nodded slowly. 'It could be. It's roughly in the line of flight from Cygnus X-1.'

'And it's *close*.'

'That's right. Eleven point two light-years away. There are only a dozen stars that are closer to us.'

'If Dr. Ruiz's theory was correct...' He stopped till the pain disappeared from her face. 'Then that must have been the

303

Cygnans' last stop before they headed for Earth. Our feathery zoo mates were the Cygnans' most recent acquisition before us.'

'But 61 Cygni was never considered to be a prime candidate for life.'

'It is now.'

'It's a double star, actually. The two suns are a K5 and a K7. Very weak. About six per cent of the luminosity of our own sun. There wouldn't be much of a biosphere for habital planets. Are you sure you understood the humanoids correctly?'

'61 Cygni has a third component,' he prompted her.

'But it isn't a star,' she said. 'It's a nonluminous body. A planet. Actually, one of the first extra-solar planets to be discovered. It's a superjovian, with a mass about twelve times Jupiter's. It . . .' She stopped. 'Oh.'

'Exactly.'

She swivelled back to the computer console so quickly that Jameson had to press her shoulder to push her back in her seat. Her hands scrabbled over the keys. Words tumbled out of her as she worked. 'Dr. Ruiz transferred big chunks of the Farside computer's astronomical library to the ship's memory before we left Earth. He wanted to be sure we had updated data. The third component of 61 Cygni was discovered over a hundred years ago when they noticed some irregularities in the proper motion of the binary. They started to discover a lot of extra-solar superjovians that way about then – most of them among the closer stars, of course. But nobody keeps tabs on them much any more. They get surveyed every few years in the automated sky sweeps, and if anybody wants to pull data out of the record for a graduate paper or anything, they can. Here we are. A check was made on it about five years ago, and then another just about a month before we launched this mission.'

They both stared avidly at the data coming up on the screen. Jameson was unable to interpret the tables of astonomical figures. 'What's it mean?' he said.

'Five years ago 61 Cygni had its usual wobble. Now it doesn't.'

'The superjovian's gone, then.'

Maybury was going over the figures. 'The Cygnans would have taken it a little more than eleven years ago. Its light ran ahead of them – but not by much of a margin. We would have seen the wobble until just before the Cygnans arrived – if we'd known enough to look for it.'

Jameson looked out the viewport. The cast-off moons of Jupiter were now the brightest objects in the sky. They were tumbled carelessly across the night, like scattered dice, still rather close together. He picked out the biggest of them, a smooth white ball, the apparent size of a golfball, that had captured its own marble-sized moon.

'That's its core,' he said. 'All that's left of a planet twelve times the mass of Jupiter. It belongs to the feathery folk. Too bad there's no way to get it back to them.'

Maybury had found something in the figures that interested her. She was making side calculations on a lightpad.

'They were astronauts,' Jameson went on. 'They made me understand that with pantomime. They were out quite a distance from their world, exploring asteroids, when the Cygnans scooped them up. They've got space flight, the same as we do. But their race doesn't have star travel yet. They were as excited by the Cygnan broomstick as Mike was. They want to go home.' He paused. 'But they don't have a home to go back to, do they?'

She made a brave effort to smile. 'Is that what you came here to ask me?'

'Yes.'

'The third component of 61 Cygni couldn't have been their home, you know. It's an unkindled star. Nothing could have lived there except creatures like the Jovians.'

'I know that. But I thought their home planet might have been a satellite of the superjovian – same as the Cygnans' was. It was big enough to have planets. Big enough, even, to have an Earth-size planet.'

'No,' she said flatly. 'That would put their planet too far away from either primary to be warmed by them. It's not at all the same situation as Cygnus X-1 and its supergiant companion. Those were two *hot* stars with a joint ecosphere, so close together that they circled one another in only four and a half days.'

'And 61 Cygni is a different story?'

She almost laughed. 'Commander, the two stars of 61 Cygni have a period of seven hundred and twenty days! They're *far apart!* They're too far apart to have a joint ecosphere. And they're both so dim that no matter which one of them the humanoids' home world orbited, it would have to be very, very close to its star. When the Cygnans made off with the super-jovian component of the system, it couldn't possibly have dragged the humanoids' planet along with it.'

'So their world is still there?' he said.

'Yes,' she said. 'It's still there.'

'Thanks,' he said. He squeezed her shoulder and got up to go.

She stopped him at the door. 'Commander Jameson...'

He turned. 'Yes?'

'Dr. Ruiz... I mean... what do you think will happen to his body? They won't just... just throw it away, will they?'

'No,' Jameson lied. 'They'll probably allow the humans to bury it in their compound. It's a closed ecology. Relatively closed, anyway.'

'That's good, then,' she said slowly. 'He'll be a part of them forever now, won't he?'

'Not just them,' he said, and left.


Sue Jarowski looked round the wreckage of Jameson's cabin, appalled. The Cygnans had torn out everything movable, including the mattress on the bunk, and messed up what was left.

'I suppose we can make it livable,' she said doubtfully. 'I'll bring my own mattress and some cushions from the lounge.' She stared sadly at the empty shelves. 'They even took your omnisound and music cards.'

'We can live without music,' Jameson said. 'I was getting tired of that damned collection anyway.'

She gave him a probing look. After a moment she said, 'Tod, don't feel too bad about Maggie. She isn't worth it. She tried to get me to send a coded laser message back to Earth today. I refused. I think she was going to report Mike for sharing the Cygnan broomstick with the Chinese.'

'She won't get very far with that. Not any more. Mike's going to be a hero when we get back. So are we all – Maggie and Gifford and Fiaccone included. We're all going to have to smile a lot at each other for the holocasts. The facts are going to be rearranged. Klein never murdered Ruiz. He was just another heroic crewman who died trying to save the human race. I never fought Chia's crowd. We were all in it together.

They're going to have diplomatic problems enough splitting up the Jovian moons and the new terrestrial planet.'

Later on, he showed her 61 Cygni through the port. 'It's very faint,' he said. 'You can just about make it out. Actually it's two stars.'

'Nice,' she said, nestling up to him. She yawned. 'Nice to know that there are a lot of little elves out there, covered with pink feathers.'

The communicator buzzed. Jameson reached out and switched on the audio.

'Commander,' Maybury's voice said. 'Did I wake you up?'

'No,' Jameson said.

'I just wanted you to know that I accumulated enough observational data. Jupiter's going to miss the Earth. It's going to pass through just where Dr. Ruiz said it would.'

'That's fine,' he said. 'That's very fine. Now go get some sleep.'


A week later they held a modest celebration in the saloon. Jupiter had crossed Earth's orbit twice, with no more effect than a few earthquakes and typhoons, and the bollixing up of the planetary tables in the Nautical Almanac. It already had passed the orbit of Saturn without incident, and was heading out of the solar system at the rate of six thousand kilometres per second, still picking up speed. It seemed to be heading for the Great Nebula in Andromeda.

'They paid for it, you know,' Mike Berry said.

'What?' Jameson said. He'd been preoccupied watching the antics of the two humanoids. They seemed to like alcohol too. They couldn't tolerate the sugars in beer or wine, or the congeners in whiskey, but chilled vodka seemed to do very nicely for them, if it wasn't mucked up with vermouth or lemon peel. Right now one of them was mixing up a new batch in a cocktail shaker, while the other was breaking up the Chinese by doing a wickedly accurate imitation of Yeh's hulking walk.

'They paid for Jupiter,' Mike said. 'They took a planet the human race couldn't use and left us an Earth-size planet – conveniently sterile – and three of the four Galilean moons. Plus they traded us their own moon for Io. I'll bet the archeologists will go crazy.'

'We didn't own Jupiter. The Jovians did,' Jameson said.

Mike went on, oblivious. 'That's five more planets in the

solar system that the human race can colonize. And Jupiter's radiation belt isn't there to keep us away.'

Jameson took a sip of his martini. Mike was only saying what had been on everybody's tongue for the last five days. As it hurtled Sunward, Jupiter had failed to hang on to its outer satellites and the two bodies the Cygnans had brought. It had managed to hang on to Io, of course, and the piece of rock known as Jupiter V.

The core of the superjovian gas giant they had ridden into the solar system was now the size of the planet Earth. It was going to be the most valuable piece of real estate in the solar system, surpassing even Mars. It could be terraformed. They could make water out of the remnants of its hydrogen and the oxides in the rocks. It was rich in iron and heavy elements. And it was heavy enough to hold on to the atmosphere that could be squeezed out of its rocks.

'And to top it all off,' Mike was saying, 'Jupiter yanked them closer to the Sun before it let go. According to Maybury, it even looks like Ganymede will end up in an elliptical orbit that'll take it inside the orbit of Mars.'

'You overlooked the biggest gift of all,' Jameson said. 'They may have given us the stars.'

Mike nodded vigorously, spilling his beer. 'I've been going over that Cygnan broomstick with Po's boys. Do you know that it runs on water? Takes about a pint – we've tried it out with the ship's stuff. Uses the hydrogen. I don't know *what* it does with the oxygen! Very efficient – almost a hundred per cent conversion to energy. It comes out as very energetic photons. They work like hadrons and scatter a hell of a lot of rho mesons. I think it's a scaled-down version of their star drive. If they can make it that small, it has to be *simple!*'

'If the Chinese have been looking at that thing, there's going to be one great big crash research programme on our side. I think you're going to be at the head of it. That's how the bureacratic mind works. You were there first. You're magic.'

'So are you,' Mike said. 'You're the only person in the world who can talk to Cygnans.'

'For the time being. There must be a few linguists around who have absolute pitch.'

'It'll be you,' Mike said in a positive tone. 'You and our pink feathered friends. With the three of you working on that Cygnan engineer we've got in the hamster cages, we ought to get enough clues to have a star drive inside of twenty years. Anyway, if I'm going to be project supervisor I won't *take* anybody but you.'

'I accept,' Jameson said, laughing.

Mike leaped to his feet, spilling more beer. "It'll be the stars, boy!" he declaimed dramatically. 'Just think of it – the stars in our lifetime!'

Heads turned in their direction. Mike lifted his glass and toasted the saloon in general.

The humanoid who had been imitating Yeh came tumbling over in a series of cartwheels. Mike scratched it behind the ears. Everybody was doing that now. It was hard to keep your hands off them.

'S-t-t-*ars!*' it chirruped in its songbird voice. 'S-t-t-ars, s-t-t-ars, t-t-t-*we!*' The two of them already had picked up a few English and Chinese words, beginning with 'no' and 'stop' and 'don't touch', and you could understand them if you listened hard.

'That's right,' Mike said, patting the silky crest. 'We'll take you home first. *Then* we'll visit Alpha Centauri.'

'Hold on there!' Jameson said. 'Don't go off half-cocked. Alpha Centauri's only four light-years away, and 61 Cygni's eleven. If we get a starship out of this, the bureaucrats who finance it are going to want instant gratification.'

People were starting to drift over, drinks in hand. Ears had perked up at the sound of what had become the most popular subject aboard the ship.

'That's right,' Quentin agreed earnestly. 'Baby steps first. That's been the whole history of the space programme, ever since Stafford and Cernan and Young circled the moon before they let Armstrong and Aldrin land.'

'Look,' Mike said. 'It's a five-year trip to Alpha Centauri. Two of that is boosting and decelerating up to light-speed, during which you knock off another light-year, right?'

'Yes, but—'

'And it's a twelve-year trip to 61 Cygni. Same two years to boost and brake. In between you travel at, say, ninety-nine point ninety-nine per cent of the speed of light.'

'What about it?'

Mike leaned back, looking smug. 'So at that speed, the time dilation effect is a hundred to one, right? *Subjective* time for the crew is maybe two years and two weeks to Alpha Centauri

309

compared to two years and *six* weeks to 61 Cygni.' He spread his hands. 'So what's the big deal?'

'You're missing the point,' Jameson said, egging him on. 'Back home in the budget department, they're waiting ten years to show results from an Alpha Centauri round trip versus twenty-four years for a return from 61 Cygni.'

'*You're* missing the point,' Mike said, grinning hugely. '61 Cygni's a sure thing! Nobody can criticize the maiden voyage. We know there's life there! And intelligent life at that!' He ruffled the humanoid's silky fur affectionately. 'And we've got two friends to introduce us.'

Quentin was still trying. 'Yeah, but listen, Mike—'

Mike sat up, an astonished expression on his face. 'Hey, just came to me! All distances are the *same!* Give or take a couple of months, anyway. We can reach *any* star within a hundred light-years in about three years of travel. The hell with them back home! If you want to spend five years travelling, you can have any star within three hundred light-years. Hell, make that ten years – no, twelve years . . .'

He stopped and looked round at the circle of faces.

Kay Thorwald said it for him. 'We own all the stars in a thousand light-years. That's what we traded Jupiter for.'

The celebration had grown suddenly quiet. Into the silence, Jameson said: 'What's the price? Do we dismantle Saturn next?'

'Hell no!' Mike said briskly. 'The Cygnans spent six million years travelling with a first generation technology. *We'll* have a second-generation technology. We'll find a better way.'

# EPILOGUE

'There's our snowball,' Jameson said. 'Let's see if we can nudge it into the cup.'

Through the forward viewscreen the comet was an enormous sphere of frozen slush, fifty miles in diameter, according to the instruments. Out here in the cometary halo, far beyond the orbit of Pluto, it had no tail. According to Maybury's calculations, it grew its tail only once every two million years or so, when its elliptical orbit took it close enough to the Sun to vaporize its sherbetlike surface.

'Right on target, Skipper,' Li said from his console in the circular control room. His English had improved a lot in ten years.

It had taken only ten years to build the first star-ship. Mike had been right. The principle behind the Cygnans' energized-photon drive was simple. The human race would have had it in another century anyway; the technical and theoretical ground-work already had been laid.

Of course, the humans had made a lot of improvements.

Sue lifted her head from the communications console to admire the view outside. The ten years had fine-etched her face, making it even more striking. Jameson was glad their daughter looked like her, not him.

'Will that really take us all the way to 61 Cygni?' she said.

'Sure,' said Mike Berry. 'It's mostly water ice. Some methane, ammonia, carbon dioxide, dissolved into it, of course, but the engine's only going to eat the hydrogen anyway. There'll even be enough of it left at the end to keep shielding us from insterstellar hydrogen. We'll use any of *that* it picks up, too. Who needs a Jupiter? We don't have to boost as much mass as the Cygnans, and we don't have to push it as hard.'

'We'll never run out of interstellar fuel,' Jameson said. 'There's a hundred billion cometary nebulae out here beyond Pluto. All our starships have to do is come out and chase them down. And we can do that on a tank of water.'

At constant one-g acceleration, it had taken less than three weeks to reach the fringes of the cometary halo and find their snowball. There would be similar swarms of unborn comets around every star, extending light-years into space and mingling with the cometary halos of their neighbours. There would always be a refuelling stop. Man would never have to vandalize the planets, as the Cygnans had done.

The two feathery humanoids chattered excitedly. They were temporarily free of their engine-room duties, and Jameson had invited them up to the control room for a look. This was a big moment for them.

Slowly, the first human starship drifted towards the comet's frozen core. It was a mere two hundred metres long, a slender needle with a hundred-metre cup at one end, so that it resembled nothing so much as a gigantic golf tee.

'Contact!' Jameson said.

The snowball settled into the cup, or the ship landed head first on the comet, depending on how you wanted to look at it. The important thing was that the tail of the ship was pointed in the right direction. Before they'd gone very far, the ship would be half buried.

By that time they got ready for turnaround, the snowball would be down to a more manageable size. The ship would be somewhere in the centre of the comet by then, firing its photons through a tunnel melted through miles of snow. All that mass around it would be more than adequate to shield it from the diminishing hail of impinging radiation, and the drive beam itself would handily ward off the interstellar hydrogen directly ahead.

There was no spin section. They would be in free fall for only a few weeks, subjective time. Maybe later ships, with farther to go, would work out a spinning cage or some other device pivoted along the axis of the needle.

The forward screen went blank. The ship's other senses took over. The humanoids had a drink with them to celebrate, then went back to the engine room.

'We've got us some friends,' Mike said, watching the pink creatures scamper down the companionway. 'Wait till their people start working on their own version of the star drive. In another ten years, we'll be roaming the galaxy together.'

Jameson switched on another outside pickup, and the viewscreen was suddenly filled with the splendour of the Great Nebula in Andromeda, a whirlpool of stars sparkling with gems of many colours.

Maybury came over for a look. "They won't get there for two million years,' she said.

'Maybe that's what they were getting up their nerve for,' Jameson said. 'The big jump. It took them six million years to work up to it.'

'They can't turn back now,' Sue said. 'We'll never see them again.'

Mike gave a short bark of a laugh. 'Want to bet? When they reach the Andromeda galaxy, we'll be waiting for them. They've only got a short headstart.'

'Two million years,' Li said thoughtfully. 'What will we be by then? What will *they* be?'

'A partnership with the descendants of the humans aboard,' Jameson said confidently. 'The Cygnans lost their purpose when they started running six million years ago. Maybe the humans will substitute theirs.'

'Some day we'll cross the gulf and rejoin them,' Maybury said, staring at the screen.

Jameson switched off Andromeda. 'Some day,' he agreed. 'Right now we have a galaxy of our own to discover.'

The engines fired.

# ABOUT THE AUTHOR

Donald Moffitt was born in Boston, and now lives in rural Maine with his wife, Ann, a native of Connecticut. A former public relations executive, industrial film maker, and ghostwriter, he has been writing fiction, on and off, for more than twenty years under an assortment of pen names, including his own, chiefly espionage novels and adventure stories in international settings. *The Jupiter Theft* is his first full-length science-fiction story and the first book of any genre to be published under his own name. 'One of the rewards of being a public relations man specializing in the technical end of large corporate accounts,' he says, 'was being allowed to hang around on the fringes of research being done in such widely disparate fields as computer technology, high-energy physics, the manned space programme, polymer chemistry, parasitology, and virology – even, on a number of happy occasions, being pressed into service as an unpaid lab assistant.' He became an enthusiastic addict of science fiction during the Golden Era, when Martians were red, Venusians green, Mercurians yellow, and 'Jovian Dawn Men' always blue. He survived to see the medium becoming respectable, and is cheered by recent signs that the fun is coming back to sf.

*And selected from the SPHERE Science Fiction list*

# THE LAVALITE WORLD
## Philip Jose Farmer

The long-awaited fifth book in the astounding World of Tiers series

The Lavalite World is a world of slow but constant change. The very landscape moves. Here mountains rise from plains or sink into rifts. New oceans form as vast hollows collapse and seas rush in. And there is only one escape from the bizarre planet: the one gateway to other universes is in the place of the Lord Urthona. Paul Janus Finnegan – also known as Kickaha – must reach it if he is to survive. And he must do so despite the Lords Urthona and Red Orc, the hired thug McKay, flesh-eating vegetation on the run, assorted strange beasts of prey, and planetary pseudopods. . . .

SCIENCE FICTION    0 7221 3475 8             £1.10

Don't miss the other superb novels in Philip José Farmer's World of Tiers series
THE MAKER OF UNIVERSES
THE GATES OF CREATION
A PRIVATE COSMOS
BEHIND THE WALLS OF TERRA

# SPACE WAR BLUES
## Richard A. Lupoff

New Alabama. A planet that's a fair reproduction of long-lost Dixie, filled with down-home, racist rednecks. The N'Alabamians have carried their tribal prejudices to the farthest reaches of the galaxy, like the other minorities expelled from Earth by the dominant Pan-Semitic Alliance. There's New Transvaal. New Cathay. And New Haiti, a black world where Papa Doc's descendants carry on the old ways.

When New Alabama and New Haiti go to war with each other, it's a bloody black-versus-white stalemate. Until the N'Haitians develop a horrific new secret weapon based on a very ancient tradition.

Imagine you're a clean-cut N'Alabamian good ol'boy, giving your all up there in the space fleet, and you suddenly realise the enemy crews aren't human at all. They're what people back on Earth used to call zombies . . .

**SCIENCE FICTION   0 7221 5671 5**          **£1.25**

And don't miss Richard Lupoff's
FOOL'S HILL
– also in SPHERE Science Fiction

# BELOVED SON
George Turner

## THE SF EPIC OF THE YEAR

2032. England has gone. The proud industrial nations have destroyed themselves. In a post-cataclysmic Australia humanity survives by ruthless genetic engineering and a cult of youth. Then, out of the stars, come strangers from the past – a space-ship crew who left before the Holocaust and have lived in a slow-down time-suspended state for over four decades.

Shattered by the bizarre civilization they find, can they – or the new world – survive that encounter . . . ?

BELOVED SON is a superb SF epic by a first-time author in the field, a brilliant depiction of a frighteningly plausible future world which has been universally acclaimed as one of the most original works for many years.

'COMPELLING . . . OFTEN BRILLIANT'
*New Statesman*

'THE BEST DIALOGUE AND CHARACTERIZATION TO COME FROM SCIENCE FICTION IN YEARS . . . THE REAL THING'
*The Spectator*

'AN EXCITING DEBUT'
*Yorkshire Post*

'REALLY BRILLIANT'
*Irish Press*

SCIENCE FICTION   0 7221 8642 8

£1.25

*And*

# DEUS IRAE
Philip K. Dick & Roger Zelazny

## AFTER THE HOLOCAUST, A NEW GOD EMERGES ...

What chance has Tibor McMasters – one limbless
heretic – against the awesome powers of the legendary
Deus Irae, the wrathful entity behind World War III?
Commissioned to paint the deity's likeness, Tibor must
first find him. And to do so he must travel across the
nightmare landscape of the post-holocaust world,
braving its terrifying mutations while his Christian
companion acts on orders to sabotage his mission ...

Philip K. Dick and Roger Zelazny, two of the most
strikingly original talents of the contemporary science
fiction scene, have produced in this, their first
collaborative work, a tour-de-force of terror,
mind-spinning ideas and grim wit.

'That they can put one in mind of *A Canticle for
Leibowitz* is surely a tribute' *The Times*

SCIENCE FICTION    0 7221 2964 5                    95p

A selection of bestsellers from SPHERE

*Fiction*

| | | |
|---|---|---|
| VIXEN 03 | Clive Cussler | £1.25 ☐ |
| THE DEATH FREAK | Clifford Irving & | |
| | Herbert Burkholz | 95p ☐ |
| WOLFSBANE | Craig Thomas | £1.25 ☐ |
| GOLDEN MOMENTS | Danielle Steel | £1.25 ☐ |
| MARILEE | Con Sellers | £1.50 ☐ |

*Film and TV Tie-Ins*

| | | |
|---|---|---|
| THE PROFESSIONALS 5: BLIND RUN | | |
| | Ken Blake | 85p ☐ |
| THE PROFESSIONALS 6: FALL GIRL | | |
| | Ken Blake | 85p ☐ |
| THE MUSIC MACHINE | Bill Stoddart | 95p ☐ |
| THE PROMISE | Danielle Steel | 95p ☐ |
| BUCK ROGERS IN THE 25th CENTURY | | |
| | Addison E. Steele | 95p ☐ |
| BUCK ROGERS 2: THAT MAN ON BETA | | |
| | Addison E. Steele | 95p ☐ |

*Non-Fiction*

| | | |
|---|---|---|
| THE THIRD WORLD WAR | General Sir John | |
| | Hackett | £1.75 ☐ |
| LIFECLOUD | Fred Hoyle & | |
| | N.C. Wickramasinghe | £1.25 ☐ |
| BARDOT: AN INTIMATE BIOGRAPHY | | |
| | Willi Frischauer | £1.00 ☐ |
| COME WIND OR WEATHER | Clare Francis | 95p ☐ |

*All Sphere Books are available at your local bookshop or newsagent, or can be ordered direct from the publisher. Just tick the titles you want and fill in the form below.*

Name ..............................................................

Address ...........................................................

......................................................................

Write to Sphere Books, Cash Sales Department, P.O. Box 11, Falmo

Cornwall TR10 9EN

Please enclose cheque or postal order to the value of the cover

UK: 25p for the first book plus 10p per copy for each ad

ordered to a maximum charge of £1.05

OVERSEAS: 40p for the first book and 12p for eac

B.F.P.O. & EIRE: 25p for the first book plus 10p po

8 books, thereafter 5p per book.

*Sphere Books reserve the right to show new retail pr*

*may differ from those previously advertised in the tex*

*increase postal rates in accordance with the GPO.*